USA TODAY bestselling author **Natalie Anderson** writes emotional contemporary romance full of sparkling banter, sizzling heat and uplifting endings—perfect for readers who love to escape with empowered heroines and arrogant alphas who are too sexy for their own good. When not writing, you'll find her wrangling her four children, three cats, two goldfish and one dog…and snuggled in a heap on the sofa with her husband at the end of the day. Follow her at natalie-anderson.com.

Clare Connelly was raised in small-town Australia among a family of avid readers. She spent much of her childhood up a tree, Mills & Boon book in hand. Clare is married to her own real-life hero, and they live in a bungalow near the sea with their two children. She is frequently found staring into space—a surefire sign that she's in the world of her characters. She has a penchant for French food and ice-cold champagne, and Mills & Boon novels continue to be her favourite ever books. Writing for Modern is a long-held dream. Clare can be contacted via clareconnelly.com or at her Facebook page.

VERY CONVENIENT VOWS

NATALIE ANDERSON

CLARE CONNELLY

MILLS & BOON

First published in Great Britain 2025
by Mills & Boon, an imprint of HarperCollins*Publishers* Ltd,
1 London Bridge Street, London, SE1 9GF

www.harpercollins.co.uk

HarperCollins*Publishers*, Macken House, 39/40 Mayor Street Upper,
Dublin 1, D01 C9W8, Ireland

Very Convenient Vows © 2025 Harlequin Enterprises ULC

Their Altar Arrangement © 2025 Natalie Anderson

Unwanted Royal Wife © 2025 Clare Connelly

ISBN: 978-0-263-34447-9

01/25

This book contains FSC™ certified paper
and other controlled sources to ensure responsible forest management.

For more information visit www.harpercollins.co.uk/green.

Printed and Bound in the UK using 100% Renewable Electricity
at CPI Group (UK) Ltd, Croydon, CR0 4YY

THEIR ALTAR ARRANGEMENT

NATALIE ANDERSON

MILLS & BOON

For the two Sorayas.

Soraya L—our daily accountability texts are the bomb.

Soraya B—your guidance is just the best.

Thank you both so very much!!!

CHAPTER ONE

ELODIE WALLACE STOOD in the heart of London. A stretch of ludicrously expensive stone residences curved before her, the city homes of many of the world's wealthiest, those supposedly important, probably corrupt, definitely powerful people. The kind of autocrats who'd do anything to ensure their wealth and power didn't just remain intact for all eternity but grew like rampant weeds through millennia—strangling anything and anyone in the way of their relentlessly upward trajectories.

Cynical? Why yes, Elodie was. Dramatic? That too.

But sometimes in life everything does happen all at once. Bad things truly happened 'in threes', and 'when it rains, it pours' wasn't a strong enough forecast—a whole hurricane had hit her world. It wasn't enough that her dream career was under threat or that her best friend's livelihood was also at risk, but her younger's sister's *life* was basically at stake.

So she would enter the den. Slay the dragon. Save the princess. Though admittedly now she was confronted by the imposing buildings that so spectacularly signposted both wealth and sticking power, she regretted not bringing backup. But both Phoebe and Bethan, her *compadres* in pursuing a life of personal liberty, needed protecting too. Phoebe was away taking the first holiday in her life, while Bethan was still fragile from a deeply wounding disillusionment. So Elodie had not told them about the call she'd taken from her sister

Ashleigh late last night, nor of the decision she'd made to come here today.

One step at a time.

The clichés would get her through, they usually did. She loved using them at work—twisting them to mean the opposite and thus confusing her customers. She stalked along the pristine path until she hit the right numeral beautifully painted in black on twin marble columns. The portico was ridiculously grand, the neoclassical architectural style exuding timeless and impenetrable exclusivity.

She registered the security cameras. They were subtly situated but still able to be seen, thus acting as deterrent as much as actual recording devices. Breaching this citadel would be a challenge. She drew breath and climbed, staring straight into the lens of the camera nearest the front door as she pressed the button.

Somewhat amazingly the door opened after only a few moments. Elodie's attention zipped to the man blocking the space. He looked like a cross between a pro wrestler and a secret service agent. Blank expression, black earpiece, built physique complete with a bulky bit in his black jacket that made her suspect he was carrying a weapon. That last might be her over-active imagination but she was pretty sure. Quelling her rising nerves, she fixed her gaze squarely on him. She'd pretend she was meant to be there, as if *she* were someone important too. She was good at pretending.

'Elodie Wallace,' she announced with the particularly precise enunciation she used at work. 'I'm here to see Ramon Fernandez.'

'Snootily confident attitude' crossed with 'bulletproof ballbreaker facade' had got her into some of the most exclusive clubs when she'd needed to destroy her own name. But, bold as she'd been on those nights, she had to be even more so now.

'Is he expecting you?' More than a touch of scepticism tarnished the man's reply.

'I'm his fiancée's sister,' Elodie elaborated crisply. 'I'm here to discuss the arrangements for this weekend's engagement party.'

The butler/bodybuilder/probable assassin might've been immaculately trained but even he failed to hide his startled moment at her answer. Elodie maintained her frigidly polite expression. Bluffing was an art form and fortunately she'd had plenty of practice. There was a pause. Though he kept his gaze on her, the man's eye muscles narrowed slightly and she sensed his attention was elsewhere. His earpiece perhaps? She tilted her chin slightly. She wasn't leaving without talking to the man she was sure was inside. She'd chain herself to one of these columns and scream like a banshee if required. Ashleigh's future literally hung in the balance.

The behemoth drew an audible breath but suddenly muttered, 'Of course.'

Was he talking to her or—?

He stepped back. 'Please come in.'

As she followed him inside she sneaked another steadying breath, unable to appreciate the sudden temperature change from the stifling summer heat outside to a cool, high-ceilinged sanctuary of an atrium.

The body-built butler gestured towards a comfortable-looking chair. 'Please take a seat.'

'I'd prefer to stand.' She smiled glacially. 'While you let him know I'm here.'

'He knows you're here.'

A prickle of fear scored its way down Elodie's spine. Had he been watching the feed from those cameras? The butler paused again, this time not even trying to hide that he was listening to someone. Elodie stood defiantly but her already erratic pulse zipped from rapid to frantic. Cold sweat slicked across her skin.

'If you'll follow me,' the man said, abandoning any attempt to hide his wide-eyed curiosity, 'Señor Fernandez is ready for you.'

She very much doubted that. Ramon Fernandez was the man Elodie's parents were bullying her baby sister into marrying and she intended to eviscerate him.

Although now she was actually *here* she realised she had little concrete idea as to *how*.

She followed the man, reluctantly impressed by the interior. She'd expected ostentatious decor—a gallery of gilt-edged frames housing priceless portraits, gleaming sculptures on plinths, luxurious rugs handmade by a city of workers a century ago...that sort of thing. But this home was sleek with black-painted walls and dark polished wooden floors, punctuated by occasional warm lights that only partially illuminated the way. It made Elodie feel as if the world were growing gloomier with every step—as if she were being led into a lair. A dark, sumptuous dwelling for a predator.

Way too fanciful... Elodie mocked herself.

This wasn't one of the escape rooms she designed and managed. Though she memorised the way as she went in case she needed to actually escape in a hurry. She tugged her blazer sleeves and swept her hands down her tailored pants. The sleek suit formed part of her armour as did the make-up she'd applied only half an hour ago. She'd had to mask the shadowy ravages of an utterly sleepless night. The bustier beneath her blazer was extremely well-fitting—literally giving strength to her spine. Black and embellished with orange and gold beads and yes, while those did completely clash with her red hair, that was deliberate too. She wanted to project fearlessness. That she was a rule breaker. Reckless. A possible threat. Indeed, she wore it to project intimidation. But it was pure projection. A ploy because deception was her trade. But today wasn't mere playful pretence, she needed the armour for real and it was burnished with rage.

'Señor Fernandez…' The butler paused just outside a wide open doorway. 'Ms Wallace is here to see you.'

'How delightful.'

A drawl. Complete mockery.

Elodie froze on the threshold, barely aware of the butler's departure behind her as the man stood up from the sleek desk that housed a bank of slimline screens.

Blue eyes. Black hair. The sharpest cheekbones she'd ever seen. Not chiselled but sliced—angular, masculine, stunning. Eagle-eyed, he stared back at her. For a timeless moment she just stared back. Then he moved. She didn't. Couldn't.

For a split second she felt a hit of *hope*. Surely this man couldn't be the monster her sister meant? Ashleigh had described him as slimy and weak. Elodie had gone online to track down his London address but there had been little else and so nothing had prepared her for the cinematic perfection of Ramon Fernandez. He looked like Hollywood's version of the ultimate, suave hero.

She blinked. It didn't help. The tuxedo amped up his attractiveness. Formal evening wear suited most men—maximised their height, breadth, length—but this suit did all that and more for him. His frame was leaner than the butler's but she suspected his muscles were no less lethal and he had an air of command the other man lacked. But it was those eyes and the aquiline features that mesmerised her.

'You're *far* too old for her,' she breathed, so stunned that her first thought simply fell out of her mouth in a puff of disbelief.

Not just too old. Too *everything*. Too wealthy. Too handsome. Too successful, surely. Because he was smug with it. She watched him stroll towards her, his demeanour relaxed yet predatory, as he calmly took in every aspect of *her* appearance. He enjoyed wielding his power and he had it in spades. Both personal and professional. *Why* on earth would a man who lived in a place like this and looked like he did, need to buy himself a teenage bride?

'Do you think?' he asked conversationally.

So it was true. He didn't even try to deny the arrangement. Bitter disappointment squashed that little leap of hope and her rage returned. But still she couldn't move.

Undeniably overwhelming, he was tall, dark, intolerably, impossibly handsome.

Yes, a cliché. But again, the cliché was flipped. Like the conundrums she created, Elodie's exterior ran at a complete counterpoint to her interior. While she projected a confident demeanour, on the inside she was terrified. This man was the same but in a far worse reverse. Beneath the beauty, this man was a beast. Angelic on the outside, a monster within. It was knowing this that caused her heart to stop altogether, right? The absolute horror before her. She almost lost her nerve.

'You realise she's only *just* turned eighteen,' she spat contemptuously.

He stopped less than a foot from her. Much closer and he'd be breaching generally accepted boundaries of polite personal space. Not that he apparently gave a damn given the arrogance oozing from him. Doubtless he considered himself not just above convention but above the law.

'You realise she only left school a few weeks ago?' she added when he still didn't bother to reply. 'She's beautiful, but she's a baby.'

His gaze dropped, lingering on the beadwork of her bustier. He was looking at her like he was assessing an item for the art collection he didn't even have. But his was a keen, knowing eye—summing up her valuation with a singular glance and to her shock and mortification a torrent of reaction released within her. She *blushed*—actually blushed. Heat rose everywhere as she endured his remorseless appraisal. Her response was fierce and uncontrolled—appalled outrage, right? Not any other kind of response.

'You have nothing to say to that?' she goaded desperately.

'I thought you wished to discuss the arrangements for the engagement party, not her age.' A cool reproof.

Her jaw dropped for a split second before her wild anger unleashed, driving her forward into the room so she stood toe to toe with the monster. 'There shouldn't *be* an engagement party! If you had *any* scruples you'd end this deal.'

He cocked his head ever so slightly and looked down his nose at her. 'Deal?'

It was that smallest curl of a smile that did it.

'I know all about it,' she derided furiously, any last self-restraint in flames. 'I know you're *paying* for your bride.'

'You think?'

How could he be so sanguine?

The intensity of her anger overrode everything. 'You're investing in my parents' hotel. Which is madness. Surely you're aware it's never been a commercial success. Some would say it's a lemon. Why do you want it?'

He remained relaxed. 'Surely you know how good I am with hotels—'

'Right, I do. So forgive me if I don't believe that you need another one. Certainly not one that isn't anywhere near the size of those already in your stable.' She glared at him.

'Perhaps I like a challenge,' he said quietly.

'You're bored? You need entertaining?' she said sarcastically. 'Join a Scrabble club. Better yet, hire a children's party entertainer.'

Something flickered in his eyes, but she couldn't quite define it and he still said nothing.

'No?' she mocked. 'Because it's another sort of filly you want, isn't it?'

His beautiful lips curved again.

She shook her head in total disbelief. 'Why do you need a wife, exactly? Is it image management? Because in case you hadn't worked it out, I'm going to be a problem here.' The only thing she could think was to shame him. She knew too well that shame was a vitriolic thing. 'I'll go to the media,' she added. 'I'll cause such a scandal, I'll—'

'Publicly embarrass your own family?'

She stared into his intense blue gaze. Clearly he didn't know that she'd already embarrassed her family on a professional level. Entirely deliberately, knowing they'd disown her. Because four years ago this had happened to *her*. She hadn't been eighteen, but nineteen when her father had driven her into the arms of a man she didn't love. He'd always been controlling—from the subjects she studied at school, to the clothes she wore, to how she spent every moment of her time. He was the head of the family and Elodie, her sister and her mother were expected to do his bidding without question. Elodie had long accepted that as normal, but in her late teens her frustration grew. Her father had never valued her as anything more than a decorative source of free labour. He'd never listened to her ideas for the hotel. And *she'd* barely paid attention to Callum Henderson. Yes, he'd been at her school, but he was three years older and honestly off her radar. Not her father's though. Son of the local mayor, monied and influential. Her father had been thrilled to recruit him as assistant manager. Elodie had been hurt her father had laughed at her own quietly voiced inclination to apply.

But Callum had gone out of his way to talk to Elodie. He'd told her about a couple of interactions between them at school. Truthfully, she'd never even remembered them. He'd listened to her ideas—even enacted a couple—presenting them to her father as his purely to get them over the line. To Elodie's surprise her father hadn't been angry about Callum taking her time—he'd told her to be nice to him. For once she seemed to have pleased him.

The proposal had come out of the blue—a rose-petal-strewn moment in front of her parents and half the hotel staff. Blindsided, there was no way she could reject Callum *publicly*. Especially not when she'd glimpsed the hard expectation in her father's eyes and realised that he hadn't just known about it but that he'd *approved* it. She'd had to say yes in the moment. And then her father wouldn't hear her misgivings. She would never 'do better' and Callum was going to invest in the much-needed hotel upgrade and she couldn't be the one to deny the rest of her family that much-needed resource; moreover, she should be *honoured* someone like him wanted someone like her.

At that point Callum hadn't even kissed her. It had never occurred to Elodie that he'd want to. But he'd been patient and persuasive. He'd promised to manage her father once they were married. And here's where Elodie had been so at fault herself. She'd been flattered because he'd listened, because he'd seemed to truly care. She'd believed him, blind to the fact that what he wanted wasn't what she really was. So swiftly she'd been swept into a situation she couldn't escape.

The gravity of her mistake hit within mere days of the marriage. Callum's promised support and freedom had been fiction while the intimacy he'd promised would develop between them hadn't. Asking to end it had been futile. Turned out appearances mattered more than anything to *both* those men and ultimately Callum was every bit as controlling as her father. In the end she'd stopped asking. She'd acted. *Badly*.

'Well?' the too good-looking tower of a man right in front of her now prompted, somehow sensing her unsteadiness. 'How far are you willing to go to stop this?'

'As far as it takes.' She blinked away the shameful memories, furious with her weakness—for thinking about herself in this moment. Because this was about Ashleigh—and she completely understood her sister's inability to say 'no' to her father. She wouldn't let her sister endure more than the unfair pressure she'd already faced.

'What's *weird* is why *you* have to go to such icky lengths to get what you want,' she pushed back on him. 'What's so repellent about you that forces you to *buy* a bride?'

That slow, wide smile curved his lips. Apparently he wasn't shamed in the least by her acidic question.

'You tell me,' he invited softly, leaning closer still. 'How repellent do *you* think I am?'

Oh, he was so *very* arrogant. She refused to respond to such a blatantly outrageous diversion. 'You need to call the wedding off.'

'But won't your family—'

'Lose the hotel?' She shrugged. 'I don't care. Ashleigh isn't for sale.'

'Ashleigh,' he echoed calmly. 'She hasn't mentioned you to me.'

Of course her sister hadn't. Elodie was an outcast for deserting her 'perfect' husband and 'perfect' life. Her parents now lived as if she'd never existed. She and Ashleigh had only remained in touch online until Ashleigh had borrowed a friend's phone last night.

'No.' Elodie's words slowed as she registered that somehow Ramon Fernandez had moved even closer to her. 'She wouldn't have dared.'

Ashleigh couldn't disobey her father. Not yet. Elodie understood that too. She'd been the same for so long.

Ramon was serious now. Finally. 'Because you're a danger to the deal.'

'Yes.'

The startling blue of his eyes thinned as his pupils flared and she found herself sinking into their dark depths. The crackling sensation across her skin was so foreign it took her too long to realise what it was. Chemistry. Sexual chemistry. To her horror she realised her heat wasn't entirely comprised of rage at all. Her pulse thundered because this wasn't some tempting tendril of intimacy. This was an untrammelled cannonball of lust suddenly running amok within her. All because he was standing so close. It was something she'd never before felt. Instant. Intense. Completely and utterly inappropriate. Horrified at the utterly unbidden rush of want, she gasped sharply. But the attraction was overpowering—and terrifyingly unstoppable.

'And you're a danger to me,' he whispered.

'Very much so.' She bluffed.

Because she knew now that the opposite was true—he was an absolute danger to her. But she couldn't seem to back away from him. She should. She should get away. She didn't need to test his measure. He thought and said and did what he wanted with no compunction and no remorse and certainly no consideration for another's feelings. And yet here she was, a heartbeat away from him.

'How, exactly?' he breathed.

That heat from deep within spread across every inch of her body and burned her skin. To her amazement a light flush echoed on his—colour scorching those angular cheekbones as his intense focus dropped to her mouth. With innate understanding she realised that he was considering kissing her. Instinctively her lips parted—that was to breathe, right? Because the shock stole her breath.

But she didn't step back. She refused to let him intimidate her. Because that's all this was—an attempt at intimidation. He was so sure of himself—enraptured with his own power—sensual and otherwise. But this close she caught a hint of his rich, oaky scent and the reason why she was even here at all began to slide from her mind as a shadowy, heated haze enveloped her. His long jet lashes lowered and suddenly his lips were but a whisper from hers.

With the last thread of resistance she remembered. Murmured, 'You would cheat on your fiancée so easily?'

His eyebrows flickered but he didn't pull back. 'You would betray your sister?'

'It's no betrayal,' she denied huskily. 'I've already told you I'll do *anything* to stop this marriage.'

She would put herself between him and her sister.

His lips twisted in triumph and he lifted his head away from her. His eyes glittered as he stared as she ran a tongue across parched lips. She realised that *he'd* been testing *her*. He hadn't *actually* intended to kiss her and that she felt *disappointment* was truly awful.

'You're not in love with her,' she accused bitterly.

'No,' he admitted with brutal candour.

Pain and fury and humiliation coalesced within her. How could he—and how could her parents—do this? Elodie wouldn't let them hurt Ashleigh in this way.

'So she's nothing but a toy?' she flared scornfully. 'A pawn in some bigger game you're playing? Just a thing to be sacrificed?'

'You think it would be so bad to be married to me?' he asked too mildly.

'Apparently I'm not the only one who thinks that, given the lengths you're having to go to get yourself a wife.'

His flash of amusement infuriated her all the more. How could he laugh? It was sickening.

'It's all about you,' she erupted. 'Your status. Your needs.'

'You don't think there'll be any benefits to her in the arrangement?'

'None that are worth it.' Not Ashleigh's innocence and liberty and dreams for her own future.

Elodie had long ago vowed never to get involved with another man again. She'd fought hard for her own freedom. She'd done horrible, necessary things. But she would suffer far more if it could save her sister from the same.

'For some unfathomable reason you want to get married,' she said. 'So perhaps it doesn't matter who the unfortunate woman is.'

He was unnervingly still, that intensity sharpening his eyes. 'You have another candidate in mind?'

Candidate. As if it were a job.

'Another poor soul, you mean?'

The devastating good looks of the man, his searing wealth, his callous lack of care and her own horrendously *animal* response to him fuelled her fury to the point where all control was lost.

'Sure,' she added acidly. 'If you want a wife so *desperately*, then you can marry *me*!'

CHAPTER TWO

JUAN RAMON FERNANDEZ clenched every muscle and made himself remain still. Not because he'd recoil but rather he was on the verge of pulling her against him and sealing the deal with an incendiary kiss!

But he did *not* want a wife. He would never *want* a wife. Yet the unpalatable truth hitting him hard was that he might very well *need* one. Soon. *That* was surely the only reason why he was almost overcome by the most inexplicable urge to grate out an expletive-laden acceptance of this fiery woman's scathing proposal. Why he'd haul her into his arms before she could change her mind. Why he had the impulse to carry her off to the nearest altar this instant—impossibly happy to! Because then he'd take her to bed.

Fortunately Elodie Wallace's very direct, very condemning blue gaze nailed him to the spot as that roar of possession swept through him.

Possession?

He'd been possessed. Momentarily gone mad. Blinking, he spun and stalked to the gleaming glass counter in the corner behind his desk.

'Would you like a drink?' he asked unevenly.

He'd pour hers and swig directly from the bottle if it wouldn't betray his loss of composure. And he was damn well clinging to that facade with a death grip.

'I'm not leaving until you agree to release Ashleigh from this sham engagement.'

He splashed four fingers of whisky into a crystal tumbler before glancing back at the flame-haired fury standing in the centre of his study. She had guts, he'd give her that. Bold as anything and beautiful with it. A little thing with a big impact. The chandelier must have been dusted recently, or perhaps Piotr had changed the bulbs because the light illuminated her so intensely it was like she gleamed from the inside out. And when she shook her head at him, all fury and scorn, her mass of red hair glittered like a waterfall of fire across her shoulders. He couldn't look away from her if he tried. Which was a further loss of control he didn't appreciate.

Oh, who was he kidding? He *fully* appreciated looking at her. A human form tempest crossed with a Siren and right now he relished the distraction she was—mitigating the rage rising within. The fact was he had no power to release her sister from an engagement he was no part of. It was another arm of his family at fault. His *aunt.* Apparently not content with the company money she received, she was willing to use her own *son* to steal the most priceless jewel in the family treasure chest.

'I mean it,' Elodie-the-Beautiful declared defiantly, her hair catching the light as she tossed her head again.

Amusement rippled through him. Amusement that he didn't ordinarily indulge in. Amusement dangerously intertwined with lust and as inappropriate as hell given the situation. He sipped his drink—another thing he didn't ordinarily indulge in—hoping it would settle the *other* urges still rippling through him, but the burn wasn't enough to clear his head. He took another, deeper draw. Then he gave in and accepted that this was no ordinary day and he was going to have to do something drastic to resolve this.

'Piotr!' Ramon called loudly. 'Change of plan for this evening,' he said brusquely the second his assistant appeared, but he kept his gaze on Elodie. 'I'm staying in. Please send my apologies, prepare dinner for two and ensure the guest suite is ready.'

That amusement tightened as he watched her jaw slacken and then in a flash her entire body stiffened with fury again.

'The guest suite?' Her query dripped with iced loathing.

'Well, I thought it might be a little soon for my room but I don't mind having you there tonight if that's what you'd prefer,' he purred.

He shouldn't have said it. Couldn't resist. Blamed the drink and set it down.

She stared open-mouthed at him. 'You're...'

Yeah. He had no words either right now. He could only inwardly curse.

Ramon would be the first to acknowledge that his regimented life could sometimes be boring, but his narrow focus was utterly deliberate. Greed—hunger for excess in *all* forms—was the family curse. His father had allowed his appetites to spiral out of control regardless of the cost to his family. Ramon had an equally rampant appetite, but he'd chosen to channel it into work. He'd relished the challenge of turning the family conglomerate he inherited too soon from overly stretched to stratospherically successful. Relationships were out. Never was he getting married. His father's rapacious genes ran through him, and he wasn't destroying any woman the way his father had destroyed his mother.

So the time Ramon offered a partner was limited. Anything long-term a definite no-go. And women didn't like coming second to work, didn't like that he travelled so much and never invited them along—so it was easy enough to keep emotional complication at bay. Nowadays on the rare occasions it got the better of him he slaked sexual hunger with a one-night stand. Maybe it had been a while. Maybe that was why when the doorbell had rung and he'd glanced at the security feed from the front door, he'd been intrigued by the bold woman staring straight into the camera. When she'd outlandishly claimed to be *his fiancée's* sister, he'd simply had to indulge the ridiculous urge to let her in. He'd been unable to resist hearing what she'd wanted to say. Turned out to be quite a lot. By admitting little and encouraging her ire, he'd grasped what was really going on.

Her sister. His cousin. His aunt making a monstrous mistake.

So yeah, he was far from bored now as he watched Elodie's lusciously full lips press together, part, then press together again.

Still no words. Right.

A wash of colour betrayed her despite the immaculate make-up and to his horror he felt an answering wash of heat suffuse his own face. Again. He'd never heard of Elodie Wallace before now but he wished he had. Wished he'd been warned that when entering her orbit he'd have an intensely sexual reaction. Her eyes were a far more vibrant blue than his and right now they were very alert. Her slick make-up didn't entirely mask the freckles over her face but it was expertly done—her long lashes were enhanced, her lips shiny—while her slender figure was showcased to perfection with that stunning outfit. In theory her black pants suit would be appropriate for any occasion but the beaded bustier she wore beneath the blazer gave him a glimpse of her breasts almost spilling from the top and was sexy as hell. Dominatrix-lite. All she was missing was a riding crop. She was here to demand what she wanted and she wasn't leaving until she got it.

'*You can marry me!*'

Her outrageous suggestion hung in the air above him like a Shakespearean dagger. A dramatic temptation that a devil within still urged him to accept because it would so neatly solve the situation that he hadn't anticipated would come to a head so soon.

'You just said you weren't leaving until Ashleigh's freedom is secured.' He mastered the mess of emotions engulfing him and broke the scalding silence with as mild an expression as he could muster. 'I need time to consider my options. You may stay while I do that or you can leave.'

Ungallant as his deception was, he had to find out as much as he could from her and he could never confide to anyone—let alone a complete stranger—that his own family had their knives out and had caught him off guard.

'But if you do choose to leave,' he added, 'then the plan currently in place will likely continue.'

'You need *time*?' she echoed incredulously. 'It should take a man like you less than two seconds to realise dragging a teenager to the altar is a more than bad idea,' she snapped. 'Yet apparently, you're incapable of rational thought on this.'

She was right and she expected him to back down. She was used to getting what she wanted. Her confident diva aura was total demonstration of the fact. Curiosity devoured his brain—all he could think about was all the things he wanted to learn about *her*. Mostly inappropriate things. He gritted his teeth and summoned some self-control.

'Your kind offer of accommodation isn't really a *choice* for me, is it?' She stepped closer until she stood toe to toe with him. 'Does it make you feel good to exert control over someone?' she asked, her voice husky and low as she glared up at him irately. 'Is that what gets you going?'

He could only stand and stare at her. Couldn't let himself so much as breathe. Because *she* was what got him going in this instant and another acerbic challenge like that would have him slip the leash.

'Is that why you want a young bride?' she challenged further, oblivious to the storm brewing within him. 'Do you think you can mould her into your ideal wife?'

He didn't want to control her. He wanted to be consumed in her fire. He was so tempted to take her in his hands and tease her more. Instead he dragged in a steadying breath and harshly demanded *information*.

'Why wouldn't Ashleigh have dared mentioned you?'

Her eyes widened.

When he'd got this inappropriately close earlier, her haughty facade had fallen and he'd seen an uncontrollable response flash—not fear but a flare of attraction that mirrored his in every way. Instant, unwanted, intense. A weakness. He saw it again now and would exploit it. Because when she was emotional she exploded and truth emerged. He had to use those tactics because he didn't trust her. Nothing personal. He didn't trust anyone, not when he came from a family gored by infighting. Not when his own father had been a master of betrayal. Not when he'd been forced to be complicit in his old man's deceit.

He'd thought the worst of all that was in the past. Thought he'd made enough amends on behalf of his gluttonous father. Apparently not. He knew his aunt Cristina had suffered as a spoiled but ignored second child, as a young woman taken advantage of by a man who'd consumed everything he could from everyone he encountered. But that she would consider doing this?

He'd thought her interest in a hotel investment in the South of England was little more than a vanity project for her son. He'd missed the off-paper condition—a *wedding*.

That told him this wasn't about Elodie's family's barely-breaking-even hotel. This was about *his* family's private island. The sanctuary his mother had retreated to in her despair and which had returned to the family trust since her death. The trust decreed that lifelong occupancy rights were granted to the most senior male of the family as long as he were *married*. While Ramon was the most senior male, he was single. If the next in line—*Cristina's son*—were to marry, then *he* could claim occupancy—and development—rights. Ramon couldn't allow that to happen because Cristina would use her son to destroy everything Ramon's mother had built there.

Ramon could mount a legal challenge to amend the trust. Should've done that already, but since his mother's death he'd buried himself even more in work and somehow three years had passed. But Ramon would protect his mother's legacy by whatever means necessary—especially now he knew he no longer had the time for a protracted legal battle.

So he *did* need to know everything about the fire-breathing beauty before him. No way would his aunt allow a woman like Elodie Wallace to enter the family—which meant Cristina didn't know about her and that could play very well into his hands. Perhaps he was the one who'd take revenge this time. Maybe he'd finally make his aunt pay for the cruelty she'd shown his mother in her grief.

'Elodie?' He caved in to temptation and gently cupped her face. 'Are you persona non grata?'

She trembled slightly at his touch but she didn't pull back. The hint of hurt crossed with courage in her eyes made his chest tighten.

Yes, he could save time, money and stress by getting married himself. The trust didn't specify that he had to *stay* married or for how long he even had to *be* married. Because in his hypocritical family, the concept of divorce supposedly didn't exist. But it would for him because there was no way in hell that he would ever marry for real. All he had to do was get married for long enough to invoke the occupancy rights. Maybe he would call Ms Elodie Wallace's bluff. Right now he wanted to do *that* more than anything.

'What did you *do*?' He provoked with a silkily patronising tone, pleased to see the instant flare in her eyes. 'What's really so dangerous about a little thing like you?'

'I lied.' She glared, finally goaded. 'I cheated. I abandoned my responsibilities.'

There was a ring of truth in her flash that he couldn't ignore.

'That bad, huh?' He tried to keep his tone light but his anger flared because he knew too well how those things damaged people. His father had lied, cheated. His mother had abandoned her responsibilities. And this woman was apparently every bit as fickle as she was beautiful and right now that pissed him off more than anything.

'Worse.' She was ferociously defiant.

'Yet here you are sweeping in to save your sister from a fate worse than death,' he snarled, because she was a contrary mix of shameless and protective.

'Because *she's* innocent.'

And Elodie wasn't. Bitterness burned. He could never, *ever* trust her. Which meant she presented one problem while being the solution to another in the one stunning package. He moved closer still, needing not just to see her reaction, but to feel it. He put his hand on her waist. A tremor instantly wracked her beautiful body, but she kept her head high, captivating *him* with her stormy gaze despite him being the one holding her. His smile was both twisted and unbidden. Without a doubt they would end up in bed together and he knew to his bones it would be mind-blowing. But that time was not now.

'Well, thank you for your honesty,' he muttered. 'It seems an appropriate time to admit that I haven't been completely forthcoming with you.'

And he still wasn't going to be entirely honest because some family secrets he could never tell. It didn't matter, she'd just admitted her prior deceit so she'd hardly care.

'*I'm* not the man intending to marry your sister,' he finally said softly. 'My cousin is.'

CHAPTER THREE

'PARDON?' ELODIE STARED at the stunning man as a rushing noise echoed in her head. She can't have heard him properly.

'My cousin is the man coercing your sister into marrying him. Well, actually, it's really his mother doing the coercing. My aunt.'

His *aunt*? She gaped. 'You're not Ramon Fernandez?'

'I am Juan Ramon Fernandez. You were seeking *Jose* Ramon,' he explained with a faintly regretful air. 'We are both known as Ramon.'

She suddenly realised he was still holding her and sharply pulled free of the hold that had been disconcertingly comforting. 'Not at all confusing.'

'The names are a family thing.' He watched her step backwards. 'My mother Daniela's family, actually. Fernandez is her name. The first Ramon was *her* father. My mother married a businessman who became CEO and took control of the Fernandez empire—continuing the family name through me was part of their deal. It is my mother's sister Cristina causing the problem. Her son—Jose Ramon Fernandez—is to marry Ashleigh.'

Stunned, Elodie tried to process all that information but it was almost as convoluted as one of her most challenging escape room clues.

Jose Ramon. Juan Ramon. Ramon. Both Fernandez.

She had it wrong. *This* man was not Ashleigh's prospective groom, that was someone else entirely—his cousin on his mother's side. And instead of doing the mental gymnastics to sort all that out, heat simply swamped her from head to toe as that illicit part deep within her pulsed with primal pleasure—

He wasn't the one. He wasn't taken. He could be hers.

Full mortification hit as she suppressed her own inner roar of possession. What was she *thinking*? She'd worked herself into a fury and she'd not even attacked the right guy and she should definitely *not* be so happy about it.

'You should have told me the moment you realised my mistake,' she growled.

He'd strung her along and allowed her to completely embarrass herself—hell, she'd all but thrown herself at the man in an attempt to show his immorality!

'I wanted to understand more about the situation—'

'You let me rage at you!' She couldn't restrain herself from raging again now. 'You let me—'

'You might have left before I could help.'

She paused, mistrustful as hell. 'You intend to help?'

'That surprises you?' His lips curved in that devastating smile. 'I think we may be able to resolve this situation to our best advantage if we work on it *together.*'

Best advantage? He spoke coolly, yet she felt an insidious warmth at the possibility of teaming up with him. But she couldn't lower her guard just because of his good looks and sudden charm. *This* Ramon was more than wealthy. He was powerful and definitely controlling. He'd just controlled the information he'd given her! He was used to being in charge—getting everything his way. And if he were anything like the controlling men she'd known, he wouldn't stand to be denied. She needed to be very, *very* careful. But she realised he'd given something away in admitting he'd wanted to understand more.

'You didn't know about the engagement plans,' she surmised.

He hesitated. 'No.'

'Yet you're this other Ramon's cousin?' Were they not close?

'Families can be complicated.' His gaze slid from her for the briefest second. 'I think Jose Ramon is as much of a pawn as your sister. He won't stand up to either his mother or your father.'

She felt a flare of pity for Jose Ramon because she had the feeling he wouldn't have a snowball's chance in hell of standing up to *this* man either. She knew how hard it was to say no to powerful people. It had taken her years to develop the skill. 'How old is he?'

'An immature twenty-two.' He cocked his head. 'How old are you?'

She ignored his question. 'Why does your aunt want him married to my sister?'

He hesitated. 'Because I have no plans to marry and they know it.'

'What's the relevance of *your* relationship status?' she asked with blunt sarcasm.

Even though that greedy part within her was utterly, keenly interested.

'It's everything.' He regarded her with that shameless arrogance. 'In a family like mine marriage is rarely about love. It's about assets and heirs and continuity of control. Some of our property is held in trusts because it is always better for assets to remain within the family. Most of the wider family are happy to let me remain in charge and do all the work as long as they get their quarterly dividends. But there are always some who'll never have enough. Cristina will never have enough.' He drew breath. 'So the pressure will continue on poor Jose Ramon to marry—if not your sister then someone else because if he beats me up the aisle then he could gain control of one particular property portfolio.'

'So this is really all a fight within your own family.'

Which meant to some extent he was still to blame for this situation. Which was good because she felt safer being angry with him.

'There are warring family factions in every generation, no?' He shrugged negligently. 'Dysfunction is often the norm.'

'In ridiculously wealthy dynasties, perhaps. I wouldn't really know.' But that wasn't quite true. Her family was dysfunctional. They didn't have the assets and heirs but they certainly had the control issue. 'So what are you going to do?'

'Well, I am seriously considering your proposal.'

'My...' She stared at him fixedly as a rush of adrenaline deafened her again. *'What?'*

'Marriage is the one thing both our families want. Perhaps we should give it to them.'

'I was speaking *facetiously*.' Yet the raw attraction burgeoning inside begged to differ.

'Were you?' He moved closer to her again.

This was bad. When he was close her brain failed and her body burned.

'How disappointing,' he added softly. 'Let's revisit it as a realistic prospect to solve our respective problems.'

'*Our* problems?' Breathless, she retreated a step. 'Sounds like this is about *your* problems which I definitely don't need to be part of.' She took another step back. 'I should go—'

'Stop.' He grabbed her hand. 'Stay. Sit.'

It wasn't his words that stopped her, but the jolt at his touch. Not an electrical current but a shot of pure desire— instantly followed by rage. She desperately hauled back her composure. 'I am not a dog you can command,' she snapped.

He paused. 'Please.'

'Not much better.'

He smiled. She was immune to the charm of it. *Immune*. She was not being dictated to by any man ever again.

'An apology might go a little way to salvaging the situation,' she muttered.

He cocked his head as he studied her thoughtfully. Right. This man apologised to no one. He didn't admit mistakes. Too arrogant to believe he even made any. And this was fast becoming too much about her and her increasingly uncontrollable insane reaction to someone she knew would be so wrong for her.

She needed to get out of here. She would figure out an alternative solution. She would break Ashleigh out of there and bring her back to London, find another job to support them both. It would be hard, but they could survive on their own together. But Juan Ramon Fernandez still had hold of her hand and somehow without her noticing he'd stepped closer again and all she could focus on was his finely tailored dinner jacket and her itchy-fingered desire to discover the heat of him beneath the starched white shirt.

'May I offer something even better,' he said smoothly. 'It's getting late. It's been a stressful evening. I get hungry when stressed. Do you? Stay and have dinner. We'll talk. Swap family horror stories—'

'And come up with an actually *practical* solution?' she interrupted.

For Ashleigh—only for Ashleigh—would she even consider this. She would ignore his charming and courteous side, stay on task, and she would never let him railroad her into anything as ridiculous as marriage.

'Precisely. I can help your sister. And you.' He gazed down at her. 'I have a couple of calls I need to make. Would you like a moment to freshen up while I do? Piotr will take you—'

'To the guest suite,' she muttered dryly. She was not thinking about his comment about her staying in *his* room. That had been way too much.

He smiled, unabashed. 'What do you say—will you stay?'

Awareness of danger feathered across her skin but the fact was she was short on time and ideas. And as he seemingly didn't want his cousin and Ashleigh's marriage either, she needed all the help she could get to stop it. Plus she didn't want to show any kind of weakness in front of him. Running away would only reveal how much he got to her. His supposed interest in her stupid proposal was little more than a joke, but even if he was serious he'd have a change of heart once he knew more about the reputation she'd cultivated in the months after she'd run out on her marriage, when she was trying to force Callum into finally accepting their separation. But once Ramon got beyond the marriage idea, perhaps they could work together. She was wary of his power, but if he were on her side, then she maybe could use it.

'I'll stay for dinner,' she said haughtily. 'But only so we can sort out this situation to my satisfaction.'

'Perfect,' he muttered soothingly and released her hand.

Weirdly, walking away from the man made her shiver. She pulled her blazer together, annoyed by the absurdly certain feeling he would sort the situation. He was the capable kind who could sort anything and everything. Even more annoying was her attraction to him. For a moment she imagined sweeping along in this velvet atmosphere wearing some gorgeous dress. Imagined being alone with Ramon Fernandez any time she felt like it. Imagined the confidence to do anything she wanted. With him. *To* him…

The effort to redirect *those* thoughts came at a cost. With every step away from him an almost blinding headache came on swiftly and strongly. Thankfully the immaculately efficient Piotr opened a door, then stood back to let her through.

'I'll be back in about twenty minutes to escort you to the dining room,' he said.

'Thank you.'

She leaned back against the door the second she closed it. Ashleigh's safety was the most important thing—the *only* thing to focus on right now.

She stared at the enormous bed—more luxurious than any hotel perfection. Not that she'd ever stayed in one of the hotels in the Fernandez empire though. Another fantasy engulfed her—of being in his room. That shocking comment had been pure temptation. Her face flamed and she chastised her wayward imagination. Her head pounded, exacerbated by not eating in hours because she'd been too nervous about her mission. And now the riot of her wholly unexpected and inappropriate response to him caused even more inner tension, resulting in a fierce pounding at her temples. She staggered into the stunning bathroom, dampened a cloth and went back to sink into the large armchair beside the bed. Closing her eyes, she pressed it to her face, desperate to relax.

Ramon tensed, his gaze narrowing on the screens in front of him that were mirroring those of two of his highly paid personal assistants who were working late in the city office. He was juggling calls with both.

'I want to see everything that's there. Go back further.'

His assistant immediately obliged, knowing better than to question, no matter how exceptional or unusual these particular instructions were.

He'd already skimmed the plans for the island that Cristina and Jose Ramon had commissioned and planned to submit for local government approval the second Jose Ramon had occupancy. Yet instead of prioritising that imminent disaster he'd fallen down the rabbit hole that was Elodie Wallace's social media profile. So *many* party pictures—not yachts and private beaches and the like—this was all clubs and bars in the city.

'There's nothing earlier,' his assistant said.

Nothing prior to the sudden rush of pictures starting about three years ago. Furthermore, the flurry of party girl activity had been updated only sporadically in the past year. Her profile picture showed her standing between two other women who looked to be a similar age. Her squad? A curvy brunette and an arctic-looking blonde. They made a stunning trio, but it was the flame-haired vixen in the centre who he couldn't help staring at. Who he felt absurdly angry about.

It didn't bother him that she'd mistaken him for his cousin. He wasn't insulted by her assumption that he would marry someone so young and who he barely knew. No, that wasn't the problem. *She* was. Specifically, his reaction to her. Her wild red hair, striking blue eyes and temperamental sass sharpened his senses. The strength with which she drew him was beyond irritating. It was her unexpected appearance, right? She'd stormed into his home—dressed to thrill—and demanded what she wanted.

So yeah, she'd got his attention. That was all. Because for years now he'd proven to himself that he was not his father. That he *didn't* have that bastard's age-old weakness for a beautiful woman. That he wouldn't ever be controlled by base urges in the way his repellent old man had been.

Ramon was better than that. Only now, in mere moments, that belief was destroyed. One look at her and he'd been stupefied. One conversation and he was almost tongue-tied. His animal instinct urged him to capture and claim. He'd been unable to resist the desire to touch her.

'She works for an escape room company,' the other assistant informed him. 'She's a hostess there.'

'Hostess?'

'You know, the one who reads the rules and then locks people in.'

And watches them try to worm their way out? Yeah. That made sense. He had the feeling she would enjoy that power trip. She liked to be in control.

'She was married.' His first assistant coughed. 'And is now divorced.'

His blood iced as the certificates appeared on the screen in front of him. 'Can you find anything about the ex?'

'Same town addresses. Presumably someone local. Looking at him now.'

There was a pause while his assistant typed.

'They went to the same school,' she said.

She'd married her high school sweetheart? Had she outgrown him? Broken his heart?

Ramon clicked the certificates away. Now he knew what she'd meant with her dramatic declaration—

'I lied. I cheated. I abandoned my responsibilities.'

He gritted his teeth. The details didn't matter. He didn't need to know anything more than the bare fact that she'd betrayed her husband. Leopards didn't change their spots.

His father had cheated on his mother many times and lied about it for years before making Ramon complicit in betrayal too. His father had tried to convince him that it was 'normal'—that Ramon would understand as he grew older. That they were very alike. And yes, Ramon looked like his father, worked like his father and had now long been stained by his father's sins.

He'd tried to protect his mother from the truth. Not only had he failed in that, she'd never forgiven him for his silence, assuming he'd known about the one betrayal that had been so much worse than Ramon could have ever imagined. His parents' marriage had been such a travesty, Ramon was never entering one of his own. At least not for real and not for long.

Fortunately, Elodie had already proven that vows didn't signify to her. Which meant the impulsive solution aired earlier might actually have legs. She'd offered herself, had she not? She would do anything for her sister. What was a little agreement—a signature here and there?

'There's no mention of her on her parents' social media profiles,' his other assistant said. 'It's as if she doesn't exist.'

Irritated, he snapped, 'And her sister?'

'Doesn't seem to be online.'

Which was weird. But Elodie's social media profile was easily accessible. Beautiful Elodie in short, form-fitting dresses—all seductive smiles, drinks in hand, nightclubs, restaurants and parties. Unsurprisingly she was accompanied by a vast assortment of men. Apparently disowned by her parents, she was a wild child. And an appallingly base part of him was pleased that Elodie Wallace knew how to have a good time.

'Enough. Thank you.' He ended the calls and remained staring at the screen full of pictures for far too long.

She would be able to hold her own with him. She was as uninterested in happy ever after as he was. She was about immediate gratification. His competitive nature surged. No one would give her a good time in the way he would. He would have her resplendent in his bed, mindless with bliss, with nothing other than sighs tumbling from her tart mouth. Because that was the element missing in all these photos. His gut instinct told him her pleasure here was superficial amusement at best. Not bone-deep satisfaction.

So maybe he would thwart his aunt and get the occupancy rights of the property the moment before she thought she'd succeeded. And in the same sweep, he would enjoy an affair with the enthusiastic and experienced Elodie Wallace.

He finally stalked along the corridor to the guest suite, anticipating her annoyance that it was more than an hour since

Piotr had shown her to the room, not a mere twenty minutes. That it was Ramon himself coming to fetch her for dinner, not his man. In part he'd wanted to test whether she'd skip out or not. He knocked on the door but got no response. Opened it and paused. She was reclined in the large armchair, a flannel folded across her eyes—was she asleep?

He moved forward, not expecting that she'd be so relaxed as if she were having a spa session at a hotel. But of course, she was a confident queen. He crouched before her. Her satiny skin tempted as did her soft-looking mouth. But there was something vulnerable in her positioning.

'Elodie.' His whisper came out gruff and he had to clear his throat.

She lifted away the cloth and looked straight into his eyes. The cloth must've been damp because much of her make-up was removed and she was disturbingly pale.

'Oh. I'm…' She made to sit up.

He frowned and pushed her back against the chair. 'You have a headache?'

'I probably look like a racoon.'

But the shadows beneath her eyes weren't streaks of mascara. She looked wary and sensitive. Interesting given her boldness earlier.

'What time is it?' She bit her lip.

'I took longer than I'd thought. Wasn't sure you'd have stayed to be honest. Turns out you're lying here looking like death.' He studied her curiously. 'Been burning the candle at both ends?'

Had she been out partying and just not updating her social media?

He heard a defiant little hitch of her breath.

'Of course, that's how I like it,' she said.

'So you have no problem sleeping wherever and whenever?' And with whomever?

He shouldn't care about that. Her past was the past and none of his business. But without doubt *he* would be her immediate future.

'Right.' She lowered her lashes but beneath them her eyes gleamed. 'It's a skill I've perfected over the years.'

'Impressive.' As was the coy death look she was shooting him now.

He watched her pull herself together before him—in two blinks she morphed back into the confident woman who'd coolly knocked down his front door. Her lashes lifted and she looked at him directly. The ambient temperature soared. Colour surged back beneath her skin. Her blush was a giveaway reaction to him that was completely beyond her control. As was his. This chemistry needed to be burned. He rose from his haunches and offered his hand. There was a small hesitation—as if she were bracing—before she took it. He locked his fingers firmly around hers—also inwardly bracing to contain his insane satisfaction—and tugged, helping her to her feet in a smooth movement.

Now they stood too close and still she met his gaze with that daring, fiery defiance. The bed beckoned. He watched, waited. Would she make the move? She was definitely sexually interested. No way was he wrong about that. Which meant any moment now she'd lift her chin and press her lips to his. He wanted her to. Badly.

But she didn't. She'd frozen as if paralysed by the crackling reaction between them. His pulse thudded—pushing him to close the gap. Resisting the urge took almost everything he had.

'I'm hungry,' she said huskily.

He dragged in a breath. She was *very* good. But this vixen had entered *his* den and he wasn't afraid to engage with her. He wasn't bored anymore either. No, now they would spar. 'Then come with me.'

CHAPTER FOUR

ELODIE HAD LITTLE choice but to accompany Ramon Fernandez down the corridor, given he didn't release her hand. Her pulse lifted, her breathing quickened and amazingly the pain in her head receded. She told herself it wasn't from his touch but rather the rush of adrenaline that his appearance had induced.

Okay, it was his touch, and she was completely out of her depth. But if he knew how much he affected her that would give him power, and Elodie never wanted anyone to have power over her again. Not emotional. Not physical. Not financial. She'd worked too hard for too long to gain her independence and her confidence. So she'd pull on her cool.

Once more she regretted coming here alone, but she'd never imagined that he'd be so attractive. She had to shake off this sense of intimacy that had deepened by virtue of him catching her resting. *Physical* distance would help but the house made that difficult. The dark colour scheme flowed into the dining room where the silverware gleamed in flickering candlelight. It was atmospheric and something smelled so good her mouth watered.

He released her hand and held a chair for her. 'Eat.'

Right now she was too hungry to think of a comeback to savage his tendency to command. Desperate to haul her scattered wits together, she did as he'd suggested and focused on the food. She would refuel her brain and then get it together.

Piotr presented the plates and then left. Salmon fillet, baby potatoes, a pretty salad—Elodie felt healthier just by looking at it. At the first mouthful she suppressed a moan. Exceptionally cooked, it wasn't rich and decadent but light and refreshing and everything she needed. She basically inhaled it. Maybe she ought to make polite conversation, but it was too hard to keep her emotions contained. Fortunately, he too seemed intently focused on stabbing the food with jerky movements. They both drank water, steering clear of the wine. Slowly she felt fortified, and by the time they moved to the elegant and refined fruit and cheese platter with an exquisite assortment of petit fours that she simply couldn't resist, she thought she might be able to handle anything.

'Better?' he asked quietly.

'Yes.' She finally dared to look at him directly and breathed in deep because it was a mistake.

He was appallingly handsome, but it was that combination of alert amusement and awareness in his eyes that minced her brain again.

'When did you find out about Ashleigh's engagement?' he asked.

'Last night.'

'You've been kept out of the loop as much as I have,' he noted softly. 'Save your sister. Marry me.'

'That's crazy,' she muttered.

The crazy thing was that she was *tempted*—purely because of her physical response to him. Her whole body was on high alert. Sex had never been a big part of her life before, so this desire was shocking and diabolical and extremely difficult to control.

'Isn't accosting someone in their own home also crazy?' he said. 'Especially when you got the wrong guy. Perhaps impulsive is a better word. Perhaps we could impulsively marry.'

'Absolutely not.'

His smile flashed. 'Are you not attracted to my brilliance? My billions? Not even my body?'

She squirmed like a fish on a hook. 'None of the above.'

'You lie a lot.'

'Your ego is astronomical.' She sipped more water. 'I don't need to create more problems for myself by entering a foolish and unnecessary marriage. Two wrongs do not make a right. And frankly, I don't believe that you really feel forced into doing something so drastic.'

'Unfortunately my aunt's duplicity forces me into action of some kind,' he said mildly. 'Cristina wants assets. I imagine she wants Jose Ramon to produce the Fernandez heir for the next generation. As I'm pushing thirty and don't have three offspring already, she hopes that I'm a lost cause and so—'

'I'm *never* having your baby.' This talk of heirs and offspring shocked her into interrupting him.

He just laughed. 'Indeed you are not. I have zero intention or desire to procreate.'

'Right. Good.'

'As we agree so easily on this, I'm confident we'll find more common ground.' He smiled, all smug confidence. 'Our marriage may well be an oasis of emotional calm.'

She stared at him incredulously.

'I will retain control of the Fernandez empire,' he said.

That's when she saw the glint of steel and realised he was lethally serious.

'But if you're without an heir—what happens then?' she asked.

'I'll ensure the succession plan is in the best interests of the company but I need to buy a little time first. Getting married is the most expedient way of achieving that.'

'But you don't need to marry *me* at all. You could marry anyone.'

'Of course I could,' he agreed.

Elodie stilled, shocked as a hot spear of jealousy stabbed deep inside her.

'But that wouldn't solve the problem within *your* family,' he added with a charming smile. 'Won't your father simply find your sister another husband she doesn't want?'

That was a *horrible* possibility.

'You need a more permanent solution for your own family drama,' Ramon said. 'I can be that solution.'

He made it sound so simple. So easy to say yes to something so insane. But Ramon Fernandez was more powerful than both her father and her ex put together, and she should be running far, far away.

'I've been married before,' she said flatly. 'I have zero intention of doing it again.'

He leaned back and studied her. 'You were nineteen.'

She glared at him. He *knew*?

'Why did it end?'

The atmosphere sharpened. When did he learn that about her—had he pried into her personal life while she'd been resting?

'You were unfaithful?' he asked harshly.

'Repeatedly,' she lied furiously.

His expression pinched. He believed her. It was important that he did. It was another layer of armour for her. She *needed* him to think she was trouble—that she was tough. That he couldn't control her.

'Which I assume is the source of your supposed danger,' he said. 'Your flightiness. Your high *needs*. Perhaps our marriage could restore your reputation?'

'I don't want to *restore* my reputation,' she snapped. 'I *like* my life. It took a lot to get my freedom and I'll fight to keep it however I have to—'

'You do realise that I'm not talking about forever?' he interrupted with a low drawl.

'You do realise that I could make your married life the worst thing ever?'

'I was rather hoping you'd suggest that.' His smile widened to full crocodile threat. 'You're everything they'd hate. My marrying you would be their worst nightmare.'

Great. Good to know her efforts to be repellent had been so successful. She breathed through the hit and pulled on a ruthless smile—drawing on the persona she'd cultivated after walking out on her marriage after only five months. The one that had finally given her ex the impetus to agree to the divorce he'd tried to delay. He'd begged her to come back but never *listened* to why she didn't want to. He'd wanted the obedient Elodie he'd first met, not the free Elodie she'd desperately needed to be.

'Because I'm a troublemaker?'

She'd played 'unfaithful wife'. Repeatedly. She'd posted 'incriminating' pictures all over social media until finally neither Callum nor her father could stand the continued public humiliation. The divorce had been expedited at last, and Elodie had been wiped from her own family's photos.

And Ramon Fernandez clearly thought he knew all about her now—knew her fickleness, flippancy, infidelity. Of course he wasn't afraid of it. Maybe the only thing that mattered to him was money.

'Because you're an independent woman who's not afraid to say what she thinks or to ask for what she wants,' he corrected.

Elodie's breath stalled as a lick of pleasure curled inside her. Independent? Not afraid? Maybe he was just being smooth but that was how she wanted him to see her. Strength mattered. And she would remain strong in front of him now.

'Unfortunately that's not going to work on my side.' She coolly denied him. 'Because *you're* not *my* family's worst nightmare.'

'No?'

Hell, no. Her father, so impressed by grandeur, by supposed social standing, would be a drooling sycophant should he ever meet *this* Ramon Fernandez.

'You supposedly have billions,' she said. 'If I were to marry you they'd be over the moon, basking in the glory of such a connection. They wouldn't care if you treated me badly. In fact they'd probably cheer you on.'

His mouth thinned. 'Which is why—when the time is right—you'll give me hell and walk out. You'll destroy me like you no doubt destroyed that other guy.'

She masked her flinch. 'As if *you* would ever allow yourself to be destroyed.'

'You see?' The crocodile smile returned. 'It's perfect. Because you do not care about marriage. You do not care about me. Neither of us will mistake this for anything more than a temporary deal to resolve family drama.' He leaned close. 'You're as bulletproof as I am.'

He was so wrong. But she couldn't ever admit that to him.

'As appealing as you've made it sound,' she said with a bored expression, 'there's not enough in it for *me.*'

'No?' His gaze sharpened. 'Then tell me, Elodie Wallace, what is it that I can do for you?'

She fought to keep her brain together and not let the new sensual ache in her body derail her completely. 'Are you really trying to offer me anything I want in return for my hand in marriage?' She shook her head and went full bluff. 'Sorry, but I already *have* everything I want.'

'No,' he scoffed. 'There's something you need. There's always something.'

'You're saying anyone can be bought?' she asked.

He was so cynical.

'You know it.' He suddenly leaned close, his blue eyes

glinting and jaw angular as he sucked in a sharp breath. 'Why not take everything that you can get from this?'

'"This"?'

'Don't pretend to be so naive,' he muttered harshly. 'Don't avoid the obvious.'

She couldn't believe the fire now in his gaze and couldn't stand the energy coursing through her. She had to move. She pushed back from the table at the exact moment he did. He moved with such rapid force the chair toppled behind him but he didn't care—he grabbed her hand instead.

People shook hands in all kinds of settings so the smallest of strokes of his thumb on her wrist shouldn't have had the effect on her that it did. But it was such a gentle caress. One he repeated—almost as if he were unconscious of the action. Except he was as aware of it as she. *Hyper*aware. Heat flooded her face and the answering splash of colour on his upper cheekbones melted her.

'*This* is the obvious?' Her voice was high and thin because she was breathless and yearning and hotter than she'd ever felt in her life.

'Has been from the moment you stormed my house.' He kept those mesmerising blue eyes on her. 'The fact is you want me as much as I want you.'

He crowded closer but she craved closer still. With a hitch of her breath, with an unconscious sway towards him she admitted it. *Invited.* His other hand landed on the small of her back—beneath her blazer. Her breasts tightened against her bodice. She gazed up at him, her lips parting as he lowered his head to hers. One kiss. Just one. Just to see.

He caught her mouth with his and in seconds it was the most sexually explicit kiss she'd ever experienced. His tongue teased then plundered, full of intent and carnal temptation. With a moan she sank against him, and his hold tightened. She gasped as his lips trailed lower, teasing the sensitive skin of her neck. Her knees weakened at the caress—such was the cliché she'd become. But in an instant she was his plaything. Somehow her blazer slipped from her shoulders to the floor. She swayed, so supple for him, so eager for his touch, and he lowered her back against the table. Their empty plates were at one end but now she was the dish on offer. And he feasted. His body was like rock and the intensity of *his* arousal turned her on even more. She was breathless with awareness of it—*ached* for it. She wanted him. Completely.

In moments they were hurtling towards a foregone conclusion. She would sleep with him. She would do *anything* with him. Frankly, he'd seduced her before even touching her and now that he had, she'd gone up in flames. Eviscerated. Inevitable. He tugged her bodice down. She sucked in a shocked breath because he was strong and bold. Her breasts were exposed to his gaze, touch, tongue, and he took quick advantage in that order.

'You are stunning, my flame-haired vixen,' he groaned huskily. 'You know how to make an impression and I so appreciate it.'

'It wasn't for you,' she moaned.

'I know,' he laughed exultantly. 'But I'm not my cousin. I'm not a weak man. I know what I want and I'm not afraid to reach for it.'

He wanted *her* and he made no effort to hide it. No effort to restrain his intense kisses, caressing her with mouth and hands and closeness—rousing her to an equally wild hunger.

This boiled down to *sex*. From the moment she'd set eyes on him the awareness had kicked in. It had been a swift, unstoppable reaction she'd never experienced before and incited a shocking greed that she couldn't control. She wrapped her leg around his hips so she could feel his hardness right where she was aching and wet. Even through the layers of clothes, the feel of him against her was shudderingly good.

He moved against her again and again in the most delicious erotic tease and suddenly she was about to lose control. She was about to—

'Oh, no,' she muttered to herself, a shocked gasping whisper. *'No!'*

'But you're so close,' he muttered hotly. 'Let me finish you—' He broke off on a growl and stepped back.

Elodie almost wept as a wave of frustration smacked into the empty space he'd left. She'd be shaking in bliss if she'd just bit her lip! For a split second longer she remained leaning back on the dining table, staring up at him. The fire in his eyes, the flush on his cheeks, the satyr-like smile on his lips…he gazed down at her so hungrily and she was stunned at how sexy *she* felt. She'd been more turned on in the last minutes than she'd ever been in her life—a breath from an orgasm she'd never experienced with another.

And it had taken him mere moments. A chill ran through her body, dousing the flame of desire. That had been too intense. Too quick. She scrambled to cover up. She'd never been as close to losing complete control of herself.

'Games, Elodie?' he growled softly. 'Of course you like to play them. But you really don't need to feign shyness.'

She wasn't playing anything, but she would let him think it while she got her head together. She needed the protection of his disapproval. If he knew how shaky and vulnerable she actually was right now, she'd be completely at his mercy.

'I'll happily play whatever games you want once we're married.' Ramon curled his hands into fists, striving to regain control of himself.

She'd surprised him by slamming on the brakes, but he'd seen the keening ache still in her expression as she'd turned away to tug the bustier back in place. He picked up her little blazer. She snatched it off him with trembling hands.

'This has been a waste of time.' She flipped her hair free and it settled in wild disarray across her shoulders.

'It has not,' he retorted, folding his arms across his chest to stop himself grabbing her back against him. 'But unlike you, I'm not one for making dramatic declarations, I'll actually *do* whatever is necessary to resolve this. The question is, will you? Or are you all talk and no action?'

'I'm taking action. By leaving. Now.'

He didn't want that, but he clamped down on his urge to restrain her with brute force. 'Running away because you can't handle the temptation?'

Twin spots of colour flooded her cheeks. She almost looked prim. 'You really think you're that irresistible?'

'I really think this chemistry is,' he threw back at her.

She stilled, stared at him with wide, wild blue eyes.

'I'm not afraid to be honest,' he growled. 'Seems you need a little more practice.'

But doubt sliced—was this just strong chemistry or was it those more *unfortunate* genetic tendencies unleashed? Ramon had vowed never to come unhinged by lust. Yet here was his very personal challenge to that. So he would show restraint. Just to prove to himself that he could—that he wasn't like his father in everything.

'Piotr will drive you home,' he said roughly. 'I'll be in touch tomorrow. We'll solidify the plan.'

'Make an actual proper plan, you mean.'

He watched her worry her lip—that's all it took to reignite the need to pull her close. He definitely wasn't alone in feeling this, but he'd slow them down and ensure this would be a controlled explosion geared to extract maximum benefit for them both.

'I guarantee that if you marry me, your sister will be released from that engagement immediately,' he said. 'And you need this to be immediately, no?'

She didn't reply, which was better than an outright refusal. He sensed she was unsettled from something more profound than the insanity of this rash proposal. He got to her. It pleased him. It made them even.

'Thank you for dinner.' She ground out the most reluctant polite goodbye ever.

He laughed. She looked angry.

'My pleasure.' He should step back. Instead, he couldn't resist temptation again. Not when she stood there so defiantly—wordlessly daring him.

One kiss. Just one more. He bent and brushed his mouth gently against hers and felt the instinctive cling of her lips to his. No denial. She couldn't. Suppressing a guttural groan, he allowed himself another taste of her exquisite softness. He cupped her face to stop himself from searching out her curves but then he couldn't resist pressing her against the wall with his body. She melted like wax against him, and damned if that wasn't every bit as good as earlier. If not even better than the raging inferno of the straight-to-orgasm encounter they'd almost had on his dining table. She was so warm. So tender. So sweet. And with another swipe of his tongue the inferno was back. He growled and ground against her—torn between keeping his head and indulging his rampant appetite. He should just take her to bed. Slake this hunger. If he asked now she would say yes. But he wanted her acceptance of something so much more.

He tore his lips from hers, leaning back to study her. Her eyes were still closed as if she was lost in the moment. As if she'd never been kissed like that in her life. And maybe it made him a fool, but he was willing to go with it because he hadn't had a kiss like that either.

'I can hardly wait till we're married,' he muttered.

Her eyes opened and looked huge—dazed. Her bold, sexy clothes and her trembling, flushed response were a study in contrasts and he decided then that he would truly take his time because her surrender would be all the more satisfying.

'We're not getting married.'

'Sure we are. That's the only way I'll give you what you want.' He would convince her properly tomorrow. He would find her weak spot, apply pressure and win.

'Sleep on it. If you can,' he challenged softly. 'I'm not going to. I'm going to lie awake all night thinking about you. Specifically what I'm going to *do* with you the second I have that band on your finger.'

CHAPTER FIVE

'YOU HAVE ONLY one hour to escape!' With dramatic effort Elodie closed the heavy door on the group of excited pre-teens and turned the lock with a loud flourish.

Her first customers were making the most of the air-conditioning to escape the suffocating heat that London could shock with in the summer. By the time she got back to reception, Bethan had arrived and was sewing final touches onto a prop for the new scenario they had planned.

'You okay?' Bethan's eyes narrowed on her. 'You look tired.'

'Just a bit distracted.' Elodie smiled to cover up. 'I'm going to work from the back office for a while, can you monitor those guys?'

'Of course.' Bethan nodded. 'I'll bring you coffee shortly.'

Elodie hugged her as she went past. 'You're the *best*.'

Try though she might, Elodie couldn't stop thinking about Ramon Fernandez. Already in sleep deficit after the disturbed night before, worrying about Ashleigh, she'd lain awake for the whole of last night as well—thinking about *him* instead of trying to find alternative solutions to help her sister. She was pathetic. But she still couldn't process what had happened between them.

Lust. Instant. Rampant. Undeniable lust.

Seemingly a normal thing for him but an absolute first for her. Most of the time she didn't think about sex, and she tried not to think about her ex-husband Callum at all. Their physical relationship had been unsatisfying at best and in truth she wasn't anywhere near as experienced as people believed. All her nightclub party pictures had been for show to provide the humiliating evidence she needed for her liberation. So the uncontrollable moments in Ramon Fernandez's home last night?

Shocking. Even more shocking, was her appetite for more.

Bethan appeared in the doorway of the office but with no coffee in hand. Instead, she had a curious expression on her face. 'Someone's here to see you. He says it's a personal matter?'

Elodie stared at Bethan, then swivelled to check the CCTV displays that showed all the escape rooms, plus the reception area. They'd barely been open ten minutes and here he was—tall, *devious* and handsome.

'Lock him in the Prohibition room,' she said softly.

'Did you say *lock* him in?' Bethan checked, startled. 'Um… I don't think he's a customer. He—'

'Deserves it,' Elodie said flatly.

'Right. Uh, I'll get him in there right away then.' Bethan backed out of the office. 'I'll stay on reception to handle those others and the next scheduled.'

Elodie clicked a few commands on the audiovisual set-up to block the Prohibition room from Bethan's monitor on reception, then switched her own view to full-size on that very room. It was only a moment before the door opened and Ramon strolled in with that relaxed, yet predatory, ruler of the universe way of his. Bethan quickly closed the door without saying a word to him.

Elodie activated the intercom system. 'You have one hour to escape.'

'Elodie.' He slowly turned a full circle in the centre of the room, his alert gaze taking in the vibrant decor. 'I am locked in?'

'That is the point of an escape room,' she said acidly.

'You think I came here to play?' He stared straight into the CCTV camera that was mounted on the wall.

'Consider it a test.'

'What happens if I fail your test?'

She'd put him in the hardest of the escape rooms. Whole teams of people struggled to work the challenges out. She was certain he'd fail. 'Then I know you're not fit for purpose.'

He smiled. 'Are you not going to give me the rules—don't I get some sort of scenario I have to work through?'

Yeah, she'd skipped the three-minute spiel she usually gave before that final line.

'How can I pass your test if it's unfair from the outset?' he added.

She gritted her teeth. 'The year is 1922. It's the Prohibition era in the States, but you're a playboy—running with the wrong crowd and trying to be a big man bootlegger. You've been lured to The Redhead, a speakeasy with a secret entrance beneath a barbershop, and locked in to be caught. If you're found here you'll forfeit your family fortune. You need to find the hidden mechanisms that will turn the basement bar back into a storeroom and then make your escape before the police catch you.'

'Did you just say I've been lured to a redhead?' His mouth twitched. 'You really do like playing games…'

'It's the name of the bar.'

Elodie put on the jazz music that signalled the start of the hour. She watched him read all the supposedly 'random' notes on the counter and take note of the patterns painted on the walls. It took him only a moment to find the 'hint' envelope stashed behind one of the decorative bottles.

'Need help so soon?' she murmured.

'I want to get out of here as fast as possible.' He speed-read the letter inside. 'An interesting job you have, watching people struggle to work out the clues. The diversions, red herrings, complications. Do you enjoy seeing them sweat?'

She did want to see him sweat, actually. 'What do you think that says about me?'

'That you like to play but you keep yourself safe. Distanced.'

'I offer assistance when required.'

'Benevolence?' His laugh was low. 'No, you just like to display your superior intellect.'

'Not superior,' she countered. 'I have the advantage only because I know the rooms inside and out.'

'Because you designed them. You've set this trap for me.'

She watched him unlock the first cabinet and gritted her teeth. He was too quick. He was going to do this in less than an hour. 'You've been doing your research.'

'I stayed up all night finding everything I could about you.'

'That would hardly have taken all night,' she said uncomfortably. What did he think he knew now?

'The night was very hard.' He grinned. 'Will you give me extra time given my performance might be impaired due to the lack of sleep you caused?'

'No.'

'I won't forget that small lack of mercy, Elodie. Maybe there'll come a time when I show you no mercy.' He stood still and stared directly into the camera. 'Here's the deal. When I escape this room—in less than an hour—you'll elope with me.'

Even though there were walls between them, she felt that look burn through her. 'You're not really in a position to make demands.'

'I have copies of your parents' accounts,' he said softly. 'You're going to want to see them.'

Her stomach dropped. 'How bad are they?'

'Can't say right now, I'm concentrating on decoding this

cipher.' He pushed a series of buttons—in the right order. The cloth providing a colourful backdrop for the musicians' platform fluttered, swallowed into a small gap in the floor and leaving a bland basement wall exposed.

'Oh, that's impressive,' he commented.

Elodie refused to feel pleasure at the praise. She clicked to another screen and adjusted the temperature of the air conditioning. Willing to play dirty to win.

Only a few moments later Ramon removed his jacket, put it on the wooden table and rolled up his sleeves. 'I appreciate your efforts to make this even more difficult for me.'

He flexed his hands and stepped forward to line up a series of cocktail glasses.

'Copa de balón...' He angled his head and read the gin bottles. Understanding he needed to read the colours in the mirror to input them in the right order. 'This business is for sale. The owner wants to retire. Meaning your job is potentially at risk. His asking price is steep.'

Elodie froze, hating him.

'It must be disappointing that you don't have the money to scrape together a bid when you're the one who's made such a difference to the bottom line with rooms like this and thus have inflated that asking price,' he added. 'You've brought in another stellar worker and everything. It must be nice to work with a friend. Bethan, right? The brunette on reception. She's in some of your social media photos.' He ran his hand over the knobs and lined them up. 'Wouldn't it be a shame if she lost her job too?'

'I'm not going to let that happen.'

'No? But the business leases this building and that's also coming up for renewal shortly. What if the landlord decides to sell? A new building owner might want to do something else with the space given it's such a central location. It could even be a good boutique hotel.' He paused. 'All that could be avoided if *you* were to buy the business.'

Elodie turned the audiovisual feed off completely. It was a calculated risk but one she had to take given he was at the three-quarter mark already. She ran down the secret fire escape passage to the compartment that was about to be flipped into the room and stepped onto the small space just in time. She heard the creak as the mechanism started. Lifting her chin, she pressed back as she was swung around on the small platform and into the room. Because what had been a shelf in front of him was now a hollow holding Elodie herself.

She met his stunned gaze with a defiant glare.

'Wow...' Ramon pressed his hand to his chest. 'Quite the jump-scare.' He regarded her with wide eyes as she stepped into the centre of the room. 'You really do know how to make an entrance. Here was me thinking the object of the exercise was to get *out* of the room.'

'There are surprises for the clients,' she muttered. 'Sometimes a mannequin, sometimes a fake skeleton—'

'Sometimes a beautiful woman.' He put his hands on her waist and pulled her flush against him. 'This is definitely an interactive experience. I—'

'Think you're done?' She stood stiffly against him.

'Yes.'

'No,' she said with some pleasure. 'It was a false finish.'

He stilled. 'So we're still locked in here?'

'You are. I can get out anytime I like.'

He gazed down at her, taking in her floor-length black skirt and high-necked fitted black shirt with its long row of pearl buttons. 'So are you a Victorian widow or scandalous witch? Either way, I like it.' He looked back into her face, his own half smile all mockery. 'I'm not sure you should have joined me in here, *cariño.*'

Elodie summoned all her strength to resist him. 'I'm not afraid of you.'

'I'm glad to hear it,' he said softly. 'I'm not afraid of you either.' He glanced into her eyes. 'Much.' He cupped her face and muttered quietly, 'Who's monitoring the cameras?'

'I turned them off.'

He stared at her for a long moment. 'Always three steps ahead, aren't you Elodie?'

She stared back at him silently.

'You want to delay my success,' he murmured. 'You're trying to distract me—'

'Because you're cheating.'

'No, I'm not.' He smiled a little bitterly and released her. 'I think that's your speciality.'

'The clues,' she gritted as he stepped back. 'You're getting them too quickly. Did you search a spoiler page online? I change up the clues frequently to counteract them.'

'I didn't look them up, you're watching my raw talent.' He focused on figuring out the final task. 'When I'm determined to achieve something, I don't let anything get in the way of my goal. Like you.'

'You know what you want and you go for it.'

'As do you.'

She wasn't his equal—but she could pretend. Because she wanted to be. She really wanted to be. If she could hold her own with Ramon Fernandez, she could hold her own with anyone.

'You use numerical patterns. Ciphers. The envelope contained a decoder,' he said. 'A colour wheel. Morse code.'

'We use many codes, trick props. But sometimes it's simply that the truth is the opposite of how it appears.'

She watched as he worked through the penultimate clue with annoying ease.

'The opposite.' He glanced across and read her expression. 'The door will unlock if I do this?' He smiled but didn't move the piece into play. 'Less than an hour. Time to keep your end of the bargain.'

There was so much that was more important than testing him like this. 'Are my parents really going to lose their hotel?'

'It's in trouble. Your ex-husband didn't do such a great job as assistant manager. You left and he stayed.'

Right. So now Ramon knew that her father had sided with her ex after she'd walked out. Callum had remained as assistant manager while both he and her father had tried to convince her to come back. Well, Callum had tried to convince her with increasingly startling desperation while her father had simply bullied and threatened. Neither liked not having complete control.

'He left once he agreed to the divorce,' she said. Once she'd publicly humiliated him too much.

'Your father hasn't made wise choices since.'

'He tends not to make wise choices.'

He thought he did. He thought he knew everything and wouldn't listen to alternative ideas. The only way was *his* way.

She watched Ramon step closer to her. 'Dad's financial issues don't make marrying off Ashleigh the right thing to do.'

Ashleigh shouldn't be driven out of the only home she'd known. Shouldn't be expunged from the family like Elodie had been.

'Don't worry, *that* wedding will not happen.'

But Ramon wanted another one. Her heart thudded.

He frowned. 'You still look worried.'

'Of course I'm worried.'

'Don't be. I'm a good guy, helping save your sister.'

'By taking advantage of—'

'*No one* takes advantage of you, Elodie Wallace. You'll get what you want as much as I will from this.'

She stared at him. What she really wanted was *selfish*.

'Say yes and you'll have more than you need to help your sister,' he said. 'You'll have your own business. You'll be able to secure Bethan's job too. I understand she also walked out on her marriage.'

'That's right.' She tilted her chin in defiance of all his damned invasive research. 'We have our own divorced wives club, actually.'

'Of course you do. Does it have a name?'

'You mean your team didn't find that out for you? FFS.'

'Quite.'

'No, that's the *name*.'

'Standing for the obvious.'

'We're the Forever Free Sisters. Meaning we're going to be free—from *marriage*—forever. None of us are making that mistake again.'

'And with me you won't be,' he said. 'You're an astute woman, why not get what you can from me?'

'My body is not for sale.'

'Sure, but your signature could be. That's all I'm paying for. Your signature on a wedding certificate.'

She swallowed. It was a little more than that. It was her name. Her honour. But she'd destroyed both of those things herself, hadn't she?

'We both have pasts. We both know what we're getting into. We both know our affair is as inevitable as our next breath,' he said harshly. 'So why not extract some additional benefit to our being together?'

He thought she was something she wasn't, but if he knew the truth of her first marriage, if he knew how she'd faked most of those photos, how inexperienced she actually was—especially compared to him—would he still suggest this?

Elodie swallowed. He was more powerful. More experienced. More everything. If she told him and if he still wanted to proceed with this crazy plan, then she would lose what little power she had. So he couldn't know.

Because she'd spent most of last night regretting that she'd stopped him touching her.

Her loss of control had been shocking. Yet because of that she now knew he wouldn't demand more than she was willing to give. Not physically. She'd inadvertently tested him in the course of her own confusion and overwhelm. He'd stopped the instant she'd asked him to. He would again. So maybe she could fake her way through this. He never need know the extent of her inexperience and along with securing Ashleigh's future, she would get something *she* wanted. Him. Just for a little while.

'Come on, Elodie.' He crowded her as he had last night. As if he couldn't stand to stay at a respectable distance from her for more than three seconds. 'You know it's going to happen.'

'Are you trying to seduce me into saying yes?'

'As if you've never seduced someone into doing something you want?' He laughed.

Right. Elodie *had* never seduced anyone. She'd flirted—but only so far—then she was very good at escaping. And she didn't get seduced. She didn't lose herself in desire and heat. Never had. But she *wanted* to know. She *wanted* to be normal. This was her secret reason to say yes. But it had to stay a secret.

The physical relationship between them was to be a separate issue. She had an opportunity to discover something for herself. And right now it was the only thing she could think about.

'You know how this game works,' he murmured. 'The stakes aren't even that high. Neither of us is going to get hurt.'

Right. What was another failed marriage to her name? Maybe hardly anyone needed to even know about it. Surely it would be brief. Just long enough to secure a safe future for her sister and ensure he had the assets he wanted.

'You're too smart to turn down a deal that benefits you and those you care about so greatly. You're a realist, Elodie. You know what you want and you know you can get it all from me.'

Affair. Benefits. No complication. No messy misunderstandings. No expectations that couldn't be met. She'd sworn not to get hurt by a man again. And she wouldn't, because this was simply an arrangement. There was nothing deeper—no emotional connection. No guilt. But he could give her something she'd never had.

He watched her hesitation with raised brows. 'It's not like you consider wedding vows to really mean anything, right?'

That hurt but at the same time helped narrow her focus. He wanted her but didn't think much of her. She could hate him a little for that. Which was good. It would protect her from his immense magnetism.

'It doesn't bother me that you broke them before,' he added. 'They mean little to me either.'

She didn't believe him. He *judged*.

'So this is to be an open marriage?' she questioned even as the idea repelled her.

'Oh, *no*.'

His immediate guttural denial made her skin prickle and he captured her in a hard embrace.

'My affairs are always monogamous.' He lifted her chin so she couldn't avoid his eyes. 'I won't cheat on you.'

The strangest sensation of trust washed over her—belief in him—a fragile thing that scared her into pushing back. Because she couldn't drown in it. She'd believed someone once before when he'd made promises.

'I don't care if you do,' she lied, purely to keep him distanced.

'To be clear,' he said harshly, 'you won't cheat on me either.' He ran his hand firmly down her back, moulding her against his rock-hard frame. 'You won't have the time or the energy to even consider it. I intend to keep you utterly exhausted.'

His heat and strength seeped into her. This was a threat she knew he'd honour. And just like that he got her. Her overwhelming physical response was unlike anything in her life.

'Wow,' she breathed to mask her trembling. 'Big promises.'

'Big enough to satisfy you.' His smile was more a baring of teeth. 'Say yes already.'

This was what she wanted. Him roused. Her on fire. To the point where thinking was impossible. There was only feeling. It compelled her to soften and lean right against him.

'Elodie?' He jerked her closer into an intimate embrace.

His hand lifted, gazing her breast. His erection dug into her lower belly. Her nipples pebbled hard against his hand. But her physical acceptance was not enough.

'Fine.'

Not the word he wanted but the meaning was the same. He grunted and smashed his mouth on hers. She moaned, bowing into him so he scooped her closer still.

The kisses destroyed her. She clawed him closer as the animal inside overtook her again so swiftly. He was so *hot* and she wanted him everywhere. He *knew* because he moved almost as fast as she needed him to—unbuttoning her blouse to press kisses down her neck while hungrily grinding his hips against hers in that shamelessly sensual dance. Hell, they were almost consummating the deal while still fully clothed and it was *so* arousing. Elodie moaned.

Ramon wedged his hand between them, sliding it beneath her waistband until he got his fingers right between her legs and she moaned into his mouth again.

'Three steps ahead again, Elodie?' he growled.

'So?' She gasped in stunned pleasure at his repeated—deeper—incursion. 'Are you going to catch up?'

He laughed and suddenly dropped to his haunches, lifting her long skirt up and out of his way in a flagrant move. She just fell back against the wall as he shoved her panties down and exposed her core to his fierce gaze. To his mouth.

'What are you doing?' she whispered harshly. But she was so shocked she just let him. So willing she actually widened her stance and bunched her skirt in her hands to hold it high. So thrilled she couldn't catch her breath.

'I'm locked in here until I satisfy your demands, no?' he growled against her.

Utterly overwhelmed, she was unable to resist the temptation he offered. *Pleasure.*

'You're stunning,' he ground huskily, trailing his fingers over her thighs.

Never in her life had she been so bold. There was no embarrassment—*nothing* could survive this heat other than the desire that fuelled it. She craved his touch. She'd been craving it all night. And it was his fault. He'd awakened this hunger and with a singular circling motion she demanded he sate it.

To her gasping delight he teased his fingers over her and his mouth followed. There was no thinking. Only feeling. Wanting. Every stroke. Every lap of his tongue. She quaked as pleasure fired along every nerve. She wanted him to devour her and he did. Until a high-pitched moan startled her back to earth.

'Oh, *no.*' She bucked her hips to break his hold as she realised that mewling cry had come from her. She'd turned off the cameras and intercom, but the walls weren't going to be soundproof enough for the explosion coming upon her.

'Bite on this,' he ordered harshly.

She blinked at him uncomprehendingly, stunned to see that he'd risen.

'You're seconds from screaming your head off,' he added gruffly. 'Bite on this.'

Her mouth slackened and he shoved his silk handkerchief in before dropping back to his knees. She moaned in mortification but now it was muffled. Helplessly, hopelessly relieved, she closed her eyes and moaned again. His broad, strong hands squeezed her thighs, parting her for his mouth. She gripped her skirt as he took her so intimately with his tongue again. His fingers teased. Filling her just enough to be devastating. She rocked her hips, wanting more of him to ride. He gave her another. Pulsing, then plunging faster and deeper, he sucked too deliciously hard right where she was too devastatingly sensitive. He pulled her under with a relentless rhythmic onslaught that destroyed the last of her defences until she lost it entirely on a shriek of surrender. She gritted her teeth into the gag, grateful it suffocated her screams and then she was so far gone she simply didn't care any more.

Because he didn't stop, even as she arched uncontrollably and sobbed in uncontrolled, feral ecstasy, he gave her more. Holding her harder, his fingers flicking faster, his mouth hot and hungry until her legs gave out. That's when he caught her, rising to his feet and pressing her body against the wall with his. She trembled uncontrollably as he took the material from her mouth, wiped his own with it before shoving it into his pocket. She watched, stunned and turned on again by the total intimacy of that act and the even more carnal one preceding it. She'd never been this intimate. Never let go of everything. Never been as out of control. And she still wasn't herself. She still wasn't done. She felt his hardness pressing against her—where she needed him. If it weren't for the clothes in the way—

'Please…' She was barely aware as the raw plea escaped her. Barely aware of what she was asking for. She simply ached, unable to bear the agony of unfulfilled lust.

'Luscious Elodie,' he growled as he pinned her. 'So hedonistic. No wonder…' He breathed out harshly. His body was primed, pressing close enough to leave an imprint on her. 'When I finally have you, it will not be in a semipublic place with the possibility of interruption at any moment. It'll be in a bed, and we'll have all night and several days beyond to indulge in each other. There'll be no distractions. No interruptions.'

She shivered at the prospect. Impossibly all the more aroused. Because she believed him. He'd given her the most intense release of her life earlier. He'd just made her brainless.

She was utterly vulnerable. Utterly exposed. He'd turned her into a writhing, hot creature desperate for his touch. Shaken by the intensity of it all, she put her hand to her face to hide. How much she still ached. She heard him mutter something and he pulled back from the blatant thrust of possession into a looser, gentler embrace.

'You'll be my sole focus. I'll be yours. Together we'll be filthy,' he said unevenly. 'But it'll be *after* the wedding.'

With a muffled sob of laughter, she rested her forehead on his chest and closed her eyes. Sure, she should straighten and take her own weight. Not lean on him like some weakling. But she was too wobbly. Still too *needy*. Lust still howled within her. If she was the confident woman he thought she was, she would prowl down his body now—freely purr on all fours, undo his trousers, tease him as he'd teased her. She would touch him. She would take him in her mouth. She would rub—

She clenched her fist, unthinkingly pressing it into Ramon's chest as she tried to stop the X-rated images in her head turning her on all over again. She'd never wanted to do that with anyone. Ever. She'd had sex only with her ex-husband and he'd never made her feel *that*. Never made her want to reciprocate in such—

How was she to have known? Why couldn't she have known? She squeezed her fist more tightly, *hating* her humiliating past. She'd never initiated sex. She'd invented reasons not to be intimate. She'd lied to her ex-husband. Repeatedly. But she'd been begging Ramon just now. *Begging.* Because the pleasure she'd just experienced, she wanted again.

A little thrown by the intensity of the storm he'd just incited, Ramon adjusted his footing to steady them both. He kept hold of her—she was trembling too much to stand on her own two feet. He covered her tightly held fist with his hand and tried to claw back his own calm while she rode out the emotion sweeping through her in a series of violent aftershocks.

She still wouldn't look at him. And she'd looked almost stricken in the immediate aftermath of her orgasm, she'd pressed her face into his shirt and hadn't lifted it since. Was she embarrassed? He shook his head to clear his thoughts. Not possible.

Yet last night her 'no' had emerged just as she'd been about to come apart on his dining table. At the time he'd thought she'd wanted him to stop but he'd realised she'd been muttering to *herself.* Today it had almost happened again until he'd thought to silence her self-consciousness. He'd wanted her to have the release. Wanted to taste it. Wanted it again now.

It was shocking how much he wanted it.

'Don't think you have to hide your hunger from me,' he growled. 'I am not so prehistoric to think a woman has any less right to pleasure than a man. You like sex. So do I.'

Her wordless, quivering response almost unravelled him. If they weren't in a semipublic place he'd be plunging balls-deep inside her right now. He tensed, battling the surging hunger *he* couldn't yet control. Winning her acquiescence to his—frankly mad—scheme had him wildly exhilarated. That's why he'd just lost his mind and gone down on her like some ravenous sex beast, right? He held her more tightly as another intense wave washed through them both. This was the most savage ache he'd ever experienced. She smelt good. Tasted good. Felt good. He wanted more. Now. Because she was still hungry too. As aroused as he.

It was unfathomable that he felt this rabid about getting her to bed. He'd thought he'd escaped his father's weakness. He'd always been able to walk away from a woman easily enough. But he'd do almost anything to have Elodie. And that *was* dangerous. She freely admitted being a liar and an adulteress. But the intensity of their sexual chemistry would be expunged and if he had to feel this kind of madness, at least it was with a woman who was experienced enough to know how it would end and who wouldn't be hurt.

'What you did before you met me is your business. Your past is your past,' he muttered, reminding himself of that reality more than anything.

That was when she lifted her head. 'I don't need your absolution.'

He released her and she immediately stepped away. But there was an interesting rush of colour beneath her skin as if she *were* embarrassed. Which didn't really make sense.

'No?' he questioned.

A spark of rebellion glittered in her pale face.

'You can still go dancing, anytime you like.' He suddenly wanted to make her strike again. 'I know you like dancing a lot.'

She straightened her blouse. 'You're not worried I might dance with other men?'

'If I'm not there your bodyguard will see off any threats.'

'My *what*?'

He smiled, happy to see her fire return. 'Naturally you'll have a bodyguard. More than one, at times.'

'You're not serious.'

Deadly, actually. 'I'm extremely wealthy. It would be remiss of me not to provide protection for you. I won't have you endangered because of your association with me.'

'They don't sound like bodyguards, more like gaolers.' She looked mutinous. 'I don't want you to control my actions.'

His amusement died. 'The *last* thing I want to do is control you.' In fact, the *only* person he wanted to control right now was himself. But that hunger sliced anew, and another truth emerged before he could stop it. 'I want to *enjoy* you.'

But if he were wholly honest, he ached for more than that. He wanted her surrender—her total submission to the passion that had ignited between them so unexpectedly. So irrationally. He didn't want control or her obedience, but he did want her to admit this was like *nothing* else she'd ever experienced.

Ego. In other words. The competitive nature that had pushed him to be top of class was on fire today. He mocked himself. He just wanted to be the best she'd ever had. He wanted to be the one she would never, ever forget. Because he already knew he was never, ever forgetting her. And that was infuriating.

But now she turned, pulling back completely. 'So how did you want to go about this? Are we to have a wedding in Vegas at two a.m.? Five minutes in a neon chapel?' She smoothed one of the silver coasters on the table needlessly. Turned and adjusted another glass.

Ramon watched her fidgeting and suspected she was more shaken by what had just happened than she wanted to admit. Frankly, so was he. They needed to get out of here and deal with everything properly. He needed to calm down.

'Sadly no, we're in too much of a hurry.' He reached for his jacket. 'Ashleigh's engagement is being announced this weekend. Isn't that why you hunted me down in the first place? I assume you have a current passport?'

'I thought you just said we weren't going to Vegas?'

'Not quite that far. We fly today. Get married tomorrow. Return before the engagement party. Our families are having a private celebration the night before and we're going to gatecrash it.'

At that she turned and shot him a mocking look. 'Why Ramon, you have a flair for the dramatic.'

'Well, you enjoy the dramatic.' He gestured around the room they were in. 'You like to create a scene.'

'A pretend one. For *other* people to enjoy.'

'Isn't that exactly what we're doing?' he drawled.

She fiddled with another prop. 'I'll need a couple of moments with Bethan.'

He smiled ruefully. 'How will she cope with your defection from the single-forever divorcees' club?'

'She'll be busy looking after the escape rooms for me and Phoebe is currently abroad. I'll fudge the reality—'

'No scruples about deceiving her?'

'I've already told you I lie. I bluff in my business all the time. So rest assured, I'm good at it.'

Yeah. Ramon slowly followed her from the room. Warned, wary but utterly willing as he took one last look at the little clue stuck on the back wall of the hidden compartment she'd appeared in.

Trust No One

He really didn't need the reminder.

CHAPTER SIX

ELODIE TOUCHED HER CHEEK, regretting her rash decision to turn up the temperature in the escape room and still battling to contain her jumbling emotions. What had just happened? *How* had that just happened? How had she lost all control, so completely? And was she really just going to go off with this man?

Yes, she was. *For Ashleigh.* She muttered her sister's name like a mantra, desperate to keep her sister uppermost in her mind—not her own ravenous desire that had materialised the moment she'd set eyes on him and apparently could overrule her common sense as easily as pie.

As she approached reception, Bethan's eyes widened.

'Are you okay?' Bethan leaned across the counter and whispered. 'You're really flushed and your blouse is—' Bethan broke off only to immediately add, 'What—'

'I'm fine,' Elodie interrupted hastily. 'But I have to go away for a few days. Can you look after the rooms? Get one of the part-timers to—'

'Go where?' Bethan gaped.

'I know it's sudden.' Elodie slapped on a reassuring smile. 'I'm working on a deal to secure our future, but I just need—'

'A deal with *him*?' Bethan shot a concerned glance over her head to where Ramon was waiting by the door. 'He doesn't look like he wants to do *business* with you, he looks like he wants to—'

'It's *fine*,' Elodie assured her urgently. She didn't want to lie to her friend. She didn't want to tell her the truth either. She would evade both options. 'Can you manage? *Please.*'

Bethan hesitated. Bethan, who was still heartbroken from the whirlwind holiday romance that had culminated in a rushed mess of a marriage, and who trusted men even less than Elodie did.

'Of course, but you stay in touch, and you call me if you need me,' Bethan whispered vehemently. '*Any time.* I'm here for you.'

Elodie squeezed her friend's shoulder. 'I know.'

Five minutes later Elodie awkwardly sat in the back of a car, avoiding meeting Ramon's far-too-smug expression. She'd caught him looking at her thoughtfully once already and now she'd finally fully recovered her self-possession she was embarrassed. But she would fake otherwise.

Be smart. Sassy. Worldly-wise. Confident...

In control, in other words.

She cleared her throat. 'Where are we going?'

'To get your passport and papers. Then we'll head to the airport.'

This was moving *fast*. But that didn't surprise her, this man was used to getting things done. 'I'm not marrying you without written confirmation of our deal.'

'I've had a prenuptial contract drawn up—'

'You were that certain I would say yes?' Her temperature ticked up again.

'I like to be prepared for all eventualities. Give me your lawyer's email and I'll send over a copy right away.'

She shot him a quelling look. 'I'm capable of reviewing a contract myself.'

'You should take independent legal advice.'

'You should assume I'm capable of looking after my own interests,' she replied coolly.

'Have it your way,' he murmured softly.

'That's how I like it,' she purred back.

There was the smallest curve to his mouth as he gazed limpidly back at her.

'So where is it?' she prompted.

His eyes gleamed and his smile deepened. 'I've put it into a series of envelopes and hidden them in various places in this car. I'll offer occasional clues, though you might find each out of order and then have to puzzle them together. The page numbers might help, but who knows.'

She gaped at him for a full second before her burgeoning amusement bubbled out. His smile became pure grin as she giggled.

'Here.' He reached into a bag at his feet and handed her a file.

She was completely grateful for the diversion. It was bad enough that he was staggeringly beautiful, but when he made her laugh like that any last resistance fled her already weak body. Paperwork would be the perfect antidote. Beside her, Ramon had pulled another file and was already reading it.

He'd moved into work mode. She could get a grip and do the same. Thankfully, she'd taken Phoebe's advice and done evening classes in business management and contracts law once she'd settled in London. She might not have made billions like Ramon, but with her wonder assistant friend's help, she had educated herself. Hopefully, once she had control of the escape rooms she would make it even more successful. She wished she could've bid for the business on her own but she didn't have the savings. And Ashleigh's call for help now meant she needed to do whatever was necessary.

She read the neatly typed pages. Several clauses caught her attention. Upon the dissolution of their marriage, the business interests of the escape rooms would be hers in entirety.

In return she would relinquish any further claim to his fortune. But there were additional benefits she'd not expected.

'You're giving money to Ashleigh?' she asked.

'My family has put immense pressure on her.' Ramon kept reading the report in front of him. 'Consider it reparation for emotional stress. This way she can choose to study or travel without having to bow to further parental pressure.'

Elodie blinked at his generosity. 'And there's a lump sum for me.'

'You can scratch that one out if you like.' He turned the page of his own document. 'It was only in case the escape room doesn't do as well as hoped once you take over, but having seen you in action today, I know you're going to kill it.'

She was stunned by his vote of confidence in her ability.

'What?' He lifted his head and gazed directly at her after a couple moments. 'You know you're good.'

Well, she hoped so but it was nice to hear someone else say it. Especially someone as successful as him. She coughed and tried to focus. 'The trust for Ashleigh is dependent on our remaining married for a minimum of six months.'

'We don't have to live together for all that time. I just want to beat the duration of your previous marriage,' he said with a softness that was actually nerve-shreddingly sharp. 'Be better than any competition. I'm a very competitive guy.'

She gritted her teeth. 'I'm astounded there's no good behaviour clause with a special reward for my doing every little thing you want.'

'But Elodie, *I'm* your reward. This you already know.' His eyes widened in mock innocence. 'And every little thing you do will be every little thing that *you* want.'

Elodie dropped her gaze to the papers on her lap, trying to deny the fact that her damned toes were curling. Response rushed through her. She snatched together some sarcasm. 'If it's to be so mind-blowing, what tears us apart? How am I to destroy you?'

'We'll work that out later.' He shrugged. 'It doesn't need to be anything dramatic. Neither of us will oppose the divorce. It'll be quick, easy, painless.'

Unlike her last. She breathed out slowly. This offer was too good to turn down. Too easy. He was right. She would get *everything* she wanted. 'You have a pen for me to sign?'

'Do it on the plane, Piotr will witness.' He nodded his head towards the window. 'Passport, papers—birth certificate, wedding, divorce. Make it snappy.'

She hadn't realised they'd pulled up at her tenement block. 'I don't need anything else?' she asked, irritated by his high-speed insistence. 'Toothbrush? Clothes?'

'We can get all that there. You have ten minutes before Piotr drives off.'

Pointedly, she didn't move a muscle because she was *not* jumping to his every little command. 'Are you sure you don't want to handcuff me to you and come inside with me?'

He stared at her, motionless. She stared back—words forgotten, intention to tease evaporated. Because this was no joke. Heat unfurled deep within and a dragging sensation in the pit of her pelvis pulled her inexorably towards him. *Everything* tightened. Just as she made to escape he leaned over her. Stopping her simply by narrowing his proximity.

'I've already promised I'll indulge any and all of your kinky urges once we're *married*,' he reprimanded softly.

Fire scorched her cheeks. Yes, she'd thrown a gauntlet. But he'd not just accepted it, he'd trounced her with only a few words. She swallowed. No doubt he'd had many affairs while she was a complete *faker*. Little more than a novice. She'd have to work harder—*smarter*—to hold her own with him. Indulge and yet somehow maintain some self-protection. Remembering this was *merely* an affair was the way.

'Go on.' He opened her door before slowly pulling back from her. 'The sooner we get to the airport, the sooner your sister is saved,' he taunted.

She furiously exited the car and stalked into her building. She *would* hold her own with him. And she would escape unscathed. The one thing that soothed her was that *he* hadn't been able to hide the fiery expression in his eyes. He felt this attraction as keenly as she. She grabbed her passport and file of important paperwork, changed into comfy jeans and a tee and threw a few other items into a small carryall. She needed his influence to free Ashleigh. He was willing to pay for that because he needed her name on a certificate so he could retain the property he wanted. Beyond that, his interest was only in her body. She had no real interest in *him* either—just *his* body. So she would have it. She was in control of this every bit as much as he was.

She would see Ashleigh safe. She would get her business. And she would have the first full-blooded affair of her life.

Ramon stared fixedly at the paperwork he'd been ignoring on his knee and willed time to move just a little faster. He did not want to see her home. Not her bedroom. He was *not* curious. And the last thing he wanted to think about was the other men she'd taken there. He'd never thought he'd ever be a jealous lover, but here he was—hating the thought of her kissing someone else. Of her letting someone else inside her home, her life, her body. He dragged in a deep breath, trying to quell the ferociousness of these utterly foreign thoughts overtaking his mind. He didn't think about any women like this. But Elodie Wallace was gorgeous and wilful, smart and infuriating and he could not *believe* that he'd lost all control of himself and gone at her in her *workplace*. He hadn't been able to resist. Which was not great.

Only what had happened had been so freaking *fantastic*

that just the flicker of memory made him hot all over again. Aching—*battling*—he grabbed his tablet and forced his focus on making notes for his assistants. Taking time away from work was extremely out of character for him. He needed to give them extensive notes.

She lied. She cheated. Abandoned responsibility.

He repeated her self-confessed litany of moral crimes. Reminding himself to remain wary. Distanced. Yes, their chemistry was spectacular, but lust would be sated. He wouldn't allow her to cause any damage. To his curling pleasure she was back within the ten minutes he'd assigned but he said nothing, and he even managed not to reach out and touch her despite the harrowing urge he had to. He ground through more briefings for his assistants and was ridiculously relieved when they finally made it to the airstrip.

'Where are we flying to?' she asked once he'd slid his tablet into his bag.

'Gibraltar.'

'Is that a private jet?' Her eyebrows lifted as she looked at the small insignia on the plane. 'Don't tell me that's your family crest.'

'Okay then.' He pursed his lips, mock pouting to remain silent.

'You don't seriously have a family crest?' She stopped ahead of the stairs and studied it more closely. 'Of course it would feature a bird of prey,' she muttered. 'But it should be *all* the apex predators in a pile fighting with each other.'

He laughed. 'That's exactly what my family is like. I'll have it amended.'

'Along with that stupid trust for your property,' she said and marched up into the plane.

'Right.' He ushered her to a seat near a small table. 'After we take off, sign the prenup. There are more forms. Some are in Spanish.'

'I don't speak Spanish.'

'Piotr will translate.'

'Can I trust him?'

'For now you have little choice. But you're quick…you'll pick Spanish up in no time,' he said soothingly.

She shot him a mutinous look. 'Are you going to teach me?'

'As if you'd allow that,' he chuckled. 'You're more likely to download an app and teach yourself.'

She didn't respond, which meant he was right. He couldn't help smiling at her determined self-sufficiency.

'Piotr will witness then get the documents ready to file.' He handed her a pen.

'Is there nothing the man can't do?' she murmured. 'Will he be flying the plane too?'

'Don't get any ideas.' Ramon felt that jealousy ripple again and tried to lighten his response. 'He has a wife and two children. And if that isn't enough to deter you from trying to seduce him, you're not his type.' He smiled. 'You're too provocative. He likes them demure.'

But Elodie's sarcastic facade had fallen away and she looked genuinely concerned. 'Does he ever get to see them?'

Ramon's defensiveness surged. 'My bodyguards are on a week-on, week-off schedule. This is his week on.'

He took a seat on the diagonal from hers. Once they'd levelled out Piotr appeared from the rear cabin along with an assistant who offered Elodie refreshment. Ramon opened up his laptop and feigned focus while she worked on the forms but he saw she did indeed scratch out the cash provision for her. He counted down the minutes until Piotr took the documents Elodie had filled in and went back to the rear cabin.

'Are you always this work-driven?' Elodie sipped from the tall glass of juice.

'You do realise how many people my companies employ?'

he gritted. Because the fact was he'd basically got nothing done, and while he could always focus on work, right now was the one exception.

'Companies?' A furrow appeared between her brows. 'Don't you mean hotels?'

'The hotels come under one company. There are several *other* companies.' He stared at her. 'Didn't you do any research on me?' Was he actually miffed by that?

'Obviously not enough seeing I didn't know you have a cousin with almost the exact same name as you. But then we can't all afford an army of assistants with the skills to hack into people's private databases.'

'Your social media profiles were all set to *public*.'

'What other companies?' she redirected pointedly.

'The luxury leather goods. The vineyards. There's a venture into a cruise line.' He slowly listed them off, rather enjoying her mounting outrage. 'Then there's the other properties.'

'You're CEO of all of them? How is that even possible? You can't oversee the work of absolutely everyone.'

'You'd be surprised how much detail I can retain on each,' he said. 'I like the variety. I need that challenge.'

Her mouth opened. Then closed. Then she sat back. For a second she'd almost looked crestfallen, which diverted him momentarily. Why would his work commitments disappoint her?

'What do you want me to wear to the wedding?' she muttered after another few minutes.

For the first time in years Ramon's brain froze. 'You can buy a dress once we get to Gibraltar,' he said stiffly.

'Ooh, are you going to give me a platinum card so I can drain all your massive accounts?'

He breathed out through clenched teeth. 'Haven't had time for that paperwork yet, darling. So sorry. Piotr will pay.'

'You mean he's going to keep me on a leash.'

Awfully, another ripple of jealousy ripped through him. He tensed—too busy battling it to answer her immediately.

'You don't have *any* requests?' she prodded, unaware of how close to the edge he was. 'Do you want something outrageous or would you prefer traditional?'

Have mercy. He closed his eyes—couldn't stand to think of her in a wedding gown—*any* gown—in this instant. She'd look stunning in anything and best of all *naked*. And he was losing his mind. He hauled his papers together and stood, inwardly swearing because they were airborne and he *desperately* needed some space.

'You can wear whatever you like,' he snapped. 'I need to work.'

Elodie stared as he strode towards the back of the plane. Okay, so he really didn't care what she wore, which she should be pleased about. She'd had her clothing choices dictated to her for most of her life—no pink, no red, no short hemlines...

Yet absurdly she had the urge to make Ramon *pay* for his disinterest. There was literally, of course. She could spend squillions on some outrageous frock, which would serve him right, it really would. Maybe he thought she'd be restrained with Piotr in tow? Or maybe she'd turn up in a bin bag. He probably wouldn't notice if she did and she'd feel rubbish. She didn't want to feel rubbish, she wanted to feel good—wanted a dress that *she* liked. Maybe she'd go shopping and pick something solely for *herself.* After all, she'd not chosen her own wedding dress in her marriage to Callum. She'd had to wear the 'fairy tale' number her father had approved of. 'Modest' and 'appropriate', it had been lacy and swamped her. She didn't want to be modest or appropriate this time.

This was definitely not a fairy tale.

Her marrying Ramon was going to be scandalous. But she

didn't care about the optics. She wanted to feel *sexy*. And she didn't want to examine her motivations for that.

She ruminated for an hour, absurdly irritated by Ramon's ability to focus on work while she was being driven to distraction at the thought of their marriage. As for all the companies he managed... His need for *challenge* and *variety*... That told her their marriage was likely lasting way *less* than six months. He'd probably be bored and ready for his next female 'challenge' in days. Sure, he'd said his affairs were monogamous but that didn't mean they lasted long. Had he had a succession of lovers before her? She didn't even know, yet here she was. Jealous.

Grumpily determined to course-correct, she opened her phone and took advantage of the onboard Wi-Fi to download a language app. Ten minutes of basic greetings later, she needed a bathroom break and headed towards the back of the plane.

That's when she heard a weird noise. She peeked through the gap in the door leading to the rear cabin. 'Oh, for...' She gritted back the rest of her mutter.

Ramon paused dictating voice messages and grinned at her. 'Something to say?'

He'd shed his stunning suit and was now clad in gym shorts and singlet, apparently sweating out his aggravations, and looked even more gorgeous while he *still* worked.

'I cannot believe you have an indoor cycle on an airplane,' she said stonily. The machine was bolted to the floor.

'It helps with jet lag.'

He was so *perfect*, wasn't he? So controlled. Physically active, he ate well, and worst of all, he was still reading a report while doing it. Multitasking with his annoying ability to concentrate.

'You really are a workaholic,' she muttered.

'You will be too once you get back.' He smiled at her patronisingly. 'Your business will be everything.'

'It wasn't a compliment.' She corrected him. 'Is money all that matters to you?'

'It's not money that drives me but the company itself. It's my heritage and my responsibility and I'm proud that I've grown it.'

'It's your baby.'

'As the escape room is yours.' He scooped up the towel on his handlebar and wiped his brow. 'Admit it. You work hard to make it thrive.'

'Yes. But unlike you I also have other things in my life.'

'Because your baby is somewhat smaller than mine. Mine is demanding.'

'You could delegate.'

'Why? What am I missing?'

'Rest and relaxation?' she quipped lightly, barely masking her deep curiosity. 'A social life?'

'Like you have? Dancing with all your men?'

'Dancing with my *friends*,' she replied nonchalantly. 'If men want to dance with us, that's fine too. It's a more fun option than *your* stress release. *Cycling.*'

He stopped pedalling. 'Well, tomorrow night I'll be riding you and I think you'll be grateful I burned some energy here already.'

She gaped at him. 'You're appalling.'

'Because you make it so worthwhile.' He hopped off the bike and moved towards her. 'For a party girl with no conscience and no cares, you blush amazingly easily.'

She locked her weak knees so she wouldn't back away from him. 'I'm not blushing. This is my natural colouring. Red.'

'Rot.' He placed the backs of his fingers against her cheek. 'You're burning up.'

'Fever.'

'Yeah, commonly known as lust.' He laughed. 'As stunning as I know we're going to be together, we're definitely waiting until our wedding night so *stop* trying to tempt me.'

She wanted to tell him he'd be waiting a long time but couldn't lie that well.

'It's my first, you know?' Sardonic amusement danced in his eyes. 'Marriage, that is. Special.'

'Are you going to wear white?' she gritted acerbically.

'I can't tell you that!' he declared with mock outrage. 'It's bad luck to see each other in our wedding finery before the ceremony.'

'Bad luck is the least of your concerns.' She turned and stomped back to the forward cabin.

She desperately tried not to stare at him when he returned to the seat beside hers a half hour later. He'd seemingly *showered* onboard and was now dressed in a different suit, smelt delicious and looked more vital and virile than ever. And she was not thinking about the bed she'd seen in that cabin at the back of the plane.

Once they'd landed, Ramon guided Elodie into the waiting car. They went straight from the airport to a civic office where they registered their intention to marry. In twenty-four hours they could proceed. Then they went to the hotel—which would also be their wedding venue. Oceanfront and opulent, their suite had the most stunning views of the sea.

'I have work to do.' Ramon set his bag by the large desk in the lounge.

So predictable.

'Good stuff,' Elodie said airily. 'You need to earn many more millions because I'm taking Piotr shopping for the outrageously expensive dress that you don't care about.'

'Did that wound?' He smiled at her dangerously. 'Don't worry darling, I care very much about what's *beneath* it.'

Elodie had to get out of there before she devolved and did something physical to him—and not in a good way.

'We need to find an evening wear specialist, Piotr. Are you up to it?' she asked the enigmatic bodyguard.

'I have a list of boutiques and phoned ahead to make several private appointments,' he answered. 'There's also a hairdresser and beautician at the hotel on standby should you like to make use of them later.'

Good grief, the man was worth his well-muscled weight in gold. 'I hope Ramon pays you ridiculously well,' she said. 'I don't know how you put up with his round-the-clock demands.'

'He's a good employer. He doesn't demand all that much.'

'He's listening in right now, isn't he? In your earpiece. And you've just earned yourself a bonus.'

'This trip is a bonus. It is the first time in three years I've known him to travel for leisure.'

Elodie paused, startled by the nugget of information she'd never have expected the utterly discreet Piotr to let fall. But this trip *wasn't* leisure. It was business. And all work and no play made Ramon Fernandez a formidable opponent.

Ninety minutes and three shops later, Elodie stood in the private changing room and stared at her reflection. The shop assistants would admire her in anything—which meant she was reliant on her own judgement. She had to please no one but *herself.* She liked her costumes at work—pretending, being in character. But this was something just for *her.*

The soft silk skimmed her body, sophisticated, sexy, sweet too. It might not please him—it might not be the bold statement he expected from her—but *she* loved it.

Energised and excited, she decided to find something equally confidence boosting to wear to the family cocktail party they were going to gatecrash to stop Ashleigh's engagement. Oh, yes, Elodie Wallace was finally on her game.

CHAPTER SEVEN

RAMON HAD MOUNTAINS of work to do, and he was not going to let a little thing like getting married disrupt his routine. He absolutely was not bothered that Elodie had been gone for more than three hours already. Yet he'd lost track of the number of times he'd gone to the suite's media room to glance out the window overlooking the hotel entrance and now here he was wandering over to do it again. His concentration was blown and pushing him into feral territory. Which was *not* him. He did not abandon all responsibility just because he wanted *sex*. He was not his father.

Only this time as he looked out the window, he spotted her walking into the hotel. His entire body responded with a savage driving urge that almost overwhelmed him. He breathed deep and glanced wide, amused to see Piotr, masking a pained expression as he walked a step behind her, laden with bags. Was she making a stand with her purchases?

He sure as hell hoped so. He couldn't wait to see the contents of them. He couldn't wait to touch her. It wasn't for the wedding that he was really holding off. It was to test his own self-control. He was determined that he wasn't a lecherous, rampantly reckless man like his father. Turns out he was exactly that. And to make it worse, he was now so tightly wound he no longer cared about the fact.

The second she appeared in the hotel suite he moved towards her. 'You must be exhausted.'

She might want to lie down—in which case he would join her. He utterly abandoned the idea of keeping his hands off her until after the wedding. The ceremony would happen regardless and was honestly irrelevant. He could and would have her. Now.

'Not at all.' Elodie evaded his approach with a swift step and a coolly proud gaze. 'I have an appointment with a hairdresser and a beautician. Possibly a make-up artist.'

He stilled, locking in place in the middle of the lounge. Every muscle burned with the urge to touch her—to provoke her the way she provoked him by merely *existing*—let alone with the levelling look that accompanied her words.

'You should cut your hair,' he muttered huskily. 'Tie it up at least.'

She froze and that levelling look of hers iced.

Ramon tried but couldn't suppress his smile because he was sure she would do the opposite. She blinked a couple times and her mouth softened. He remained rock-still as she walked over until she stood right in front of him. Which yes, was another thing he'd desperately wanted. She rose on tiptoe, bringing her lips dangerously close to his ear. He went from rock-still to diamond-hard.

'Is that your juvenile way of saying you like my hair long and loose?' she murmured.

Of course she had him. '*You're* the one who likes things to mean the opposite of what's true.'

Her eyes gleamed. 'I'll do my hair how I want.'

'Great,' he croaked in total capitulation. 'Can't wait.'

Because he'd weave his hands into her hair *however* she styled it—he was desperate to feel its silky length and wrap himself in her fire. Pleasure flashed in her eyes as with a tilt of her chin she shot him the smallest smile. Helplessly he watched her leave with a sway to her hips utterly designed to aggravate and arouse him even more.

He couldn't stand to remain cooped up inside while she was out. He left the hotel, turned down a couple of streets, vaguely taking in the shop fronts. He didn't shop in person. His assistants ensured the clothes he needed were in ready supply, knowing his preferred brands. His tailor made house calls for fittings. He never had need to purchase anything personal.

But one sign caught his eye, the window pulled him closer, and a quixotic impulse pushed him inside. He couldn't recall being in a jewellery store. Had never bought anything for himself or anyone else. Such gestures were meaningless— his father had showered his mother with sparkling gifts and flowery attentions to hide his infidelity. She'd believed him, accepted them. Ramon had refused to treat dates with trinkets. But this deal with Elodie was different. It was a tease. He would get something to provoke her. Only then one item caught his eye and it wasn't a provocation.

It was perfect.

Almost two hours later he stood by the window overlooking the sea and considered making the leap. He needed to cool off somehow. He'd been dressed and waiting for her to appear from her room for more than fifteen minutes. No one kept him waiting. Ever. Yet here he was, almost bursting out of his skin from the agony and irritation of waiting. He finally heard the door open and spun.

'Oh, were you waiting? So sorry.' Her voice was breathy as she sauntered towards him, head high, eyes glinting.

Once again Ramon couldn't stop the smile spreading across his face. 'You really do like playing games.'

She was pure party girl in a backless, short, scarlet, sexy as hell, form-fitting dress. Her hair was left long and loose and the urge to run his hands through it was going to destroy him.

'I'm not the only game-player here.' Her gaze swept down his sleek tuxedo.

'You suit red,' he muttered.

'My father said I should never wear it.'

'Is that why you wore little else for a while?' He moved closer as her eyes flashed. 'In all those pictures in those clubs,' he said, explaining how he'd seen them. 'You don't like being told what you can and cannot do.'

'Maybe I got a little sick of it,' she said quietly.

'If he dictated what you were allowed to wear then I don't blame you for rebelling.'

She turned her head slightly away from him.

'It was more than what you could wear, huh?' Her father really was the controlling type.

She nodded and glanced back. 'I think I'll be overly reactive now when people try to issue instructions.'

'No, you?' He'd chuckle if he weren't so strung out. 'So, are you wearing red for our wedding?'

Her lashes fluttered, suddenly coy. 'I thought we were keeping such details secret.'

Anticipation pulled every muscle tight. But she backed away, held up her phone and snapped a selfie with the view of the ocean in the background.

'You're updating your social media profile?' he mocked.

'Sending a proof-of-life picture to my friends,' she replied primly. 'I go silent for more than twenty-four hours and there'll be an international incident.'

'They'll launch a divorced wives rescue mission?'

'Exactly.'

'You don't want me in the picture?' He prowled closer.

'And give up our element of surprise?' She shook her head. 'No *way*.'

Right. He stilled—he was the one surprised. He'd got so caught up in baiting her he'd forgotten the reason *why* they were getting married at all.

Elodie wasn't hungry enough to do the divine dinner justice. She didn't need the fuel—she was running on something else—something she couldn't quite handle.

'I have something for you.' He put a small square box on the table once the waiting staff had removed their plates.

She wasn't just out of her depth and struggling to stay afloat. She was sunk in concrete.

'Aren't you going to open it?'

'Not if it's what I think it is.'

'We're getting married, Elodie. You do need the trimmings.'

'*Trimmings?* Am I some celebratory dinner to be served up on a table?'

His grin was wolfish and she snatched up the box in annoyance at her own ability to make appalling *double-entendres*.

'Don't panic,' he said a few moments later as she stared at the ring in stunned silence. 'It's artificially grown in a lab. Machine-made. Not worth anywhere as much as you're thinking.'

'So it's as fake as this marriage is going to be?' She tried to match his droll tone. 'All that glitters is most definitely not gold.'

'Such a pity, isn't it?' he muttered wickedly.

Elodie had seen a fair amount of costume jewellery because they used it in the escape rooms all the time and Bethan could turn pound shop items into trinkets that looked like they were worth millions. But this *looked* an absolute treasure—full throttle dramatic. So she had the feeling this ruby wasn't lab grown and nor were the diamonds surrounding it. She lifted her gaze, all faux insouciance. 'Yes. It's disappointing that it won't be worth much when I sell it in a few months.'

'You won't sell it,' Ramon purred. 'You're a magpie. You like collecting shiny, worthless things—'

'To feed my shiny worthless soul?' She managed to slide the ring onto her finger despite her cold sweat, and lifted her hand to see the stones catch the light. 'Careful, you'll increase my appetite for more trinkets. I might demand actually *valuable* ones, then you'll be in trouble.'

He just laughed.

She couldn't take her eyes off the ring. It was a statement piece. Definitely unusual and one of a kind. Panic subsumed her. 'It's not a family heirloom, is it?' She looked up at him. 'Not your mother's or anything inappropriate like that?'

He actually recoiled. 'Why on earth would you think it was my *mother's*?'

'Well, when did you have the chance to buy it? When did? *Oh!*' She broke off, suddenly feeling a fool. 'Piotr has exquisite taste. Please thank him for choosing so well.'

The strangest expression crossed Ramon's face—a quixotic blend of admiration and indignation. 'You vexatious wretch.'

'Forgive me if I don't believe for a second that you took time out of your precious work schedule to choose something so unimportant.' Elodie smiled.

He drank almost the entire glass of ice-cold water in one go before sucking in a breath. 'I'm going to make you pay for that.'

'I can hardly wait.' She faked cool but her breathlessness betrayed her.

Had he chosen it? She looked at it again, still doubting his word on its artificial origins. But her clueless question made her realise she didn't know anywhere near enough about him. She had no idea where his parents were, let alone what they would think of their son marrying a complete stranger. He hadn't mentioned them at all. 'What will she think of this?'

'Who?' he frowned.

'Your mother. What's she going to think of your sudden marriage?'

He froze. Then rallied. 'Both my parents are dead. They won't think anything.'

'Sorry.' She felt terrible but at the same time it was hardly her fault—the man had more walls than a Renaissance hedge maze. 'I didn't know—'

'And you don't really need to.'

'I disagree,' she said flatly. She'd never been as argumentative with anyone in her life. 'But if we're to have everyone believe this marriage is real—for the duration—then I am going to need to, aren't I? I don't even know how old you are, let alone when your birthday is. I'll put my foot in it from the start.'

'Did you not read the marriage forms?' he replied coolly. 'I'm twenty-nine. Scorpio. My father died when I was eighteen. My mother when I was twenty-five. I'm their only child. I took over the family business when my father died and have done very little else. I live for my work.'

And he didn't want to share anything more. Okay, she got it—even if it sounded somewhat sad. 'I'm twenty-four. Also a Scorpio. That's all we need to know, right?'

To her relief his smile returned.

Elodie barely slept. Ramon had kept his distance completely after dinner. He'd quietly accompanied her back to the suite and immediately disappeared into his own room. Probably to do more work. She'd been absurdly disappointed. She'd thought she'd read hunger for *her* in his eyes before dinner but he'd backed off completely. Was this not going to be an affair—if he was that hot for her, why the delay?

Early the next morning she got out of bed and drew back the curtains. It was a stunning day and there were too many hours to fill before the ceremony. She had to move. In the lounge Ramon was nowhere to be seen. He was probably unnecessarily observing those wedding traditions—ridiculous given this wasn't a *real* wedding.

She went back to her bedroom and dressed in jeans and tee. When she went back out into the lounge she found Piotr waiting. His prescience was uncanny.

'I'd like to go for a walk, is that allowed?'

'I will accompany you discreetly.'

She rolled her eyes. 'You don't need to walk three feet behind.'

But Piotr obviously had his orders as she ambled through the town. Around her people were going about their business, tourists were taking photos, students in groups, office workers hurried to grab coffees—it was all so normal. What she and Ramon were doing really was ridiculous—who got married mid-afternoon on a *Thursday*?

She wandered along the shady side of a street she'd not ventured down yesterday in the great dress hunt, and paused by a jewellery store. She couldn't resist entering—drawn to a large glass case on the rear wall. Just the one piece was displayed. She put her hand to her chest as she stared at it. Four strands of what looked like diamonds sat flat on the back of the neck, while at the front they were woven into an intricate diamond knot—further embellished with yet more gleaming stones. If they actually *were* diamonds this one necklace would probably cost about the same as a large-sized house. Sure enough, there was no obvious price tag—which meant it would be astronomical and there was no way she could ever wear anything like it.

'You like this necklace, *señora*?'

Startled, Elodie turned as the jeweller approached. She saw his sweeping glance take her in—lingering on the fingers she'd spread just below her collarbones. He'd seen the ruby ring. She dropped her hand. No doubt the man would instantly recognise it as 'artificial'. Sure enough, his demeanour subtly changed. But to her surprise he went from merely polite, to pure sycophant.

'Would you like to try it on?' He opened the cabinet and lifted out the glittering piece before she could say no.

'Just…briefly,' she agreed weakly.

Moments later she gazed at her reflection, her resolve weakening. Maybe she would amp up her gold-digger facade? Only it wasn't that. Honestly? She loved the cool weight and drama of it. She'd never thought she'd go for something so intense or so couture but it would contrast beautifully with the light simplicity of the dress she'd chosen. But there was no way she would spend that amount of Ramon's money.

The jeweller regarded her speculatively. 'It is sublime on you.'

'Yes, but I can't…' She made the man remove the necklace.

Piotr materialised beside her. 'Do you need assistance, Ms Wallace?'

'I don't think so.' She smiled at him ruefully. 'I could never buy it.'

Piotr studied her impassively. 'What if you could borrow it? With your permission I will inquire.'

'Um—'

Piotr turned and addressed the jeweller in staccato bursts of rapid Spanish that she didn't understand a word of. After some time he turned back to her. 'I will supply a borrow bond and return it immediately after the ceremony. We'll take it with us now.'

'*Really?*' She was stunned.

The jeweller put the necklace into a velvet-lined travel case that Piotr slid into his jacket pocket in return for a swipe of one of those cards.

Five minutes later she couldn't resist a quiet plea to the

taciturn bodyguard. 'We don't have to tell Ramon we've borrowed it, do we?'

She wanted to let her temporary husband think she'd spent a stupid amount of his money—just a tiny tease. She swore she almost caught a smile from Piotr.

'My instructions are to assist you any way necessary, Ms Wallace. You can trust that I will take care of your best interests.'

She did trust him, actually. He was a marvel.

Back at the hotel the hairdresser and make-up artist were waiting. Two hours later she stared at her reflection. A veil the hairdresser had produced added a touch more 'bridal', the necklace delivered a wallop of luxury, while the sky-high heels would give her a chance to look Ramon directly in the eyes.

But really all this was for *her*. Last time it had been everything someone else wanted. But this was all for herself and she was going to indulge in the fantasy of it because it sure as hell was never, *ever* happening again.

Piotr arrived and actually smiled as he offered her his arm like the big brother she'd never had.

The hotel had a stunning private deck that was built right over the stunning blue sea. Enormous white sails screened them from the sun overhead and Elodie breathed in deeply as she walked towards her groom. On her first wedding day she'd been anxious and awkward and scared of screwing up. This was vastly different. It wasn't meant to be momentous— she could relax—but the flutters in her belly begged to differ.

Ramon was waiting for her beneath a fresh floral arch and was indeed wearing white. His linen suit, perfect for the blazing mid-afternoon heat, accentuated his tanned skin and the vivid blue of his eyes. Excitement trammelled through her at the sight of him. She desperately, *dangerously*, wanted him.

This was simply a *deal*. There shouldn't be any emotion,

hell, he mightn't even particularly like her and she didn't want to let herself think that he *could* because it would tempt her to like him back. He was far too easy to like already. Yet suddenly it was impossible not to smile.

Ramon couldn't speak. She looked immaculate. This was simply another of her costumes except he couldn't quite believe it. With a helpless shrug he fell into the fantasy. Her dress had the thinnest of straps and skimmed her slim figure—the pale pink accentuated her stunning hair and was so very pretty. The veil was short and didn't cover her face, which he appreciated because her eyes were shining. She looked so damned fresh and *sincere*. He saw her shaky breath as she took her place beside him. She was either a supremely talented actress or she really was nervous. He reached out and took her hand. Tightened his grip when he felt her tremble. They were in this together. Just for a little while.

He repeated the promises, deeply satisfied as she echoed them, laughed when she struggled to put the wedding band on him.

'I wasn't prepared,' she muttered as the celebrant turned to deal with the paperwork. 'I didn't realise you'd wear one.'

'It's a symbol of my taken status,' he said, and winked.

'You could just adjust your social media settings. It would've been cheaper.'

'But money is no object.' His attention lingered on the diamond collar she wore around her neck. The irony of it being rope-like wasn't lost on him.

She flushed almost self-consciously and touched the knot at the base of her throat. 'I thought I'd better up the sparkle, like the greedy little magpie I am.'

'The ruby ring was not enough for you?' he murmured.

'I need to look sufficiently worthy for you. Plus, I can sell them both later and make bank.'

'Enterprising.' Ramon decided then and there that he would have her naked in his bed wearing nothing but that collar tonight. It would satisfy him immensely. And yes, he might even have to tie her there. This was only a short-term pretence so he would indulge in it while he could.

Before the celebrant could say the words he kissed her. She melted right against him but it wasn't *nearly* enough.

He'd bring forward the flight plan. He quietly moved to speak with Piotr, listened as his man explained a few salient points. Smiled. After giving Piotr a couple extra instructions he moved back to Elodie and used the photographer as pretext to pull her close again. He couldn't resist stealing another kiss. Then he gripped her hand tightly in his and walked her out of the hotel to the waiting car.

'Where are we going?' She looked more nervous now than she had just before the ceremony. 'Somewhere for more photos?'

'No.' He quelled his amusement. 'We're going to the airport.'

'The airport? Now?' Her voice went pitchy. 'We're not staying in Gibraltar?'

'You're disappointed?' He leaned closer, curious to see how she'd play this.

'I haven't even been to the beach.'

'I'll take you to another beach sometime. One that's more private. Indulge your craving for a naked roll in the waves there.'

Her mouth opened. Closed. She took a breath. 'We're not even stopping to get changed?'

'The flight isn't that long.'

'But—'

'We need to get back to break up your sister's engagement, remember?' he said smoothly. 'There's no time to lose.'

Her tension mounted. He almost felt sorry for her, except

she'd teased him one time too many today—just by existing—and he *really* wanted to call her bluff.

'We can't leave yet.' She glanced around as they arrived
at the airport. 'I need Piotr to run an errand.'

'He's busy tending to *my* errands. He'll meet us here shortly.'

'Well, *I* need to run one.'

'Can't it wait until we get back to London?' He guided
her towards the plane. 'Come on, we need to get moving.'

'We can't.' She stopped dead on the tarmac and gripped
his arm desperately. 'I'll get arrested.'

He stared down at her, feigning confusion. 'What? Why?'

'Because it's on loan.' She paled.

'Sorry?'

'The necklace. I can't leave Gibraltar wearing it. I promised to have it returned the moment the ceremony was over.'

Ramon couldn't hold back his amusement a second longer. 'You mean you didn't buy it?'

'Of course not!' she snapped. 'I would *never* spend so
much on anything. Not my money. And definitely not *yours*!'

He stared down at her, his smile fading as he absorbed
her genuine agitation—not so much from the fear of taking the diamonds from the country but that he would really
think she would spend so much of his money. And she hadn't
spent any at all, had she? Piotr had informed him that Elodie
had very determinedly paid for her dress, shoes and acces-
sories all herself.

'Well, I did,' he muttered roughly.

'What?' She breathed hectically.

'I bought it,' he growled. 'It suits you.'

Her eyes widened. 'Piotr said I could trust him.'

She'd been honest about the necklace and deeply concerned not to deceive the retailer. Or him. Which pleased
him an odd amount. Her sweet panic compelled him to admit
the truth.

'You can,' Ramon said, as he pulled her onto the plane. 'He didn't tell me it was on loan until after the ceremony. He was forced to when I asked him to get ready to leave sooner than I'd originally said. So I sent him to pay for it.'

She perched on the edge of a seat and didn't look any more relieved. 'How much did it cost?' she asked.

'I've no idea.' He slumped into the seat opposite hers.

'You don't know how much it costs?' She looked appalled.

'Apparently nor do you,' he said. 'And honestly, I don't *care* how much it costs.'

A flash of fury sharpened her eyes and her hands went to her neck.

'Keep it on,' he ordered sharply.

She froze, then lowered her hands.

Utterly goaded by her fierce glare he leaned forward. 'I'm taking you to my bed the moment we land back in London. And in that bed I will take you wearing nothing but those diamonds, Elodie. I've been fantasising about that from the second I saw you in that dress today. Which also is delectable by the way. So don't remove a thing, because *I* want to do it.' He paused to release a stressed sigh. 'Please.'

'You're going to…' She breathed in with apparent difficulty.

'Have you. Yes. My bed. Time. Space. Privacy. So we endure the flight back. It's only three hours. Can you cope?' He was furious with both her and his descent into monosyllabic sentences.

She flushed. Her gaze fixed on him. Struggling as much as he.

They remained silent while the attendant got the flight ready and Piotr returned. Remained silent as the plane taxied down the runway and took off. And the moment they levelled out, Ramon stood to remove his jacket.

'Don't take it off,' Elodie ordered in a thin voice.

He stilled.

She lifted her chin and met his gaze squarely. 'I want to do it. Don't remove a thing.'

He sat back down. 'You like making me sweat?'

'I think it's only fair.'

Ramon stared at her. Siren. Temptress. So bloody beautiful. And finally—for now—*his*. He watched her erratic breathing, the sheen on her skin, the way she squirmed in her seat as he stared. As for the undeniable evidence of her arousal gifted to him by the sharp peaks of her luscious breasts—his body was like a rock.

'Let's play something,' he suggested tightly. Except the only games he could think of were highly inappropriate.

'You're not going to work?' she muttered.

'Currently not capable,' he conceded through gritted teeth.

Another flush of desire stained her skin. She reached into the bag the attendant had delivered and pulled out a spiral-bound notebook. 'Help me design a room I'm working on.'

He reached for a bottle of mineral water and took a moment to mentally calibrate. 'What's the theme?'

'Honeymoon suite.'

'Right.' He half laughed. 'Let me guess. Runaway bride?'

Her pout curved. 'Intriguing, don't you think? She's desperate to escape.'

'Boring. Flip it—why not a runaway groom?'

'Would he be such a coward?' She stared into his eyes.

Ramon had the feeling he should be running away right now. His want for her was insanely intense. 'Why is it okay for *her* to run away?' he pointed out tensely. 'Why wouldn't she stay and fight for her man?'

'Maybe it's not a marriage she actually wants.' She rolled her eyes. 'Who generally has the power or control in a relationship? Statistics suggest it isn't the bride. Sometimes the only way out is to escape. It's quickest, easiest. Safest.'

'Okay,' he said softly, quelling the sharp ache in his ribs that her words engendered. 'Talk me through what you have so far.'

He listened as she outlined the full 'scenario'—the few props and tricks she'd already had—then began throwing outrageous suggestions at her because he needed to lighten the mood. She swiftly matched him. They debated the merits of virtual reality and of incorporating light projections into the room.

'What if they have to evade noxious gas—you could have fun with dry ice. They'd have to put on masks. It would be fully immersive. People love wholly immersive.'

'Do they?' She laughed. 'You'll be suggesting dive tanks and flood rooms next.'

The hours literally flew by. By the time they landed, Elodie had scribbled several pages of notes while Ramon had laughed more than he had in the last decade. Which made him sober up the second he realised it.

'You're very creative, Ms Wallace,' he said softly.

She wriggled her ring-clad fingers at him. 'Not Ms anymore.'

No. She was his wilful wife, and he was damn well having his wedding night.

CHAPTER EIGHT

ELODIE STEPPED INTO the house and heard Ramon close the door behind them. The conversation that had bubbled so easily between them for hours on the flight had evaporated and she felt so awkward that even breathing seemed difficult and un-natural. Energy, adrenaline, anticipation all coursed through her, rendering her uncoordinated. But they were finally here and now it would happen. Only she didn't know how to start. Should she undress? Only he'd said he wanted to do that. Should she walk straight to his room? Only she didn't actually know which one that was. She was so skittish she stumbled on her high-heel sandals. Only he must've been right behind her because he caught her and swung her into his arms.

'Nicely done,' he murmured sardonically and tossed her lightly to pull her closer.

'You think I tripped deliberately?' She wished she *had* thought of it because she was appallingly happy to be pressed against him like this.

'I think you're very good at playing your part.' He walked swiftly down the corridor.

'Right. This isn't real,' she reminded her thudding heart with a breathless murmur.

'And yet.' He set her down on her feet. 'This is the only wedding night I'll ever have.'

'You really don't want to fall in love? Marry again later—for life?'

'No.' A smile curled his lips. 'So indulge me in the fantasy of tonight.'

'You're into role-play.'

'And you're not?' His humour flashed.

More than he would ever know. But she had no idea how to fake worldliness in this moment.

'This is so elegant.' He tracked a finger along the neckline of her silk slip dress. 'As for that diamond collar. As for *you*...'

Her heart was going to beat right out of her chest any moment. She couldn't take her gaze off him as he tangled his fingers in her hair and tilted her head back. She arched towards him. He liked her dress. Her necklace. He wanted *her*. Which was such an immense relief because he was *all* she wanted.

'Feels like I've been waiting forever for this. Going to take you apart, Elodie,' he swore. 'Going to make you come harder than you've ever come in your life.'

'Get on with it then,' she breathed. 'Enough talking.'

But she stilled as that anticipation paralysed her. He was overwhelming and she really didn't know where to begin. There was a curious smile in his eyes as he studied her. Next moment he lifted her onto the bed. A haze enveloped her as he stood above her. She wanted to touch him but couldn't reach, couldn't find the strength to do anything but moan. Her fingers fluttered. Then she couldn't do anything as he caressed her. His fingers trailed all over her until her hips lifted through no choice of her own. She rippled, undulating on the bed, meeting his tender, teasing strokes. So easily he made her a mindless creature who craved anything he cared to give her—from the lightest kisses, to the briefest of touches. When even this—the mere play of his skilled hand—destroyed her. He didn't even have to *kiss* her to have her so completely his.

She was in awe as his potent sexuality overpowered everything—until she was aroused in a way she'd never been—wanting things she'd never wanted and twisting restlessly until he took pity on her and kissed her through the silk dress. It was no less of an intimacy—of a torture.

'Ramon!' She wanted him closer.

He slid her dress up, slid her lace panties down. His smile was feral as he watched her arch to meet his hand and let her have just a finger. It wasn't enough and yet she shook with need. There was only now. Only him. In that moment he was all there would *ever* be for her.

'I can't take any more.' She trembled. 'Please, Ramon. *Please.*'

He was flushed and breathing hard, revelling in her escalation. 'What do you want?'

She shook her head, only able to gasp his name. She wanted to hold him. To feel his whole body against hers. Skin to skin. But he just teased her—devastatingly—watching her lose control at his touch.

'*Tell* me,' he groaned. A plea as much as a dare.

Singular words tumbled from her in an incoherent erotic mess. But he didn't do as she begged. He just kept teasing her with that devilish touch until she thrashed beneath him then utterly strung out, she arched one last time.

'Oh, no...' she shuddered.

'You don't like that?' he rasped. 'You don't want—?'

'I want you *inside* me...' she moaned.

But it was too late. She shuddered as waves of bliss tumbled over her until, wrecked, all she could do was gasp for air. He chuckled and slowly nudged the thin straps from her shoulders. Soon she wore only the diamonds. He touched them, then lifted his gaze. She was simply a puddle of goo in the heat of his blue eyes.

She didn't strip him. Yeah, that threat had been completely hollow. She couldn't even move. She was still quivering too much. He stepped back and yanked off his jacket and shirt, shedding shoes, trousers, boxers. He even remembered to use protection when she'd not even thought of it. She was just stunned—only able to watch because Ramon was genetically *blessed*. He was beautiful and so terrifyingly, fantastically *focused*. On her. She couldn't handle the intensity of her rising desire.

And he seemed to know because he helped. He was gentle as he joined her on the bed, pulling her closer. She moaned almost helplessly as he braced above her. He slid his hands beneath her, holding her so he could sink deep in a powerful thrust. She cried out, unable to hold back the delight as he filled her. His beautiful face stiffened as his jaw locked.

'Happy now?' he gritted.

So happy she choked back a sob and closed her eyes to hide her tears. The only thing she could manage was to kiss him. His moan as he pressed deeper into her was guttural. It was so slow. So perfect. Every inch of her skin tingled. Every muscle was like jelly, wrecked from the shuddering tension between bliss and need. The sensation—to her bones—was exquisite. He swept his hand down her arm, pressing his palm to hers, locking their fingers together.

His blue eyes blazed into hers. 'I knew we'd be good but *this*—'

Yeah. Ecstasy competed with overwhelm. All she wanted was to pull him closer still. Finally she found her strength. She wrapped her legs around him, kissing him long and deep. Something unleashed within her. Something *he* unleashed. Not just pleasure but power, she found purpose in her own body. She was meant to be here—meant to be like this—with him. She welcomed it. Wanted more. Braced closer. Everything melded as they made love.

He closed his eyes and hissed. They were locked together, fighting to get closer still. Best feeling. Ever. Best moment of her life. Ever. She didn't want it to end. Ever. But his draw was too strong, the drive between them inexorable and her next release simply sneaked up. The savage cry was pulled from her soul and she shook in his arms. They tightened—so very tightly. He gripped her and growled as he thrust hard one last time. She clung to him as he shuddered in her arms. She never wanted to let him go. She would hold him like this always.

Ramon didn't want to move. Couldn't, actually. Elodie was draped over him, her legs entangled with his. Soft, warm, utterly asleep. They were nestled together and apparently had been the entire night. So much for all his threats of prowess. There'd been no acrobatics. It had hardly been a sexual marathon. He'd been shattered on a level he didn't recognise by that one encounter then slept like nothing else. She was still knocked out.

He wriggled to glance at his clock, stunned to realise the time. He roused his will—the discipline that saw him rise early. Always. That's how he caught up on issues from the other side of the globe that had come in overnight. He needed to do that now. So he ignored the inner scream to stay and keep cuddling her and steeled himself. Stole out of the bed and went to shower in a bathroom further away so he didn't disturb her. Though she was so asleep he doubted she'd wake.

He turned the water to cold because the desire he'd thought would ebb, had only done the opposite. He was hot as hell and it was everything he didn't want.

His father had been ridden by urges, unable to control impulse or appetite. He'd wanted everything and had no compunction in going for it all. He'd groomed Ramon to be his heir. In everything. Once when Ramon had accompanied him on a business trip, he'd walked in on his father with his 'assistant'. Not an image Ramon ever wanted to recall. Nor was the 'man-to-man' talk his father had then had with him.

'These things are minor. Mean nothing. There's no need to hurt your mother. It's never anyone she knows, never at

home. You play away—you understand? As long as you're discreet—'

As if that made it okay somehow.

To the world—indeed to Ramon up until that moment—it seemed his father had *adored* his mother. Ramon suspected his father *believed* that he loved her. But his greed and conceit led him to think he could have more—to have everything and anything and anyone he wanted. And he did. Less than a year later his father had died while in the company of one of his lovers. Ramon had moved mountains to keep that horrible secret safe from his mother and he'd succeeded until her own sister—Cristina—had revealed something far worse.

Ramon was a lot like his father—fully *success* driven. He'd feared it would take nothing to tip into that same world of greed and excess, so he restrained himself. Never made promises he couldn't keep—never allowed a lover to consume his thoughts or influence his choices. He'd never intended to marry and definitely didn't need heirs to dump his driven nature onto. He'd relished his work and would work until the day he died. It had satisfied him completely.

Until he'd met her.

Now Ramon finally understood why and how his father had just 'needed more'. Elodie Wallace had activated his libidinous gene. All he could think about was going back to bed and taking up from where last night had ended. Because it had been amazing. Yet their intimacy had gone differently to how he'd expected. She'd talked a big game but the second he'd actually touched her she'd rapidly become so overwhelmed it was almost as if she'd been *shy*. Her fingers had curled in and she'd only been able to gasp as he'd tasted her. She'd certainly been *sweet*. He'd been happy to take the lead and in doing so it had become evident that she adored sex. Which was good. Being as insatiable as each other meant they could burn this out. For his own peace of mind he needed it to burn out *quickly.*

He looked in on her and mentally willed her to wake. She didn't. She was so deep in slumber that he felt like a stalker. He went back to his office, printed off the document that had arrived in his inbox, spent an hour reading it before realising not one word had sunk in. Then he returned to his bedroom—delighted to see her sharp eyes open. He could only see to her shoulders because she was snuggled beneath the sheet. Her hair was somewhat wild and her face flushed, and she was still wearing the diamond necklace.

'You should send another proof-of-life picture,' he said huskily. 'You look...'

Beautiful. Like an utterly irresistible living jewel.

'What?' She eyed him warily.

'Cute,' he completely understated, reaching for some defence against his weakness. 'Didn't expect you'd be so cuddly.'

She stiffened. 'Apologies if I overstepped.'

'No, you were sweet. I slept well.'

Her expression pinched. 'So glad.'

He laughed. 'And you didn't?' He tossed the papers beside her and thrust his hands back in his pockets. He could practice self-restraint. Sure he could.

'What's this?' she looked sniffy.

'Your wedding present.'

She scanned the first page. 'You've bought the building? Not just the business?' She nudged the offending document with a single finger until it fell from the bed to the floor. 'This is more than we agreed,' she said coldly.

His adrenaline surged. She wanted to reject it. She wasn't just reactive or responsive, but volatile as hell. He liked it— liked that she let him know the second she was unhappy about something. That at moments like this, she held nothing back.

'Spectacular as it was, this isn't a bonus for last night.' He couldn't resist stepping closer. 'Consider it payment for your vow of obedience yesterday.'

'What?' She sat bolt upright, clutching the sheet to her beautiful body. 'I never vowed obedience.'

'Didn't you understand the Spanish?' he inquired innocently. 'I think it had a slightly different meaning.'

'Rubbish.'

'It is so easy to aggravate you.' He laughed again. 'Now you own the building you can really go to town. Put in that flood room and you can drown the most annoying customers.'

'Don't put ideas in my head.'

'You already have ideas. Sadly, there isn't the time to enact them right now. That is why I'm keeping my distance. Your temptress wiles will not work on me this morning.'

Who was he kidding. He was going to act on them.

'Wiles?' She held the sheet to her neck and awkwardly swivelled to get out of bed, dragging the linen with her across the room. 'I'm not doing anything. You're the one with the apparent need to *flex*.'

Yeah, he had no idea why he'd thought he should get dressed earlier. Dumbest idea ever. And if she still wanted him to take the lead, he'd do so. Happily. He trod on the edge of the sheet. She stopped seven paces from the bed. Tugged. He didn't relent—rather, he took two handfuls of the thing and pulled it right off her. Delighted when she was suddenly naked before him.

She glared even as colour tinged her from top to toe. Only then she flicked her hair and turned her back. Possessive fire destroyed his soul.

'Don't turn away from me.' He was on her in two paces and spun her to face him. Embarrassingly, his words were a strangled plea. 'Look at me,' he muttered breathlessly. 'Right at me.'

'Why?'

Because she couldn't hide her response to him when she faced him and he needed that desperately. Because he didn't want her to shut him out. He needed to see the heat and longing she couldn't suppress. For *him*.

'So you can't pretend to yourself that it isn't me who does this to you,' he growled. 'That it's *me* you want more of.'

Yeah, he got off on that in a way he wasn't sure was altogether healthy. More than a desire, it was a desperate need. He growled, pushing out that disturbing thought. He'd reduce her to that writhing beauty again—squirming and sighing at his touch— where the only word she could utter was his name. That was all he needed.

'Egotist.' But she faced him and her body flushed with desire.

He stripped off his tee, observing with keen pleasure the colour flame across her face. 'Yeah, but you can't deny it.'

He shoved down his jeans and she stepped towards him. He went in low, scooped her up and tumbled her back to the bed. This time there were few preliminaries. No matter. He was hard. She was hot and wet. He gazed into her eyes as he thrust home. He liked the excitement she couldn't hide from him. Liked seeing her lose total control the second before he lost his.

It was over far too quickly. But this time he wasn't wiped out. He was energised.

'Not enough,' he muttered.

He filled the bath and took her in there. Propelled her to the kitchen for sustenance and ended up taking her there again too. Then he'd had to carry her back to bed where hours passed in a haze of sexual hunger and fulfilment which was exactly what he needed. They would burn this out.

He woke with a start. Swore as he blinked at the time.

'Wake up, *cariño*.' He shook her shoulders gently. 'Get dressed for the evening. We'll take the helicopter.'

CHAPTER NINE

ELODIE COMBED HER HAIR, trying to convince herself she had herself together—as if this were the sort of thing she did on the daily. Being transported in chauffeured cars and private planes accompanied by bodyguards because she was accompanying a stupendously wealthy man was no problem...and actually all that she *could* handle.

But facing her father for the first time in years? That was the emotional catastrophe causing her nausea right now. Not Ramon. Not the fact that he'd got out of bed early this morning without her even being aware of it. Not that he'd showered and dressed and continued his campaign of corporate domination while she had no idea what time it was or where her panties were. She'd thought she'd finally got herself together after the incredible experience he'd given her last night but then he'd flummoxed her with the gift of the building and then they'd spent most of the day in bed.

Shockingly, it wasn't enough. She'd thought last night would salve her sensual ache, not make it *worse*. But it was definitely worse even *after* today's luxurious sensual marathon. And the problem was that if everything went to plan tonight, both their other 'needs' would be met. Ashleigh's engagement would be ended while Ramon would have the paperwork to secure that property. There'd be no reason for their 'marriage' to last that much longer. She was sure he wasn't serious about the six months. From the little she could gather online, the man had short relationships and not many because he was ruthlessly focused on his work.

So actually Ramon totally bothered her. Or rather the feelings he aroused in her did. And now she had to face her *father* as well and she hadn't faced him in years.

She would need every ounce of armour to get through the ordeal. She built it from the ground up—shoes, dress, jewellery, make-up, hair. She knew the purple gown was striking, especially with the diamonds glittering and the fake ruby gleaming. It ought to be too much but for an occasion like this it was perfectly over the top. She stepped out to meet him, eyes widening when she saw his suit. Immaculately tailored, it was the colour of her ruby engagement ring. Again, it should clash with her purple, but they were a match. Sartorially. Sexually.

That hunger in her awakened anew. 'I'm impressed,' she muttered almost grudgingly.

'At last,' he said dryly before flashing her a wicked grin. 'I like dressing up for you, Elodie. I like you dressing up for me. I like *undressing* you even more. But all our efforts will have been for nothing if we don't even make it out the door. '

He made her laugh. If he'd really done it to please her it had worked.

She ran her thumb over the back of her ring. 'You really think your cousin will call off this engagement just because you're married?'

'I'm certain he will.'

Quelling those rising nerves, she stared out of the window of the helicopter and then in the car, not bothered that Ramon worked the entire time. It gave her a chance to practice breathing. She needed to—her lungs grew more constricted the nearer they got.

'How long since you've been back?' He broke into her spiralling thoughts.

She realised the car was approaching her parents' place and went cold all over. 'Over three years.'

The hotel's former seaside glory was long gone. Honestly, she was surprised it was still standing. Her father—for all his loud bluster—wasn't the best businessman, cut corners on upkeep and it was probably only because of the stunning views and the proximity to the sea that it had survived this long. Well, that and the tireless work her mother and sister did behind the scenes.

'You didn't miss it?' He watched her.

'The beach, absolutely.' But not the endless unpaid shifts as housemaid. She felt bad she'd left her sister to do that on her own.

'I moved to London and fell on my feet at that job at the escape room. I was so lucky.'

She'd met Phoebe there on one of her first shifts when Phoebe had been a guest on a corporate team-building day. It had been the start of the best friendship. And she'd grown confidence in discovering she was good at the work. The increasing responsibility and the respect the owner had given her had proven it. But all that confidence fled from her now.

'How are we going to do this?' She had to actively draw in a breath.

'As quickly as possible,' Ramon said. 'So I can have you alone again.' He took her hand and gave it a comforting squeeze.

But as they walked inside she felt as if she were walking into an icebox. Never had she been so cold. He slowed on their way through the reception area and frowned at the frames behind the counter.

'You're excluded from family photos?'

'They trade on it being a family hotel.' Elodie winced. 'My behaviour was not "family-friendly".'

Ramon turned to her. 'But still—'

'We're *possessions* to him, not really people.' She let go of his hand to rub the tension from her forehead. It was hard to explain how it happened, how someone could have control over others in such an overwhelming, undeniable way. 'It was important we make him look good—that we didn't disrespect him, that we made him proud. His word was law—there was no compromise. He wasn't willing to listen to alternative ideas. Not from me anyway.'

Ramon rolled his shoulders. 'Your mother didn't stand up to him? Your ex-husband?'

She dropped her hand and straightened. 'It doesn't matter—I shouldn't need anyone to stand up for me. I should be able to handle it myself.'

She moved. There was no point delaying this. Ramon walked beside her as she moved towards the private function room. The door was ajar and she heard a polite laugh. When they walked in almost everyone in the room turned. She caught Ashleigh's eye and inwardly winced at her sister's desperate look of relief. But then she saw her father's expression—shock, swiftly followed by rage. Yeah, he didn't like surprises. Didn't like not knowing what was going on—because that made his control vulnerable.

But suddenly Elodie wasn't the capable, confident person she'd thought she'd become. She was a girl again. Afraid of displeasing the man who demanded complete obedience over everything. In a nanosecond she was entirely paralysed.

Her father stepped forward. 'Who are—?'

'Ramon Fernandez,' Ramon interrupted coolly. 'Elodie's husband.'

Everyone stared—stunned—including Elodie, because she hadn't expected him to just come out with it like that. But of course Ramon was nothing if not quick once he'd decided upon an action.

'Full marks for dramatic entrance, no?' he murmured as

he put a firm hand on her back and guided her forward to claim centre space in the room.

Elodie shot him a brittle smile of appreciation and cowardly as it was, allowed him to take the lead. He wasn't a cat amongst the pigeons, he was a panther. Sleek and predatory and totally at ease, and she was so grateful because he gave her a chance to breathe.

'You're…*what*?' her father asked.

'With two such happy occasions this is the perfect time for us all to reunite, don't you agree?' Ramon picked up a cocktail and raised the glass.

No one agreed. No one said anything. But life began to trickle back into Elodie.

'I wasn't aware of it until recently, but it is amazing to consider our families' double connection.' Ramon sipped before immediately setting the glass down as if the taste had displeased him. 'Of course Elodie and I don't want to overshadow your upcoming celebrations, cousin.' Ramon appeared regretful as he turned to the young man on the other side of her father. 'Perhaps you ought to consider delaying your announcement—'

'*What?*' Elodie's father turned puce.

'Better still,' Ramon continued, unperturbed by the interruption. 'Cancel it completely.'

And that was definitely an order, not a suggestion.

Elodie had thought it would amuse Ramon to do this; instead she sensed he was actually battling a deep anger that went beyond her understanding.

'You're not… You can't…' Her father stepped forward. 'You're—'

'Ramon Fernandez,' Ramon repeated patiently. 'Chair of Fernandez Group Holdings. Your daughter Elodie's husband.'

Ashleigh had covered her mouth with her hand and had

been slowly edging closer and closer to Elodie this whole time. 'Elodie?'

'One celebration at a time, I think,' Ramon said as if it were all settled. 'After all, Ashleigh is young. She hasn't had much opportunity to see the world. Don't you agree?'

Again, no one agreed.

Elodie looked at the well-dressed woman standing alongside her mother. It had to be Ramon's aunt. She was younger than Elodie had imagined her to be—formidable and clearly furious. His cousin's face was awash with colour and he fidgeted until his mother said something sharp in Spanish that stilled him.

'Ashleigh.' Ramon turned and addressed her sister in a far gentler tone. 'It would be our pleasure if you would join Elodie and me in London. Take a break from the pressures here. Would you like that?'

Ashleigh's eyes widened.

'Ash—'

'Don't interrupt, Dad.' Elodie finally remembered she had a spine and spoke firmly. 'This is her choice.'

She looked her ruddy-faced father in the eyes and felt a completely foreign calm enter, easing her lungs as she stared him down. And for once he fell silent.

'Is that okay?' Ashleigh breathed right beside her. 'Would that be okay?'

'Of course. Go pack a bag.' Elodie nodded. 'Be quick.'

Her father's eyes narrowed, taking in her dress, her diamonds. 'You're really married?'

'Yes.'

It really seemed to be taking him a while to process it. Elodie glanced just beyond him to where her mother stood a step back. She'd paled but remained silent as always in any kind of 'situation'. Elodie willed her to say *something*, to speak up just for once. But she didn't. Maybe she never would. Maybe she'd been browbeaten too long. That was when Elodie's heart ached.

'I'll take care of her, Mum,' she said softly.

She should have got Ashleigh away sooner.

'What about the engagement party?' Her father spoke before her mother could even open her mouth. 'We have people coming—'

'As I said, cancel it,' Ramon ordered harshly. 'If you're relying on *either* of your daughters' matrimonial statuses to boost your business, then you might want to revisit your business plan.'

But Elodie's father had no shame. 'It's very kind of you to take Ashleigh on a holiday.' The switch to sycophant was laughably swift. 'Perhaps you and Elodie will soon visit us again and stay. It would be nice to get to know you.'

Nice? Elodie gaped. His volte-face was completely mortifying and yet so predictable. Always he turned to the *man*—especially if he had money.

But Ramon turned to her. 'That's entirely Elodie's decision.'

Elodie met his gaze. It was her time to say something, anything—*all* the things—but in the end there was little to say at all.

'I don't think I'll be back,' she said quietly.

There was a sharp silence.

Elodie wanted to leave, indeed she turned but then that stylish woman who'd been so quiet stepped towards Ramon.

'You can't let him have anything, can you?'

Ramon barely glanced her way. 'She's eighteen, Cristina, what were you thinking?'

'That she's fortunate to make such a good marriage so young.'

Ramon's dismissive stance didn't fool Elodie. She sensed that the anger she'd seen moments before was now rage.

'Neither Ashleigh nor Jose Ramon ought to endure such extreme parental pressure,' Ramon said harshly.

His aunt laughed. It was the bitterest thing Elodie had ever heard.

'As if you're doing this for him?' Cristina scoffed. '*You* got *everything.* Why shouldn't he inherit something? Isn't he *owed* that?'

'You think I got everything?' Ramon shot back. 'I inherited isolation and pressure. I sacrificed everything to prove myself worthy.'

Elodie moved closer and slid her hand into his.

'Are your dividends and allowances not enough?' he added. 'I can make adjustments if you need, but Jose Ramon is *owed* his liberty. Give him space to find a job for himself. A wife for himself. One he wants when he's actually *ready.*'

'Like you have?' his aunt questioned sarcastically.

'Exactly,' he snapped.

'You're every bit as selfish as your father,' she spat. 'A dog in the manger. You don't want it but you don't want anyone else to have it either. You haven't been there in *years*—'

'Actually, Elodie and I are going there for our honeymoon.' Ramon's grip on Elodie's fingers tightened. 'And now we've seen you to offer our congratulations—or should that be *commiserations*—we can leave immediately.'

CHAPTER TEN

ELODIE BIT THE inside of her lip, holding back a million questions. What had Ramon's aunt been on about? Why was there so much animosity between them? Where was it that Ramon was supposedly taking her tomorrow? And *what* honeymoon?

He didn't explain. Didn't actually speak to her. He was too busy talking with Ashleigh for the entire journey back to London. Light, easy conversation—never mentioning her father or his family and the horrible experience they'd all just endured.

Elodie battled to suppress her rising jealousy because she knew if it were just the two of them travelling, Ramon would have his head in work for the duration. Once they got to his Belgravia house she took Ashleigh to a guest room and settled her in. Piotr then proved his worth again by delivering them snacks, so it was well more than an hour before she left her sister and went in search of Ramon. He was in his home office staring out the window into the dimly lit street. Residual emotion emanated from him, compelling Elodie closer.

'Ashleigh has everything she needs?' he asked roughly.

'Yes, thank you.'

'She's very polite,' he muttered. 'Hopefully spending some time with you will cure her of a lifetime of mute compliance. She could do with some of your spirit.' He fidgeted with his cuffs. 'Did it take long for you to recover yours?'

Elodie stopped moving towards him.

'You froze when you saw your father.' He speared her with that intent gaze.

Yeah, she'd gone full 'rabbit in the headlights'. She was close to that again now as embarrassment—and wariness—surged.

'Only for a moment,' he added softly. 'Then you were back.'

She nodded. Because he'd been beside her and he'd stepped in for that second when she couldn't speak. She cleared her throat, wanting to move forward. 'What's this place your aunt meant?'

His mouth compressed. 'A private island off the coast of Spain. Lifelong occupancy rights go to the eldest married male of the family. It's for his personal use. Wider family can only visit upon his invitation.'

'Sounds exclusive and somewhat unfair.'

'Life isn't fair,' he said briefly.

Okay then. 'Your father held the previous occupancy rights?'

'Right.'

'And now, because you're married, you do,' she said. He must have wanted to keep it very much. 'What's on the island?'

'Lizards. Not much else.'

He clearly wanted to talk about the place as little as she wanted to talk about her father, but she hovered, unable to walk away from him.

He sighed heavily. 'As Cristina pointed out, I haven't been there in years. There truly hasn't been the time, but I need to go first thing. You're welcome to join me but it's not mandatory.'

'You told her that we're going there for our honeymoon.'

He winced. 'Yes, but—'

'You need her to believe this marriage is real,' she said. 'Otherwise she might contest those rights.'

He looked to the ceiling. A muscle in his jaw flicked. 'I'd

like you to have the *choice*, Elodie. I don't have the stomach to be another man who bullies you into doing something you don't really want.'

Her innards iced.

'You turned *white*,' he added gruffly. 'You—'

'Survived.' She interrupted because she did *not* want to go there with him. She did not want to revisit how weak and vulnerable she'd been for all those years under her father's thumb. She pushed out a tight breath. 'This island has a nice beach, right?'

He shot her a keen look, then *almost* smiled.

Warmth flowed back inside her. 'It's no hardship to visit a nice beach,' she added gently.

'Just for a few days. Five, max. Ashleigh too,' he invited. 'She's only just got here and she needs you. Plus she'll be good company because I'll need to—'

'Work,' Elodie interrupted with a laugh. 'Sure, I'll ask her.'

But Ashleigh looked appalled when Elodie went to her a few minutes later.

'I am *not* coming on your honeymoon!' she whisper-screeched. 'I shouldn't have come here *now*—'

'Of course you should have. I want you here. Please, Ash—'

But Ashleigh point-blank refused, and in the end Elodie phoned Bethan, who immediately offered for Ashleigh to stay with her. As Phoebe—Bethan's flatmate and the third member of the FFS club—was still in Italy, she would love the company. Elodie simply loved her friend.

Naturally Ramon retreated into work mode for the entire trip but his expression grew from remote to thunderous the nearer they got to the island and she didn't think it was because of the report he was supposedly reading. Seeing him so off balance wasn't just surprising, it was actually upsetting. Elodie would talk to him about it, only he clearly didn't want to. And why would he—they were 'married' but it was a *temporary* arrangement. He didn't want compassion from her, nor any other kind of emotion other than sexual attraction. And she didn't want to feel anything else, either. She was strong and independent and alone and that's how she intended to stay. Always.

Yet his spiralling mood mattered to her.

At last they got through the final leg of the journey—a short hop from the mainland by helicopter, then Elodie scurried to keep pace with him up the path to the stunning stone house at the top of the hill.

'I'll set up a workspace,' he said tersely. 'I have things to do before the close of day in the States.'

'Sure.'

She refused to pry and determinedly explored the house instead. She would keep their affair on the superficial, sexual level it was supposed to be.

The home was smaller than she'd expected—more cottage than mansion. The kitchen was stocked with the healthy, high-quality food he enjoyed. She went out the wide glass doors and took in the views of the sea. It was isolated and utterly beautiful.

There were no staff onsite. Not—she suspected—because he wanted to be alone with her, but because he didn't want anyone else here. Despite its undeniable beauty, he didn't want to be here *himself.* She figured his reasons had to be deeply painful. Had he spent time here as a child? With both his parents now dead, were those memories too much? Or had something horrible happened here?

The guy buried himself in work constantly. It was what he was doing now, in fact—total emotional avoidance mode. But in that argument with his aunt he'd said he'd sacrificed everything to prove himself. What had he meant by that?

She turned back to the house, suddenly needing to check on him.

He was in the lounge, sprawled back in a low-slung chair—a glass dangling from his hand, watching her approach with a moody gaze. For whatever reason he was definitely hurting, and an answering emotion rippled within her. He didn't appear to have got much work done in the hour since she'd left him to get on with it. Maybe he needed a different 'escape' than what his work could offer.

'Time for a break?' she said lightly.

'I don't need a break,' he said belligerently. 'What is it you say? A change is as good as a holiday? I visit a different company property and it is refreshing. I am constantly refreshed.'

But this wasn't a company property. This was a personal one.

'Oh, yes,' she said dryly. 'Your mood is so revitalised.'

His annoyance visibly deepened. 'You enjoy the endless creativity of your escape scenarios. We are very similar, no?' He snaked out a hand as she passed, catching her wrist and tugging her into his lap. 'We both like *this*...'

His glass fell to the floor and he growled as she softened against him.

'But you're all bark and no bite,' he muttered huskily, holding her too tightly for her to slip off his lap. 'Where's the seductress who drives men wild?'

He thought she was some amazing lover—that's what she'd implied, right? But now he was watching her with those very astute eyes and she felt hot and embarrassed because she so *wasn't* and had her faking it failed?

'Most men like to be in charge.' Her coquettish reply fell flat because she mumbled it.

'Men who are in charge all the time sometimes like to relinquish the reins,' he countered. 'Besides, I thought *you* liked to be in charge. Isn't that your everything?'

Elodie didn't know how to answer him without admitting her inexperience. But she couldn't stop herself gazing back into his beautiful blue eyes. He looked so tired. So tortured. Her heart rose and she gently cupped his jaw, soothing her fingers over his rough stubble. He worked too hard.

'Ravish me, Elodie.' He suddenly groaned. 'Make me your slave.'

The anguish in his expression made her realise this wasn't some test. He was hurting and her own heart ached in response.

'Ramon,' she reproached him gently. He had—she realised—done *everything* she'd asked of him. 'Are you not already?'

'So do what you want with me,' he breathed.

He sat like stone, but he was burning hot and he needed this from her. And she needed to give it. She scooted off his lap and moved to kneel on the floor before him. She hadn't stripped him on their wedding night because she'd been lost to his ministrations but now it was his turn to succumb to the vulnerability of being so intimately exposed. She would strip him entirely—slough off the bitterness until there was nothing but this heat between them. Because it was pure and so good, it couldn't be wrong. And because at the core of him there was hurt and it echoed within her. He was hurt and alone and she knew exactly how much that sucked. So she would take him to a place where his brain no longer functioned. It wasn't just a balm…it was absolute bliss. And she would do this because she wanted it too. She wanted him entirely.

His breathing shuddered as she unbuttoned his shirt and traced her hands over his muscled chest, tracking her finger through the light dusting of hair. She battled with his belt and jeans and in the end pulled him so he moved down from the chair to the floor with her. Then she could strip him completely, drawing it out, savouring his strength, his deeply male beauty. She touched him everywhere in all the ways she'd secretly dreamed of for days. She wanted to find out all his most sensitive spots and torment him. To please him. And as he grew restless, and his breathing quickened, and that one part of him strained… Elodie smiled.

He watched her avidly with heavy-lidded eyes. He liked looking, just as she liked looking at him. So she slowly slipped her own dress off, her underwear too. He wanted to look? Well, she would let him. She prowled on all fours, engaging as the animal he reduced her to. Not degraded in any sense, but fully provocative because she wanted to *play* with him.

'Don't turn your back on me.'

His strangled groan made her cringe. Too late she remembered what he'd said when she'd turned from him before. He'd wanted her to face him, to know it was him—as if she would *ever* be thinking of anyone else?

But when she froze, he suddenly moved. He rose and scooped her into his arms and carried her into another room. But he didn't put her on a bed; instead it was the floor again.

'We can do it how you want, but we'll do it here,' he growled.

She glanced up and saw he'd put her before a floor-to-ceiling mirror. Elodie burned, hardly wanting to look at herself in this moment but in the same second she met his gaze in the mirror. She saw his muscles flex as he knelt behind her. His hands swept from her shoulders down her waist to rest on her hips and her flush spread.

'I want to see your face,' he gritted. 'Every time I'm inside you.'

'Why?' She shouldn't have asked. She was afraid he'd make another comment about making sure she knew who she was with, and she didn't want that hurt right now.

'Because you're so bloody beautiful.'

He cupped her breast and possessively slid his other hand between her legs. His gaze was pinned to hers as he stroked her—watching her every reaction even as he felt it. She saw the triumphant lift of his chin as she began to quake.

'Watch,' he muttered fiercely. 'Watch how beautiful you are.'

But she dropped to all fours and he took her just as she began to scream and that made her scream even more. He ground her name as he ground deeper into her. It was frantic and hard and relentless and so freaking good she just screamed more as he pounded into her again and again and again. He was fierce and she'd never, ever felt as hot or as wild. She'd never wanted anything as much as she wanted him like this—primal and free—and so she pushed back on him, bucking her hips and tossing her head and he grabbed her hips harder. She *adored* it, screaming his name until finally he finished with a raw growl and a powerful thrust that almost made her pass out with pleasure. Indeed, she slid completely to the carpet and he slumped right over the top of her.

Together they gasped for air until suddenly he growled and lifted his weight off her.

'I cannot *believe* your ex let you go,' he muttered harshly.

Elodie chilled and turned her head away from him—hating that Ramon had reminded her of *him* in this moment. Because Callum hadn't *wanted* to let her go. Not because they'd been good in bed together but because he'd turned out to be as controlling as her father. Yes, he'd wanted her—but ultimately as a possession, not a person. She hadn't realised that he'd been interested in her since *school* days. She hadn't realised that he'd built up a fantasy of their future that couldn't ever become real. Hadn't realised that the chemistry that he'd assured her would develop, hadn't. When she'd distanced herself from him intimately, he'd insisted she show affection in public so no one would know that there were problems in private. He'd started to insist on more and more and she didn't want Ramon—or anyone—to know any of that now.

'I've changed,' she said coldly. 'I've got better at it since then.'

'Then why didn't any of your other lovers try to collar you for good?' Ramon challenged her. 'You're an opiate, Elodie. I can't get enough.'

She glared at him. Apparently he was still angry, and now so was she. Because she couldn't get enough either.

'Have at me then,' she snapped. 'Because I'm not satisfied.'

His eyes flared. 'Really?'

'Yes!'

Ramon was in an even more horrendous mood when he woke. He left Elodie's warmth and stalked to the kitchen to make coffee. He hated being here. Wouldn't have come if it weren't for Cristina's jibes. But she only wanted this island because she wanted to destroy every last thing her sister had loved and she was using her son to do it. As if what she'd done after his father's death wasn't enough? Yet apparently still she sought vengeance for all those years of being in the shadow—wronged, silenced, embittered. He growled in annoyance at the memories that surfaced. He definitely shouldn't have come here. They'd leave as soon as possible.

He sucked in a breath. Elodie wouldn't be thrilled. Elodie who he couldn't get a read on. Elodie who was hot and wild and who he couldn't resist when her face was flushed and her fiery hair a tumbling mess. She was a tornado and he couldn't believe she'd been controlled by her own father, that she'd married young to some guy who hadn't been able to give her what she needed. But she had. Hell, he'd seen her freeze in front of her father. Yet something niggled at him—

what she said and how she acted didn't quite add up and it set him even further on edge.

'Out of practice, *cariño*?' He set the coffee down beside her when she finally stirred. 'I thought you had no problem partying all night.'

She didn't answer, merely sipped the coffee and stared back at him.

Yeah, he was being a jerk. He'd been a jerk last night. Then he'd had the most passionate night of his life, and yet here he was, still being a jerk. The sooner they got out of here the better.

'Pack your bag—wheels up in twenty.' He backed away from her.

'We're *leaving*?' She sat her coffee cup down with a clatter. 'Already?'

'I've done all I need to here,' he said roughly.

Cristina would know from the flight records that he'd been here. He could blame the trip's brevity on work. It would have to do.

'By turning up for two minutes—just long enough to prove you were here? Well, good for you,' she said sarcastically. '*I* haven't even been down to the beach.' She scrunched down in the bed. 'What happened to five days? It hasn't even been twenty-four hours.'

He saw her slight wince as she moved and realised she was tender from their encounter last night. Fire licked, distracting and tempting. It had been sensational—the most erotic experience ever, and she'd been right with him, pushing him every bit as he'd pushed her. She pushed him differently now.

'You can't make me get on another plane,' she said mutinously. 'I've flown back and forth across the continent this week too many times already. Your carbon footprint must be *monstrous*.'

'I offset it with carbon credits from several forestry plantations,' he snapped back—adrenaline rippled through him at her challenge.

This was what he needed. Sparring with her stopped the worst memories resurfacing.

Grief. Betrayal. Abandonment.

None of it he wanted to feel ever again. This was why he didn't come here. Why he didn't let anyone close. Yet he found safety in Elodie's sarcasm, heat in the sexual tension that twisted them together.

'Of course you do.' She shot him a look from over the sheet. 'You have answers for everything.'

Not quite. He didn't really have answers for why the last forty-eight hours had been such a roller-coaster of the most fantastic and freaking awful moments ever.

'You keep bringing me to beautiful beaches and not giving me a chance to swim.' She glared at him.

'I'll take you to a better beach sometime.'

She shook her head disbelievingly. 'Promises, promises.'

The bitterness in her answer was more than sarcasm and hit harder than he expected.

'I haven't the time to waste here,' he gritted, battling the bad feeling. 'I've got work to do. Be ready to go in an hour.'

He left her, desperate to pull himself together. He even manned up and stepped outside. A long time ago this place had been a haven. He'd enjoyed summer holidays here with both his parents before he'd realised the betrayal. It was the one place his father never brought any of his lovers. Which eventually made it the one place his mother felt safe. After his father had died and the worst exposed, she'd come here and never left again. Ramon had tried to get her to at least visit other places. Tried to get her to accept help. Never could. He'd stand here and watch her walking down this path towards the dunes and her damned beloved lizards. He'd noticed her thinning frame but she'd denied his concern. Denied him so much. Her time. Her forgiveness. She wouldn't let him help. Wouldn't let him care for her. She'd been furious when he'd brought a doctor—another betrayal.

Ramon lasted less than twenty minutes before turning back to the house. Elodie was dressed, sitting on the deck and eating an ice cream.

'For breakfast?' A chuckle escaped even though he couldn't feel less like laughing. 'Where'd you even find it?'

'Freezer.' She offered it to him.

'I don't eat sweet things.'

'Maybe you ought to.' She blinked oh-so-innocently.

'Not good for me.'

'All or nothing?' Her eyebrows lifted. 'You're afraid of losing control.'

He slung himself down beside her and faced the sea, so he didn't have to look into her eyes.

'I lost control with you last night,' he admitted gruffly.

He saw the little raw spots on her knees and knew they were from the plush carpet. He wanted to kiss them.

'I was too rough.' He coughed.

'No, you weren't. I liked it.' She licked her ice cream. 'I incited it.'

Was that why she looked impishly pleased with herself? She'd not had control of her situation for years. It seemed she liked having a little control with him.

He couldn't resist touching the small wounds. 'I don't like to see you hurt.' Not even a little.

'I hardly think they'll scar.'

'But I bet they sting.' His words had as well. He'd been rude. He regretted it. He frowned at the sea, unsure how to say any of that—unsure why he even wanted to.

'This place poisons you,' she said softly. 'It's beautiful but your mood is ugly every second we're here.'

His whole body felt tight.

'Do you even want this island?'

He rubbed the back of his neck. 'It's an environmentally sound investment.'

'There are plenty of other ways you could greenwash your financial reports,' she said sceptically. 'There's more to it. Why put so much effort into securing this when you clearly *hate* it here?' She reached out and touched his shoulder so he was compelled to meet her concerned gaze. 'Is it just because you don't want your aunt to have it?'

Ramon didn't discuss any of this with anyone. Ever. But Elodie wasn't anyone. She was…

He didn't know what she was. But that night in Cornwall he'd been shocked to see her pallor when she'd first faced her father. He'd instinctively stepped forward and spoken first. After a moment she'd joined him. And when Cristina had snapped at him Elodie had slipped her hand into his. For once he'd not been alone. It might've only been an act, but they'd felt like a *team*. He hadn't had that support before and he couldn't resist reaching for it again.

'My mother moved to this island permanently after my father died,' he admitted.

Elodie's eyes widened, then softened. 'She was grieving?'

'She became a recluse.'

His mother hadn't just been heartbroken, she'd fallen apart. Unable to stand the brutal betrayals of her husband and her sister. And of Ramon.

'This place became her life. She worked to restore the environment to pristine status, made it predator free. It's why there's no development here aside from the cottage,' he muttered. 'It's literally a lizard habitat.'

She'd banned all visitors—made it difficult for even Ramon to visit. She'd raged at him for keeping silent about his father's infidelity. Rejected him from the day of his father's funeral. Told him he was his father's son—not hers.

He'd never won her forgiveness and all those betrayals had been a cancer, slowly destroying her until another cancer had come.

Elodie fiddled with the stick from her ice cream. 'So she stayed here the whole time until she—'

'Died. Yeah.' He snatched a little breath. 'Cancer. Sudden and unstoppable. Four years ago.' He didn't want to see the sympathy in Elodie's eyes so he kept talking—distracting himself with other detail. 'She didn't say she had any symptoms. Didn't give me a chance to get her help. It was weeks between diagnosis and death.'

'Ramon, I'm really sorry.'

He shook his head. 'My dad was a glutton. Food. Alcohol. Work. But especially women. There were lots. Mama was oblivious because he'd carefully have those affairs when travelling for work. Then he'd come back and spoil her. He did all the things a besotted husband should do. Gave her all the *gifts*. All the attention.'

'But you knew?' Elodie asked.

Bitterness enveloped him. 'From about fifteen I began travelling with him. He was preparing me. And when I walked in on him with an "assistant", it was a little hard for him to deny. We had a "chat" after. He said I needed to protect my mother in the same way he did—that she didn't need to know. I thought I'd shielded her from it, but after he died she found out in the cruellest way.'

'After?'

He nodded, but didn't elaborate on those awful details. He'd already shared far more than he'd ever thought he would and that last was too awful to utter aloud. 'That's when she moved here permanently.'

'Leaving you alone to take on the company.'

'I was the heir.'

She looked concerned. 'But it was a lot. Your dad had just

died, your mother retreated here, and that company wasn't like some small family business. You were alone with all that pressure as well as—'

'I was fine. The work was good. She didn't want me here anyway,' he snapped.

Really, the company had saved him more than he'd saved it. It was one thing he could control and where his energy could be safely expended. He put in time and focus and the rewards were tangible. Numbers were black and white. He'd become addicted to their constant improvement. He couldn't fix his mother. Couldn't fix his aunt. Or his cousin. The only guarantee he could give all of them was *financial* security. And so he had.

'Ramon—'

'My work guaranteed that she could stay here and hope-fully gave her some peace of mind that her family company was safe.' He closed his eyes. 'She could be here and do what she wanted. But she lived a harder life than she had to. She wouldn't let me make any improvements. Wouldn't tell me anything she really needed.'

She'd shut him out so completely that she hadn't even told him she was in physical pain. It had devastated him when he'd finally found out—far too late.

'It must have been awful to have her so isolated, knowing she was hurting from the loss of your father and finding out that horrible truth,' Elodie said quietly.

The empathy in her eyes was too much. He jerked free of her touch and swung back to face the sea.

'I've had workers in periodically to keep the place tidy but haven't been back since. Jose Ramon has drawn up plans to build a hotel here and turn it into a party island. DJs, end-less thumping. I guess Cristina wanted to help him secure it.' He sighed. 'But my mother put the ecosystem here ahead of everything, including her own life, and I can't let it be destroyed.'

'Have you talked to Jose Ramon about that?'

'He's not interested in talking to me. All his life he's been told that I'm the big bad bully who gets everything he wants.'

'Told that by your aunt?' Elodie guessed. 'Why is she so angry with you?'

Ramon couldn't utter that hideous complication aloud. He bowed his head, clenching his fists as bitterness overwhelmed him.

'Come on, let's get out of here.' Elodie suddenly rose to her feet. 'You shouldn't have to stay in a situation that makes you unhappy. You requested the helicopter, right?'

'Yeah.' He stood but he was confused. 'So we'll go—'

'Home.'

Home. With her. Right. His breathing stalled.

'I mean…' Her gaze dropped from his. 'Ashleigh's there.'

Of course. She wanted to see her sister. He frowned, remembering how muted Ashleigh had been, how silent Elodie herself had fallen for those first moments in Cornwall when he'd had the smallest glimpse into her background.

'Ramon?' She reached up and smoothed his frown. 'It will be okay. You're smart, you'll come up with a creative solution to resolve this with your family.'

Yeah, well, he hadn't yet. Not in all these years. 'Your faith in my problem-solving skills is misplaced.'

'You forget I watched you figure out my hardest escape room clues in less than half an hour.' She smiled at him a little sadly. 'But I think this place holds nothing but bad memories for you. I know you want to protect her work, but it hurts you to be here now. So let's go.'

His mouth gummed. He couldn't actually move. He felt like he'd been cracked open and if he moved a muscle, he'd fall apart completely. Because she was right. So right. What was *happening*? She was listening. She was seeing. She was caring. And he was *drowning* in it to the point where he couldn't seem to function at all.

She cupped his face. 'It's not weak. It's not running away. It's not avoidance.'

'No?' he whispered, devastated. 'I've been avoiding this place for *years*. I should have pushed for the terms of the trust to be changed. Look at what's happened because I didn't.'

'Nothing all that bad has happened,' she answered calmly. 'We stopped that stupid engagement. It's okay.' She spoke so softly. 'It hasn't been the right time for you to deal with this place. Maybe it'll never be easy. Maybe you'll need help with it. That's okay too. But your earlier instinct to leave was right. You don't need to suffer more by staying here.'

She sharply inhaled and suddenly spoke low and fast and fierce. 'What your father did wasn't your fault. *He* betrayed your mother and he put you in an impossible position forcing you to choose loyalties and keep his secrets from her. You just wanted to *protect* her and in the end you couldn't. But that wasn't your fault either. She chose to cut herself off—this place is how she did that. And honestly, she abandoned you too. So no wonder you hate it here,' she whispered harshly. 'You leaving now is self-care.'

The rush of gratitude was so real and so unfamiliar that he couldn't speak.

'Come on.' She took his hand again and tugged. Hard. He just followed.

Ten minutes later they waited at the helipad.

'Self-care, huh?' He mulled. 'That's what you did when you left Cornwall?'

'I guess.'

His gut tightened but he turned to her because he suddenly needed to know. 'Your father was always domineering?' He braced. 'Violent?'

His heart stopped as she paled.

'Not too bad. Not as we got older,' she breathed. 'But he still threatened. Mum was anxious that we please him. She couldn't stand up to him and we didn't either. We had to look good, perform, improve the family position. But never actually think for ourselves.' She shot him a colourless smile. 'He wasn't interested in my ideas, but I actually have quite good ideas.'

'I know you do,' Ramon muttered helplessly. 'He should have listened. *Valued* you for *everything* else. Never hurt you.' Impotent fury swept through him. 'Didn't your husband see it?'

Her expression pinched. 'Callum said marrying him would make it better. That he loved me, he'd help push my ideas, stand up to my father and that we'd—'

She broke off and cleared her throat. Ramon knew there was something more she'd left unsaid and wished she'd trust him enough to say it.

'But he didn't?' Ramon pressed. 'He stayed there even after you left?'

'Until he accepted that the divorce was inevitable,' she whispered.

An unbearable tension built inside. 'He really didn't want to let you go, huh?'

Elodie shook her head. 'But Callum made many promises that he didn't keep long before I left him.' Her glance skittered from his again. 'Lots of people don't deliver on their promises.'

That was true. But Ramon was increasingly bothered by the feeling that his wife Elodie *wasn't* one of them.

CHAPTER ELEVEN

BACK IN LONDON, Elodie was touched by Ramon's kindness towards Ashleigh. He put a chauffeur and car at her disposal, inquired about her favourite food, arranged tours of tertiary options and offered every possible comfort, giving her freedom, security, funding. He was unquestioningly generous. Elodie returned to work, energised by the astonishing reality that she owned not just the business but the whole building.

Bethan pounced on her the second she walked in, wanting to know all. Her friend was an incurable romantic, but Elodie couldn't open up to her about Ramon. Their deal was confidential and besides, he was far more complicated than she'd first thought. His arrogance was partly a protective facade. He'd been hurt—his father's infidelity, his mother's heartbreak and the burdens that had been put on him. No wonder he kept those who remained at a distance when he'd been let down by the people who should have protected him. She understood how that felt. Her father hadn't truly cared for her, while Callum had been full of it. He'd told her he loved her, that he would stand up for her, that he'd be patient. But the Elodie he'd wanted had been a figment of his imagination—one he'd got fixated on. He'd wanted little more than a decorative accompaniment and in the end he'd tried to dictate her life every bit as much as her father had.

She almost wished she could tell Ramon the truth about her break-up with Callum, but he had enough on his plate. She was already testing his generosity by having Ashleigh to stay. And would he even be interested? This was only a temporary agreement—all physical, not emotional. The only sort of affair he ever had and the kind he thought *she* had all the time too. If she told him she actually didn't, then he might wonder why she'd agreed to their fake wedding so easily in the first place. Might worry she wouldn't be able to really handle it—that she was somehow more vulnerable because of her inexperience. He was arrogant enough to think she'd catch feelings for him and she knew he'd run from *that* in a flash.

And the thing was, *she* didn't want things to change at all from how they were now. She relished this—night after night of banter, their verbal jousting, the foreplay before they made intensely physical demands of each other. So she'd keep quiet. She'd make the most of it while it lasted. Because it *was* going to end.

A few nights later Ramon returned home so late Elodie was already in bed, reading. She caught the moodiness in his eyes. 'Something wrong?'

'I have to travel tomorrow.'

'I thought you liked travelling.'

'I also like sleeping with you.'

She felt a shiver of risk but couldn't resist. 'You don't see a solution?'

'I see a very obvious one.' He sat on the edge of the bed beside her with a wry smile. 'The question is whether you're willing to endure more time in an airplane?'

Pleasure washed through her but she didn't want to give away her complete excitement at the prospect of accompanying him. 'How long?'

'We'd be away about ten days. A whirlwind visit of a few of our hotels. I need to check in on them.' He took the book from her and set it on the bedside table. 'You could check out all the escape rooms in the cities, call it a research trip.'

She couldn't answer. Her heart was beating too fast. She wanted to say yes too much, too easily—wanted *time* with him—more than she should when this was only supposed to be *temporary*. Which was exactly why she couldn't deny herself.

'Bethan did a good job of running the place last week.' He stroked a strand of her hair and made that heat lick through her. 'Ashleigh might want to help her out on the front of house—would be something to occupy her while she works out which course she wants to enrol in. She could invite a friend to stay here, an assistant could move in too—she wouldn't need to be lonely. You'll call her lots. She'll be safe.'

'Are you managing my business for me?' she teased breathlessly.

'Your business is my business.' His finger traced down her neck and drew a little circle in that space between her collarbones.

Right now—for now—he wanted her to come with him and she couldn't say no.

'Mi casa es su casa.' His finger dipped lower, a direct line down between her breasts.

What's yours is mine. He had all the expressions and used them well. She reminded herself again that this was merely banter, just the light tease that they'd fallen into so easily from the start. But buried in a secret chamber deep in her heart was the burgeoning wish that he actually meant it.

'You should pack your bikini.' His eyes twinkled as he played his trump card and took a side detour to her straining nipple.

Elodie grabbed hold of his marauding hand and tugged him down to the bed with her. 'You mean you're *finally* letting me loose on a beach?'

The next morning—having laughed at Ashleigh's wholehearted reassurance that she was living her best life *ever* and Elodie could definitely please *go*—Elodie was surprised to see an additional twelve or so people board his plane with them. Personal assistants, alternate bodyguards and business analysts, apparently. All of whom were top-level Fernandez employees.

Seated in the private front cabin with Ramon, Elodie was fascinated to watch their interactions with him throughout the flight. They came solo or in small groups for short, sharply efficient meetings. Unfailingly professional, they offered Elodie a polite smile before briefing Ramon on various issues with laser-like focus. Unlike her father, Ramon actively listened, in fact he demanded intelligent input and robust debate before issuing instructions. There was no personal chat before the employees then headed to the rear cabin to work on Ramon's directive. Elodie thought they seemed nice, but none were actually *friendly* with him. Not even the loyal Piotr seemed to have that status.

It struck her as somewhat sad. Ramon was surrounded by all these people who shielded him from everyone else. Yet they were distant from him themselves. Was it just so he could focus on work—as if he was some high-performance professional? Really, she increasingly thought he was a man who had only half a life. Ramon would laugh at her if she suggested it. He thought he had it so very *together*—he loved his work and he had everything he wanted.

But maybe he didn't have all he really *needed*.

Paris, France

'Are you going to spend all my money at the shops?' Ramon knew she wouldn't, he just couldn't resist provoking her.

'Every. Cent.'

'Liar,' he mocked.

'Enjoy your meetings.' She blew him a kiss and sauntered out the door.

Indeed, the only money she spent was entrance fees to various galleries, museums, attractions for her and the bodyguard he'd insisted accompany her. She filled her day happily—returning late in the evening with shining eyes. But *he'd* paced the hotel room, impatient for her return, concentration shot. He hadn't seen half the galleries she mentioned. Didn't like missing out. So the next morning he pushed out a meeting so he could go with her to an escape room, which took far too long given both of them were useless, with only basic school-level French.

Then he took her back to the hotel and endured meetings that went on far too long. He raced back to their suite the second he could. She was working on a puzzle on the sofa. He couldn't resist sinking beside her and sliding his hand into her pants—he'd been dreaming of that all afternoon. Her little moan was magic and he leaned in to steal the kiss he probably should have started with. He slowed down, teased her, making her come before he lifted her to ride him. Her hair was a tangled mess of fire, curtaining them both in an insanely hot world until their orgasms tore through them and they tumbled into a heap of limbs.

'Bed,' he murmured sleepily. 'We have an early flight tomorrow.'

Rome, Italy

'Come on, let's go out for dessert.' Ramon hauled her to her feet when he got back to the suite after another day of long meetings. But he was challenging himself to delay their dive into bed and now, knowing Elodie had a weakness for ice cream, he had the urge to please her in a way outside of the bedroom.

'You're actually going to have something?' she marvelled.

Walking in the warm evening, her joyous appreciation of

the architecture made him smile. Then the gelato bar had her drooling, but she frowned when he didn't order one for himself.

'I thought you were going to have something sweet?' She licked her rapidly melting treat.

'I am.' He leaned close and licked her lips. 'Very sweet.'

It was disarmingly easy to flirt with her. Her blushing responses were growing more adorable—indeed her *shyness* seemed to be growing, which was the oddest thing. She didn't always pin him with that fearless gaze. Often times now her glance skittered away as if she couldn't bear to look at him too long. Naturally that only made him tease her more.

Vis, Croatia

'You promised a *beach*.' She looked at him balefully.

'I'm told it's a *beautiful* beach,' he assured her firmly. 'We just have to jump down to get to it.'

'Jump off a *cliff*?' She shuddered. 'Have you not been down there?'

He shook his head. 'One of my army of assistants recommended it.'

She'd teased him about the number of people in the back of the plane that they'd barely seen in the last two days—because he'd been avoiding work on a scale utterly unlike him. But now she knew the extent of his assistants and bodyguards and it seemed she wasn't so much impressed as amused.

With a sigh Elodie swept her hair up into a ponytail and secured it with an elastic. He couldn't resist running his hand down the length of it.

'Not so bad tied up?' She turned her head archly.

'You. Tied up. Yeah, definitely not so bad,' he drawled.

Colour whipped into her cheeks, but his laugh became a cough when she shed her shorts and tee.

'Scarlet bikini?' he gasped.

Scarlet and skimpy and she was going to give him a heart attack.

'People tend to stare at me so I might as well give them something to really look at.'

'Why do you think they stare?'

'I think it's the red hair.' She shook her ponytail ruefully. 'Loud and out of control. I guess they think *I'm* like that as well.'

'I think you're very in control. Most of the time.' He winked at her. 'I think you give people what they expect. You play up to it.' Her past had hurt her, so she'd toughened up. He didn't blame her in the least. 'What's real and what's the armour, Elodie?' He jerked his head towards the cliffs. 'How brave are you really?'

'You like to challenge me,' she muttered.

'I like seeing you enjoy yourself.' He held out his hand. 'Do it with me.'

She held his hand painfully tightly. He gripped hers as hard back and grinned. Twelve long seconds later they surfaced.

'My bikini slipped.' She giggled as she grabbed her top before it could float away and eyed him accusingly. 'Which is what you wanted!'

Buenos Aires, Argentina

'You really like dancing,' Ramon murmured.

She'd been entranced by the tango display but now the performance was over and the club's resident DJ had taken to the decks. Revellers were crowding the floor and Ramon ached.

'Yes, I do.' Elodie sipped her drink and nodded. 'No lie. It's liberating. I like being alone in a crowd but knowing we're all feeling the same beat. It's the safest place to express myself. It's sexy.'

She was sexy.

'Go on then,' he dared her huskily.

She disappeared into the crowd but soon enough he spotted her in the middle of the crowd. She had such sensual physicality—in tune with her body, dancing unconditionally, unreservedly, and he could only stare. But eventually she came over, the tease obvious in her eyes.

'You only like to watch?'

Her cheeks were flushed and there was a sheen to her satiny skin and how could he resist?

'You like to challenge me,' he growled, echoing her words from the other day.

She smiled. Remembering. He'd known she would.

'I like seeing you enjoy yourself.' She held out her hand. 'Do it with me.'

Which is how Ramon, who hadn't gone dancing in more than a decade, found himself in the middle of a packed-out club floor. Liberated and laughing. Until he wasn't laughing and he could hear nothing but the music, feel nothing but the beat and the heat—driving him to move closer to her. It was more than two hours later before they made it back to the hotel. To a cool shower. Then long moments more—dancing of a different kind.

'Is this liberating?' he breathed as he buried deep inside her. 'Sexy?'

'*Si,*' she sighed. 'Yes.'

'Look, fluent in my first language already.'

Somewhere over the Atlantic

The less than two-week trip had spilled into three when Ramon extended the trip in South America, purely because she'd never been there before and he'd been enjoying her wide-eyed enthusiasm. But there could be no more prevaricating, he had to fly back to London. Duty called. But he sprawled next to her on the wide sofa, his safety belt loosely fastened in his lap. He ought to be working but simply didn't. It wasn't that he was too tired, he was too *relaxed*. A very different thing.

He idly watched her scribble in the spiral bound notebook that had been new at the beginning of this trip. It was fat now—filled with ideas, pictures, postcards. She was industrious and if that small smile on her face was to be believed, happy. So, he realised with a warmth unlike any other, was he. They were both quiet—no drama between them, no playful banter even. Just *peace*. She sketched and he watched, oddly content when he was effectively being the laziest he'd ever been in his life—letting his mind rest.

But his mind never really rested. Being back in London meant work would ramp up. And other responsibilities were pressing.

'It's the annual Fernandez Family Foundation gala tomorrow night.' He finally admitted the event that was forcing their return. 'It's a good opportunity to introduce you to the rest of them.'

She stopped sketching. 'Surely I'm not sticking around long enough to need introductions to everyone.'

He tensed. Not around long enough? What did she mean by that?

She avoided meeting his gaze. 'I don't think it's appropriate.'

Well, that was ridiculous. 'You're not that much of a provocateur, Elodie,' he said dryly. 'So you've been to a few nightclubs? You've not got any kind of criminal record. How awful for a young person to have had some fun in her life. If they're going to judge you for that then they need to take a long look in the mirror.'

'I thought I was a gold-digger. Only with you for money. I don't have a heart.'

'That's why you offered yourself as a replacement bride for your younger sister,' he drawled. 'The one with a missing heart is me.'

'But if you have no heart, why did you accept my offer?'

'Because I'm greedy.'

'You're *paying*. You're the one losing.'

'It's not money I'm greedy for.'

She sat back. 'You could get sex anytime you want.'

Yeah, but it wasn't sex he was talking about. Not entirely. Not anymore. And even if it was, he didn't want that with anyone else either. He wasn't going without her and he suddenly didn't know what to say. Because *none* of this he was willing to admit when *she* was only using *him* for hot sex. Right?

'I thought I was supposed to be their worst nightmare,' she added in his silence.

Defensiveness—protectiveness of her—rose in an unstoppable wave.

'Because you're not afraid to call out bullshit when you see it,' he snapped. 'Not because you might have partied hard when you finally got your personal freedom. I would've done the same if I'd been stifled by my family my whole life.' He shook his head at the stupidity of her concerns. 'No one's expecting a nun.' He growled. 'And I'm sorry if this comes as a shock but I wasn't a virgin on our wedding night either.'

Her eyes widened and she lost colour.

He gritted his teeth. She'd said she'd cheated on her first husband, and he knew too well the damage infidelity inflicted. Cheaters were selfish. But what he couldn't wrangle his head around was that *Elodie* didn't seem that all selfish now. Seeing Ashleigh so quiet and compliant was sobering because the thought of his fiery Elodie ever being like that appalled him. And while he couldn't stand to imagine the details, had never thought he could ever understand someone cheating, he had to acknowledge that she'd been young. Maybe she'd felt trapped. Maybe he couldn't judge what he didn't know, but his stomach ached and he sucked in a breath and shoved those thoughts away.

'We're *married*,' he said, trying to haul himself back together. 'It's made it to the society pages. Which means it's a little late to keep it a secret.'

'And too soon to reveal the truth?' she asked.

That wave of protectiveness morphed into panic. Did she mean end their marriage? Absolutely too soon. He hadn't done a thing about resolving the future of that island. He'd had no problem organising the contracts for the wedding, for purchasing the escape room, but as yet he'd done nothing about amending that damned trust. He couldn't yet—he justified—Cristina might think his marriage a fraud if he made changes now and he really didn't want to meet with her and Jose Ramon to find another way through. It would be much better to maintain the marriage for the full six months he'd rashly suggested and consolidate his occupancy rights that way.

'Sometimes the truth makes things worse,' he said, avoiding answering Elodie directly.

'So what's your solution?' she asked. 'If the truth is too painful, the secrets too devastating, how do you work around that? Do you live with lies?'

Funny that she asked that when she was the self-confessed liar. But he knew the answer. 'You don't let anyone close enough to hurt you that badly again.'

He saw her immediate withdrawal and tensed.

'Isn't that what you do now?' He defied her wistful expression. 'With your friends and your vows to be free forever? That's a pact to protect yourselves. Staying single keeps things simple.'

'Then why do you want me to show up to this gala as your *wife*?'

Because he wanted her with him! Because he didn't want to face them alone! But realising both those facts made him bristle with rejection. He grasped for another reason. 'It's the trust.'

'The island you can't stand?' she said sceptically.

'I can't let Cristina destroy that as well.'

'As well as what?'

He couldn't stand Elodie's direct gaze, but he couldn't seem to break the hold she had over him. The bitterness had been building inside him for years and as he stared at her the poison spilled suddenly, stupidly easy. 'As well as destroying my mother's life when she told her that Jose Ramon is my father's other son.'

Elodie gaped. *'What?'*

'My father had an affair with my mother's sister.' He folded his arms tightly across his chest. 'Jose Ramon is their child.'

'But your aunt Cristina is quite young—'

'I *know*,' he groaned. Younger even than Elodie had been when she'd entered that unhappy marriage. 'She was eighteen when she had Jose Ramon. She never said who the father was. Never married.' Ramon's guts twisted. 'I *know* she was a victim. I know she'd felt overshadowed by her older sister. My mother was high-achieving and beautiful and I can only think resentment damaged Cristina, because she exposed the truth just after his funeral.'

He shrivelled inwardly, remembering the horror of those moments. His mother had been frantic. Disbelieving. Near hysterical she'd turned to him—begged him to tell her it wasn't true—because his father would *never* have cheated on her. But Ramon had been too shocked to be able to respond. And he couldn't reassure her, he *couldn't* confirm his father's fidelity because he'd known about the *others*. But not that one. *He'd* been so sickened by Cristina's revelation he'd been stunned to silence. And no matter what he said from then on, no matter how many times he tried, his mother never believed that he hadn't known it all, all along. She'd never forgiven him for saying nothing. She'd left for the island later that day and never returned. Ramon had lost both parents that day.

'I never understood why Cristina waited until *then* to say anything,' he said huskily. 'It wasn't to punish my father—he was dead. It could only have been to hurt my mother. Cristina wanted revenge and took it in the cruellest moment.'

Ramon couldn't forgive her for that, even when he knew how complicated the entire mess was. That ultimately it was all his father's fault.

'And now you're paying her back for that by not letting Jose Ramon have this island.'

'Does he really even want it?' Ramon flung back defensively. 'Or does Cristina just want to destroy the last thing that was precious to my mother?' He stared at Elodie, not wanting to see judgement in her eyes. 'Do you blame me for wanting to stop her? You wanted revenge on your family.'

She shook her head. 'I wanted to save my sister.'

He drew breath. Yes. That had fascinated him. Elodie's ready willingness to sacrifice herself to help her sister was so different to his family dynamic. But surely there'd been more to her choice to marry him. 'Not only that. You knew turning up with me on your arm, that your father would be furious to be thwarted at the missed opportunity to form a valuable connection with me.'

'Is that your ego talking again?'

'Be honest. You liked it.'

'I liked it,' she agreed. 'But not because it was revenge.'

'No?'

She looked at him intently. 'What I liked was that for the first time I didn't have to face them *alone*.'

Ramon tensed his arms to stop himself softening. But that was how he'd felt too. 'You don't count Ashleigh?' he asked gruffly.

'I had to protect her. I don't have to protect you, you're strong enough to fight alongside me. You're stronger than all of them.'

He shook his head. He didn't want to accept that she was more noble than he. 'But you didn't want me to bail him out financially. You wanted him to see you thriving in a world of wealth while he lost his precious deal. Is that not revenge, Elodie?'

'You make me sound horrible.'

'You're human. He hurt you. Isn't it natural to want to strike back?'

'Maybe I was wrong not to let you help him. Maybe if he doesn't have to struggle, he won't hurt anyone else.'

'Unless he's greedy,' Ramon said heavily. 'Unless he has a bottomless appetite for accumulating things and not caring about anyone in his way. That was *my* father. That *is* my aunt. And if your father's like either of them then you have a problem because it'll never be enough. He'll never stop.'

'You don't think he'll ever change?'

'Does anyone? People remain fundamentally the same. Their flaws can't be miraculously fixed.'

'People can grow. Learn from their mistakes. Get better.' She straightened proudly, her gaze falling just short of his. 'I'm not the person I was when I married Callum.'

'No?' A terrible regret built inside him. 'You wouldn't let yourself agree to a marriage you don't really want?'

She turned on him fiercely. 'I asked you.'

'But—'

'This is *different*. I get something *I* want out of this.' She threw her shoulders back. 'I have an element of power. Of *choice*.'

He was silent because more than anything he wanted her to keep choosing him, and that was doubly shocking.

'We're all shaped by our experiences, right?' Her voice softened. 'Sometimes we can grow beyond hurt and thrive but maybe some people can't get past the damage and end up stunted. I think revenge only perpetuates the problem. It all becomes a never-ending cycle of pain and payment. An eye for an eye only hurts everyone.'

She was naive, wasn't she? Or—horrible doubt bit—was she right?

'So you would have me turn the other cheek to Cristina?' he swallowed tightly.

'I don't know. Maybe she'll never get over the past. But Jose Ramon is young, maybe all this bitterness doesn't need to infect the next generation.'

'She wouldn't let me anywhere near him.' Arms still crossed, Ramon curled his hands into fists and pressed them more tightly into his sides. 'Said I was too much like my father and she didn't want my influence on him. I was so angry anyway, so busy getting the company on track that I stayed as far away from them both as possible. I just made sure she got the money they were both owed. He doesn't need the island. He should find his own project,' Ramon muttered. 'Shake off the family interference. He's old enough—'

'But he might not be secure enough. Not everyone is as independent as you,' Elodie said.

'You are,' he countered. 'You survived, totally on your own once you ran away.'

'Not totally alone. I have friends who support me.' She frowned. '*You're* the one who's totally alone.'

'I have an army of highly skilled assistants.'

'Do they offer emotional support?' she challenged. 'Or do they help you keep everyone else at a distance?'

'I don't need emotional support.'

'*Everyone* needs emotional support.'

'Okay, fine,' he snapped grumpily. 'Emotionally support me then. Come to this damned gala. I would like you there with me!'

He stared at her, stunned by his own outburst. What was he *doing*? Since when did he ask anyone for touch, for company, for comfort the way he asked her? It had slipped out of him unbidden, yet so easily.

But before he could pull back, she was there—soft and warm, her lips an inch from his—as she promised, 'Of course I will.'

CHAPTER TWELVE

ELODIE HAD FASTENED the diamonds around her neck and checked her appearance. She'd opted for black, not wanting to draw additional attention tonight. She actually wanted to look *appropriate*. When he'd first mentioned the gala she'd been reluctant but she would go there for him. She wished Ashleigh was here so they could catch up but Bethan had taken her to Edinburgh for a long weekend as a surprise treat. Her friend was truly the best.

'Going for the black widow look?' Ramon teased when he walked up behind her. 'My relatives would adore you if you followed through on that.'

She turned. He looked sharp as ever in the dark dinner suit. 'I don't think they'd want me to kill off the man responsible for their gravy train.'

But as they walked out of the house a shiver of trepidation rippled through her.

'Nervous?'

'Why would I be?' She drew on her old confident armour. 'I'm not scared. I like a party.'

'Such bravado, Elodie,' he jeered softly. 'It's the *family* that scares you.'

'Yeah, well, you have to admit they were pretty fearsome in Cornwall.'

'Don't worry, tonight is too public for much drama. They'll all act as if everything is just fine.'

But she looked at him more closely and saw he was paler than normal. Was he nervous too? She wouldn't blame him. Ramon was even more alone than she'd imagined. What he'd told her was shockingly sad but she was deeply touched that he'd trusted her enough to share something so personal and painful. Maybe she could—*should*—be more honest with him too. But she knew Ramon better now—knew he was honourable and protective, and if he found out she wasn't as worldly and as experienced as she'd made out, he'd definitely be bothered about their fake marriage deal. He felt bad about enough already—his father's treatment of his mother, her isolation and emotional abandonment of him, the awful mess of his aunt and his father and his unacknowledged half-brother. She didn't want to add to that. But honestly, she was mostly afraid that he would end their affair immediately, and now it wasn't that she wasn't ready for that *yet*, but that she might *never* be ready to let him go.

She shivered again.

'You sure you're okay?' Ramon wrapped his arms around her and pulled her into a bear hug.

Pure safety, security, support. She knew she could step back at any time and he'd release her, but instead she leaned even closer against him. She didn't want to escape. Didn't want to be alone. Not anymore. She drew on his strength and wistfully hoped that somehow he too drew on something from her.

'I'm good,' she whispered.

He pulled back with a devastatingly tender smile and held the door for her. Her heart somersaulted in her chest and she suddenly knew she *had* to talk to him. Had to be honest. Her heart compelled it for herself. *She* didn't want to hold back anything from him anymore. She would be brave and tell him *everything*. But she would face his family with him first. That was the one thing he really needed from her now.

Ramón couldn't get his head around the fact that he'd been married to Elodie for more than a month because it had truly passed in the blink of an eye. But he knew she couldn't resist ice cream. Her preference for green tea over black. Her enjoyment of detective shows. Her other 'tells' had become more obvious too. He knew when she was thinking about kissing him, when she was about to come, when she was nervous—like when jumping from those rocks. She'd awed him when she pushed through with courage then and it was what she was doing now—looking stunningly dangerous in that black evening gown despite desperately snuggling in to him only moments ago. He ached to draw her back into his arms. She'd given him a comfort he hadn't felt in years and she'd helped him face his past. Maybe he might even resolve that mess properly soon.

But for now he enjoyed watching her gracefully enter the car. She had that aloof, unattainable but sexy air down pat. Her enigmatic focus intrigued him. She liked to set puzzles and throw red herrings everywhere but actually was a puzzle herself. She could be flirtatious, confident, brash yet in the next moment blush awkwardly, flustered and jittery. She could hold men at arm's length. And did. Including him sometimes. In short, she fascinated him and he wanted to know more. *Should* know more. But he'd not had the stomach to ask about her past lovers. It had suited him to think of her as being as bulletproof as him. It had made his own plan palatable.

But no one was bulletproof.

He'd been *lazy* and frankly jealous. He'd chosen not to question the nuances of her first marriage. What had happened? Her father had to have approved it and didn't want her divorce, so had he bullied her into it like he'd just tried with her younger sister? And where was the ex in all this, why hadn't the jerk had Elodie's back?

Ramon had been so blinded by lust he'd not stopped to discover the subtleties. He thought back to those party photos on her social media. Maybe it was all wishful thinking, but he was sure there hadn't been the sparkle in her eyes that there was when she was out with him. She'd posed—performative. Had it all been a front to hide heartbreak?

Now he wanted to know why, to *understand* everything. Why had she embraced such overt hedonism? Had she felt so oppressed she needed to discover herself?

She was loyal to her friends. To her sister. Even to him. Yet she'd apparently cheated on her husband. The Elodie he'd seen, the one he'd touched, the one he *knew*, didn't seem likely to do that. Although she'd admitted that she wasn't the same person she was when she married the first time. So what happened to make her walk out on him?

Ramon had tested her only once with a stupid question about her husband letting her go, but she'd said nothing. Had her silence been another demonstration of her innate loyalty?

So somehow, as they were driven through the heart of London, he voiced his deepest worry out loud. 'Did you fall in love with him?'

She shot him a confused look. 'With who?'

'The man you left your first husband for.'

'I…' Colour scalded her skin, only to ebb as violently quickly, leaving her waxen. 'I don't think now's the right time to talk about that.'

Yeah, rubbish timing. His impulse control had *completely* gone. He bit the inside of his cheek. Because even if she'd loved the guy, it obviously hadn't worked out and she'd then dated a string of others. Which shouldn't—didn't—matter. The double standard of sexual desire should be left in the last century and maybe he shouldn't be wondering about her past. It was irrelevant to now, right? To his future.

Their future.

Yeah, *there* was the bother. He wanted more with her and somehow the facts she'd presented about her past *needed* scrutiny, because he really had the feeling she was holding back on him. His father had kept so much from his mother for so long and he hated the idea that he might not know Elodie properly—not in the way he *thought* he did. He couldn't bear to be blindsided by anyone.

He gritted his teeth as they entered the gala. The place went fully silent for a second as literally everyone stared. Because she was beside him—his unbelievably beautiful wife. Yet something felt off-kilter. He tensed even more, sensing threat. It was probably just in his head. Honestly, he didn't know who he was anymore—couldn't believe the impulsivity that he couldn't control. Since when did he travel with anyone? Take not just hours, but whole days to his own leisure? Since when did he let anyone in his life for longer than a meeting? When did he hang out with anyone? And since when did he strike her with inappropriately personal questions at the worst possible moment?

Her tension was obvious too and he mentally kicked himself. As if this evening wasn't going to be stressful enough? But there was music playing and a few people were on the dance floor.

'Shall we?' He gestured to the too well-lit space. 'It's safe on the dance floor, right?'

But this wasn't arms-in-the-air free-form fun, this was formal, and she didn't relax.

'I'll be back in a moment.' She pushed away from him after only a few minutes, disappearing in the direction of the rest rooms.

Ramon picked up a drink from a tray and prowled to the

edge of the room, unwilling to engage with his wider family yet. He'd wait for her return. While he didn't want to be alone in facing them, he didn't want *her* to be either.

'Why would you want to dance with her when so many other men already have?'

'Pardon?' Ramon turned, unable to believe his ears. He didn't recognise the belligerent-looking man who'd appeared beside him. 'And you are?'

'Callum Henderson. Elodie was my wife first.'

Ramon gaped. What on earth was her ex doing here? How had he got in? He glanced across the room and even from this distance saw Jose Ramon's moody defiance and Cristina's glittering gaze. His guts twisted. This was *too* much.

He hauled his wits together and faced Callum. 'You think that entitles you to pass comment on her now?'

'Take it from someone who knows her well. She's never satisfied.'

Something purely animal ran through Ramon. 'Maybe in your company. Not mine.'

Callum flushed. Good. He was a jerk. Treating Elodie as a possession. A prize. Not a whole person. And maybe Ramon's reply had bought into it but he'd been stunned into snapping back.

Now Callum's gaze turned nasty. 'Yeah, well, she won't give you the heir you want.'

Ramon almost choked. He didn't want an heir. But of course, that side of the family thought he did. Heirs and assets. It was all that mattered to them. Yet suddenly the image of a sweet little girl with fire-engine-red hair popped into his head—disarming him completely. Goosebumps peppered his skin as his wayward imagination fed him another future child—a son. More red hair. Smiles. Playfulness. Elodie would have such fun playing games with them and he would have such fun joining in. And he just wanted to grab her and get the hell out of here because he *really* needed to talk to her.

'But you already know she's probably infertile,' Callum added venomously. 'All that time with women's troubles.'

'What?' Ramon responded before thinking. *'What?'*

Callum's features sharpened as if he'd sensed a chink in Ramon's armour. And yeah, there was a chink. A huge one. Did Elodie have health issues she hadn't told him about?

'You have no right to discuss my personal business, Callum.' Elodie's voice came from behind him.

Ramon turned, immediately shocked by her pallor. Her sapphire eyes were sharp as blades, but she couldn't hide the pain in their depths. Not from him. He chilled, then menace filled him. He was wild with Callum, but even more horrified that *he* might have hurt her somehow and he didn't know.

'What are you doing here?' Elodie asked her ex-husband bluntly.

Ramon whipped his head and watched the way Callum looked at her. He knew then. He just *knew.* Callum couldn't drag his attention away from her. Couldn't hide the wild emotion in his eyes. Ramon knew the feeling. Jealousy burned as he saw how much this man still wanted her. Hell, he probably still thought he loved her. And how had he shown that—by not wanting to let her go? By getting angry because he couldn't control her? If his current behaviour was any indication, when Callum couldn't get what he wanted he got ugly about it.

'I wanted to see for myself,' Callum said roughly. 'I'd heard you finally landed a wealthy one. The husband of your dreams. Are you happy at last?'

Bile burned the back of Ramon's throat. The jerk thought she was a money-hungry predator? *She* wasn't the predator. She'd spent most of her life surrounded by controlling men.

'Yes,' Elodie replied in a brittle, bored tone that sounded nothing like her. 'Ramon's able to satisfy my every need.'

There was the same inflection in her answer that he'd put in his—the stamp of their sexual cohesion. He felt that animal emotion rush on him again but quickly quelled it. Because Elodie put on a show. She masked her hurt. This was vixen Elodie up front and centre and suddenly he wasn't sure what to believe.

She turned and walked away from them both, her head high and her fiery hair gleaming in the light. Ramon swiftly stepped to match her pace. Confused. She'd said nothing to him about her health. Nothing. And he was furious.

She turned the corner, drawing them from the line of sight.

'Is that why you asked me about leaving him earlier?' She whipped round to face him the second they got behind a tall column. 'Because you knew he'd be here?' She tossed her head. 'Why would you—'

'Of course I didn't invite him,' he interrupted. Doubly furious she'd even think it possible. 'I think Jose Ramon brought him. Wanted to create drama.'

Wanted to create chaos. Spoilt and petulant, he'd wanted to wreck Ramon's perceived happiness.

'What?' Elodie gazed up at him and the anger in her eyes bloomed into something he didn't want to see from her. Pity.

'He's *that* angry…?' She shook her head sadly. 'He must be really hurt.'

'You feel sorry for him?' Right now Ramon was feeling sorry for himself.

'I do.' She sighed deeply. 'It must be impossible to be compared to you. And won't Cristina have put him up to it anyway? The poor kid doesn't stand a chance.'

She reached for a glass from a passing waiter and pasted on a smile. Ramon paused, momentarily in awe of her self-control. He just wanted to smash something. What should have been a boring, slightly tense evening had rapidly descended into one of the worst nights of his life. He lasted barely ten minutes more before grabbing her hand and sweeping her from the room. He saw the looks of consternation on the guests' faces as they left but he didn't give a damn about what anyone thought. He wasn't waiting a second longer before demanding the truth from Elodie.

CHAPTER THIRTEEN

ELODIE SAT RIGID in the corner of the car, repelled by her own cowardice. Ramon was terrifyingly silent for the entire journey but she knew there was no escaping the coming reckoning. It was her own fault for lying for so long. Now he knew things she'd hoped she'd never have to admit to anyone *ever*.

As soon as they got home he went to the kitchen and poured a large glass of water.

'You want one?' he asked huskily.

'No thanks.' Her throat was too tight to swallow.

He leaned back against the counter, gripping the glass with white knuckles. 'I'm sorry my family tried to humiliate you. It was cruel. I'll talk to them. They went too far.'

There wasn't just anger in his eyes but worry. She gripped her hands together as shame swamped her.

'Callum shouldn't have been there. Shouldn't have said any of that.' Ramon coughed. 'Are you okay?'

'I'm fine.'

He drained the glass and set it down. 'Is what he said true?'

That Ramon was the 'husband of her dreams'?

'That you have fertility problems,' he whispered.

Right now she was more afraid of telling the truth than she'd ever been of lying, but she had to reassure Ramon. He was wide-eyed and ashen. Too late she remembered that his mother hadn't told him about her cancer symptoms.

'No.' Her mouth gummed. 'Not true.'

'You're not unwell?' he pushed. 'You're really okay.'

'Yes. Healthy,' she mumbled. 'Truly, I'm fine.'

He jerkily shoved his hands in his pockets. 'But you told Callum you—'

'I lied.'

He expelled a huge breath. *'Why?'*

Elodie stared hard at her tightly laced fingers and hated herself. 'Because I didn't want to sleep with him. I told him I had a lot of pain with an irregular, difficult cycle. That was an excuse he could accept.'

Ramon was silent for so long that she had to look up, needing to see how angry he was.

'You should have been able to just say no,' he breathed.

'I was his *wife*.'

'Elodie—'

'I was young, okay? I didn't know how to assert myself then. Callum said he loved me, he promised that he'd help me handle Dad. He had me on some pedestal, said he would be patient and that I'd feel more for him given enough time, and I got swept up in believing him because I *wanted* to. I thought he was my knight, you know? A guy who could cope with my father while also being someone he approved of. I was a childish *fool*.' She flushed. 'And Callum only loved the *idea* of me, not the reality of me because I just disappointed him.'

Ramon muttered something unintelligible but Elodie shook her head—he'd asked and she wouldn't stop now. She'd tell him.

'We didn't sleep together until after the wedding,' she said angrily. 'It wasn't great, and I soon made those excuses because I didn't want to tell him that I didn't...'

'You didn't want to hurt his pride so you lied about your *health*?' Ramon looked shell-shocked.

'I thought it was just how I was,' she mumbled.

'That you didn't enjoy sex?'

Ramon's incredulous expression burned her to cinders.

'I know I'm an awful person,' she said. 'I know it was my fault. I know it was awful to lie.'

'You never should have had to.' Ramon's mouth pinched. 'And was it really a lie? Pain isn't always physical…it can be emotional too.'

Elodie winced. 'I think he genuinely thought we could make it work. He wasn't violent. He just wanted me to be something I wasn't. I could never please him, but he tried—'

'I cannot believe you think you have to defend him.' He breathed in sharply. 'You did what you needed to do to survive. Anyone would.'

She twisted her hands. Did he not think she was terrible for lying?

'So when you met someone you did feel turned on by,' Ramon asked, 'you couldn't resist?'

She froze on the edge of the precipice she'd dreaded. As determined as she'd been earlier, *this* truth made her very vulnerable. She was terrified of his reaction. That it would lead to her *rejection*.

'Elodie?' Ramon's brain creaked, struggling to process the weight of what she'd just told him. Why hadn't he asked? Why had he avoided even thinking about this? Of course her first marriage hadn't been great, otherwise she'd have stayed with the guy. Of course she'd run out on him when she'd met someone she'd actually *wanted*.

'That *is* what happened, isn't it?' he prompted.

She said nothing. She wasn't just reluctant to reply, she was basically paralysed.

He moved towards her, urgency driving him as an outrageous suspicion hit. An impossibility. But now he remembered that time in her escape room when she'd breathlessly questioned what he was doing when he'd dropped to his knees. He'd thought she was acting it up, but maybe she'd really not known. Maybe she'd really not had a man do that before.

Not possible. Just not possible.

'You fell for another man, realised what you'd been missing out on, left Callum for him—no?' Ramon pressed, really wanting that to be right.

She stared at her locked hands again.

'*When* did you meet the other man?' he growled.

Her head turned from him. 'Callum could accept that we weren't intimate in private, but he insisted I show him affection in public. He insisted on more and more—like how I dressed and what I said and stuff. Eventually I told him I wanted out. He resisted that idea. I thought my only choice was to run.' She cleared her throat. 'They tried to make me come home. Dad was furious. Callum went kind of crazy. I got desperate. I figured he'd stop coming after me if I was a complete...' She spread her hands, then knotted her fingers together again. 'If I was with other guys it would put him off.'

Ramon stared at her fixedly. So she'd become a party girl to push away her possessive husband. All those photos of her dancing with all those guys had been a performance. And she still hadn't actually answered him properly. Had there *ever* been a guy she'd actually *wanted*?

'How many men have you slept with?' he asked bluntly.

She went rigid. 'That's irrelevant.'

'I disagree.' It wasn't the number that concerned him, rather her ability to answer. Honestly. 'What's your body count?'

'Define body count.' She glared at him angrily. 'Because right now I'm very close to murdering you.'

The most preposterous notion had taken hold of Ramon only he was suddenly certain it wasn't that far-fetched at all. 'I'm not talking a few kisses on a nightclub floor. I want to know exactly how many men you've taken to bed.'

'Well, you can want all you like, I'm not telling.'

Right. He suddenly felt murderous himself. 'Would it really kill you to be completely honest with me? Just this once?'

'Why does it matter so much?' She whitened. 'Will you even believe me if I even tell you? If I admit to the sanctimonious, perfect Ramon Fernandez himself that I've only slept with my ex-husband and the current one?' She stepped forward. 'That's right,' she spat. '*Two*. You and him.' She dragged in a broken breath and pushed back on him in true Elodie style. 'How many women have you slept with?'

This wasn't about him. He'd never hidden the truth so deliberately. 'So your supposed infidelity, the *reason* for your divorce—?'

'You don't have to go all the way to be unfaithful,' she snapped. 'I *was* unfaithful.'

No. She'd enacted an escape plan. Because her first husband had resisted her leaving and her father had pressured her into returning, she'd acted out. But it had been an act. She hadn't cheated at all.

He gaped at her—so incredibly hurt and he didn't know why. She really *was* into role-play. He just had it all back to front.

'You engineered everything so they'd think poorly of you. So others would judge you. All your wild partying ways and supposed promiscuity, all those photos—a new partner every night, dancing with so *many* different men.' Bitterness filled him. This made sense now. This made total sense. 'I can't believe I didn't realise sooner.'

'How could you have?'

'You *blush*, Elodie. The first time I took you to bed you barely knew what you were doing. No wonder you didn't—' He broke off, registering the humiliation welling in her eyes.

But then she blinked and lifted her chin. 'Didn't…?'

Of course she would fight on.

Ramon didn't finish the thought aloud. He was too bitter. Too bloody *broken*.

Everything he'd believed was in ruins. He'd thought they were alike in what they wanted, in their ability to see this stupid marriage through, that they were mutually experienced enough to handle this affair. But he'd just begun to think that maybe there was *more* between them. Hell, he'd actually tried to understand her past infidelity. But *none* of it was as she'd portrayed. She hadn't even been unfaithful. She hadn't been anything like what she'd said she was.

And maybe all he really was to her was the first guy she'd actually got off with. He sure as hell couldn't be anything more when she'd shared so little of her real self with him. Indeed, she'd only told him the truth tonight because Callum's outburst had caught her out.

It was like when he'd caught his father with that assistant. When Cristina had revealed her affair with his father and the truth about Jose Ramon. When he'd bullied his mother's doctor into breaking his patient confidentiality clause and admitting to him that she had end-stage cancer.

Once more the world he'd thought he'd known was in ruins and it *shredded* him. He couldn't stand that Elodie had held back on him this whole time. She hadn't *chosen* to tell him the truth. Hadn't *trusted* him. Hadn't *cared* enough to open up.

But *he* had. He'd really started to think differently about his future with her. But who knows how long she would've gone on letting him think things that weren't true?

The realisation pressed on his chest. An anchor, drowning him.

'Why are you so bothered about a stupid number?' Her breathing shortened. 'It shouldn't matter. I thought that you were happy to take me as I am.'

'But you're *not* as you made yourself out to be.' How could he believe a word she said now? When she'd held back from him even in the one place where he'd thought they were completely intimate.

'You said yourself my past is my past.' Her voice rose. 'What does it matter if it isn't as colourful as everyone else thinks. It's not their business and nor is it yours and—'

'I don't *care* who you have or haven't slept with!' he roared. '*That* is not the issue!'

'Then what *is*?' Elodie cried.

This was going so much worse than she'd feared. But of course Ramon didn't care how many men she'd slept with. It was irrelevant. He wasn't jealous or possessive because he didn't really care about *her*. He'd never considered an actual future with her and never would.

'It's the *lie* that matters,' he said shortly.

But he'd just accepted the fact that she'd lied to Callum. So when was one lie okay and another not? And she hadn't so much lied as much as not spoken up. 'Your pride has taken a hit because you didn't know every last little thing about me?'

He stared at her. He looked dreadful—not just angry, but deeply bitter. 'Honesty matters to me, Elodie.'

'Really?' Her emotions slipped and she called him out. 'You're the one who entered a fake marriage purely to keep control of some property you don't even want.'

'The honesty required was between *us*.'

But honesty took trust. Which took time. 'You didn't even tell me about that island at the beginning. Nor would I have expected you to. And you shouldn't have expected me to tell you everything either. Relationships don't work that way,' she said.

'Do we actually have a relationship?'

She hesitated, suddenly terrified about how to answer that. 'We have a *partnership*. We are in the midst of an affair. We're physically intimate…' She didn't know how else to define it. 'Trust needs to be *earned*, right? I don't trust easily. You don't trust at *all*—'

'How can you say that? I told you things I've never told *anyone*. And you let me. You listened. Empathised even. You let me think…' He trailed off.

She froze, hating his anger. She had to try to explain why she'd been quiet—why she'd been so *afraid*. 'I needed you to think I could handle it. That I knew what I was getting into. If you knew what had really happened, you would have had such power over me. I couldn't let anyone have that—'

'Because you didn't trust me.'

'I didn't *know* you then.'

'And nothing has happened in the last few weeks to make you change your opinion—maybe believe that maybe you could begin to trust me?'

She breathed, unable to answer. The fact was even though she'd wanted to, she'd been too scared. She'd worried he mightn't react well. She'd been right to worry. Because he wasn't. He was prickly and doubtful and he wasn't going to believe her if she said any of what she truly thought and wanted now.

'And you still don't,' he said softly. 'You're still playing your part. Bulletproof, brave Elodie. So self-sacrificing.'

She wasn't. She was selfish. She'd wanted Ramon. She'd wanted this affair with him. She still did. In fact, she wanted *more*. But he was furious and pushing her away so quickly, so easily—and that told her everything.

'I'm used to betrayal, Elodie. And I knew you played games. But I thought that at least in *bed* you were honest with me.'

She *had* been honest with him there—she hadn't held *anything* back. It had been impossible to. Couldn't he feel that? Defensive, she pushed back hard because this was just hurt pride for him. 'Does it make you feel guilty to know I wasn't as sexually experienced as you thought? Because don't. It was good, Ramon.'

'You don't need to pacify me with half-truths Elodie. I'm not him. You don't need to protect *my* feelings.'

Because he didn't really care? Right. 'You think I was lying about that just then?'

'It's what you do.' He nodded.

He didn't believe her. Wouldn't ever.

'You pretend to be something you're not and fool everyone around you in some sort of warped protection mode so you can escape any possible threat,' he said.

'While you're perfect?' she flung back at him, so hurt she sought to wound with her words. 'A workaholic who can't stand emotional intimacy. Who basically uses bodyguards and assistants as human shields so no one can possibly get close. You've virtually shut yourself in a panic room because you're afraid of getting close to people and you don't even *want* to escape.'

He turned white. 'At last I know what you really think of me.'

Because of course he believed *that*—the worst thing she could think to throw at him in the fury of her hurt. 'No, you have no idea. *None.*'

Because it was only coming to her now—belatedly and disastrously. Because facing his anger like this was the last thing she ever wanted. Because she couldn't stand to feel as if she were less than in his eyes. To have him lose faith in her. But the three feet between them was an insurmountable gulf. And this had become so much more than a game to her. This had become *everything*. At the worst possible moment she realised how deeply she'd fallen in love with him. Panicked—lost in a maze of her own making—*she* was the one locked in a room from which there was no escape. Not without pain. Not without leaving her heart behind.

Ramon had prised her open so effortlessly, yet how could she tell him that now? He wasn't going to believe her. And more than that, he didn't *want* it.

The last month had meant little to him. He'd probably only taken her with him on that trip because he'd not trusted her to stay home alone, not because he'd really wanted her there with him. She'd been such a fool. It had always and only been a hot affair for him—nothing more.

'Yet you've nothing else to add?' he asked heavily. 'Okay, Elodie. You win.'

She stared. Unmoving. Uncomprehending.

'You've secured Ashleigh's freedom but at heart you've always wanted your own. You have it. Immediately.'

'Meaning?'

'Go home. It's over.'

CHAPTER FOURTEEN

THERE WERE TIMES in life when a girl really needed her friends and Elodie was fortunate enough to have really good friends. She'd escaped the house the second after Ramon had stormed out of the kitchen. She'd hailed a cab and gone to Phoebe's. Phoebe had bitten back the billion questions Elodie knew she wanted to ask. She'd just led Elodie to Bethan's empty room and tucked her into bed.

The next morning she'd messaged Piotr who'd taken pity on her. Or maybe he was just following orders because he'd packed her and Ashleigh's things and dropped them at the escape room at a time when Elodie could avoid him. She'd moved back to her own tiny apartment in North London and then Ashleigh had returned from her trip with Bethan. She'd sat next to her on the sofa and they'd binge-watched a serial killer series. They were at the penultimate episode when to their mutual astonishment their *mother* had shown up. She'd been wary and tearful and apologetic and told them that she didn't want to lose both daughters, that she'd asked their father to sell the hotel, that she was sorry for never standing up for them...

Ashleigh had been amazed. Elodie had been too shell-shocked to even take it in. But Ashleigh had opted to go stay with her mother at a hotel in the city for a while. The moment they left Phoebe and Bethan had arrived with three tubs of Elodie's favourite brand of ice cream.

'I never even got to ask how Italy was,' Elodie apologised to Phoebe. 'Was it amazing?'

'It was.' Phoebe smiled.

'Yeah?' Elodie nudged her with a grin. Phoebe did still have a post-holiday radiance about her even though it was a few weeks now since she'd got back. 'And the new job's going well?'

'It's full-on.' Phoebe nodded. 'There's a rumour that it's a takeover target.'

'Oh, no—'

'I'll be *fine*.' Phoebe chuckled. 'Don't worry about me, we're here for *you*.'

'Exactly.' Bethan grabbed Elodie's hand. 'Are you okay?'

'I'm really sad,' she admitted huskily. 'I liked him.'

'Have you told *him* that?' Bethan asked gently.

Elodie winced.

'If I could go back in time that's the one thing I'd do differently.' Bethan opened the next tub of ice cream. 'I'd tell him.'

Yeah, Bethan had been utterly in love with the man she'd married and was taking a long time to get over her heartbreak in discovering that he hadn't felt the same.

'I don't think Ramon wants to hear it,' Elodie muttered.

'Then write it,' Phoebe suggested. 'At least then you'll have been honest. That's for yourself as much as for him. How he responds is over to him.'

Two days later an envelope arrived at the escape room with the Fernandez crest in the corner. Elodie ripped it open, her heart pounding, Phoebe's idea of writing a letter echoing in her head.

But it wasn't a letter from Ramon. Only legal documents. The paperwork had been transferred and the escape room business was now in her name. There was no accompanying note. It was nothing to him, apparently. To spend money on a business, on a building, on Ashleigh's independence. To let Elodie leave without so much as an actual goodbye.

She stared at the contracts. She could sell both the business and the building and pay him back immediately, but she wanted to prove herself first—that she could make it even more popular, that she was good at this job. She would regard this as a business loan and Ramon was the investor. She drew up a payment plan, factored in interest. Doubtless he wouldn't care less whether she did or didn't but *she* cared, and sure, it might take her years to pay him back completely, but she was damn well going to. She was already at work on a new themed room and Bethan was busy making stunning props. Maybe she'd eventually expand—she might never make multinational Fernandez-type status—but she could do national. Pushing towards that would keep her busy.

She *needed* to be busy. She needed to have no time to think at *all*. Which was exactly what he did, right?

He hid from everything that hurt by focusing on work. And now he had everything he wanted. Control of all the family assets that mattered to him. Complete emotional independence.

But he did still *feel*. In fact he was as volatile as she—passionate about things that mattered to him. He'd endured the bitterness of his father's infidelity, his mother's withdrawal, his wider family's drama. And he'd blown up the minute he'd found out that she'd kept some truth from him. Because maybe he'd been *hurt* that she had.

That thought gave her a spark of hope—the impetus to at least *try*. She took a fresh sheet of plain paper. Maybe it wouldn't matter what she said or did henceforth. Maybe he would never believe her—never have faith or trust in her. But she needed to tell him how she truly felt.

For years she'd swallowed everything back, obeying her father, not causing problems for her mother. When she'd finally tried to speak up—to end it with Callum—neither he nor her father had listened. She'd stopped speaking up about anything intimate, deciding never to let anyone in like that again.

But Ramon wasn't anyone. He deserved more. He'd given her so much. The courage to do this would be the most important thing yet.

Ramon avoided coming home for more than a week. Elodie had escaped the second she had the chance. He'd gone to cool off and by the time he got back she'd gone.

He'd told her to, hadn't he. And so she had. Destroyed him.

The next day Piotr had informed him that he'd taken her gear to her. Ramon had at least known she was safe. That afternoon he'd boarded a plane to find Cristina and Jose Ramon. Dealing with that lifetime's worth of drama was easier than dealing with the absence of Elodie.

It hadn't been easy—in fact it had been horrible. Ramon had strived to remain businesslike, stressing that they needed to find a civil way forward. He'd not mentioned Elodie, yet Jose Ramon had seemed subdued and for once willing to engage. Maybe Ramon's early departure from the foundation gala had impacted more than he'd realised. Ramon had bypassed Cristina and asked Jose Ramon directly what he really wanted. He'd offered to support him in a management apprenticeship role at one of the hotels if he was interested. Surprisingly, Jose Ramon had agreed. Even more surprisingly, Ramon's offer had seemed enough to placate Cristina. They'd agreed to amend the terms of the trust for the island, which meant no protracted legal battles in its future. Maybe things were never going to be great there, but not great was a lot better than fully vicious.

Trouble was, none of this helped Ramon sleep any better. None of it made him able to fully focus on his work again.

When he got back to London an hour before dawn days later the house was simply hollow. He spotted the small rectangular case in his dressing room when he went to get changed. The diamond collar gleamed on the velvet lining.

Her ruby ring and wedding band were nestled in the centre of it. He touched the stone and regretted it immediately. It was cold when it wasn't on her skin. Of course she'd not taken them to sell for the money. She didn't want them—didn't want *him*. He slammed the lid down, wilfully ignoring the fact that he was still wearing the ring she'd struggled to put on him.

He'd get Piotr to get rid of the lot later. Piotr who'd been emanating waves of disapproval like a silent doom machine ever since that horrible night. He stalked to the kitchen to grab some water. Closed his eyes and sagged back against the counter as that horrible conversation replayed in his head.

He'd been *brutal*. He hadn't stopped to think. He'd just reacted. He couldn't control himself around her. Never had been able to. And nor could she. That chemistry *hadn't* been pretence.

For all his supposed intelligence, he'd not seen the truth of her even when the clues were there. In hindsight it was so *obvious*. But Elodie's silence still burned like betrayal. Hadn't she started to trust him? Surely he wasn't just anyone? But maybe it wasn't only that she didn't trust *him*. Maybe she didn't trust her own judgement—or even her own worth. Her own father hadn't valued her. Her ex hadn't stood up for her—hadn't paid attention to her desires. Of course she was cautious of controlling men and she saw Ramon as the ultimate in controlling.

Maybe it hadn't been fair of him to be so impatient with her. Maybe his anger hadn't been rational but reactive. *Emotional*.

Only a month ago he'd have scoffed at the idea that he'd ever be emotional. Or ever need emotional *support*. He was fine. Strong. Calm. Capable.

He so wasn't.

Now he saw that instead of being like his father, he'd withdrawn like his mother—from family, from intimacy, from basically everything but his work. Until Elodie had stormed his house. She'd challenged him. Teased him. Kissed him. Listened to him. She'd absolutely got to him. And he'd pulled her close. Taken her with him. Given her not things, but time. *Himself.* Something he'd never given anyone. He couldn't admit it before but she'd put him at such risk.

He'd wanted to be close to her. That's why it had hurt so much when he'd found out all she'd held back. But she *had* given him a lot already—companionship, compassion, *fun*. He'd revelled in her blossoming physical pleasure, enjoyed her boundless creativity and he ached for her to succeed. God, he wanted to be alongside watching while she did.

And why on earth had he *ever* worried he'd be an unfaithful jerk like his father? Elodie kept him not just wholly occupied, but absolutely captivated. There was nothing and no one else he wanted or would ever want. He wanted to be with her *now*, the only one with her henceforth. Her last, in other words. He wanted her to be his forever. He'd wanted her to love him. Because he loved her. But he hadn't said any of that. Instead, he'd been a coward the first chance he could.

He'd sent her away.

Like an idiot.

But what horrified him most was the realisation he was in danger of being as *unforgiving* as his mother had been with him. He knew how much that *hurt*, how much it had destroyed for them both. He never wanted to do that to Elodie. Or to himself. He was suddenly so very sorry.

Ramon straightened. He did not stand about doing nothing. Ever. He formulated a plan and enacted it immediately. He was so preoccupied that he didn't notice the piece of paper wedged beneath the rug at the front door as he strode out of the house.

Nothing was going to stop him now.

CHAPTER FIFTEEN

'THAT PACKAGE HAS ARRIVED.' Bethan glanced up as Elodie walked in. 'I've put it in the room we've stripped out.'

'Really?' Elodie frowned. 'It's that big?'

'Uh…yeah.' Bethan followed her, oddly fidgety for someone generally serene.

Elodie walked into the room they'd prepped for a new escape scenario. It was completely empty save for one thing.

'Welcome to my escape room.' He spread his hands.

She heard the door close behind her but she was too busy staring at him to have the nous to move. Ramon didn't have the decency to look even slightly unhappy or unkempt; in fact she'd never seen him look as handsome. He was clean-shaven, his hair neatly trimmed, and his suit showcased his tall, muscular frame to bone-melting perfection. She was suddenly, horribly conscious that this morning she'd decided to rot in bed for the day and it was only because Bethan had phoned to tell her about a delivery that she'd bothered to come in. She'd thrown on a ratty pair of jeans, too depressed to make much effort when she planned to be in the back office and not see anyone all day.

'Bethan!' She called for her friend to come back and unlock the door.

But she knew Bethan was still a romantic, despite being devastated by that Greek jerk she'd married, and doubtless thought she was *helping*.

'It's not locked,' Ramon said. 'You can walk out of here any time you like. But I hope you won't. Yet.'

'It's hardly an escape room then, is it,' she said stiffly, glancing anywhere but at him. 'There's at least a narrative. Some clues. A puzzle to solve. There's literally nothing in here.'

'There's me. And you.'

No puzzle. Only pain.

'Apparently this is my building now, and I'd like you to leave.'

'Is this another instance where the opposite is true?' he challenged softly. 'The opposite was true of a lot of what you let me believe.'

She closed her eyes. It was too late for this. 'Ramon... I don't want to hurt any more.'

It hurt to look at him. It hurt to hear him. It hurt to hold everything in.

'You know we need to talk.' He moved a step nearer.

'You could have just phoned.'

'Would you have answered?' His mouth twisted. 'I couldn't take the risk. And hopefully you'll find it harder to refuse me in person.'

'You arrogant—'

'I find it impossible to think when I'm with you. Which gives you the upper hand completely, by the way. And unfortunately I needed time to think and realise the blindingly obvious. So can you please be patient—'

'Patient? I wrote to you over a *week* ago and there's been nothing.' She'd been crying herself to sleep every night and she was sick of it.

'Wrote me what?' He frowned. 'I never got a letter. Was it a letter? When? Where did you send it to?'

Her legs emptied of strength. 'I put it through your door.'

'I didn't get it. I swear.' He cocked his head and stared hard at her as if trying to read her mind. 'What did it say?'

'That I'm regarding your purchase of the business as a loan. I'm going to pay you back.' She locked her knees to stop herself from shaking.

'Oh.' His face fell.

'I don't want your help. Or your charity or anything. It might take me decades but I'm paying you back.'

'You don't want anything from me at all.' He turned ashen.

'I want *plenty*. Just not that,' she mumbled. 'There was more in the letter.'

More than she wanted to have to *say*. But she was going to. Just as soon as she got her thundering heart under control so she could hear herself think.

'You know when you appeared at my home that afternoon, all fierce outrage, I seized whatever excuse I could to get close to you,' he said. 'And I ran with it—far further than I intended, further than maybe I should have. But I don't re-gret it. I can't. I only regret letting you go. I *never* should have let you go.'

She still couldn't hear herself think. Because she couldn't think. She could only stare at him.

'It never occurred to me that you wouldn't stand up to anyone else the way you stand up to me. You've never been afraid to challenge me, Elodie. It's always been like that with us and I never want you to change. But when it came to it the other night, you backed off.'

Because she hadn't always been bold. She hadn't chal-lenged any man the way she'd challenged Ramon. She'd not got close enough to any—all that was a facade. She'd built confidence in fronting the escape room and she'd taken that persona to confront him that day in London. But then *he'd* made her spark even more. There'd been something about only him that night. Animal magnetism had made her *reck-less* and she'd reaped the rewards of their chemistry.

She ached for more of that now. But there was so much more to *them* now.

'It took a lot to get out of your father's control,' Ramon said huskily. 'Then Callum's control. It took a lot for you to build an independent life. A good life. You were worried I'd be controlling too. Control is a thing for us both.' He shook his head at her sadly. 'But the only person I'll ever try to control is myself. Never you. But I do want to be with you. Watch you—working, dancing, laughing, doing the things you love—going all in with full dramatic flair.'

'I do want to be with you.'

That was the bit she heard. The bit she needed for that final notch of belief.

'From the second I first saw you, you pushed all my buttons. I wanted to be a worthy adversary,' she admitted softly. 'I thought if I could hold my own against you, I could do anything. Handle anyone. That would mean that I was finally *there*.' She blinked rapidly to stop the tears that were rising. 'You were the most powerful man I'd ever met and I wanted to get the better of you but the thing is, I'm better *because* of you. When you're alongside me, I'm brave. I can even jump off a cliff. You made me believe I could do anything.'

'Except trust me with your truth.' He looked so sad.

'I should have told you everything sooner, but I didn't think you really wanted to know.'

'Part of me didn't.' He spread his hands. 'I wanted to pretend this was something so much smaller than what it is. I didn't want to face the reality of how deeply I'd fallen—how much you meant to me.'

'You deny yourself too much,' she whispered. 'The sweet things. The fun.'

'I certainly tried to deny the truth of how I felt about you.' He took another step towards her. 'You're a sweetheart, Elodie, and I know the choices you made always come from good intentions, but I hadn't shown you—or told you—that I'm here for you. That I'm here for when *you're* ready to talk to me. I know you weren't ready the other night and I reacted badly. I'm so deeply sorry about that.'

She bit her lip. 'You wouldn't have married me if you'd known from the start. I did what I thought I had to do.'

'To protect Ashleigh,' he said.

'Not only that. But to get what *I* wanted,' she whispered. 'I wanted an affair with you and that was the only way you'd let it happen. You wouldn't have even suggested it if you'd known. You'd have thought I wasn't up to it.'

'I don't think I could have resisted, actually. I can't resist you at all.' He reached out and brushed back a strand of her hair. 'You teased me. You were vexing. And you were right. I've been locked away and you shocked a huge part of me back to life. You're loyal, Elodie. Loyal and loving but you should also have fun. So should I.' He smiled at her. '*You're* my sweet thing. You're my fun. You're everything I want—'

'Don't—'

'Be honest with you?' He crowded in and cradled her face in his hands. 'Be really, truly honest with you? Don't you want to believe me?' he whispered. 'I'd get on my knees if I thought that's what you wanted. But I think you want something else. So I'll be at your side, I'll have your six, and I'll go toe to toe when you want me to challenge you head-on.'

It was what she wanted. *Everything* she wanted from him.

'I'm *here* for you, *cariño*.' He leaned close, touching the tip of her nose with his. 'Right here. Because I love you.'

'You're the sun in my universe, Ramon, but I got burned.'

'Then let me kiss it better.' He folded her into his arms and pressed her body to the length of his. 'I've missed you. I need you. I want you back.'

She closed her eyes and let him take her weight completely. His arms tightened even more and it was *heaven*.

'You *thrill* me,' she muttered against his chest. 'I just want you more and more. I fell in lust with you instantly even though you were arrogant and annoying, I just wanted you on a cellular level because you challenged me in every way.

You're different to anyone I'd ever met and I'm every bit as greedy as you once thought me,' she said. 'But not for money. Not even lust. Well, not just lust. It's *you*. I couldn't stop myself from going for every moment I could get with you. From getting as close to you as possible. And it was so good I was scared of losing it. So I stayed silent. I'm sorry.' She pushed so she could look up into his eyes even though tears half blinded her. 'I'm really sorry.'

He shook his head and kissed her as he answered. 'You've nothing to be sorry for.'

'Please take me home,' she whispered.

Which is how, only a few minutes after nine in the morning, Elodie abandoned her work for the day. Bethan smiled but said nothing. Piotr actually smiled too as he opened the car door for them, but he also said nothing.

Ramon too was silent as they were driven home, and if anything he looked more anxious than the moment she'd seen him waiting for her in that empty room. She felt his deep breathing and realised he was exercising restraint.

The moment they got inside he crushed her to him again and tremors wracked his strong body. 'I was scared you'd never be here with me again.'

He stepped back only to scoop her into his arms.

'Not the guest suite,' she teased, delighted when an amused smile cracked his strained expression.

'Never.' He set her down and stared at her in wonder. 'I've been a wreck without you.'

'You don't *look* a wreck.' She pressed her hand on his jaw, appreciating the close shave that displayed his angular features.

'I wanted to make an effort for you. But while I might be okay on the outside, I'm a mess in the middle.'

'Could've given me a heads-up so I could have dressed for you.' She gestured at her old jeans. 'I'm just a mess.'

'You're always beautiful.' That wicked smile creased the

corners of his eyes and he slipped the shirt over her head. 'However you are.'

'Yeah? I still think I should get out of these old jeans.'

He laughed. 'I've got a three-piece suit to get off. *Cufflinks.*' He shuddered. 'I don't know what I was thinking.'

'I'll help.'

But his clothes were too well made to be torn despite frantic attempts, stifled swearwords, laughter and groans. In the end they were still half dressed when the desperate drive to reconnect overtook them. They tumbled to the bed and the relief of holding him, of being held, overwhelmed her.

'I've missed you so much.' He kissed away her tears. 'I need you *cariño.* I love you. I want you now and always.'

She could feel his intensity. Knew he meant it. But he wasn't making another move.

'Then touch me,' she whispered as her heart filled. 'Because I feel *everything* with you and it's so good.'

'Yes.'

Eventually they wriggled out of those last items of clothing and cuddled close. It was going to be another delicious day in his bed. Elodie's very favourite kind of day.

'I know you're going to be busy with the escape rooms, but do you think you might travel with me sometimes? I know it's a lot, I'll try to reduce it,' Ramon muttered idly. 'I hate being apart from you.'

'Yes.' She snuggled closer. 'Same.'

'I'm bringing Jose Ramon onboard.'

She propped her chin on his chest to look at his face. 'You are?'

'He says that's what he really wants. Cristina has agreed. I think she might back off him a bit actually. He and I might be able to move forward.'

'That's good.' She smoothed his frown. 'You guys share

a father, but you're each your own person. Not carbon copies of him.'

'Yeah, I know I'm not like him now. Never will be.' He ran his hand down her arm. 'We're going to leave the island as a conservation project and for private family use only. *All* the family. I guess we'll use a booking system. Oh.' He suddenly slid out of the bed. 'Forgot something.' He tousled his hair as he padded away from the bed. '*Two* things.'

He returned in only a few minutes holding her envelope. She sat up as he ripped it open and skim-read her neatly typed promise to repay him for the business and the building.

'No.' He tossed that page over his shoulder with a dramatic flourish.

Elodie summoned courage as he paused over the handwritten page she'd included beneath the promissory note. 'You don't need to read that. I'm brave enough to say it to your face.'

'I want to read it. You wrote it for me.' He flashed the page towards her. 'You even drew a code.'

'Yeah, but I don't have to hide the truth in a pile of clues for you to decipher now.' She smiled tremulously. 'I want to be with you. I want to trust you. I love you.'

'I'm so glad.' He lifted his other hand and unfurled his fist.

Her ruby engagement ring glittered in his palm. Her eyes watered. 'It's not artificially grown, is it?'

'No.' He smiled tenderly. 'It's the real thing. *This* is the real thing.'

He'd also retrieved her wedding band, and as he slid them both back on her finger she saw he still wore his.

'I couldn't take it off,' he said quietly when she touched it. 'There's nothing fake about my feelings for you. Nothing fake about our marriage.'

'So we're not getting divorced?' she breathed.

'Never.' He nudged her shoulder. 'You're stuck with me.'

She pulled him down and pressed her mouth to his with a laughing sob. 'I should think so!'

CHAPTER SIXTEEN

Almost three years later

> *Don't open the third drawer of the second desk in the first room.*

RAMON EYED THE card poking out of their closed bedroom door with amusement. He recognised the handwriting. And he was totally going to open the third drawer of the second desk in the first room.

He'd been away two nights but as Elodie was in the middle of an escape room refit, she'd opted not to travel with him on this trip. He'd missed her and he was beyond glad to be back—even more so now he knew he was in for an evening of amusement with his deliciously creative wife.

He'd jettisoned some of his work so he had more time at home. Ashleigh was halfway through a degree up in Edinburgh. And amazingly his relationship with Jose Ramon had improved. His aunt was wary and that was unlikely to change, but it was at least better.

In the third drawer he found a cupcake with a birthday candle. On the base of which was a sticker: *Games Aplenty*.

The games room, obviously. They'd set one up not long after she'd moved back in permanently—part home office for her, playroom for them both. They pitted their wits against each other with board games, card games, codes, ciphers and the occasional use of handcuffs and blindfold. It was Ramon's second favourite room in the house. Their bedroom being the first, of course.

'I know you're here,' he called out. 'Probably watching me fumble around like a fool because you've set up hidden cameras.

Elodie had used some of her usual tricks to send him on a wild goose chase around his own home to find her. One clue meant the opposite: he was told to 'reflect'—in other words hold the clue to the mirror. The *second* time he went into the games room, she was reclined on the plush chaise longue that was also a new addition. She held a stopwatch—timing him. She must've been hidden behind the curtain the first time. *Minx.* But he didn't mind because she was wearing the pink silk wedding dress and the diamond collar and—if his eagle eyes didn't deceive him—nothing else. No underwear, no shoes. He paused, transfixed by the queen of hearts. He adored her—all this about her.

'Should I get on my knees?' he muttered, sinking to the floor beside her before she could answer.

Her eyebrow arched coyly. 'I love how fast you are.'

He hesitated, eyes narrowing. 'Maybe you're *not* a clue. Too obvious. You're a diversion. Dangerous.'

The look of chagrin mixed with delight on her face confirmed it. He stood up again and scouted the room for something else that he'd missed the first time. Something that was out of place. It wasn't hard to spot. A faux Fabergé-style egg was artfully placed on a low table. Bethan's work, no doubt—delicate and clever. He carefully clicked the lock and it opened. He stared at the wrapped date nestled on the silk cushioning inside. He pulled out the date and set the egg back on the shelf. He unwrapped the date and waggled it at her with a what he hoped was a bemused look.

'You need a clue?' She teased archly. 'Sure. I love you.'

Her voice was a touch breathless. His chest tightened; he would make her more so. Because he knew that while she meant it, she also played with him.

'Red herring,' he teased back.

She giggled and her whisper this time came with a self-conscious shrug. 'I couldn't think much beyond the literal…'

He paused. He was holding a date. Literally.

'So we're celebrating an actual *date*…' He swung back towards her. He slid his hands up her silken legs in a teasing gesture, aching to push the pretty dress out of the way so he could feast on the treasure he adored beneath. But he knew her outfit was another clue. 'It's not our wedding anniversary.' He kissed her knee and remembered the cupcake with its singular birthday candle. 'Not your birthday. Nor mine.'

She smiled. Her eyes were luminous.

'Yet this is a very *important* date…'

Elodie shivered as she watched him work through the silliest, most important clues she'd ever come up with. The man was far more than her match. She loved this—having him return to her. Travelling with him. Living a life so full of laughter and joy, she'd never have imagined it to be possible.

'You're here, another delicacy for me to enjoy.' He cocked his head. 'I think I *am* meant to unwrap you.'

'Well, duh…' She was sitting here in all her finery, basically begging him to ravish her.

His eyes glinted. 'A double cross. You weren't the diversion, you're the goal.'

He opted not to go from the hem, but slipped the slim straps from her. Lowering the silk so her breasts were exposed. She was so sensitive. Bursting with the secret she wanted him to work out. He cupped her breasts. She shimmied on the soft cushion, wanting her dress to slip further. He got the message. She arched her hips so he could slide the silk down to her ankles. That was when he sat back and studied her—now naked aside from the diamond collar.

'Temporary tattoo.' With his forefinger he slowly traced the Roman numerals she'd stuck on her skin. It tickled and her lower stomach quivered. 'Two numbers,' he said.

She held her breath now.

'Aside from the numbers themselves, I suspect their positioning is significant.' He breathed. 'You think these things through. Your belly.' He looked up, his gaze burning directly into hers. 'Day and month. This is just over seven months in the future.'

'Yes.'

'The egg was a clue on more than one level.' His hand cupped her belly.

'Yes.'

'You're having my baby.' His voice roughened with possessiveness.

Her 'yes' was smothered by his kiss.

Ramon could be fast. Decisive. Powerful. All of which was exactly what she needed him to be in this moment. He had her on the floor beside him, stirred to desperation in seconds. Because the embers always burned hot and it took the lightest of breaths to fan the flames high.

'You're not showing yet, but it won't be long.' He gasped as she battled to undo his damned trousers. 'Oh, Elodie, I'm so excited.'

'Me too.' She was caught between laughing and crying. 'I'm so glad I asked you to marry me—'

'If you consider it *asking*,' he said, and ground into her with a growl of satisfaction. 'More like you demanded. Best moment of my life. I love it when you demand that I do things with you.'

'I have some more demands right now.' She arched, happily pinned by his weight.

'Go on then.' He pressed deep and gazed down at her with the most adoring smile she'd ever seen.

She curled her arm around his neck and huskily gave the orders she needed him to fill. 'Love me hard. Love me always. Never let me go.'

'You mean you haven't got the message *yet*?' he breathed. 'There's no escaping how much I adore you. You're mine.' He punctuated the claim with a deep thrust. 'I'm yours.' His hands laced with hers. 'We're locked together forever, darling.'

'Yes.'

* * * * *

Were you swept off your feet by
Their Altar Arrangement*?*

Then you'll love the next two instalments in
the Convenient Wives Club trilogy, coming soon!

And don't miss these other stories
by Natalie Anderson!

The Boss's Stolen Bride
Impossible Heir for the King
Back to Claim His Crown
My One-Night Heir
Billion-Dollar Dating Game

Available now!

UNWANTED ROYAL WIFE

CLARE CONNELLY

MILLS & BOON

CHAPTER ONE

NOT ONCE IN the five months since marrying the heir to the throne of Cavalonia had Rosie come close to considering it a love match. Nor, however, had she realised quite how much she would hate her husband, perhaps for the chief reason that Rosie had never hated anyone before in her entire life. And yet here she was, married to a man she couldn't stand, walking a constant tightrope of faking affection as necessary for the public, and barely looking at him when they were alone—which was rarely ever. After all, if she hated His Royal Highness Sebastian al Morova with every fibre of her being, then the same could surely be said of his feelings for her.

'You wished to be informed when His Highness arrived?' Laurena, Rosie's most trusted aid and advisor spoke softly into the large and elaborately furnished office Rosie had claimed upon becoming the princess of this small yet wealthy and respected kingdom.

'He's here?' Her voice, usually poised and calm, took on a thicker quality.

'Yes, ma'am. He arrived ten minutes ago. On the bike.'

Rosie gritted her teeth. There were many things she'd attempted to explain to her husband since their engagement was formalised—after all, a large part of their marriage was based on her supposed ability to reform his ways and turn him into a suitable heir to the throne—but the damned motorbike was apparently non-negotiable. In fact, despite her efforts, most things in Sebastian's life had turned out to be. He had an infuriating habit of listening as Rosie calmly and thoroughly explained why things were done a certain way, his expression always blank, impossible for her to interpret or understand, then smirking. Just the smallest lift of one side of his mouth, barely a flicker, really, but enough to convey not only his disdain for her and her advice, but also their marriage.

She expelled a rough sigh, her nostrils flaring with a hint of frustration. If he would only listen to her, she knew she could help him be more successful with the people of the country, could help him be welcomed, regardless of his husky American drawl and years of estrangement from the king.

'He's on his way to me?'

'No, ma'am. He's going to see the king first.'

'Of course he is.' She squeezed the fingers of one hand into a fist. Rosie had planned to tell Sebastian about the king's episode herself. Though there was no love lost between them, informing Sebastian of his grandfather's health scare seemed to fall into the box of duties a wife might be expected to fulfil. The king would have wanted her to break it to Sebastian.

Not that theirs was a love match either.

Sebastian was tolerated by the king—allowed his unwelcome but necessary return to the country and palace after the unexpected death of the king's younger child.

While Fabrizio lived, the king had been confident the erstwhile royal would marry and settle down, one day producing the babies necessary to continue their line. Fabrizio, though, had been on a downward spiral for many years, and had wrapped his sports car around a tree in the early hours of the morning after partying all night. Though exiled from Cavalonia, an exception had been made for Sebastian and his mother, Maria—the king's only surviving child—to attend the funeral, and directly after, Sebastian had struck.

You need an heir: well, now you have one. All it will take for me to walk away from my life in the States and take up my place in Cavalonia is the assurance that my mother will be free to return to this country, that her exile will be permanently revoked.

The king could have accepted then and there. Sebastian held many cards, but the king had understood how badly he wanted to bring his mother home, and so he'd wielded a bargaining chip of his own, demanding that in order for Sebastian to be named Prince of Cavalonia, he would first need to marry a bride of the king's choosing. He was not going to risk history repeating itself—losing Fabrizio in such a manner had made the king cautious, and even more determined to exercise control. Control he exerted over everyone in his sphere, even Rosie.

But that wasn't entirely fair. This loveless marriage of convenience had appealed to her too, even as she'd decided that her husband was as unlikable as he was drop-dead gorgeous. The sheer fact she found his personality repellent had assured her the marriage would be a safe haven. No risk of caring for someone like him, no risk of letting his physical charms overwhelm her. No risk of being like one of her father's mistresses, stupid in lust, discarded when it suited him. No. There was no risk of attachment here: She had married for the kingdom, for the good she could do it, and she'd leave on her terms, when she'd achieved what she wanted, and was confident Sebastian was ready to rule in his own right.

Rosie drew her clear gaze back to Laurena's face. 'He knows I asked him to come?'

'Yes.'

She sighed again, softly this time. 'Then he's been informed by someone else.'

'The palace leaks,' Laurena confirmed.

'Even to him?'

'I suspect especially to him. He is, after all, next in line to rule. There are many who would seek to curry favour with him by proving their loyalty at every turn—particularly when the king's health is—' Laurena tapered off, wincing sympathetically. She didn't need to finish the sentence. Rosie had been with the king since the early hours of the morning, when his chief advisor had called to let her know he had required defibrillation to deal with another incidence of arrhythmia. He'd suffered from this for years, but since Fabrizio's death, he seemed to have lost the ability to fight. Or the will.

Rosie's blue eyes glittered like the stunning Adriatic Sea just visible in the distance, beyond the thriving capital city. Laurena was, as always, right. 'Fine,' Rosie tamped down on her impatience and employed a voice with as much calm authority as she could muster. 'Please have him come to me as soon as he's finished.'

'Of course.' Laurena dipped her head slightly in a deferential bow as she left the room.

It was an hour later when the heavy oak door to her office pushed inwards. She didn't turn around to confirm it was Sebastian; she didn't need to. There wasn't a single soul on earth besides her husband who would be presumptuous enough to invade her private space without waiting for an invitation. The shock of their first meeting, shortly after the

king had implored her to marry Sebastian, had also made
her senses hyperaware, and everything about the man had
been imprinted on her. She'd been struck by his size—so
tall with broad shoulders that had been filled out by his
years on the rowing squad of the elite Ivy League college
he'd attended on an academic scholarship; he looked like
the kind of man that could fell ancient trees with his bare
hands. And for all he'd been raised in America, there was
no mistaking his Cavalonian heritage: He had a deep cara-
mel tan, black eyes, thick lashes and bore the same cheekbones as the king—high and angular, as if carved by a
master craftsman. His obvious physical appeal had set her
on edge; she wasn't prepared to marry a man she was at
risk of being attracted to. But then he'd spoken, and he'd
been so arrogant and rude, so dismissive of the king, she'd
realised there was no risk here, and never would be.

Dislike frothed in her belly, the sensation familiar. She
didn't bother to conceal the enmity from her features as
she turned to face him, lifting one slim hand to check her
blond hair was still neatly tucked into a low bun. Her stomach clenched, the same dislike churning in a way that made
her wonder just how long she could keep this up.

They hadn't agreed on a time limit for their marriage.
For Rosie, she'd been handed, almost literally, the keys to
the kingdom. In exchange for marrying Sebastian, she had
been granted an enormous amount of latitude to spend time
and money working on her key charities and projects. It was
everything she'd wanted. But having to pretend to be in a relationship with this man was already starting to wear thin…

'Wife,' he said, in that horrible way he had, the way he
used the term just to irritate her.

She tried not to rise to the bait, but on this day, of all
days, her usual composure deserted her. 'I'm not in the

mood,' she responded, lifting her fingers to her temple and pressing there lightly. 'I take it you've seen the king?'

Sebastian's eyes were as dark as the night sky that now draped the kingdom. They gave nothing away when they locked to hers. 'Yes.'

'How is he?'

'As usual.'

'Oh, good!' Her enthusiasm and relief were genuine, and so consuming that she missed the way something like displeasure sparked in Sebastian's eyes. 'I'm so glad. He was very pale when I left him to nap this afternoon.'

Sebastian's jaw was naturally square, almost as if chiselled from the marble that formed the cliffs to the east of the country, dropping away down to the ocean in parts. But in this moment, it was particularly geometric, as though he was holding it that way on purpose.

'He was not pale. In fact, he was rather lucid. Full of interesting ideas. I presume he has already discussed them with you?' Something curled in Sebastian's voice, something that might have set off alarm bells if Rosie weren't so intent on hearing this good news about the king.

'I presume,' Sebastian continued, 'because you and he discuss practically everything. It's hard to imagine my grandfather coming up with a single idea that you hadn't planted as a seed in his mind.'

That accusation, though not new, got her attention. 'That's doing a disservice to him, me and our relationship.'

Sebastian stood very still, his whole body held as tight as his jaw. He wore a suit, jet black with a snow-white shirt and a stiff collar, and yet, he didn't look remotely formal. He never looked as though the fabric contained him; not as it was supposed to, anyhow. He was too big for that, his physique kept in shape by a love of the outdoors. She couldn't open a newspaper without seeing a paparazzi photograph of him sprinting through one of the nature reserves in the capital city, and those same newspapers delighted in commenting on his prowess as an athlete—they surely exaggerated how far he ran each morning.

'Is it?'

She'd been thinking about his body to the point she'd lost focus on their conversation. Her cheeks felt warm as she forced herself to concentrate.

'I must admit, I was surprised by his suggestion. You were the one who insisted children would not form part of our marriage.'

The world seemed to grind to a halt. She was conscious of the pulse in her veins, thready and weak, then far too fast and overpowering. She could hear blood washing through the fine capillaries of her ears, like a terrifying drum. 'Children,' she repeated, eyes wide, struggling to compute his statement.

'I clearly remember the paragraph you inserted into our agreement. In terms of the line of succession, no children, but you would divorce me in due course, allowing me to marry someone else and beget however many heirs I desired. Or words to that effect,' he drawled.

Rosie's skin paled. It had been a bone of some serious contention with the king. He hadn't wanted another scandal, another divorce, but Rosie had been adamant. She wasn't going to risk pregnancy, nor was she going to risk any kind of emotional attachment to her husband. This was a clean and simple arrangement, a practical marriage she had agreed to enter into purely because of how important it was to the king, and how it would benefit the kingdom. She had some boundaries though, and this was one of them. The king had reluctantly agreed, Sebastian hadn't seemed concerned, and Rosie had taken it as a victory. 'You're only twenty-nine—you have plenty of time.'

'But the king is sick.'

She shook her head, refusing to listen to that argument. 'He's getting better.'

'In fact, he is far worse than I realised. He has been for a long time.' Something tightened in Sebastian's features. 'And even then, he didn't think to bring my mother home. To bring me home.'

Rosie toyed with her wedding ring. She felt her husband's anger, and she could even understand it. What she didn't appreciate was that anger being channelled at her. As if she would call the king's wayward, exiled daughter and grandson to inform them of his declining health without the express consent of the king!

'He wants us to have a child.' Sebastian tamed whatever emotions were running riot inside of him with apparent ease, offering Rosie a look that was rapier sharp. 'And soon.'

She gasped as panic surged in her body. 'It's…it's not possible.'

Curiosity sparked in Sebastian's gaze, and then something else, something that surprised her for how human it was: sympathy. His voice even took a gentler tone as he enquired, 'You can't conceive?'

Rosie hadn't expected him to possess anything like a 'gentle' tone. She blinked, clearing away the strange feeling his apparent kindness had invoked and tried to concentrate. 'I don't mean that. I presume I can.' That was true. There was no reason to believe what had happened to Juliet Marrone would happen to Rosie, but somehow, Rosie had just always *known* that they were alike in this way. Her mother's stroke, so soon after giving birth, had rendered her in a vegetative state that had persisted for Rosie's entire life. She bit down on her lip. 'I just—don't want to. Especially not with you.'

'Your husband?'

She rolled her eyes. 'You know what I mean. This isn't a real marriage—we're not a real couple.'

'How true.'

'How could we possibly have a baby together? We hate one another.'

'I don't hate you, Rosalind.'

Her eyes widened. 'No need to lie to protect my feelings,' she said with a firm shake of her head. 'We both know what this marriage is.'

'I hate that you agreed to this,' he contradicted, gesturing around the room. 'I hate that you do whatever the king asks. And I hate that he chose you for me.'

She flinched a little.

'I am curious as to your feelings, however. Why should you hate me?'

Her stomach churned uncomfortably. It was a question she'd never asked herself and certainly hadn't expected him to ask. She settled on the first answer she could think of that made sense, and convinced herself that it was right. 'Because you openly despise the king, a man I love.'

Sebastian's lips formed a tight line. 'And unless that changes, you will always hate me?'

'Of course,' she spat. 'So, you see, even if I wanted children—and I really don't—I know how important it would be to give them a happy home. A loving home. That's not what we are, and you've just said we never will be!' she added triumphantly.

'Strangely,' he drawled, 'this might be the first time we're in agreement.'

Relief flooded her as she exhaled. 'Then we'll tell him "no".'

Silence rolled around the room. Her nerves stretched taut.

Sebastian drew a hand through his thick, dark hair. 'Unfortunately, I am also in agreement with the king. The country needs an heir. If he were to die—and he might at any point—I am not considered to be a trusted pair of hands.'

Her mouth felt unnaturally dry. 'You will be.'

'In time, yes. But for now, I'm an outsider, courtesy of my grandfather exiling my mother and me twenty-five years ago.'

'You never miss a chance to blame him for that, do you?'

'Who else is to blame?'

Rosie kept her mouth shut. This wasn't the time to go into the ancient history of their family drama.

'A child, born here, to someone like you, will calm the people and the parliament. It will legitimise my place.'

'Your place is legitimate. You were born to a princess of Cavalonia…'

'You and I both know that's not true. If it *were*,' he continued, moving a step closer, 'I would not have needed to marry you.'

She flinched a little at the insult inherent in his statement. But he was right. The king had insisted on their marriage because she was already a recognisable and beloved figure in the royal palace, having been accompanying the king for years as his aide, and because the king knew she would work hard to groom Sebastian for the shoes he was expected to fill.

'I have no interest in forcing you to do something you are set against. Deciding to have children is a deeply personal matter—the decision is yours.'

Her eyes widened at this unexpected show of reason. 'Then my answer is no.'

'I understand.'

She couldn't believe how reasonable he was being! 'Thank you.'

'Unfortunately,' he continued as though she hadn't spoken. 'It means I will have to start the ball rolling on our divorce. It's not ideal—and there'll be a PR disaster to clean up given the brevity of our marriage—but I'm sure the palace machinery will know how to handle it.'

'A divorce?'

Her back straightened. Her first thought was of the schools she was midway through developing in the least financially prosperous regions of the country—schools that would herald amazing opportunities for students who might otherwise be condemned to live out their lives in the same straitened circumstances as their parents. Who would complete them if she were not princess? Would the funding be withdrawn? The schools were her pet project; she'd fought for them, tooth and nail. Sending billions of dollars into low-tax areas hadn't been particularly popular with the parliament, but Rosie had been determined. How quickly would the plans be scuttled if she were not at the helm?

'We're *not* getting divorced.'

For the briefest moment, sympathy softened Sebastian's autocratic face. 'We are caught between a rock and a hard place. This has nothing to do with the king's wishes and everything to do with the sense of his suggestion. It's abundantly clear an heir is needed. But I have no interest in forcing you to be the mother of my child. So, what do we do, wife?'

'I just can't see why this has become such an urgent issue. We discussed all this at the time of formalising our engagement. The contracts—'

'I did not perceive the urgency of the king's health,' Sebastian interrupted, a spark of irritation in his voice. 'Had

I known how ongoing and serious his health matters were, I would have thought more about the question of children.'

'You think I should have told you?'

Something tightened in his face. 'I think *he* should have told me.'

It was yet another nail in the coffin, Rosie thought sadly. Their relationship had suffered so many—could it endure any more betrayals?

'Your king would like a great-grandchild. Losing my uncle as he did, and now facing his own mortality, naturally he fears his time is coming to an end. This is an issue he wants resolved as a matter of priority.'

She shuddered. The thought of the king's death was impossible for Rosie to contemplate. Even that morning, when she'd seen him so ashen and weak, she'd been *sure* he'd recover. He had to. He was King Renee, capable of everything—and at seventy-four, he was far too young to die.

'He'll be around for decades,' she said with false bravado.

Sebastian's eyes narrowed but he didn't argue the point. 'If you don't wish to have a baby—and of course that's your prerogative—I'll need to marry someone who does. You must see that.'

Rosie glanced sideways, towards the window. The city glittered. It was one of her favourite views, the sparkly buildings a mix of old—delightful, ancient homes and churches—combined with the very new and impressive— huge high-rises that seemed to reach right into the sky. Now it brought her no comfort, nor joy. Her heart was sinking, panic making her palms sweat. She thought of her mother, always asleep, unanimated, all because of Rosie's birth.

'I can't,' she moaned softly, turning back to face him.

'Then you have a decision to make.' His voice was emotionless, as though he didn't care either way. And that, she supposed, was true. 'Either we deliver my grandfather the heir he desperately wants to see—the heir our country needs—or we end this marriage.'

'You'd like that, wouldn't you?'

His eyes locked to hers and the air between them seemed to spark. She ignored it, just as she had the first moment she'd laid eyes on him and was hit with how handsome he was. She drew strength from the anger coursing through her and from the impotence of her position, from the betrayal that the king had discussed this with Sebastian before talking to Rosie. If Renee had come to her with this idea, she could have talked him around, gently guided him away from the necessity of considering a child just yet.

'This marriage was not my idea,' he pointed out. Then, after a beat, his eyes shuttered, revealing nothing. 'But we *are* married, Rosalind. You are my wife. We said our vows in front of thousands of people, not even half a year ago. It would be my preference to maintain the appearance of this farce. My grandfather's too.'

'You discussed the possibility of divorce?'

'If you were not amenable to falling pregnant, I suggested it might be necessary.'

'And what did he say?'

'He agreed.'

Rosie sucked in a sharp breath.

'You're surprised?' Sebastian said with a short, harsh laugh. 'Do you feel betrayed by the old man?'

She hated it when he called the king that; it reeked of disrespect.

'Need I remind you that he exiled his own *daughter*?'

Rosie played with the necklace she wore, a fine platinum chain with a string of diamonds in the centre.

'For that man, nothing matters more than his will being obeyed, and right now, he wants us to have a baby.'

Rosie's eyes squeezed shut. 'I can't believe it.'

She loved Renee. She had worked for him for five years, worked closely, on a great many projects. She thought it was mutual. She believed he loved her too.

'Relax, wife,' Sebastian ground out, and when Rosie opened her eyes, it was to see Sebastian had crossed the room and was standing right in front of her, so close she could see the handful of freckles that ran across the bridge of his nose. They were tiny, not noticeable unless you were up close like this, because his tan all but concealed them. They'd reminded Rosie, the first day she'd noticed them, of stars in the heavens, as if a constellation had been plucked down and scattered across his face. 'He told me the last thing he wants is for us to separate—the choice, he insisted, was to be yours, and I agree with him.'

She dropped her head forward, a thousand thoughts running through her mind, scattered and chaotic, totally unlike Rosie's usually clear and precise approach to problem solving. On the one hand, she'd worked for the king for a long time. She could go back to her old job, couldn't she? Perhaps continue with her pet projects in that capacity?

But no.

If Sebastian were to remarry—and he would do so swiftly, she had no doubt—then the new princess wouldn't want Rosie hanging around the palace, never mind that their marriage had been strictly business.

Whatever funds she needed for her work would surely be allocated to that princess, and not to her.

She shook her head at the impossible situation she found herself in, and chose, rather than answering, to go on the attack. To push Sebastian to face his own doubts, rather than needling her about her own.

'You don't want this, surely?'

'To have a baby with you?'

She nodded quickly.

'I want my birthright,' he responded, each word a staccato pulse, and for one of the first times since knowing him, she felt his regal bloodlines reverberate around the room. No, that wasn't quite right. Prior to returning home to Cavalonia and negotiating the terms for his exiled mother's readmission to the royal family, Sebastian had established himself as a king amongst men—in the business world, at least. Far from wasting his life lamenting his expulsion from this country, he'd made his first billion before he was twenty-three years old and had since gone from strength to strength. But this was different. When he spoke now of birthright, she *felt* it. The justness of his claim on this palace, this life. She felt the importance of his place here, and his duty to this country.

She felt her own duty too.

She loved Cavalonia. She loved the people, the history, the culture; she was immensely patriotic. She'd worked tirelessly for the king, had even walked away from a serious relationship because her fiancé had expected her to stop working, once they were married. She'd sacrificed everything to be where she was. Was she willing, even, to sacrifice her life? And what then of her baby? What of her work? Was there a way she could do this and ensure her child would be cared for, no matter what? Having grown up without the presence of a mother, and with a father who had become increasingly less reliable, she knew she couldn't bring a child into the world without certain guarantees. But could Prince Sebastian give her those assurances? Would he promise to love their baby enough for two parents?

'I need to think,' she said, quietly, not meeting his eyes.

She was surprised when he reached out and touched her chin, his strong, commanding fingers tilting her face towards his, forcing her to face him head-on. His voice, though, was low and soft, as if he understood the magnitude of this decision. Not just for himself, but for Rosie too. 'Think fast, wife. The king will not wait long for our answer.'

CHAPTER TWO

HE STORMED FROM the palace with long strides that conveyed, to anyone who dared look at the prince, the strength of his emotions.

He hated this place.

He had hated it for a long time.

His childhood memories of the palace were all troubled. Thoughts of his grandfather tainted by that last awful week, when his mother had fought with her father constantly, and Sebastian, a boy of only four, had listened to their screaming matches without understanding the content, but perceiving, in that way children could, that it was very serious. Somehow, he'd known his life was about to change forever.

In America, he'd initially refused to think of his life here at all. Avoiding feelings he didn't like, emotions that weakened him, like the dull ache of rejection. Of knowing that he was dispensable—his grandfather had easily cut him from his life without a backwards glance, as had his own father. When Sebastian's mother had left him, Sebastian's father had chosen to forget his son existed. At first, he'd missed his father and grandfather as one might a lost limb. He'd ached for them, for the time they'd used to spend together. But missing them had hurt too much. It had made him miserable and flooded his little body with a deep sense of worthlessness, so he did everything he could not to give those feelings power over him.

But bit by bit, with age, certain things had forced their way into his consciousness. The strangest things, like facsimiles of memories, really. Rather than being of anything important or specific, they were always transient—like the way the sun lit the marble floor of his childhood home, or the smell of the spruce trees that grew near the lawn, or the sound of the waves, crashing against the shore. He remembered the feeling of that too, his feet digging into the sand as wave after wave rolled over him; he'd laughed at the sensation. There were glimpses of his father and grandfather too, memories he hated, because they were good, warm and happy, which made a mockery of how they'd treated him afterwards.

He had been exiled, along with his mother, as a little boy. Punished for her sins, perhaps used as leverage to force her to relent. She hadn't. And though he was now back, it didn't undo the pain and hurt that his grandfather had caused. Sebastian had been permanently altered by the insecurity that came from rejection: it had made him careful and cynical, and determined never again to put himself in a position of such weakness and vulnerability. He had once loved with the happy abandon of a little boy, the innocence of a child who expected to always be loved in return. He would never make that mistake again. As a man, he had grown to crave control.

No wonder he found it galling to have been manipulated into marrying the woman his bastard of a grandfather had hand chosen.

Rosalind.

Beautiful, prim, untouchable, judgemental Rosalind.

His lips tightened in a firm line as he stepped out of

the east corridor and approached his gleaming black bike, gravel crunching underfoot as he reached the thing.

It wasn't like the prospect of a baby was his ideal development either. He'd married Rosalind out of sheer necessity. The old king had made it obvious that the only way he'd return Sebastian to the order of succession and revoke his mother's exiled status was if Sebastian agreed to take the hand of a woman of the king's choosing. And the king had chosen a woman who was clearly cut from the same cloth as himself.

At least, Sebastian thought with a frown, he'd thought as much until tonight.

Until tonight, his every interaction with his wife had shown her to be a ruthless, power-hungry person who put ambition above all else. Just like the king, who'd cared more about his wounded pride than his daughter's happiness.

And Rosie had married a man she didn't know, for the sake of power, money and influence. Look at how she'd lobbied to double her discretionary budget, so she could funnel the money into whichever project she deemed worthy.

At least Sebastian could say he'd acted out of love. He'd married at the king's behest because it was the only way to get his mother home and to return himself to the order of succession. Personal power had been beside the point: he'd had enough of that in his life in America. This was about righting a wrong; about forcing the king to acknowledge that he'd erred.

Except, that hadn't happened. There had been no apology, no explanation, no admitting he'd been wrong. No matter. They were back in Cavalonia and one day, Sebastian would be king; this would all be worth it.

What if Rosie didn't agree to have his baby?

It was her choice; utterly and completely. He knew many

women who'd chosen not to have children, many couples who'd opted out of procreating. Each person had their own views on this matter and were it not for the necessity of be-getting a royal heir, Sebastian doubted he'd have wanted a child of his own either. But his was not a normal life. When he'd returned to Cavalonia, he'd been mindful of the freedoms he'd be giving up. His privacy was invaded constantly, his time was scheduled from dawn to dusk, but all of this he accepted, because it was his duty. So too was the fathering of children.

But what if she *did* agree?

His parents' marriage had been miserable. Though he'd only been four when his mother had left, he had core memories of their arguments, and a pervasive sense of what it had been like to live in a desperately unhappy home. How could he, in good conscience, consider having a child under very similar circumstances?

He and Rosalind didn't like one another. They were barely civil when in the same room. How could they share a child and conceal their dislike?

With the question hanging in his mind, he straddled the bike, unaware of the pair of bright blue eyes that were trained on him from a second-story window. He reached for the helmet, dropped it onto his head, but he didn't start the bike yet. The helmet sliding into place felt almost like a weight—the weight of the entire world—and for a moment he let himself admit, just to himself, how much he *didn't* want this. How much he wished he was free to choose.

The very faint hope Rosie had cherished that the prince had been mistaken faded abruptly the next morning.

'You must have a child.' The king's voice was hoarse. Though his heart was back in rhythm, he was tired, just like the last time. She tried not to think about the surgery he'd had, which had been supposed to correct this biological programming error, nor about the fact it appeared to have failed. 'I cannot risk what will happen if I'm gone.'

'You're not going anywhere,' Rosie murmured.

'Listen to me.' An old hand, gnarled in the way the trees in the very middle of the forest became, pressed into hers. She stared at it, wondering why she hadn't noticed how much he'd aged in recent years? He was *not* old, and yet his body seemed to be betraying him. 'I do not trust him. He is too like his mother, and like the man who raised him. He is not like you or me. He does not live by a code of loyalty; he does not love this country. Not like we do.'

Rosie tried not to betray her thoughts on this. She hated her husband, but she wasn't sure that the king's charges were entirely fair. There was something about Sebastian that spoke of a deep loyalty—to his mother, if not the country.

'If I were to die tomorrow, do you think your marriage would survive?'

Rosie's eyes widened. The thought hadn't occurred to her, which made Rosie feel both naive and foolish. While she knew theirs was not a long-term marriage, she had expected it to end on *her* terms, when she was ready. When she'd finished the work she'd started. Control of this was important to Rosie and she had fought hard for it in their marriage documents. She bristled now at the idea that she might be maneuvered out of Sebastian's life when it suited *him* and not her.

'He suffered this union only as a way to secure his inheritance—we both know that.'

They *did* both know that, but acknowledging the truth so baldly did little for Rosie's ego. Was that why she'd ignored the prospect of being cast aside if the king were to pass away?

'Without me here, he would divorce you, and go on to rule with no tempering force in his life. He would be completely unchallenged in all things. I cannot allow that to happen.'

Rosie's heart tightened. The king was painting a bleak picture. 'I do not believe he would necessarily be so callous.'

'Don't you?' The king's voice was heavy with cynicism. 'You must have a child. Even he would not be able to cast you aside then.' Rosie shook her head in instinctive rejection of the whole idea. 'Better yet, have two. Three.'

She gasped. 'Stop.'

'I'm sorry.' The king's eyes swept shut. Rosie stared at him, her heart hurting at his visible decline. She loved him, but he was far from perfect, and this request was proof of that. But was he wrong?

When she'd agreed to this marriage, it had been for two reasons. Firstly, it had given her a chance to make the kind of difference she'd always dreamed of, to truly improve the lives of the most disadvantaged in the land, just as her mother had wanted to do. But secondly, she'd agreed because she loved her country. Because she was proud of where she came from and of who she was, and she would have done anything for Cavalonia's future.

Even this?

Could she have a child with a man she disliked so intensely? Could she ensure that child would be loved and protected no matter what?

'I need to think,' she said, for the second time in twenty-four hours, but deep down, Rosalind knew that she'd already accepted the necessity of this. Not only accepted, but was allowing herself, despite the fears that had gripped her for a long time, to feel a hint of something like excitement.

As terrified as she was of the medical implications of being pregnant, if she allowed herself to think beyond that, and imagine holding a baby in her arms, of staring down at their sweet face and downy head, her heart threatened to burst with a love she'd never known possible. She could see the advantages of falling pregnant, but this went beyond duty.

A baby.

If she were lucky—and she didn't dare allow herself to hope—she would have a daughter or son. Someone to love as she'd never loved before. As a child, she'd dreamed of what it would have been like, had her mother not been in a vegetative state. She imagined the games they might have played, the books they'd have read together. Sharing pots of tea and cuddling watching movies. How different her life might have been with someone to love so unconditionally, and now she allowed herself to imagine again. To hope. To pray.

But the hope did not last long.

Rosie had spent a lifetime knowing what had happened to her mother and why, and she couldn't shake the feeling that the same fate awaited her.

And yet, she had to do this. Weirdly, she *wanted* to do this. Now all that was left was to tell her husband...

It was strange, Rosie thought, as she was ushered into an oppressive wood-panelled study, that she hadn't ever been to her husband's home. Or perhaps it wasn't strange, so much as telling. Theirs was a marriage with very clearly delineated territories. Hers included the palace, from which the king ruled. His was this smaller royal house in the centre of the city's historic district. Ornate and impressive, it was nonetheless on a far less grand scale.

She wondered, as she glanced around the room, seeing very few traces of the occupant's personality, what his home had been like in America. Somehow, she suspected it had been the opposite of this. He struck her as a man who would opt for sleek metal and glass over history and pomp.

Did he hate living here? Was he miserable? Or had his desire to become king overridden everything else?

'Wife.' His voice was low and throbbed with something that pulled strangely at her belly. She turned slowly, needing a moment to calm her fluttering nerves. For what she'd mentally accepted as necessary was still an enormous step to take—and to take with this man, of all people.

'Why do you call me that?'

One side of his lips lifted in that cynical half smile she hated so much. 'You are my wife.'

'Yes. But I'm also Rosie,' she pointed out. 'You could call me by my name.'

'Your name is Rosalind.'

'No one calls me that.'

'Why not?'

Her eyes widened. Was that the first question he'd ever asked her of a personal nature? Her stomach dropped to her toes. Caught off guard, she prevaricated. His dark eyes bore into hers, his expression showing a hint of impatience.

'I guess because it's a mouthful.'

'Three syllables? How does that differ from Sebastian?'

She toyed with her fingers. 'Are you always called Sebastian? Surely some people shorten it to Seb?'

'Do I look like a man who would be called Seb?'

Despite herself, a smile lifted her lips. 'Not really.'

'Well, wife. What can I do for you?'

Her heart sped up dangerously; her fingers fidgeted more. 'I've been thinking about our…matter.'

'The matter of you falling pregnant?' he prompted, with a brief darkening of his tone.

She nodded quickly, wishing this conversation could be over.

'I've been thinking about it too.' His American accent was a drawl, pouring over her spine in a way that was jarring and unwelcome. 'Maybe it's a bad idea.'

Her eyes widened. 'You were the one who was convinced it was necessary.'

'We don't know one another,' he pointed out. 'And we don't like one another. Bringing a child into an unhappy marriage is not something to be done lightly. Trust me, I speak from experience.'

She'd heard about his mother's first marriage from the king. She knew that the princess had been unhappy with her husband, but also that she'd been young and, according to Renee, quite unreasonable in her expectations. The same could not be said for Rosie.

'I'm so glad you brought that up. I've been thinking the same thing.'

'Then your answer is "no"?'

'No. That's not what I'm saying. None of this is ideal, yet here we are—married—and with the king in failing health.' Her voice broke a little. 'The best thing for the country would be to provide a stable line of succession.' She took a step towards him without realising it. 'You were right— we have to do this.'

His eyes glittered when they met hers. Another step forward, though Rosie wasn't sure whether that was her or Sebastian. They were toe to toe, just as they'd been in her study the night before.

'You've changed your tune.'

'Yes.'

'Last night you seemed pretty set against the idea.'

'I was.'

'And now you're arguing the other side.'

'I told you I needed to think it through.'

'Which makes me, if I'm honest, a little apprehensive.'

'Why? Because I'm giving you what you asked for?'

'Because there must be some hidden benefit to you in this.'

'Not hidden,' she responded archly. 'I intend for us to negotiate new terms before I conceive.'

'Ah.' He nodded once, lifting a hand to rub his chin. 'Here it is. What would you like this time?'

'There is a lot to consider,' she said calmly. She had experience dealing with the more bombastic members of the king's staff, many of whom had resented her quick ascension to the position of king's advisor. She was used to ignoring belittling comments; even when issued from her husband, they failed to hurt. 'Such as the mechanics of me falling pregnant, where we'll live once we've had the baby, what expectations of privacy the child will have and what will happen to the child if either of us dies or becomes otherwise incapacitated. On top of that, I need to know we can work together, to co-parent without this…animosity… that surrounds us becoming a part of our baby's life.' She sucked in a breath. 'I would also like some protections for the projects I'm undertaking. No matter what happens—if, for example, I were to die as a result of having this baby, or if you were to decide you could dispense with me once our baby was born, I would like to know that funding will continue for the charities I currently oversee.'

His expression was kept carefully immovable, but something swirled in the depths of his eyes, something that caused her belly to churn.

'We would live here—definitely not at the palace. I hate that place. Royal children have a high guarantee of privacy, that's a legal requirement, as I'm sure you're aware. Your charities—I will need to see what you're working on, but I can't see a problem with that request.'

She expelled a slow, shaking breath.

He continued, 'I would also like to avoid bringing a child into a marriage that is as flawed as ours. I don't know a way around that, but I agree, we have to discuss it. Suffice it to say, the fact we're in agreement as to the importance of finding a way to work together bodes well.'

She nodded slowly.

'As for the mechanics, I presume you're familiar with how one falls pregnant?'

Heat flushed her cheeks. 'In the ordinary course of things, yes. But there are alternatives, such as IVF.'

'IVF?' he repeated, as though it hadn't occurred to him.

'We're not a couple,' she pointed out. 'I'm not going to have sex with you just because we need a baby.'

'Heaven forbid you should let a little fun be a part this.'

'Fun?' she repeated, then furrowed her brow. 'I'm not having sex with someone like you.'

'Someone like me?' he repeated.

She was mesmerised by the freckles on his nose, or perhaps they were easier to look at than his dark black eyes, so deep she felt as though she might drown in their depths.

'What exactly does that mean?' He pressed a finger to her chin, just as he had the night before, but this time, she'd half been expecting it, and a thrill of relief caught her totally off guard. She should have hated his touch, not secretly revelled in it.

'It means you're not my type.'

His eyes narrowed. 'Let me guess. The men you usually sleep with are…academics.'

'You went to an Ivy League college on a full scholarship,' she pointed out. 'What's the difference?'

Up close, his mocking smile was even more infuriating. 'By academic, I meant more of a pushover.'

'You mean weak?'

'Sure.'

'Why do you think that's who I'd be attracted to?'

'Just a feeling I have.'

'Based on…'

'Based on you being someone who never has a hair out of place. I bet when you have sex it's always a neat, passionless affair with a neat, passionless man.'

She refused to acknowledge the truth of his statement, nor how inferior it made her feel. She'd seen movies; she'd read books. She knew what sex was *supposed* to be like. The fact it had always been a pretty tame scenario for Rosie was something she'd refused to feel bad about. If anything, she liked that. Even in bed, she never lost control, she never risked succumbing to the madness of desire. When she answered, her voice emerged prim. 'Have you spent much time imagining my sex life?'

'From time to time.'

She drew in a sharp breath, heat flooding her veins no matter how hard she tried to ignore it. 'Why?'

'I like to amuse myself, imagining my prim, perfect wife "letting herself go".'

'Wow, you really are an incredible asshole.'

'Thank you.'

'That's not a compliment.'

'Nonetheless—'

'And I bet sex for you is all animalistic and untamed,'

she interrupted, two red dots in her cheeks showing anger. 'I bet you rip one another's clothes off in your desperation to come together.'

'That's the best case, yeah.'

'Well, not for me. I prefer things in my life to be more measured,' she said with the appearance of a shudder. Her mind, though, was running away from her, populating an image of Sebastian tearing her blouse from her body, and in a terrifying contrast to what she *should* have felt at the very idea, her nipples tightened against the lace of her bra, silently inviting his notice, wanting his touch.

She took a step backwards, her whole body igniting with a strange, overcharged awareness. Of *him*. This was a disaster.

'Why?' He echoed her movements, so they were close again. She didn't step away. He smelled of wood, like pine or cedar, heavy and oaked, just like his study.

'Why?' she repeated, no longer able to follow the conversation.

'What would happen if I kissed you now?'

'Why would you kiss me?'

'Because I'm your husband?'

'And? You've been my husband for five months and with the exception of our wedding day, we've never come close to kissing. Try again.'

He laughed. A short bark that made her skin flush with goosebumps.

'And because I want to.'

Her heart slammed into her ribs. It was an answer she hadn't expected. 'You do?'

'Sure.'

She bit down into her lower lip, eyes locked to his. 'Why?'

'Why not?'

And damn it, Rosie couldn't think of a single reason *not* to kiss him. A kiss was just a kiss. Not sex. Not a baby. It was just a kiss, a brushing of lips, just as it had been on their wedding day. Brief contact then over and done with. True, she'd been surprised by the spark that had spiralled through her even then, but she'd controlled her response to him, just as she would now. He had laid down the gauntlet, and Rosie wasn't going to be the one to back away, if only because she wanted to prove to them both how much a non-issue physical desire was between them.

'Fine,' she said, with a tone of feigned nonchalance. 'Let's kiss. Whatever. Maybe then you'll see that you're not my type, and I'm not yours.'

CHAPTER THREE

HIS RESPONSE WAS a quick flicker of that mocking smile and then his head lowered. Slowly. Painfully slowly.

So slowly that she theoretically had plenty of time to rediscover her sanity. To push him away and tell him wild horses couldn't make her want this. But she didn't. Instead, she held her breath, impatience flaring in the pit of her stomach, her fingers tingling with adrenaline and need, until finally, his lips pressed to hers.

Not brushed. Pressed. With actual pressure. It was a kiss that showed, in that moment, his anger, and she felt it too. A spark, a whip, a burst of flame. But then, there was something else. He moved. Not just his mouth, but his body, closing the distance between them, and one hand came around to the back of her head, his fingers tangling in the neat bun she wore, while his other hand pressed to the desk just behind her, forming a sort of cage with his big, broad frame. His powerful legs were on either side of her body and her bottom connected with the edge of his desk; she hadn't even realised how close it was.

Of their own volition, her hands lifted, her fingers curling in the fabric of his shirt, holding him, as he deepened the kiss, his mouth moving now in a way that was enquiring, as if he was asking her questions and her lips were responding in a way so much more meaningful than speech.

All controlled.

All bearable.

Until it wasn't. Until something sparked in Sebastian, or perhaps in Rosie. Maybe in them both, simultaneously. It was signalled by a small groan, low in Rosie's throat, as something he did with his tongue sent her nerves into a palpitation and she couldn't help but say his name, pushing the three syllables into his mouth. He paused, his body stiff and straight, and then he kissed her hard. Much harder than he had at first. This was a kiss that was the culmination of every ounce of his strength and need; it was a kiss that shook Rosie to her core, because she'd never known one like it. There was nothing chaste nor civilised about this—it spoke of all the raw animalism she'd felt in her husband from the first moment they'd met. He kissed her as though she was something he wanted to taste, every single inch of. He kissed her as though it was the only way to save his life, or hers, or perhaps even the universe.

The weight of his body pushed hers backwards onto the desk. She felt things beneath her—pens, a notebook—she didn't care. She just wanted to freeze time and hold on to this one single moment. It had nothing to do with Sebastian, and everything to do with Rosie, who hadn't conceptualised pleasure could be so complete and all-consuming.

She moaned again, pulling at his shirt, holding him right where he was, but Sebastian had other ideas. He broke the kiss and she almost cried out, but it was not to pull away. Instead, he dragged his mouth lower, over her chin, towards her decolletage, and as if he'd been hardwired into her most private fantasies, his big, strong hands gripped the silk of her shirt and pulled at it, so the buttons flew across the room with an overly loud tinkling sound as each hit a surface. He grinned. Not sarcastic. It was the first time she'd seen something like a real smile, and it took her breath away for how beautiful it was.

'May I?' he asked, voice husky as his finger traced a line around the edge of her breast.

She wasn't even sure what he was asking but she nodded, delirious and over-hot now. She writhed when he pushed the silk of her bra down. Not removing it, but rather liberating her breasts from the cups with that same rough need that had seen him destroy her shirt. She didn't have time to feel self-conscious. Having consented to his touch, she submitted completely, as his hands roamed her flesh, pulling, feeling, tweaking, tormenting, and then his mouth followed suit, his tongue lashing her, his warm, wet mouth sucking at her nipples until she was incandescent with a need that fired her blood like a volcano might. She swore—unusual for Rosie—the curse tumbling from her mouth, as she lifted one leg onto the edge of the desk, the skirt she wore ripping at the seam. A hand moved from one of her breasts to the thigh that had been exposed by the split, only her stockings were a regrettable barrier. His fingers crept higher, to the elasticised waistband, and he glanced up at her, another smile, this one only just very barely mocking.

'Why am I not surprised?'

She heard the hint of teasing and flushed to the roots of her hair, finding it hard to hold his eyes. She glanced away from him, her eyes landing on an ancient mirror across the room. The sight of them terrified her. She looked so wanton, so alive. So awoken by desire. Her skin was flushed, her breasts creamy white and her nipples taut, pale pink. Her stomach was bare, exposed to his touch, and yet he looked exactly the same, in his suit and shirt, unchanged by what was happening to them. To her. It was everything she'd promised herself she'd never be! Oh, heavens...

'Sebastian…' She said his name with uncertainty now. Everything felt strange, different. The world was tilting weirdly beneath her, with all her usual suppositions nowhere to be found. She wouldn't let this happen to her! She was not like the women her father had destroyed.

He pulled up a little, eyes fixing to hers with an expression she couldn't understand.

'Not so prim after all,' he said, with a hint of approval. She wanted to deny that, but how could she?

'I'm as surprised as you,' she admitted after a beat, her hands still curled in his shirt, as though she couldn't allow this to be over yet despite her deepest fears. Her body thrummed with need, heat building between her legs. But Sebastian was as canny as he was skilled. He pulled away regardless of her obvious desire, looking down at her now with cool composure. Oh, how she envied him! Only the slight colour in his cheekbones conveyed any hint that he might also have been a little undone by their passionate encounter. Where was her control now?

'Do you still think IVF is how we should conceive our child, Rosalind? Or have you had a change of heart?'

Her voice shuddered a little as she fought to find a thread of common sense. 'We both know our hearts have nothing to do with what just happened.'

'True,' he agreed with something like approval.

He brought his body back over hers, his hands braced on either side of the desk, his eyes boring into her own. 'Email me a list of your projects, and the funding you require, as well as any other terms. Once we've come to an arrangement regarding your requirements, we can decide the…how did you put it? Mechanics of conception.' He leaned closer to her, then dropped his mouth to her breast. 'My vote is for the old-fashioned way, but you're welcome to convince me otherwise.'

* * *

Why had he stopped? he thought, as the ice-cold water of his shower pummelled his still rock-hard body. His state of arousal wasn't helped by the images of Rosalind that kept flashing into his mind despite his attempts to keep her firmly in a box. No matter how much he tried to impose his usual sense of discipline, he couldn't help imagining her in here with him, her back to the wall as the shower rained down on her.

He remembered the way she'd tried so hard to resume her prim exterior, turning away from him as she'd pulled her clothes back on. He'd felt a rush of adrenalin at the sight of her shirt, at the way she'd fashioned a knot to hold it together then demurely buttoned her blazer in place, concealing, to anyone other than him, the state of her outfit. When she'd left, hair neatened back into that bun, she'd looked so much like his prim, perfect wife once more that he'd wanted to grab her wrist and drag her back against his body and kiss her all over again. He'd liked the way she sounded when she moaned into his mouth, the way her body had trembled against his. He'd liked it, even when he'd been surprised enough to acknowledge he hadn't expected it.

Sex was about chemistry for Sebastian.

Rosie had been right, when she'd accused him of indulging in wild and untamed sexual encounters. That's how it should be. If he was attracted to a woman and she was attracted to him, and they shared the necessary chemistry and had no expectations of a deeper commitment, then he was all for no-holds-barred sex. Two consenting adults who felt the same way could have a lot of fun in the bedroom, or wherever they came together. At least, that's how it had been in America, before he'd returned to this life, and his role as king. Before he'd spent six months without anything other than his own hand for relief.

What a pleasant surprise it was to discover that his wife was someone he actually did share chemistry with after all.

That she wasn't untouchable and cold.

That she might even be a perfect match for him in bed.

What did it matter that they didn't like each other? Since when had personality compatibility been a factor in choosing his lovers? He'd had sex with women he'd just met before, women he never intended to see again. All he cared about was that they were sober, single and consenting.

Rosalind had been consenting.

Sober.

And while she wasn't single, she was his wife…

She wasn't naive enough to pretend her dreams had nothing to do with her decision. Being tormented for two nights in a row with memories of her husband's touch, the weight of his body pressing down on hers, the feeling of his mouth on her breasts, had stirred Princess Rosie's blood to a fever pitch, and seen her waking each morning with pink cheeks and an almost unbearable sense of disappointment to find herself alone in bed. She'd never craved someone in her life; she'd always avoided that. But just a taste of the fire Sebastian could stir in her belly, and she found herself wanting more. Much, much more…

It suddenly seemed incredibly silly to even contemplate using IVF to conceive their baby.

They were married, for goodness' sake, and they were two adults, well able to decide who they slept with and why. For Rosie, desiring someone as she did Sebastian was just about as good a reason as she needed, but the only way she'd allow herself to give in to that desire was if she remained committed to her determination not to lose herself to him.

Rosie had seen firsthand how destructive unrequited love

could be. Watching her father seduce woman after woman after woman, looking for someone to fill a whole in his bed whilst never relinquishing the grip Rosie's comatose mother still had on his heart. She'd seen these women fall hard for her father's charms and be badly burned in the process. As a teenager, Rosie had started to realise just how one-sided these affairs were, with some disastrous, devastating consequences. For some reason, her father had managed to hold all the cards, with each and every woman, and when the relationship no longer suited him, he'd abruptly ended it, somehow forgetting everything about his one-time lover, even her name.

For Rosie, it hadn't been so simple.

She'd met the women too. She'd gotten to know them. When their hearts had broken, hers couldn't help but be touched, softening with sympathy and pity. Sometimes, she'd even tried to warn them away from him, but they'd never believed her—he was too charming.

Rosie had watched their hearts break and sworn to herself that she would never put herself in such a foolish position. If she got married, it would be a totally rational arrangement. A friendship, or a business partnership. No children, just a satisfying arrangement where neither herself, nor her husband, could be injured.

She frowned, reflecting on the engagement she'd entered into, before notions of marrying Sebastian had been on the cards. She'd liked Robert, had even thought she loved him, but not enough to meet his demands that she give up her career to support him in his. What an arrogant pig! Or perhaps he wasn't. Perhaps what he wanted was his version of a partnership, but it had terrified Rosie. There were two things that mattered more to Rosie than anything else: her career, and her independence. Robert had wanted to take away both.

She'd run a mile.

Straight into the arms, metaphorically at least, of Prince Sebastian, who'd barely given her a second glance since their wedding, except on the handful of public occasions when it had been necessary to pose as a happy couple.

Had they touched? She found herself pondering, as her hand idled down her flat stomach, towards her sex, hunger building in the pit of her belly. They *must* have touched at some point. A brushing of hands, shoulders, bodies. But try as she might, she couldn't imagine any physical contact beyond their wedding day, and other feelings had overwhelmed her then, making it impossible for her to recognise the desire that must have been wrapping around her and squeezing tight.

Perhaps it had been squeezing her this whole time, and she'd instinctively been running from it, out of fear of being just like one of her father's mistresses?

Nothing could have prepared her for their encounter at his home.

She hadn't expected his touch nor kiss, nor anything else, but she wasn't sorry it had happened.

Maybe Rosie and Sebastian had simply found a way to have their cake and eat it too…

'Laurena, would you please get a message to my husband?'

'Of course, Your Highness. What would you like me to say?'

'Ask him to join me for dinner this evening.'

'Dinner?' Laurena almost spluttered, then caught herself, reverting to the professional visage she usually represented. 'What time?'

Rosie's cheeks flushed. She opted for eight o'clock. Late enough to increase the likelihood he might spend the night.

'At the palace?'

She considered that too. It would make sense for him to come here, yet something inside of her rejected that idea. He'd said he hated it here—his home was therefore an easier option. And deep down, there was a part of Rosie that relished the thought of being somewhere other than here too.

'On second thought, tell Sebastian I'd like to join *him* for dinner.'

'Of course, Your Highness. Shall I lay out any particular outfit for you?'

Rosie considered that. He'd called her prim, and it had raised her hackles, but what choice did she have? There were strict protocols around how to dress as a princess of Cavalonia. She could hardly turn up at his house in a slinky dress and stiletto heels.

Unless...

A smile tilted her lips as she shook her head absentmindedly. 'Leave it with me. Thank you, Laurena,' she dismissed, wondering at the way her pulse was suddenly erratic.

Sebastian was torn. He didn't particularly like being dictated to by anyone, let alone Rosalind, and yet, he'd be lying if he said he wasn't looking forward to seeing her again.

He poured himself a small measure of Scotch and cradled it in the palm of his hand as his clock struck eight. His body tensed in anticipation. His mind raced.

Dinner was not a proposition, and yet it was promising. Promising?

How had his feelings towards his wife changed so much in seventy-two hours? He had disliked her three days ago. And he still did. She was manipulative, power hungry and worshipped the ground his grandfather walked on.

Or was it that his grandfather clearly loved Rosalind,

whereas he had dropped Sebastian like a hot potato? Probably a bit of both. He wasn't someone to give in to jealousy, and yet he'd felt it. Rejection. Surprise. That he'd been so clearly usurped, the place of beloved grandchild taken by someone who was not even related to the king.

He still despised her, he reassured himself. He just desired her, as well. And desire he was familiar with; desire he could control—he had many years of experience with that.

None of this was a problem.

With that reassurance, he threw back the Scotch and allowed himself to enjoy the anticipation of seeing her again, and stripping away those defences of hers, one pleasurable encounter at a time, until she was eating out of the palm of his hand...

CHAPTER FOUR

IT HAD BEEN easy to feel confident as she'd come up with this scheme, but now that she was here in Sebastian's living room, that confidence was in short supply. As was her belief in what she was about to suggest.

Or rather, agree to.

She fidgeted with her fingers, aware that it was by far her least regal habit, something the king had repeatedly tried to make her stop doing. She had become more adept at hiding the gesture, but now she surrendered to it completely.

Was he enjoying keeping her waiting? Was this a game he was playing?

More than likely.

Just because they'd shared a passionate kiss didn't mean he'd changed. He was still arrogant, rude, disrespectful: the last man on earth she could bring herself to *like*. Which was wonderful. Just wonderful! Because it meant she was at no risk of losing her heart, no matter how overwhelming their desire was. What a safe crush to nurture!

'Wife.'

She ground her teeth. 'Husband.'

His grin lit a fire in her blood, a fire she was determined to control. She blinked away as she stood, regretting her outfit selection now. Beneath the three-quarter length wool coat she wore was a dress she'd bought whilst dating Robert. Then, she'd simply been working for the king and there had been no expectation surrounding how she dressed in her own time. Nor had there been a hint of paparazzi interest in her comings and goings, no likelihood that a photo of her in an outfit like this might appear on the front pages of the tabloids the following day.

He stepped towards her, eyes locked to hers, and she held her breath. Was he going to kiss her? To say hello?

Did she want him to?

Yes, she wanted him to. But not yet. Not until they'd talked. As if to signal that, she took a neat step backwards, and he paused immediately.

'I came to discuss our new…deal,' she said, a little breathlessly.

'Is that why you came, Rosalind?' he asked after a beat, his tone lightly mocking, the double entendre sending sparks through her veins.

'We need to agree to the details,' she continued, valiantly. 'Before anything else…happens.'

He arched a brow.

'Like the other night,' she clarified, heat in her cheeks.

'Ah, yes. Heaven forbid we should finish what we started before there's a signed contract in place.'

'We're talking about making a baby,' she reminded him. 'That's serious.'

'I'm aware of that.'

'You're the one who reminded me about the importance of bringing a child into a marriage like ours. We need guard rails in place, for the sake of that child.'

His eyes narrowed and she thought he was going to argue but to her surprise, he simply dipped his head. 'Would you like a drink?'

'I'd kill for one,' she said on a shaky laugh.

His eyes skimmed her face. 'What would you like?'

'Champagne feels appropriate—to toast this development.'

'The baby, or us having sex?'

She blinked at his statement, heat swirling through her. 'That's a little presumptuous, isn't it?'

His eyes taunted her. 'Is it?'

She glanced away, unable to respond.

'Champagne it is.'

Her gaze drifted back to his as he moved to a bar in the corner and slid an expensive bottle from a small fridge, expertly removing the foil and then popping the cork, catching it in his hand and stifling most of the noise. He poured two glasses, carrying one across to her. When she took it, their fingers brushed, and Rosie's breath snagged in her throat. She took a big gulp simply to bring moisture back to her mouth.

'Okay. We should talk about the details.'

His eyes skimmed her face. 'Already?'

She floundered. 'Well, yes.'

'What's your rush? No conversational foreplay?'

'Stop it,' she said, but a smile teased her lips.

'Stop what?'

'Baiting me.'

'Is that what I'm doing?'

'You know it is.'

He lifted one shoulder. 'You don't enjoy flirting?'

'Evidently, not like you.'

'Meaning?'

'You just seem like someone who does this sort of thing—' she gestured to the bar, the open bottle of champagne '—a lot.'

His lips quirked to one side. 'I took our marriage vows

seriously, Rosalind. I haven't been with another woman since we were married.'

Her lips parted in a circle of surprise.

'You don't believe me?'

'Actually, I do. I mean, why lie? I just didn't expect that.'

'Is that your way of telling me you've been sleeping around at the palace?'

She laughed at how preposterous that was. 'Erm, no. For a start, even if I'd wanted to, I can't see any way I could have.'

'You're right. The media follows your every move.'

She grimaced. 'It's been a long time since they've had a princess.'

'And you're their darling.'

'At least for now,' she said with a hint of rare cynicism. 'I'm sorry.' She lifted her palms in a gesture that echoed her apology. 'I don't mean to sound ungrateful. I'm just aware that it is a bit of a sport, to build someone up and then tear them down. I'm still waiting for the other shoe to drop.'

'As you should. Your perception is spot on.'

Her eyes glittered when they met his. 'Your mother had a lot of that dished out to her when she left Cavalonia.'

'When she left her husband, when she left the country, when she missed any of the king's milestone events—never mind the fact she was legally exiled, cut off by her father for the sin of having abandoned a miserable, failing marriage.'

Rosalind chose her words with care. She'd heard only the king's view, had seen only his pain when events passed without his daughter's and grandson's presence. 'I think he'd have liked to heal the breach long before this,' she said gently.

Sebastian's lips formed a line of disapproval. 'You're wrong.'

'Why do you say that?'

'Because the estrangement was all his doing. He sent her from the palace. She would have chosen to stay here and marry Mark.'

'Impossible,' Rosie said with a shake of her head. 'Your grandfather couldn't have sanctioned that.'

'Why not?'

'For many reasons, and you know it.'

'You're speaking like his mouthpiece,' Sebastian responded. 'Worse, you're speaking like a throwback.'

'And you're speaking like an American,' she was baited to reply, then raised her hand once more in another gesture of apology. 'You're speaking like someone from a culture with far more freedom, far more respect for love and personal choice. That's not how it was here back then. That's still not how it is—not really. You know that. Cavalonia is a deeply traditional society. Your grandfather was only expecting your mother to uphold the beliefs he had respected all his life.'

'Times change,' Sebastian ground out.

'Not here,' Rosie responded with a lift of one shoulder. 'Not really.'

But Sebastian was calm again, in control of his emotions. 'Tell me, Rosalind, have you travelled?'

Her eyes ran over his face, momentarily jarred by the change of subject. 'I—a little. Why?'

'I mean, have you *really* travelled? Spent time in other cultures and countries, seen how other people live?'

'Enough to know there's a whole spectrum of societies and values, and that Cavalonia is probably in the middle.'

His nostrils flared. 'What business does a father have—whether king or not—to dictate how his daughter should live her life?'

'It is the obligation of anyone born to that position…' she trailed off, tried again. 'Do you think he enjoyed imposing exile on his daughter? Do you think he would have gone through with it if he'd thought she would actually leave?'

'What did he expect?' Sebastian snapped his fingers. 'That she would hear the threat of exile and decide to stay here, married to a man twenty years her senior who quite clearly hated her? Who treated her with contempt? Who barely acknowledged me?'

'Yes,' she replied simply. 'I suppose that's what he did expect.'

'And what would you have done in her situation, Rosalind?'

'Isn't that obvious? I'm married to you.'

His eyes widened, as though he'd never considered the parallels in their situations.

'But I walked into this,' she reassured him, taking a sip of her champagne. 'I chose this life—I chose this marriage—knowing you would never care for me, and that I would never care for you. Believe me, Sebastian, that's exactly what I wanted.'

'Because of the financial recompense?'

She shook her head. 'You've accused me of that before, you know. It's as untrue now as it was then.'

'It just seems antithetical, to marry for money. I'm surprised any woman in the twenty-first century would choose that, especially someone like you.'

'Someone like me?'

'You're smart, educated—you already had a great job.'

'You don't know me,' she said with a shrug. 'Money is part of why I agreed to this, but not money for myself. Money makes the world go round and as a princess I have at my command a small fortune to use and do good with.'

She moved closer without realizing it, drawn to him by the passion for philanthropy that had motivated her for a long time. 'Do you have any idea how satisfying it is to wake up each morning and know that I'm making a real difference in people's lives? Your grandfather knew what that would mean to me. He offered me something I desperately wanted. I just took it.'

'Manipulated you, you mean?'

Exasperation tempered her emotions. 'I suppose if you want to see the worst in his actions, you could call it that. But I don't. I think he's pragmatic, and he saw in me a woman who would move heaven and earth to change the world. He saw a way to give me more than I had ever dreamt of.'

'What a shame I had to be a part of the deal. Tell me, did it ever occur to you that you could have cut out the middleman and simply married him?'

Shock turned her blood to ice. 'Never mind that he's almost fifty years my senior?'

'I have no doubt you would enjoy marriage to him more than you have been enjoying marriage to me.'

'I barely see you. So far, this marriage ticks all my boxes.'

'Not quite,' he contradicted. 'But I suspect we're going to address that soon enough.' He was close enough now to touch her, because she'd kept moving forward, and he lifted a finger, brushing it over the soft skin of her cheek. Her body responded with a flash of awareness that was akin to lightning bolts firing in her skin.

But how could she want him even after he'd made the preposterous suggestion of her marrying King Renee?

Because this was just about desire, she reminded herself, glad for that. Because desire meant *nothing*. She could want him and hate him all at once, and hate held its own magical protective qualities. She was not in any danger of losing her heart nor head, even if she thought he was sexier than anyone else alive.

Still, she refused to be like one of her father's mistresses and let the situation get away from her. Rosie was a smart, switched-on woman. She chose who she wanted in her life and on what terms. If they were going to do this, she intended to retain control.

'We need to talk,' she said, proud of her assertiveness even when her voice trembled a little. 'It's important.'

'Sometimes action is better than words.'

'This is about so much more than action though. We can't just create a child then work out on the fly what happens next.'

His expression showed something she didn't comprehend, but a moment later, he stepped away from her, moving to his champagne and taking a sip. 'You're a planner?'

'With something like this? Naturally.'

He gestured to one of the sofas, waited until she'd sat down, then took a seat in the armchair opposite. She couldn't help but notice the length of his legs, the strength and command conveyed by his masculine pose, and her heart rate went up despite her best efforts.

'Okay, let's talk.' His voice held a command.

'I have a baby. But what comes next?'

He leaned forward, elbows braced on his knees. 'That would depend on you.'

'Me?'

'What do you want?'

She expelled a deep breath. She couldn't tell him her deepest fear—that she might die in delivery—but she could look for assurances in other ways. All that mattered was that her baby would be okay, no matter what. 'Well, I don't know you, Sebastian. And what I do know—' She hesitated.

'You don't like.'

She nodded a little awkwardly. 'But we're talking about having a baby. That's huge. It's a lifelong commitment and I need to know that we're on the same page. That we would want the same things.'

'I would defer to your judgement in whatever areas mattered most to you.'

'That sounds like you're just trying not to pick a fight.'

'I'm trying to be reasonable.'

'You need a baby that badly, huh?'

He dipped his head in silent concession.

'Okay. So, here's the deal. If we're going to do this, I need something from you first.'

He arched a brow, his expression otherwise taut. 'Go on.'

'I need us to get to know one another.'

He made a sound that was halfway between a laugh and a groan. 'Is that all?'

'I'm serious.' Either they'd end up raising the baby together, or he'd end up as a single father. Either way, she needed to know him, and know that she could trust him, before she committed. 'This is a deal-breaker.' She leaned forward a little. 'What do you think?'

What did he think?

He thought it was an entirely reasonable suggestion, so there was no explanation for the way he wanted to argue with her. Why shouldn't they get to know one another? She was right. They were talking about creating a life, a child, and one way or another, if they had a baby together, they'd need to be in each other's lives.

Having vague but traumatic memories of his parents' arguments, he knew that finding a way to work together made sense. But he didn't like it, because he didn't like her.

He didn't like her role in the king's life, didn't like her loyalty to him. What if they got to know one another and this animosity deepened?

Then wasn't that better to know now, before they conceived a child?

Only, he needed this child—enough to put almost everything else out of his mind. Whilst he'd raised the question of divorce, to do so—and remarry—would take time, and what Sebastian needed was an heir as quickly as he could produce one. Never again would he allow insecurity to hang over his head, nor his mother's. They belonged in Cavalonia, and if the only way to ensure that was to have a baby with the woman the king had chosen to be Sebastian's wife, then that's what he'd do.

It would still be Rosie's choice. Of course it would be—he wasn't comfortable with anything else. But what if he made the idea of having a baby with him too appealing to decline? He knew she was attracted to him; their physical chemistry had been a welcome surprise to them both. So why not capitalise on that? Perhaps the desire they'd shared would do the heavy lifting and help make up her mind.

Suddenly, the idea of seducing Rosie until she couldn't wait to say yes to a baby overtook every other thought.

'Fine,' he said with a slight narrowing of his eyes and a firm commitment to this course of action. 'Let's get to know each other. We'll take a week, and at the end of it, we'll tell the king our decision.'

CHAPTER FIVE

ROSIE HAD PRESUMED he meant a week of coffee dates, or private lunches. A week of short but important conversations, filled with the kind of information exchange a longer acquaintance would have naturally shaken out.

She had *not* expected the car that had arrived at the palace that morning, nor the hastily communicated explanation from Laurena: 'His Highness is taking you away for the week. No, I don't know where. I've packed a range of things to cover all eventualities. He did say there would be no risk of press intrusion.'

Rosie's first instinct had been to refuse to go. She had a job and a life here that could not easily be put aside.

But wasn't he just trying to fulfil her request? And wasn't it better to take a whole week and really get to know one another before entering into parenthood? Besides, she had presumed he would be taking her to one of the many palaces in the country, somewhere familiar, from which she could continue with her work remotely, and see him in between times.

How wrong she'd been.

The car had conveyed her to the royal airstrip, where a private jet had been waiting. Not bearing the royal crest of Cavalonia, but rather emblazoned with *Al Morova* in big, bold golden letters down one side. The tail was painted a glossy black.

She stared at the plane, and the flurry of activity surrounding it, with a strange feeling in her chest. Her heart was both sinking and fluttering, and a thousand butterflies seemed to be battering the lining of her stomach. Her fingers fidgeted at her sides as she walked towards the steps; Sebastian was waiting at the top, in conversation with the pilot.

As she approached, he nodded once. Not exactly a gesture of friendship nor affection, but a sign of approval that Rosie found somehow warming. Oh, how low her expectations were!

'Where are we going?'

He smirked. 'You'll see.'

'A surprise?'

'Sure.'

'I didn't expect that.'

He gestured into the plane—every bit as lavishly decorated as the royal fleet—and indicated for her to take a seat.

Getting to know one another was sensible and wise. Why then did she have an immediate instinct to back right out of this whole thing? Suddenly, despite the enormity of the plane's surrounds, the grandeur and space, she felt as though all she was conscious of was her husband. And for almost half a year, she'd accepted him as exactly that—her husband—and found she was quite capable of ignoring him. Of minimising the importance of that role.

Now he was all she saw and deep down, that scared her.

He moved with an athleticism that was almost feral, a confident gait that would have been at home in a jungle. He was pure muscle and instinct, and though he'd spent most of his life in America, when she looked at him, she could not mistake his rich Cavalonian heritage: that he was the by-product of two of the oldest, most noble families in the land. She couldn't pretend his features weren't carved by the same hand that had been carving the features of the royal family for as far back as the country had existed. When he took a seat opposite her but pulled out a large tablet and began to work silently, Rosie was glad. Glad that she could sit back and be ignored—even when she wasn't capable of doing the same to him.

Except, the reprieve barely lasted. They were not in the air long enough. Forty minutes at most. The plane lifted, cruised south, and then tacked west, towards the ocean, before beginning a descent just rapid enough to convince Rosie her stomach had been surrendered somewhere at the edge of a dreamy cloud.

'Nervous flyer?' he asked, when she pressed a hand to her blouse.

'Not usually.' She flashed him a tight smile. 'I used to be, but I have to travel more and more these days. I'm used to it.' She leaned forward, towards the windows, craning to get a view of where they were, and realised she didn't recognise it. In fact, there was very little to recognise. An island that was covered in so much wild vegetation it looked almost untouched, surrounded by glimmering sea.

'Where are we?'

'It's called Vedrina,' he said.

'Serenity?'

He nodded. 'I didn't name it. The island was called this when I bought it.'

'You bought an island?'

His expression was implacable, his mouth grim. 'Some years ago.'

She let out a low whistle but said nothing more. Curiosity, though, fluttered in her breast, and she stepped off the plane with anticipation, looking around to have her first impression confirmed. An airstrip had been carved into the earth, but it was surrounded on all sides by a lush and thick forest. Her eyes chased the trees, looking for a hint of the ocean that she knew to be just beyond it, and seeing nothing.

In contrast to the way she'd been brought to the airport in the Cavalonian capital city, a simple black four-wheel drive was waiting on the tarmac, and there was a distinct lack of staff. Staff was something Rosie mostly took for granted. Even before her marriage, she'd existed in the palace bubble, and it was not uncommon to walk into a room and have up to ten members of the household milling about, carrying on with their duties. Now that she was a princess, she was seldom alone. From the women who took care of her personal requirements, to her office staff, to the king's team, she was often with people. Many people.

She glanced up at Sebastian, wondering if he perceived the absence of staff as strange, but didn't see anything in his features to give that away. Besides which, not having an army of servants waiting at the airport didn't mean his home wouldn't be well staffed. She doubted someone like him did many—if any—of the domestic duties on his own.

'What are you waiting for, wife?' he asked, but just like on the plane, that simple word, the reminder of their state of being married, set something off in her pulse that was impossible to quell. A tremble, a rushing, like water racing towards the edge of a cliff and then over it, bubbling and babbling the whole way down.

'I'm not waiting,' she denied, looking around once more, hoping to see someone else—anyone. But there was only the attendant from the plane, busily pushing their bags into the back of the car, before returning to the aircraft.

'This is the only car?'

'Do you see another?'

She tilted him a glance, her tone wry when she spoke. 'That's what worries me.'

'Why should you be worried?' He was close enough that she could reach out and touch him if she wanted to. She didn't. But a light breeze lifted off the Ionian Sea and fanned her hair across her face. They both reached for it at the same time, their fingers brushing, and she startled from the jolt of electricity.

'Sebastian...' She heard her voice, heard the plea in it, hadn't realised she'd been going to do any such thing.

'Come on,' he responded, tone gruff. She swallowed past a strange thickness in her throat. 'Let's get this over with.'

It was like being doused in ice-cold water. Whatever flutterings and rushings of her pulse she'd been convinced she felt a moment ago, she now experienced nothing but disbelief that she'd gotten herself into this situation. Every so often, she thought back to the fateful afternoon when the king had presented her with this plan, had begged her to help him. He wanted to bring his daughter and grandson home but couldn't do it without her. She was the only person he trusted to ensure the kingdom would be in good hands. His request alone would have been enough to ensure her compliance, but he'd sweetened the deal with just the right lures. Rosie had found herself agreeing even before she'd contemplated the way Sebastian seemed to have broken all of her previously held thoughts about men and masculinity. He was unlike anyone she'd ever known, and she'd felt that, strongly, from the first moment they'd met.

He hadn't been wrong, when he'd suggested she favoured a more cerebral type.

And while Sebastian was intelligent, he was so much more, and it was the *more* that set her nerves on edge. Rosie liked to be in control of every aspect of her life, but she'd known from the first moment of meeting Sebastian that he would never be controlled by anyone.

He was his own man, running on his own instincts.

She spun her wedding ring on her finger as she walked towards the car. To her surprise, Sebastian strode ahead of her and opened the front passenger door.

He ruined the effect of the chivalrous gesture with a slightly mocking, 'Princess,' as she swept past him and into the seat. She threw him a glare, and would have pulled the door shut, but before she could do any such thing, he reached for the seatbelt and drew it across her, buckling it into place. It was so unexpected. His body was so close to hers, his face just an inch above. A small gasp escaped her before she could stop it, and her eyes widened. He glanced at her, something in his features that made her pulse race.

She could tell that he wanted to mock her. To tease her. To say something condescending. But whatever flames were igniting Rosie's bloodstream were also firing through Sebastian.

'Don't look at me like that,' he muttered. 'Not here.'

'Not here?' she repeated, mainly because she couldn't think of anything else coherent to offer.

'Do not look at me like that, when we are here on my island, completely alone.'

'We're not alone,' she said, thinking of how warm his breath was against her cheek. 'There's your pilot and flight crew.'

'They're not staying.'

'Oh.' Her tongue darted out, tracing a line over her lower lip. She asked the question that had been plaguing her since they touched down. 'Your staff?'

'No.'

'No?'

'Not here.'

'Oh.'

'We're alone.' He lifted his thumb and brushed it over her lower lip. 'And it does not matter to me that you and I don't like one another—if you look at me as though you're imagining me naked, I will make love to you as soon as we get to the house.'

Her eyes widened, her heart speeding up. 'I—'

He dropped his hand from her lips to her breast, his fingers running over her with possessive heat.

'And while I would enjoy that immensely, it's not why we're here.'

'It's not?' she asked, almost petulant sounding, and she could have kicked herself for revealing how much she did want to be ravaged by him.

His lips tilted into a half smile. 'We're getting to know one another, remember?'

Can't we do both? She bit back the question just in time.

'Disappointed?' he asked, moving his hand lower still, over her stomach, towards her thigh. He traced a circle there, eyes latched on hers.

She shook her head a little, but knew he'd seen through her response.

Sure enough, he grinned. 'Are you sure?' His hand moved towards her sex. She drew in a sharp breath as he ruched her skirt up and nudged aside the lace of her thong, so his fingers could glance across her most intimate flesh.

'Sebastian,' she cried out, the touch so welcome and so overwhelming at the same time. 'You can't—the pilots—'

But his body was shielding hers from sight, and besides, the windows were heavily tinted. She groaned then and told herself not to say another word. Not to say anything that might cause him to stop what he was doing.

'God, Sebastian,' she groaned, pressing back into the seat as he moved his finger faster, his body so close, he was invading every single one of her senses: filling her eyes, her nostrils, her soul. She cried out as pleasure built, so hard and fast, wrapping around her, making her nerve endings reverberate and dance with jubilant need until finally the banks of her pleasure burst, and she was saying his name over and over, her eyes filling with stars now, her whole body trembling.

He pulled away from her a little, removing his hand but leaving her skirt ruched at her thighs, so she saw her legs and felt a strange sense of being out of her own body at how unfamiliar and exposed she was.

'I did not see this coming,' he said darkly. 'But it works. We work. And I'm glad about it. There should be some silver lining to this farce of a marriage, shouldn't there?' He leaned down and then pressed a hard, brief kiss to her mouth, a kiss that was also a promise of more to come. Her stomach twisted and her breath burned in her lungs.

A moment later, he was gone, out of her personal space, closing her car door and coming around to the driver's side. He climbed in as though nothing had happened, but an errant glance in his direction showed the clear evidence of his desire for her, his beige trousers doing little to hide the force of his physical response. Heat flushed her cheeks, and she forced her gaze to the windscreen, and the forest beyond them.

The island was beautiful, but not in the ways Rosie might have expected. It was a tribute to the natural world. Everything had been preserved, and as they drove, and Rosie recovered from the orgasm she'd just delighted in, Sebastian enumerated the species that were home to the island. From the bird life to the monkeys to the seals that had a habitat on the western side of the island, in the ancient caves there, he spoke about the place with a passion that had Rosie finding it impossible to look away.

'You come here often?' she guessed, because he seemed to know everything about it.

'I used to.'

'Used to?'

'Before returning to Cavalonia.'

She frowned. 'Is it not part of Cavalonia?'

'No. It's in Italian jurisdiction, despite its proximity to Cavalonia.'

Before she could comment, the forest began to clear, and a house came into view. The most beautiful house Rosie had ever seen, and placed right on the edge of the beach, so the bottom steps were covered in a light film of sand.

'Oh...' She exhaled a small sigh.

The house was large and built in a traditional style of stone, which had been rendered a pale terracotta colour. The roof was red, the doors were a glossy white, and there were terraces on many windows. More greenery was here, though flowers formed a border around a grove of citrus trees, sitting beside what looked to be a potager.

'It's beautiful,' she said.

Sebastian eyed the building and then looked beyond it, his eyes landing on the horizon. Rosie followed his gaze, to the land mass clearly visible, across the expanse of sea. 'Cavalonia?'

He turned to face her, eyes hiding his feelings. 'For a long time, I thought my mother would never be granted access to her home. And so I bought this place. If she couldn't be there, at least she could see it.'

Rosie's heart stammered at his thoughtfulness—at how

kind he had been to the mother he clearly adored. She toyed with her necklace, sliding the pendant from side to side. 'You must have wanted to come to Cavalonia very badly.'

'Not really.'

She glanced at him, raising a brow.

'I was very angry with my grandfather.'

'You're still angry with him,' Rosie said gently.

He turned to face her. 'Wouldn't you be?'

It was a simple—but unnerving—question. Rosie had heard all about the estrangement, from King Renee. She knew that Maria al Morova had been married at a young age and in a lavish, fairytale ceremony that all of Europe had tuned in to watch. According to the king, Maria's husband had been older but doted on her, and his ancient bloodline and experience in government meant their relationship was just what the country needed. But Maria had fallen in love with a visiting American diplomat, and their affair had been in all the scandal sheets across the country.

Renee had begged her to break it off—she had a son to consider—but Maria had been determined. A week later, she'd been exiled and on her way to America, the little boy then pictured clutching her hand now returned to Cavalonia as an angry prince.

'I don't know,' she answered honestly. 'Maybe.'

His lip twisted. 'Are you close to your father, Rosalind?'

She bit down on her lip, eyes clouding. 'That's…complicated.'

Sebastian scanned her face. 'Would you forgive him, if he were to push you out of his life? Is there anything you could do that would cause him to cease seeing you?'

'I don't know,' Rosie answered honestly.

'Yes, you do. It is not how it's supposed to be. A parent

loves their child and advocates for them, no matter what. That, at least, has been my experience.'

'With your mother, but what about your own father?'

Sebastian's eyes narrowed and his face jerked a little, as though she'd hit him. 'What about him?'

'You don't see him, nor speak to him.'

'When my mother left, he told her we were dead to him and left the country. He has been true to his word. At no point in the past twenty-five years has he attempted any communication with me.'

'Then not all parents fight for their children,' she pointed out, but sympathy took the sting out of her words. She reached over and put a hand on his leg. 'I'm sorry about your father. He sounds like a piece of work.'

'I don't remember him,' Sebastian said without emotion, and yet she felt something in the depths of his words, something he was hiding from her, wishing her not to see. 'To all intents and purposes, Mark was my father.'

'He died quite recently?' she prompted, even though she wanted to avoid hurting Sebastian. They were here to get to know one another, and this seemed like something she should understand.

'Almost two years ago.'

'I'm sorry,' she said quietly.

'He was sick and seeing him like that was—' Sebastian's eyes probed hers, as if he might find the word he sought buried in her gaze. 'Difficult. In the end, his death was a relief.'

She flinched a little, though she understood the sentiment. Grieving a mother who lived in a comatose state brought with it a deep understanding of life, death and the grey area in between.

'Mark raised me, taught me how to ride a bike and shoot hoops, how to drive a car, how to use my mind to win just about any argument I want. He taught me to be patient when I was bursting at the seams with excitement about something, he taught me to appreciate things like art and classical music because, he said, they were a link to history and the past, and the best way to understand ourselves and our futures. And he showed me every day of his life that his family—my mother and I—was his reason for living. He was the very best of men—the fact my grandfather couldn't see that just shows how blinkered his vision was.'

A lump had formed in Rosie's throat at this description of his childhood, and yet his criticism of the king made it hard for her to say anything other than, 'We'll have to agree to disagree.'

'You are truly going to keep defending him on this?'

'I don't need to defend his actions,' she demurred.

'And yet you do, constantly.'

She sighed. 'I think his commitment to his country is admirable. I think he's sacrificed a lot, personally, because of his position as king. I think he made hard decisions that cost him dearly, but which he felt were right for the people of Cavalonia.'

'He was wrong,' Sebastian replied flatly.

'The scandal—' Rosie murmured, but Sebastian interrupted her.

'Would have blown over. They always do. Look at Fabrizio's life—he was plagued by scandals and bad behaviour, and yet he was not disinherited.'

'He was the only heir remaining.'

'There was me,' Sebastian contradicted with an intensity to his voice that pulled at Rosie. 'There was my mother.'

Their eyes locked and the air between them sparked with emotional energy, *zap zap zip*.

Rosie bit into her lip again, not sure what to say to that.

Perhaps Sebastian was right, perhaps the king was. 'It's ancient history,' she said, earning a wry half smile from Sebastian.

'That was Mark's point. History is a part of us. You and I are married because of this "ancient history", and now we are cementing that by trying to fall pregnant. Imagine if my mother had been free to stay, to raise me here, for me to grow as the assumed heir.'

His eyes scanned her face, his expression thoughtful. 'Imagine if she'd been here all along, a part of Fabrizio's life. If Mark had been a part of his life, if *I* had been. Would Fabrizio have turned into such a foolhardy, headstrong, risk-taking man?'

Rosie's lips pulled to the side. 'We'll never know.'

'I know.' He pressed his fingers to the centre of his chest. 'I know that my grandfather threw a blade through many, many lives when he chose cruelty towards his own daughter instead of offering understanding.'

She shook her head slowly, wanting to deny that, to argue on the king's behalf. But the more Sebastian spoke, the more she saw some sense in what he was saying. 'I think we're both right,' she said after a pause. 'You think he threw a blade through everyone's lives, well, I suppose he did. But isn't it also true that he did so because he believed it was right for the country?'

Sebastian's lips compressed. 'You cannot honestly believe that.'

'Why not?'

His nostrils flared as he expelled a sharp breath. 'He does not deserve the faith you have in him.'

'Or maybe it's just what he deserves.'

'No.' He reached over, a frown on his face. 'You're far too good for him, and if you are not careful, he will ruin your life as he did my mother's.' His frown deepened. 'Perhaps he already has.'

It was a cryptic comment that hung between them for a second, but when Rosie went to respond, Sebastian turned and pushed out of the car.

Sebastian didn't want to think of Mark. Of the man who'd raised him to be the best version of himself, who he feared he might be letting down by being back here in Cavalonia. Had he thrown his mother to the wolves by returning? Or had he done what Mark would have wanted?

On his deathbed, Mark had spoken of how hard it had been for Maria. He'd intimated that he regretted having been the catalyst for her exile, even though their marriage had been so happy.

And then he'd died, and Sebastian had been abandoned again, floundering in a way he'd thought was far behind him, grief-stricken like he had been as a child. Not rejected this time by choice but abandoned all the same. It had been a salient reminder about the transient nature of connections, about the importance of protecting himself from that kind of loss, and it was a lesson he intended to keep firmly in his sights.

Even if he became a father?

The thought flooded his veins with ice, because to become a parent was to assume an obligation of love, wasn't it? And what then? Risk was inherent in that; risk was everywhere. Sebastian wouldn't allow himself to be weakened by their child. This baby would be a means to an end, just as Rosalind was. It was all about the kingdom, nothing more. But nor would he abandon his baby. Never would he allow them to feel insecure or unwanted. Sebastian would not have the mistakes of the past be repeated—he was not the king, and he was not his father. Mark lived on in Sebastian in a way that had little to do with biology and everything to do with the sheer force of Mark's will, and his desire to mould Sebastian into a man who was better than the king, better than his birth father.

Sebastian could only hope that Mark's faith was not misplaced, that this marriage and potential pregnancy weren't a betrayal of the values Mark had instilled.

But of course, they weren't. If Rosalind didn't comprehend the nature of their marriage, if she secretly harboured a desire for more than he would offer, then he might have seen a problem. But she was as pragmatic about all this as he was, and for that he was very grateful.

CHAPTER SIX

INSIDE, THE HOUSE was every bit as charming as outside, with its high ceilings and wide corridors, and rooms that were generously proportioned and decorated in a manner that was comfortable without being ostentatious. It was not the kind of billionaire bolt hole she would have expected Sebastian al Morova to own, but she liked it all the more for its authenticity.

'There's nothing else on the island?' she asked with a shake of her head, as she stepped onto the deck at the front of the house and looked towards the ocean, then to the mountain behind them.

'There is a lighthouse,' he said, 'on the other side. We can hike to it tomorrow if you're interested.'

Her stomach dropped to her toes. He was really planning to spend the time here *with* her. Getting to know her, per her request.

'I—I like hiking,' she said after a beat.

'Do you get to do much of it?'

'Not since our marriage.'

He glanced at her in that unnerving way of his, as though looking straight inside her.

'I don't get much space from the paparazzi,' she pointed out. 'The palace is my sanctuary.'

'Of course.'

Except, there was more he wasn't saying, more he was thinking, and she wanted to pull at that string and understand him better. Their marriage was a flashpoint though. To discuss it was to discuss its origins, and that led them to the king, which inevitably caused them to argue, and so she steered clear of the conversation.

'Does your mother like it here?'

Sebastian's lips quirked to the side. 'She never actually came.'

'But you bought it for her.'

'From the minute I mentioned the island, and its proximity to Cavalonia, she told me how hard she would find that. To be close enough to see her home, but never travel to it. *I'm better here, my love, where I know I am welcome, even though I do not feel that I belong.*'

Rosie's heart twisted. 'But you were happy in America?'

He eyed Rosie with something like the animosity that had defined almost every single one of their encounters. 'We made do.'

She furrowed her brow. 'You had friends, I imagine?'

'Yes.'

'You sure as heck made yourself a success.'

'But I always knew I wasn't where I should have been. This—' he gestured to the mainland '—is my birthright, and more than that, it is in my soul.'

Rosie blinked away, frowning. When she'd agreed to this marriage, there had been many reasons, but in the back of her mind was the one the king kept hammering her with. *He is not suitable. He doesn't love the country like we do. How can he be trusted?* He'd said it again, when discussing the possibility of Rosie's pregnancy.

But Sebastian spoke like a man who cared very deeply for Cavalonia, who saw it unequivocally as a duty and honour to stand here as crown prince of their country. Or maybe it was pride, she reasoned. Maybe he was just the kind of alpha male who didn't like having what he saw as 'his' taken away from him? Maybe it was to avenge his mother? In any event, he was here, they were married, and it didn't matter how he felt about the country. Rosie was there to make sure he became the best prince, and one day king, that he possibly could be.

'Do you also like to swim?' he asked, turning to face her then, surprising her with the easy, relaxed tone in his voice. As though they hadn't just been discussing Sebastian having been uprooted from his life as a young boy.

She glanced at the beach and realised, for the first time, how warm the day was. Sweat had begun to trickle between her breasts, but she'd been so focused on her conversation with Sebastian that she hadn't even noticed. She nodded once. 'I do laps a few times a week.'

'Lap swimming is fine, but it is not this.' He gestured to the ocean. 'Care for a dip?'

'A dip?' she said, laughing a little, at the unexpected question, then sobering, as Sebastian began to lift his shirt off his head, revealing a tanned, chiselled abdomen that made her mouth go instantly dry. 'I don't have any bathers,' she said huskily.

'Look around you, princess. Who would notice?'

She paled. 'You mean for me to swim naked?'

He stepped out of his trousers, so he was only in a pair of white boxers that left little to the imagination and did wonders for his tan.

'I meant for you to keep your underwear on, but it's your call. Naked is also fine.'

Her mouth opened and closed as she sought for how to respond, but the truth was, she was very hot, and the water looked so inviting. 'I couldn't possibly,' she murmured, with true regret, sounding utterly regal and prim, just as he'd accused her of before this had all begun.

His eyes were laced with sardonic mockery. 'Suit yourself, wife.' He didn't walk away though. Not before he caught her chin with his finger and thumb and tilted her face, his eyes boring into hers. His expression changed, sobered. Gone was any hint of mockery and in its place was something else. Frustration? Impatience? Confusion?

'I didn't want to marry you,' he said after a beat. 'At the time, I thought there would be nothing good in our marriage—it was just a means to an end.' His gaze dropped to her lips before piercing her eyes once more. 'And yet, here we are, and I find I can't stop wanting to kiss you. I didn't expect it.'

Her heart dropped to her toes. 'Me neither,' she said, but even as the words left her lips, she wondered if that was true. Hadn't she found him impossibly desirable from their first meeting? She'd hated the way he'd addressed the king, and she'd felt Sebastian's anger at his situation, and the demands being made by Renee. She'd felt that anger being levelled at her too. But she'd also trembled, in the very core of her being, with awareness of him as a man.

She was not surprised that now, being thrown together like this, sparks were flying. She just knew she had to hold on to some semblance of control. She would not fall in lust— or worse, love—for a man who would never love her back.

'You can kiss me anytime you want,' she said with a challenge in her eyes. 'It doesn't change the fact that this marriage was a means to an end, for both of us.'

'Careful, Princess,' he muttered, moving his mouth closer to hers, so she felt the air hissing from his lips. 'If you tell me I can kiss you anytime I want, I might not stop.'

She lifted her fingers to his shoulders, warm from the sun. 'Why do you think I'd want you to stop?'

His laugh was throaty and raw, and it pushed into her mouth when he kissed her, just as he'd said he would.

Her whole body exploded on a wave of need and suddenly, all thoughts of swimming flew from her mind, as did the whole concept of control.

She knew she should be smarter, wiser, should keep hold of some perspective, but the moment their bodies pressed together, his so warm and strong and nearly naked, was the moment she almost forgot to breathe, let alone think.

His kiss was like the beating of a drum, waking up something inside of her, something that had lain dormant a long time. He'd been right about the kinds of men she'd gone for in the past: men she liked but didn't lust, didn't crave. Men who were no threat to her. She'd avoided anything approaching a flame and had missed out on understanding what fun it was to play with fire. For surely that's what they were doing?

His tongue lashed hers, his kiss an invasion in every way, but a welcome one. It was an invasion that made her toes curl and her breasts tingle. She pushed against him, needing there to be absolutely no space between their bodies, needing to feel every piece of him. She lifted her arms around his neck, her fingers toying with the hair at his nape, as one leg lifted, and her ankle pressed into his calf muscle.

'Sebastian,' she groaned, when he stopped kissing her and dragged his mouth to her throat, his stubble—something she'd once told him, right after they'd married, that he should get rid of to appear more princely—a delight against her sensitive flesh.

He lifted her easily and she wrapped her legs around his waist, his mouth still teasing her as he stepped back inside the house. The walls were thick stone and therefore it was instantly cooler here. Only a few paces inside, he eased her back to standing, his fingers pushing at her silken blouse. Just as he had been in his office a few nights earlier, he was impatient, and a button came loose. He swore, offered her a look close to apology. 'That was unintentional.'

'I don't mind,' she promised huskily. And she didn't. His hunger for her, so appreciable, was an incredible aphrodisiac—as if she needed it. He threw her shirt across the room before unclasping her bra and tossing it away likewise, his breath a rugged sound of relief as he stared at her naked torso, warming her with his gaze, rather than his touch.

'Sebastian,' she said, again, needing him to go back to kissing her, to touching her. Needing him. 'Please.'

'Please kiss you?' he teased, reaching for the waistband of her skirt and pulling her towards him.

She nodded, giving up on playing it cool, on pretending she wasn't burning up with need for him.

'And don't stop?' he muttered, mocking a little.

She nodded.

He pushed at her skirt, sliding it down her hips and taking her underwear with it, so within seconds, she was naked, and even in the throes of desire, it occurred to Rosie that he'd never seen her naked—not fully. She didn't feel self-conscious though, so much as excited, and when he took a single step backwards to allow him to look at her better, something shifted inside of her. He looked as though he had never seen a woman before, or as if he was committing every piece of her to memory. He looked as if she were his, and always would be, and even though she knew that wasn't true—this was just convenient desire because they needed a baby, a means to an end, just like their marriage—it still lit something in the centre of her being.

'You are beautiful,' he said with a shake of his head, as if only just realising it. 'What a gift the king chose for me.'

She ignored the acid in his remark, and she ignored the reference to King Renee, whom she didn't want to think about right now.

'My turn,' she said, her voice thick, gesturing towards his boxer briefs.

His eyes held hers, latched with a hint of cynicism, but he shook his head slowly. 'Not yet.'

'Why not?' She pouted.

'Because when I am naked, I am going to find it impossible not to take you.' She gasped a little. 'And before I do, I want to taste you.'

'What do you mean?' she asked, her mind not computing.

Instead of answering, he knelt before her, one glance at her face showing the amused tilt of his lips before he pressed his mouth to her sex, parting her with his tongue to find her most sensitive cluster of nerves and teasing her there, right where he had in the car with his hands.

She tilted her head back on a long, all-consuming moan, her fingers tangling in his hair, needing to hold on for balance, because the feeling of his tongue brushing her sex was so intimate and overpowering that she wasn't sure she could possibly stay standing. 'God, Sebastian,' she cried out, her body wracked with pleasure. 'Please don't stop,' she said, her knees weak, her whole body awash with flame.

He didn't answer; how could he? His mouth was otherwise engaged, and he took her instructions very seriously—he wasn't going to stop until she exploded, and Rosie could feel that building again, wave after wave of pleasure spreading through her body.

His fingers dug into her buttocks, holding her steady, support she badly needed, and she closed her eyes as desire crested into satisfaction and she was riding the biggest, most incredible tide of her life, the explosion and release of this pleasure flooding her from every angle.

He held her as she came against his mouth, feeling her release, her body wracked with trembles, and then he pulled back, catching her eye and grinning before standing, eyes holding hers.

'And to think, all these months I have thought you too prim to enjoy sex.'

She didn't tell him that up until a few days ago, he'd been right. Her eyes dropped to the floor, heat flooding her cheeks. The self-consciousness she hadn't felt earlier was back now, washing over her. 'I—'

'Don't overthink it,' he challenged, as if he instinctively knew what she was feeling. 'Now it's your turn.'

Her eyes widened as she stared at his nether regions and imagined taking him into her mouth.

'God, not that,' he muttered, then swore under his breath. 'I meant to see me naked. What kind of misogynist do you think I am?'

'Oh.' Relief flooded her veins. 'It's not that I don't want to. I mean, I just don't know... I've never...' She trailed off into nothing, but the look in his eyes when they met hers ignited something else inside of her. Something that had nothing to do with sex. She felt a spark and had to look away, because the intensity of his curiosity was too much to bear.

'I would never ask you to do anything you weren't comfortable with.'

The assurance did something funny to her insides. She had always seen the worst in her husband because of his volatile relationship with the king. It was easy to think him arrogant, rude, dismissive, discourteous and disrespectful, and those beliefs had shaped her whole attitude towards him. But like a crack forming under the pressure of a body of water, she felt something shift inside of her to see this side of him. To realise that he was respectful of women, that he was being—at least in this situation—respectful of her.

And she deserved that, she reminded herself forcibly. For whom she was, but also because of her determination to never be used and mistreated the way her father's women had been.

'Thank you,' she murmured into the throbbing silence.

He shook his head dismissively. 'This is not something you thank someone for, Rosalind. No one should ever pressure you into anything.'

Her chest hurt a little. She realised how much she liked hearing him say her name—her full name, which was unusual, because she'd been Rosie for as long as she could remember to just about everyone.

She took a step towards him then, compelled by an unabated need for him as well as pulled by something almost mystical, a hand at her back, metaphorically, seemed to guide her to him, and the moment their bodies collided, they were kissing once more, a tangle of limbs, fingers brushing flesh, mouths nipping and tasting, desperate need making them move fast. Sebastian lifted Rosie, this time cradling her against his chest and carrying her through the house to a room with a large bed in the centre and a stunning view of the ocean from windows on two sides of the room. She was conscious of the blinding blue beyond them, the line of the horizon where the ocean met the land of Cavalonia and then the sky above, the sun cutting a golden path through the room, lighting up the tiles as if with gold, and then she was conscious only of Sebastian, as he brought his body over hers, kissing her and parting her legs, teasing her with his arousal until she was incandescent with need for him.

He paused though, and on the threshold of entering her, broke away to grab a condom, which he unfurled on his length while staring down at her, his chest moving hard with each ragged breath.

'But we—' She frowned, thinking of the baby they'd discussed.

'Not yet.' He shook his head, and her insides seemed to roll. There was no time to analyse that, because with the protection in place, he was back, and this time, there was no hesitation. The same desperate hunger that had overtaken Rosie had slammed into Sebastian, and he thrust into her hard, with a guttural cry that filled the room. He stayed where he was, very still, filling her completely, then pushed up onto his elbow to stare into her eyes. 'Okay?' he asked, in a solicitous tone she hadn't expected.

She nodded, incapable of speech. The pleasure she felt at being so totally possessed defied explanation or under-standing. She knew only that she could easily become ad-dicted to this feeling, and even in her desire-addled state, she knew she would have to guard against that.

'You're sure?'

'God, yes, Sebastian, I'm sure. Please, just…please…'

He grinned then, and it was the sexiest grin she'd ever seen, enough to turn her blood to lava. She arched her back and he began to move, each shift of his hips changing his position, pleasuring her in new and different ways. Her hands ran over his back, cupped his bottom, held him, and as he moved, he kissed her, his tongue duelling with hers as he dominated her completely. Every sense she possessed was trained on him, aware of him, responding to him until she couldn't think straight, wasn't even conscious of any-thing but the sound of their bodies coming together and her cries filling the room.

Pleasure built and broke over and over again—it was as though he possessed some magical button that guaranteed her completion. She was almost hyperventilating with euphoria before he finally found his own release, his body shuddering with the force of his orgasm, before coming to rest on hers, his weight a welcome, heady sensation on its own.

They lay there for some time, with the light breeze from the ocean brushing over their naked bodies, their breathing fast at first and then slowing, but eventually, Sebastian pushed up onto his elbow and rolled to the side, facing Rosie.

'Well,' he drawled, reaching out a hand and tracing a line around her nipple with indolent possession. 'That was a nice way to start the week.'

A week. She'd almost forgotten that they'd agreed to spend so long together.

And that he'd brought her to this island.

If she'd thought anything, it would have been how on earth they'd spend the time, but she found it hard to be worried about that.

'You were right about me, you know,' she said, tilting her face towards his.

He flicked her nipple, and she gasped, the pleasure like an arrow travelling through her bloodstream. 'About what, in particular?'

'It's not…usually like that for me.'

'Sex?'

Heat stained her cheeks. 'Not that I have a lot of experience,' she explained, not meeting his eyes. 'But in the past, I suppose you could say I had a type, and it's never been predicated on a need to…rip someone's clothes off.'

'Why not?'

But she wasn't willing to discuss that. Her father's affairs were something she'd had to process and make her peace with. She wasn't sure she could adequately explain them to someone like Sebastian anyway, nor that he'd understand why she'd been so badly affected.

'I was just more comfortable with that.'

'With being bored?'

She rolled her eyes. 'I didn't say it was boring.'

'Yes, you did. Just not in so many words.'

She laughed then. 'Are you fishing for compliments, Your Highness? Do you need me to tell you that's the most fun I've ever had in bed?'

'No,' he said with a grin, and her gut lurched; danger sirens blared in the back of her mind, but she wilfully ignored them. Sex was sex, nothing more. 'But a guy doesn't ever get sick of hearing that.'

Rosie's lips pulled to the side, the smirk hiding a strange little dart of pain somewhere in her chest. 'I suppose women tell you how good you are all the time?'

'Is that your way of asking about my relationship history?'

Rosie's eyes widened. Had she been so transparent? 'God, no.' She sat up straight, dislodging his hand from her chest, pulling her long blond hair over one shoulder. 'I'm really not interested in the women you've been with. I'm sure there were a lot.'

He was quiet, and from where she sat, she couldn't see his reaction. Eventually, he responded, his voice deep. 'And does that bother you, wife?'

God. She loved hearing him say 'Rosalind', but hearing 'wife' was somehow even more compelling after what they'd just done. Her heart leapt into her throat, and she felt a stifling need to be alone, to try to understand what was happening.

'Not at all. Just like I'm sure you don't care about the men I was with before you. That's not what we are.'

'True.' His voice rang with non-concern. 'But it's natural to be curious.'

'I'm not curious.'

'Liar,' he laughed, standing, coming around to the side of the bed nearest to Rosie and holding out his hand. 'Come swimming with me.'

She looked longingly towards the water, imagining how delightful it would feel against her skin, how wonderful the sense of relief given the heat of the day. But even though she'd come to the island to get to know him, swimming with him seemed too intimate after what they'd just done. She needed space and the room to re-establish her boundaries, to reinforce her strength and independence before she had to face him again. She just wished her voice hadn't emerged so prim and proper when she'd offered a small shake of her head and said, 'Please, go on without me. I'm not in the mood for swimming.'

CHAPTER SEVEN

ROSIE MANAGED TO avoid him for the better part of the day, so by the time they were reunited in the kitchen that evening, her equilibrium had returned, and she was once again content that she could be married to someone like Sebastian, make love to him as necessary, but still not lose sight of all the reasons she had for avoiding any real reliance on him.

'You cook?' she asked with obvious surprise, as he placed a couple of steaks into a pan.

He eyed her with a look that set her pulse racing far faster than was safe. She ducked her hands beneath the kitchen bench, in case the heartrate monitor on her watch gave her away.

'You're surprised?'

She lifted one shoulder. 'I suppose I am.'

'Why?'

She gestured towards him with a flick of her wrist. 'You just don't seem like the type?'

His expression was faintly mocking, reminding her of the tension that had characterised so much of their marriage. She sat a little straighter.

'I wasn't raised royal,' he reminded her.

'No, but you're still…you.'

He lifted one thick, dark brow. 'Which means I'm incapable of cooking?'

She rolled her eyes. 'You're just so...'

'Yes?' he drawled, turning away from her so he could turn the steaks over, a sizzle and spark demarcating the action, before he turned back to her and braced his palms on the counter, regarding her with an expression that further sped up her pulse.

'You're just not really the domestic type.'

'Cooking is just a part of life. Or rather, it was.'

'You don't cook now?'

'Only occasionally.'

She pressed one elbow into the counter and rested her chin in the palm of her hand, watching as he neatly chopped a potato into cubes. 'Do you enjoy it?'

He pulled another potato out and began to slice it. 'I never thought about it like that. When I was growing up, it was part of what was expected of me.'

'By whom?'

'Mark.' A grin tugged at his lips. 'My mother *was* most definitely raised royal, and besides a few traditional recipes she'd been taught in theory, she couldn't so much as peel this potato.'

Rosie found herself smiling at the recollection.

'So most of the domestic things fell to Mark, when we moved to the States. I was still young, just a kid, but even then, he'd get me a stool so I could reach the counter, hand me a small paring knife and show me how to use it safely. I learned to cook at his side.'

'American meals?'

'Actually, he was obsessed with making Cavalonian food. He knew how much my mother missed it and wanted to please her. He felt a great burden of responsibility, I think, all his life, for having been instrumental in ruining her marriage.'

Rosie considered that. 'It doesn't sound to me as though he ruined her marriage, but rather just offered her a life raft.'

Sebastian's eyes flicked to hers, his expression inscrutable. 'Could it be that you're beginning to see things my way?'

'I see things through the lens of history, and from an outsider's perspective. But you and King Renee have both said she was unhappy, that her husband was considerably older. Plus, he had the temerity to turn his back on his own son, so I'm inclined to think him a pretty cold-hearted person. It's easy to believe their marriage was miserable, and that the fault for that was not your mother's.' She leaned forward a little, as Sebastian tipped the cubed potatoes into a pot of boiling, salted water, then turned back to her. 'If it hadn't been for Mark, she either would have lived a miserable life—and you would have been doomed to share that fate—or she might have left him anyway.'

'Do you think your precious king shares your opinion?'

She compressed her lips, his irritation raising her defensive hackles even when she knew he had every right to feel as he did.

'What sorts of dishes would he make?' she asked, wilfully refusing to be drawn into an argument about the king's thoughts. She was actually enjoying talking to him and didn't want the mood to tank over something that had happened twenty-five years earlier.

Sebastian returned to the chopping board and now turned his hand to spinach, which he'd rinsed earlier. He chopped it roughly, then did the same to several cloves of garlic.

'Stuffed courgettes, rolled eggplants, spiced mince, pita bread and dips, charcoal octopus, all of the desserts—my mother has a phenomenal sweet tooth. As a child, in the palace, she often ate only chocolate crepes for breakfast.'

Rosie laughed, trying to reconcile a little girl who would be able to sweet-talk her way into never-ending desserts with the quiet, slim woman she'd been introduced to at their wedding.

'You've only met her once, haven't you?' Sebastian said, as if reading her mind.

She nodded. 'On our wedding day.'

'And she was not herself then,' he admitted a little uneasily.

'She didn't approve of the marriage?'

'It was more the pressure of being on television, of being back, it was a difficult day for her.'

'Does she know about us?' Rosie asked, wondering why that suddenly mattered so much to her.

'You mean that her father bullied us both into this marriage?'

'I find it hard to imagine anyone bullying you with any success.'

'*Manipulated* is a better word, you're right.'

She sighed softly.

'Yes. She knows our marriage was a requirement of her return. I tried to hide it from her, but she knows her father all too well. She guessed. I didn't want to lie to her.'

'And I suppose she would hardly have believed it to be anything other than an arranged marriage, given how soon after the funeral we were engaged.'

'She knows her father,' he repeated. 'She remembers her own marriage arrangements, and the feeling that she'd climbed onto a juggernaut.'

'Did she try to talk you out of it?' She sat very still, not betraying the strange emotions coursing through her.

'Yes.' He turned his back on her then, so he could add the spinach and garlic to a frying pan on the stove, to which he added white wine and cream then lowered the heat. 'She begged me not to go through with it. With Mark, she'd found true love. She wanted that for me.'

Rosie's heart fell to her feet. 'But you didn't?'

'There are many types of love. I love her—she loves this country. I wanted her to be able to come home.'

'But she loves you too. She probably didn't welcome your sacrifice.'

'It's not exactly a sacrifice,' he said, and her heart began to race in a way she hated. She sucked in a breath, trying to calm her rioting feelings. He wasn't talking about her, and she didn't want him to be. 'I got to come home too, to become crown prince, and one day king. I have dated more women than I can remember, and not once have I been tempted to describe it as "love". If I was going to meet some mystical soulmate, I would have done so by now. My life is fine without that.'

Rosie was conscious of every single cell in her body. Every rush of blood, every breath in and out, every flicker of expression on her face. She felt as though he must be too, as though he must be able to read her self-consciousness, even when she couldn't explain what was at the root of it. She wasn't sure she bought his easy dismissal of the idea of love. He'd dated a lot, that was true, but it seemed unlikely that none of those relationships had led to something more serious. Most people were wired to seek connection; Rosie was not—she'd made herself this way. And Sebastian?

'I suspect,' he drawled, 'the sacrifice has all been on your part.'

She moved her hand from her chin and placed it in her lap, bringing her attention back to their conversation. 'The trade-off was worth it.'

'In what way?' he asked, the question relaxed. But Rosie could hear something in his voice, the persistent question he couldn't make out. Why had she gone along with this? That really bothered him. Well, they were here to get to know one another, and she had no issue with explaining this part of her history to him.

'I always remember a story my father told me, a long time ago, about my mother.'

Sebastian flicked the heat off the steak, then came back to the bench, still and watchful.

'On their second date, when they still barely knew one another, they went to a pizza bar near the university, and sat at a small table on the sidewalk. My father described it as one of the most perfect nights—the stars were shining brightly, a busker down the street sang beautifully, the pizza was delicious, and my mother smelled of sweet almonds. He told me he knew he loved her, even then.'

Sebastian's expression didn't change.

'But towards the end of the night, a tear rolled down my mother's cheek. My father put a hand on hers, and asked her what was wrong? Why was she crying, on such a perfect night?'

Rosie reached for her glass of wine and took a sip.

'She looked across the street and spoke softly. *"No one in Cavalonia should have to live like that, Grieg."* My father followed her gaze and saw a young woman with a little boy, perhaps three or four. Before he could think of what to say, my mother had stood and gone to the pizza bar, where she ordered a large pizza and bought a bottle of water and some cakes too. He watched as she carried the bag of food from the counter, and across the street to where the homeless family was sitting against the wall. On their next date, he found out that she'd gone back to them every day since, taking food, clothes, books for the little boy. She didn't have much money, but she had a heart that was bigger than all of Cavalonia.'

Silence stretched between them, but Rosie didn't feel it. She was in the past, thinking of her mother.

'She was studying to become a human rights lawyer when they met. Her purpose was the improvements of others' lives. I've always wanted to be like her, to make her proud.'

She jerked her gaze back to Sebastian's face, and when she spoke her voice was thickened by emotion. 'Working for the king gave me a chance to help, in some way. I could influence policy and get to know key players in the government. But as princess, I have so much more reach, more power. Some of the things I'm working on will make a huge difference for our people. For many of them, I hope.'

'And that was your trade-off?' he asked, turning away from her and removing the steaks from the pan before using a slotted spoon to lift the potatoes from the water and place them in the same oil. They splattered and he turned the heat back up on high. She watched, mesmerised by his confidence and economy of movement.

'I'm not interested in relationships,' she said. 'So much like you, I didn't find the idea of a pragmatic marriage to be much of a sacrifice at all.'

'You're younger than I am,' he said thoughtfully.

'Yes, and?'

'I've spent more than ten years having relationships, getting to know women—more than enough time to know that I do not want a love match. You, however, are inexperienced.'

Her brows lifted. 'Gee, thanks.'

'It's a statement of fact. You've said as much yourself, many times.'

'I've been engaged,' she pointed out. 'If I wanted a normal marriage, I could have had it.' Though she never intended that marriage to be normal either.

'You were engaged?' he repeated, eyes locking on hers with an intensity that made her blood throb. 'To whom?'

'A man named Robert.'

He scanned her face, frowning a little. 'How come I don't know this?'

She laughed softly. 'Isn't that the point of this week? We know *nothing* about one another, besides the bare minimum. Why should you have known about Robert?'

'Why didn't you marry him?'

'It turns out, we had different ideas about what our marriage would look like.'

'In what way?'

'He wanted me to quit my job,' she murmured.

Sebastian's expression showed clear surprise.

'He had a huge role in an international bank, and thought I'd be an excellent asset to him. In the same ways I helped the king, I think he wanted me to help him. I wasn't interested in dovetailing my professional life to suit his. We broke up.'

'Did you love him?'

'I thought we would be happy together. And I thought he loved me, enough to never hurt me.'

Sebastian's eyes narrowed, and Rosie winced. The statement was too telling, revealed too much. 'You've been hurt before?'

She glanced down at the counter, studying the flecks of white in the marble surface. 'No.'

'Then why should you think he'd hurt you?'

She shook her head. 'It doesn't matter.'

He reached across the bench, his finger pressing lightly to her chin, in that way he had that made it impossible for her to hide. 'You want me to get to know you, but only the parts of you you're happy to share.'

'So?'

'It doesn't work like that.'

'It can work however we want it to.'

'I want you to answer my questions. All of them.'

Imperious. Commanding. Demanding. Effortlessly regal.

Her insides slicked with heat at the tone of his voice, but more than that, at the fact he was willing to fight for this. That he really wanted to understand her and wasn't just paying lip-service to her condition that they really get to know one another.

'And I suppose you'll do the same? You'll answer any question I might have?'

'That would be fair,' he said with a nod of his head.

'Which isn't exactly an agreement.'

'Your penchant for precision is fascinating.'

'Perhaps it's that I don't really trust you?'

'And why is that?' he asked, moving around the counter, suddenly standing right beside her, so big and huge, his presence as well as his physicality. 'Could it be that my dear grandfather has tainted your opinion of me?'

'Don't forget, I've spent five months married to you and the only interactions we've had have been openly hostile. Neither of us has made the effort to be civilised with the other, until now.'

'Is that what we're being?' he asked, a wry smile on his handsome face. 'I don't feel civilised, if I'm honest. Right now, I feel about as uncivilised as ever before.' His hands dropped to her thighs, and she gasped. 'Does that bother you?'

She stared up at him, her pulse a torrent, and gave in to the instincts that were running rampant inside of her. Slowly, she shook her head. 'I think you're feeling exactly as I am.'

'Let's see about that,' he muttered, and a moment later, he'd scooped her up and lifted her over one shoulder, his legs moving with strong command to the bedroom they'd occupied earlier, and Rosie had never been so glad to see a bed in her life.

* * *

She was softer than silk, sweeter than molasses. He kissed her until he could hardly breathe, until his body and senses were filled with her. Knowing she was showering just down the hall, while he started dinner, and not joining her, not touching her, had required monumental discipline.

This trip was about convincing her that she could trust him, that having a baby together would work. He needed this pregnancy to ensure his place on the throne. Without it, he knew he was vulnerable to civil unrest, that his grandfather could pull the rug out from under him at any point, and pass the throne to a distant cousin, just as he'd threatened when Sebastian had questioned the need for marriage to Rosalind.

This trip was supposed to be about him seducing her, and instead, alone with his wife on this serene island, his need for her was robbing him of all common sense. All he could think about was her beautiful body, and how desperate he was to bury himself inside of her whenever he could.

And? You've been celibate almost six months. No wonder you're as horny as a schoolboy, his brain pointed out, reassuring him when he needed it most.

Sebastian had been single a long time, but never really alone. His life in New York had been filled with beautiful, glamorous women, his bed never empty unless he chose that. This had been the longest stint of celibacy since he'd lost his virginity. He'd have probably wanted to sleep with whichever woman ended up alone with him, given the circumstances.

He reassured himself with that as he entered his wife, grabbing hold of the certainty that this was nothing special. She was nothing special to him. This was still just an inconveniently arranged marriage, and the baby he intended for them to conceive, if she agreed to it, had one purpose, and one purpose only: to cement his place on the throne.

But pleasure was wrapping around him, and every cry she uttered, every time she sighed his name, drove all other women from his mind, and made it hard for him to think of anyone he'd ever slept with before. It was as if they'd all just been rehearsals for this.

He groaned as he buried his head in the curve of her neck and thought only of the physical perfection of this, only of the act of two hungry bodies coming together once more. All the rest was immaterial: they'd made their deal, they knew the terms. They were both safe from any complications—because this was a marriage born of negotiation, not need, and when this week was over, he would go back to the comfortable distance he'd enjoyed from his wife, and these wild, overwhelming moments of desire would seem almost like a dream.

Rosie thought she was dreaming. Or flying. Or falling. She couldn't tell. She was floating though, nowhere near earth, the rushing of her pulse echoed by the pounding of waves against the shore, beyond the open windows of Sebastian's bedroom. Pleasure washed through her, all the way to her toes and fingertips.

She stretched languidly beneath him, feeling his body shift, and smiled to herself at the silver lining of their marriage. To think, she'd initially wanted to avoid sleeping with him altogether. What she would have missed out on, if she'd stuck to her guns! For Rosie had held no conception that sex could be like this; she'd simply had no idea.

The swirling contentment wrapping around her meant that at first, she didn't hear it. It was Sebastian pulling away from her at speed, stepping off the bed, that had her sitting up and recognising the high-pitched wail of something.

A smoke alarm!

Dinner!

She grimaced as she reached for a sheet and wrapped it around herself toga style and walked as quickly as she could back to the kitchen, to see plumes of smoke emanating from the stovetop. Sebastian, naked and spectacular, stood with one frying pan tilted over the rubbish bin and coughed a little.

'The good news is the steaks are fine.' He glanced at her with a slightly sheepish expression then indicated the charred pan. 'The bad news is, we'll be eating them on their own.'

She waved a hand through the air. 'Vegetables are over-rated,' she lied, thinking with remorse of the perfectly crispy golden potatoes he'd been frying. 'Let's have sandwiches instead.'

While he cleaned up the wasteland of pots and pans and opened all of the windows to let the smoky air escape, Rosie removed lettuce, tomato, onion, cheese and mayonnaise from the fridge and began to prepare two steak sandwiches on ciabatta.

'Come on,' he said, when she sliced through both sandwiches. 'Let's eat on the terrace. The house stinks.'

She grinned as she placed the sandwiches on two plates.

'Something funny?'

'I was just thinking, that yeah, it does stink. But it was kind of worth it.'

He arched a brow. 'Just kind of?'

'Okay, really worth it,' she said on a laugh.

'Better.' And then, he surprised her by brushing his lips over her brow. 'And I completely agree.'

CHAPTER EIGHT

THERE WERE MANY things she loved about the island, but one in particular was impossible to ignore. It hit her between the eyes at every turn.

Here, she was free.

Truly free in a way she wasn't sure she'd ever been, and especially not since marrying Sebastian.

She stopped walking and stood, arms outstretched, face tilted to the sunshine, a smile on her face as she felt every sense burst to life. The sun was warm, the breeze cool, the water beneath them pristine as it continued its predictable, reassuring roll towards the crystalline coastline. In the distance, their beloved Cavalonia was a familiar landmass with buildings huddled to the edge.

'Do you need a break?'

Sebastian's deep voice broke through her silent reverie. She blinked open her eyes and fixed him with her gaze, shaking her head. 'I don't *need* a break. I just wanted to take one to enjoy this.'

He looked around, as if to understand what she was talking about.

She let out an exasperated laugh. 'It's just so beautiful. And do you know what else?'

'Surprise me.'

'No paparazzi,' she pointed out. 'It doesn't matter that I'm wearing yoga pants and a loose top.'

'Or that you've got mud on your cheek?' he asked with a teasing tone.

She lifted a hand to her face and dashed at it. 'Or that my hair is messy from where I got into a fight with a branch and the branch won.'

'The path needs maintenance,' he said, eyes lifting to her head, frowning.

'The path is perfect. It's all perfect.'

He looked around then, and now she knew he wasn't just trying to see it from her perspective, he really was.

'I suppose I've always looked beyond the island, rather than at it,' he said. 'Most of my memories of visiting this place are not good ones.'

'No?'

They began to walk once more, the climb to the top of the hill gruelling in a way Rosie found pleasant.

'I have spent countless nights on that deck, looking towards Cavalonia, and hating. Hating my grandfather, my father, even the country and people,' he admitted, 'though that was probably childish.'

She glanced towards the archipelago. 'You hated me,' she pointed out thoughtfully.

'Disliked,' he reminded her.

'Past tense?'

He turned to face her, scanning her features thoughtfully. 'It's hard to say now, isn't it?'

She cleared her throat and glanced away, something about the depth of his perceptiveness unnerving. 'Were you tempted to sell the place?'

'Why?'

'Well, you bought it for your mother, and she didn't want

to come here. It brought you little pleasure when you visited. Why keep it?'

'Hatred can be very motivating.'

She considered that, but it was hard for a heart like Rosie's, built in exactly the same good-and-kind way as her mother's had been, to comprehend the sentiment. 'In what way?'

He made a scoffing sound. 'You really cannot imagine how much it meant to me, to prove myself to the king? To my father? Both men cut me from their lives, as though I was nothing. As though I was worthless. Do you not think my success, professionally, was something I achieved because I wanted to prove them wrong? Because I hated, with every single cell of my DNA?'

Her voice faltered a little, the vehemence in his making it hard to think straight. 'I think,' she said, choosing her words carefully, 'you would always have been a success.' And to her surprise—and his—she reached down and weaved their fingers together, the contact sending awareness zipping through her veins. She squeezed his hand and then dropped it.

But a moment later, Sebastian reached for it once more, holding on as they walked. 'You sound like my mother.'

She pulled a face and he laughed. Conversation closed. But something in his words stuck with her, and as they travelled across the island on foot, it occurred to her that the man she married really did have a darkness within him. She wondered if there was nothing he would stop at to achieve his aims? And his aims had centred, for a very long time, on reclaiming what he saw as his, what had been taken from him: the right to rule Cavalonia.

'I don't want to disturb them,' she said, nonetheless stepping dangerously close to the edge of the cave and crouching down, gripping the rocks so she could balance carefully and see beneath them.

'You won't. They're sunning themselves and wouldn't care if twenty Rosalinds came to spy.'

'They're beautiful,' she said, honestly.

'No, they're not,' he laughed gruffly. 'They're quite possibly some of the ugliest marine animals to exist, but they're endangered, and harmless, and this is their home.'

She threw him an exasperated look. 'How can you call them ugly?' She pointed to one seal, out on a more distant rock, who was almost glaring at the others. 'Look, that one even reminds me of someone,' she said, tapping a finger exaggeratedly to her chin. 'Dark hair, soulful eyes, brooding expression...'

'Careful, wife. I will find ways to make you pay for that.'

She laughed with delight, and he ignored the strange tightening in his chest. He was playing a part, that was all. Making her relax to see that they could make co-parenthood work. He was just doing it so well that sometimes even he forgot his main priority was ensuring his place on the throne.

'Soulful eyes?' he muttered, as she stood, dusting her hands on the front of her pants and coming to stand with him. 'Really?'

'Sure. When you're not staring daggers at me, I'd say they're very soulful.'

'Is that what I do?'

'All the time.' She lifted her hand and cupped his cheek; their height difference meant she had to stand on the tips of her toes and her breasts crushed against his chest. Suddenly, he regretted the impulse to suggest this hike. He wanted to be home with her. Then again, what did four walls and a mattress matter? This island was private; she was his wife. Anticipation began to tighten in his body. 'At least, you used to.'

His gut churned. He didn't like her use of the past tense. Rather, he didn't like the supposition that anything between them had fundamentally changed.

And yet it had.

When they returned to Cavalonia, he hoped it would be with her agreement to try for a baby, and he hoped that was something they'd be able to achieve, and do together, without the animosity they'd shared for so long impacting the baby's life. But this was not the beginning of a relationship. He needed her to understand that, even as he knew he couldn't say anything that would jeopardise this tenuous peace they'd forged. He simply had to trust his ability to manage things as required. He didn't want to hurt Rosalind. When they were back in Cavalonia, he'd work out how to establish the necessary boundaries to create the kind of relationship with which he was comfortable, and he would do so delicately, respecting whatever she might want at that point.

Satisfied that he could manage this, and that his intentions were better than at times he suspected, he wrapped his arms around her waist and held her to his chest.

'Want to swim?'

She glanced towards the water, her body beaded in a fine covering of perspiration. 'Yes,' she agreed without hesitation. 'I'd like that.'

The water was even better than she'd hoped. Having walked all morning, her body was sore and her skin over-warm. She sank into the sea gratefully, flipping onto her back and spreading her arms and legs like a starfish, floating and staring up at the sky. She could hear Sebastian near her, the sound of his feet underwater causing little ripples that vibrated all around.

They were not so deep that he couldn't stand, and she wasn't at all surprised when his fingers curved around her ankles and drew her to his waist, wrapping her legs around him easily. She smiled at the feeling of nearness, of his proximity to her; she simply smiled because she was happy.

His hand came around her spine, lifting her from the water, and then he kissed her, the taste of the ocean mingling with the now-familiar rush of adrenaline that filled her body and mouth when they came together.

She wasn't sure she'd ever grow tired of this, and the prospect of trying for a baby was now something she relished.

Except—

Again, she remembered the way he'd spoken of his hatred, and how it had fuelled him, and she shivered despite the sensual warmth flooding her, because it was a darkness so totally unfamiliar to her, so troubling for how easily he'd allowed it to motivate him.

His hand ran down her spine, and slipped inside the elastic of her underpants, making it hard to hold on to that thought. She would wade through her perceptions another time, not now. Now was for this, for pleasure, for enjoyment. He spun her around as he kissed her, and dipped them lower into the water, so they were buried to their necks, his touch running over her. Here in the ocean, beneath the surface, there was a weightlessness to the experience and yet somehow, every graze of his skin against hers seemed hyper-charged. Or perhaps it was that she was hypersensitive? When he squeezed her nipples, she cried out in agony and ecstasy, the delirious pleasure-pain almost impossible to bear, but it was quickly overwhelmed by sheer delight as he moved his hand between her legs and found the piece of her that seemed to guarantee, always, pleasure, when he was mastering her.

His name was an incantation, and surrounded by the ocean, bathed in sunlight and watched by the forest of this ancient land, it seemed to take on an almost primeval magic. It was as though every time she said his name, something stirred in the bones of this place, something sacred and special, something that forged a new part of her, a strength, an understanding, a need she accepted now only Sebastian could answer.

It was enough to terrify her, but not then. Then, she simply surrendered to it, but in the back of her mind, she knew she was moving dangerously close to experiencing what her father had invoked in the women he'd used to forget his grief, the women she'd always promised herself she'd never be like.

But Sebastian wasn't using her. No more than she was using him.

They'd both been honest about what they wanted; there was no harm here. They were getting to know one another, and if doing so resulted in a mutual need, then so what? They'd cross that bridge when they got to it. Maybe they'd even cross it together, she thought, as pleasure wrapped around her and wouldn't let go, tipping her over the edge of the abyss on a loud cry of release, torn from the very centre of her soul.

The first night on the island there'd been smoke, and now there was fire, putting Rosie in mind of that old idiom. She drew her knees to her chest and rested her cheek against them, watching as Sebastian stoked the bonfire, before stalking back to her. The day had been warm, and the night was sultry, yet there was a breeze that made the fire not completely unpleasant. If anything, this island off the coast of Cavalonia felt almost tropical.

She sighed before she could stop herself, contentment shifting through her. 'I didn't realise how badly I needed a holiday,' she said, as Sebastian sat beside her. 'I don't remember the last time I really just let go like this. In fact, I don't think I've looked at my phone since we got here.' The thought had her sitting up straight, shocked that she could have been so carefree. Her phone was, ordinarily, her lifeline. It tethered her to the palace, the king, her job, her world—her mother, and even her father.

'Relax,' he drawled, partially misunderstanding her panic response. 'I have a phone. If his precious highness needed you for anything, I'm sure one of his minions would have reached out to me.'

She studied him thoughtfully. 'You hate his minions too?'

His smile was tight-lipped. 'We were talking about you.' He lifted a hand and curved her hair behind her ear. 'Why so long between holidays?'

She let him get away with the change of subject. 'For a long time, I was studying,' she said. 'And in the term breaks, I'd work. I was lucky enough to get an internship at the palace—'

'Working for the king?' he interrupted.

'No, initially I was working for an advisor to Fabrizio,' she corrected. 'But someone recognised my interest in policy and shuffled me into the king's department, as a government liaison at first.'

'You must have been very young to have such a position?'

'Yes, I was. I felt it. But at the same time, I had good instincts for it. That probably sounds incredibly immodest—'

'I don't have time nor interest in false modesty. I don't find it hard to believe you were excellent in this role.'

'Really?' This kind of pleasure—a reaction to his instant praise—was hard to ignore. 'Why?'

'Now who's fishing for compliments?'

She flushed to the roots of her hair.

'You're naturally diplomatic, thoughtful, measured, intelligent and well-informed. But stubborn too. I think you'd have whatever conversation you needed to have, for as long as it took to get your opponent to see things your way.'

She laughed softly at his characterisation. 'I am stubborn,' she agreed, 'but only with things I care about.'

'And you felt your agenda was in sync with the king's?'

'It was never my agenda,' she corrected gently. 'But always his.'

'You haven't shaped his choices in recent years? I read an article the other day about an uptick in palace-driven philanthropy. Tell me your fingerprints aren't on those initiatives?'

She bit into her lip. 'Everything is his decision.'

'But you influence him.'

'We talk a lot. Most of the time, he sees my perspective on things.'

'Or you make him see it,' Sebastian said, and she wondered at the tone in his voice. Jealousy? Irritation? She didn't know, but she didn't like the direction their conversation had taken.

'Did you know my uncle well?'

Sadness washed over her. 'I knew him,' she said, cautious for a reason she couldn't fathom.

'What was he like?'

She tilted her face towards Sebastian. 'When I first started working for the king, he was simply...carefree. Your grandfather has an incredible work ethic. He wakes with the sun, reads briefs, reports, writes his own letters, takes meetings all day, opens his doors to the public every week to hear their matters of concern, and then works into the evening, usually on the phone to foreign diplomats, securing relationships. He's always working. I know he'd hoped your uncle would start taking some of the load. Fabrizio was thirty-six when he died, and thirty-two when I first met him.'

'Old enough to take an active role,' Sebastian agreed.

'He wasn't interested in much, beyond the ceremonial events.'

'He liked to dress up,' Sebastian responded with disapproval, and Rosie couldn't entirely disagree.

'He liked the pomp of his position,' she said, nodding.

'But left the real work to others.'

'I've often wondered—' she said, and then broke off, because she'd been about to admit to this man something she'd never said to another soul, something that smacked of disloyalty to the king. And Sebastian was no fan of the older man. Far be it from Rosie to give him more grist for the mill.

'What have you wondered, *cara*?'

She glanced at him, the word striking something in her chest. She dismissed it; he'd just tossed a term of endearment into conversation as people often did. It meant nothing. But it succeeded in throwing her enough off her game to answer honestly, even when she knew she shouldn't discuss this.

'I only saw them together a handful of times, not often enough to judge, I'm sure.'

'But' he prompted.

She grimaced. 'Your grandfather could be very short with Fabrizio. Condescending, at times. I couldn't understand it. With me, he has always been so patient and considerate. I have never once had him lose his temper towards me. But with Fabrizio, he could be almost cold. And I sometimes wondered if Fabrizio hadn't simply decided to give up. To give up on being the man the king needed him to be, to give up on trying to impress him. Instead, he settled for doing the bare minimum, coasted through life, and eventually, to his death.'

Sebastian made a grunting noise that was hard to interpret, and they sat together in a heavy silence, with only the flickering of flames chattering in the background.

Eventually, though, Sebastian spoke. 'And yet, still you defend him.'

'As I said, to me…' She sighed. 'It wasn't my place to get involved in his relationship with his son. I will say that he loved him very much. When Fabrizio died, it was as though a part of the king had died too.' A tear rolled down her cheek; she dashed it away. 'I sat with him all night—I couldn't bear to leave him. He was bereft, Sebastian. Bereft. And it wasn't just about Fabrizio, but your mother too, and his wife. He kept saying their names, over and over again. A family of four, reduced to one man—'

'Except that's not true,' Sebastian ground out, standing with obvious frustration and stalking towards the fire. His face and body were cast into shadow and light by the amber glow. 'He still has a daughter, he has a grandson. We are here, in Cavalonia and even now, he makes no effort at amends. If he was as distraught as you say, then how can he have failed to reach out? Even when Fabrizio died, it was me who approached him with a way to come home. Would he have just left us there, in America, despite this purported grief?'

'I don't know,' she answered honestly, and at the look on

Sebastian's face, she stirred, standing and walking slowly towards him. The sand was cool underfoot, in contrast to the warmth thrown by the fire. 'I respect the king a great deal, but he's not perfect. I suppose where his emotions are involved, he might be far from it.'

Sebastian's nostrils flared and in the light of the fire, he looked quite ferocious. '*Basta*. Enough. We cannot talk about him. You are like a broken record, no matter what evidence contradicts your feelings on the matter. You refuse to see him as he truly is, and I refuse to accept that. This is not one of those situations in which you will eventually convince me to see things your way.'

She startled at his anger, took a step backwards and Sebastian closed his eyes on another heavy breath.

'I wasn't trying to—' she said, softly.

'Weren't you?'

She bit down into her lip and looked across at him. Frustration warred with sadness, and also resignation. 'Fine.' She threw her hands in the air. 'Have it your way. Go on hating him, Sebastian. Go on hating him, even when that hatred is eating you alive. Who knows, maybe you'll make another ten billion by the time you're forty. Hate, hate, hate even when it's destroying you.'

'Do I look destroyed?' he demanded and damn it if her eyes didn't devour him at the invitation he issued. Even when anger was chewing through her, there was also, always, lust.

She ground her teeth. 'You look…' But what could she say? 'I don't care,' she muttered. 'If you don't want us to talk about him, then stop bringing the king up.'

'Did I?'

She frowned. She couldn't remember how the conversation had begun, in truth. 'That's the problem,' she replied with obvious frustration. 'All roads lead back to him. He's too much a part of you, your history, your life, and he's a huge part of me, my life, my work. You ask me about myself, and more likely than not, my answer's going to involve him in some way. I'm not close to my father. I barely see him. Over the last few years, the king has become—has come to mean—so much more to me than I can explain. I love him, Sebastian. Faults or not, he's like family to me.'

Sebastian turned away from her, his face angled so she could see the stern set of his features in profile.

'Then I feel truly sorry for you. If there's one thing I know for certain, it's that the king is the last man on earth who deserves anything like love—from you, or anyone else.'

CHAPTER NINE

HE WAITED UNTIL the last of the flames had died down, turning the heap of timber into a glowing pile that some-how perfectly matched the smouldering in his gut. Sure, it was a safety concern, but with the tide inching forwards, it wouldn't be long before the wreckage of their bonfire would be swallowed up by the ocean. Staying out here on the beach had more to do with avoidance, and Sebastian hated that. He'd never been someone to walk away from a problem—or an argument. In fact, he rarely argued.

His eyes lingered on a large piece of driftwood they'd added to the pile that was now a ferocious orange, like a child might draw a dragon's breath, and rubbed a hand over the back of his neck. That was the problem.

Far from being the prim little wallflower ice princess he'd expected, he'd discovered that his wife had a pulse after all. And she managed to get under his skin every time they were together—either by making him need her to the point of distraction, or by defending the king to him, in a manner that was unfailingly going to raise his hackles. So they argued.

When had Sebastian ever argued with a woman he'd been sleeping with?

Or anyone?

In business, he was cold. Cold detachment was the way

he succeeded. Emotion was the death knell to clarity and Sebastian valued clear thinking above all else. Even his interactions with the king had been calm, despite Sebastian's long-held anger towards the other man. He'd still been able to separate those feelings out and deliver his assessment of their situation without emotions weakening him.

Why couldn't he do that with Rosalind? What was it about her that managed to needle him to the point of breaking down the rigid reinforcements he usually kept around anything approaching a feeling?

Was it just their proximity?

The island had been his idea—a way to fast-track her requirement that they 'get to know one another' and bring her to a decision about this pregnancy. He'd thought it would be like any of his business negotiations—that he could keep his eye on the prize and manage the situation to achieve his outcome. Hell, he'd done it enough times in the professional world. He was nothing if not determined.

But none of the people he'd negotiated with in the past had been anything like Rosalind.

Had he been foolish to think he could put his wife's demands in the same box as a corporate negotiation? To put *her* in the same box as he might a professional adversary? While he was a titan of the business world, he knew nothing about personal relationships—not beyond the physical—and what Rosalind was trying to do was build a relationship of sorts with him.

It was everything he'd been running from his whole adult life.

Relating with someone. Getting to know them. Playing the long game. Being in one another's lives, no matter what. Just the idea of that made Sebastian's throat feel as though it was constricting; he could hardly breathe. The idea of letting this happen with Rosalind—of coming to enjoy spending time with her, to even like sparring with her—turned his blood cold.

Sebastian jerked to standing, striding towards the embers with his hands thrust deep into his pockets. As he'd expected, the water had begun to lap the far side of what had been their bonfire, turning orange to black with a frothy whisper. The moon hit the dark ocean, highlighting the peaks of the waves. His eyes chased the milky shadow for a moment, and then he sighed, admitting to himself that he was as out of his depth as if he'd chased that moonlight all the way out into the middle of the Ionian Sea.

But what could he do?

Quit?

Admit defeat and leave?

Admit he was afraid of what this could be, if he let it, and run far away?

Every cell in his body fought against that. He was not a quitter, and he'd never wanted—or needed—anything as much as he did this baby.

He didn't trust the king, and he didn't know if he trusted his wife. At least, he didn't trust her not to fall in with whatever the king demanded, no matter what she personally thought. Her loyalty to the old man was akin to brainwashing—she might want to build a relationship with Sebastian, but it would never withstand her unwavering faith in the king, when the king was singlehandedly responsible for having destroyed Maria's life, and removing Sebastian from the country that ran in his blood.

And yet despite his love for Cavalonia and his certainty that ruling it was his birthright, his position remained tenuous. Marriage to Rosalind had engendered some goodwill from the people, but he needed this baby to guarantee his position—and to know that his child would enjoy their birthright. When he was king, Sebastian would ensure it was written into legislation: no man would ever be able to take such rights away from what should be theirs indisputably.

There was very little choice then but to stick to his plan.

She'd wanted them to get to know each other, and they were. Only he'd never intended to reveal so much about himself to her. Seduction, yes. But why did it bother him so much that she didn't understand why he hated his grandfather? Why did he want to explain how awful it had been, as a young boy, to feel as though he'd done something wrong, that his grandfather and father had refused to see him again? Why couldn't she understand how that had shaped him?

Why did he need her to? Why did he want her to not only understand him but also to approve of him?

Sebastian had never wanted to bare his soul to a woman he'd been sleeping with. He hadn't needed anyone else to agree with him that he'd been treated badly. So, why did he want Rosie to be on his side, in his corner?

It drove him wild; he had to get a grip. There was no advantage in fighting with Rosalind, and she would never see things his way. She had married him at the king's behest—she was loyal to him, not Sebastian. And so what? He didn't need her. He didn't need anyone.

But fighting was to be avoided, for the simple reason it might reduce the likelihood of Rosalind agreeing to fall pregnant with his heir. It was up to Sebastian to keep a level head from now on, to avoid conversations that were incendiary, and he could think of one simple way to do that: he would ask about Rosalind. He would ask all the questions, direct the conversation, and at the first sign of her wanting to discuss the king, he'd divert their discussion elsewhere.

He would regain control of this situation and any wayward thoughts and wants that might creep in...

With renewed determination, he took a few paces back towards the house, scooped up the blanket they'd been sitting on and set his sights on what he hoped to achieve this week. A baby was all that mattered.

Knots had formed in Rosie's stomach overnight. She'd slept badly, frustrated by their argument, replaying it, wondering what she could do to fix things between the king and his grandson, wondering if it was her place, and what good could come from her trying?

But she *had to* try.

Because she loved the king and she... Rosie frowned. She, what? She didn't love Sebastian. Far from it! But she hated to see anyone in the kind of turmoil he was clearly in, and over something that had happened so long ago.

In the early light of the new day, she pushed out of bed, ignoring the pang in her chest at the other side of the bed, which was empty—they'd shared his room the night before, but Rosie hadn't felt right presuming to go to sleep there.

Was it really the case that this family rift was ancient history? It was easy for Rosie to say that, given that the argument had happened so long ago. But hadn't it kept happening? With Maria in exile, and Sebastian separated from the country he'd only known as a young boy? Hadn't it kept happening every day he felt estranged from his culture, his people, saw his mother grieving, felt her pain at the rejection from her own father?

She hadn't been prepared to see this side of him, to see beyond the veil of his arrogance to what motivated it. The ruthless need to succeed in all things was clearly motivated by the pain he'd endured. How could she know that, as she did now, and not feel differently about him?

Rosie toyed with her fingers, frustrated in a way she couldn't explain, and padded softly out of the bedroom in search of a cup of coffee. In the kitchen, she flicked on only the small light in the range hood, not wanting to wake Sebastian, and set about making a coffee as quietly as she could.

So it wasn't as simple as relegating their argument to the past.

Even the king, she was sure, had felt the echoes of his decision, long past having made it. Once he'd even called Rosie 'Maria', then closed his eyes as if it was the worst thing he could have said. She didn't look at all like the former princess, which just showed how much Maria had been on the king's mind, even then.

Why couldn't they work out a way past this?

They'd lost so much time because of those decisions, but now Maria and Sebastian were back, and there was the opportunity to come together once more as a real family. To start the healing process, before it was too late.

Stricken, she glanced out of the window at the exact moment the front door quietly creaked open and she gripped her coffee cup with both hands, her heart in her throat. An intruder? On his private island?

Well, it might have been private, but it was surrounded by water and last she'd checked, boats could go just about anywhere they wanted. Could someone have made their way to his home?

With her pulse racing, she silently placed down her mug and grabbed the nearest thing she could find—a pepper grinder—and tiptoed out of the kitchen, her back to the wall as she crept closer and closer to the front door. And bumped headfirst—or rather was bumped into by—a big, broad, sweaty, practically naked body.

And screamed, her eyes shut—so much for defending them with a pepper grinder.

'*Cara, cara*, stop, it's okay.'

Sebastian's voice flooded her body, and the relief was immediate, if somewhat short-lived. She opened her eyes and stared up at him, mouth dry. 'I thought you were still asleep. I thought, I heard the door, and I thought—' She closed her eyes again. 'It's you.'

'Yes, it's me,' he responded, one side of his lips quirking upwards. 'It's just me.'

But Sebastian could never be 'just' anything, she admitted to herself, all too aware of his state of undress.

'You're not wearing anything.'

'I'm wearing something.'

'Not anything much,' she amended.

'I've been for a run.'

'At this hour?'

'I always wake early.'

'Of course you do.'

'What does that mean?'

Her voice was still trembling. 'Just that you're not someone I can imagine sleeping in. Or relaxing.'

'Haven't we been relaxing, these last few days?'

She stared up at him, frowning. They'd been spending time together on a secluded island, but Rosie would have described it as the exact opposite of relaxing. With Sebastian, there was an energy that kept her constantly on guard. She felt everything tighten inside of her, shaking her head a little. 'I don't know.'

'No,' he agreed, even though she hadn't exactly explained what she was thinking. 'No one can reach the island, Rosalind. You are safe here.' He caught her chin, lifting her face towards his. 'Do you think I would ever expose you to danger?'

Her heart soared at that question, at the implicit promise of protection, and of something else that might underpin it—that he cared about her. But no one cared about her, really. No one but the king. Even her father had found Rosie too difficult to spend time with as she'd grown older, because of how similar to her mother she was. He looked at Rosie and saw Juliet, and his grief threatened to destroy them both.

But Sebastian didn't care about Rosie. Her safety had to do with her position in the royal family, his obligation to her—on paper at least—as a husband, and his need for a quickly delivered heir.

'How do you know?' she asked, merely because she felt she had to say something, while her mind was spinning in a thousand different directions.

'Because I have made it safe.'

'How?'

'There are patrol boats out there,' he said, nodding. 'Watching the perimeter.'

Her eyes widened. 'Boats that could see us? That could have seen us in the water the other day?'

'No. They are my private staff, not the Cavalonian army. I have trusted this team for a long time.'

Her heart began to settle.

'On top of that, the house has heavy security surrounding it. Any unexpected activity immediately sets off an alarm.'

She shivered. Had he done that for her?

As if reading her thoughts, he said, 'Whenever I am on the island, it is monitored. Even before I was a prince, I held the kind of net worth that might make me a target. It seemed a sensible precaution to take. Now it is doubly so.'

'Yes,' she said, feeling the pepper grinder in her hand, running her fingertips over the smoothness.

'Though I'm glad to see you armed yourself for potential danger,' he drawled. 'And even more glad that you didn't use it against me.'

Her lips twisted in a self-deprecating grimace. 'It's just a pepper grinder. I doubt it would have inflicted much damage.'

'It's heavy and easy to wield. You did well.'

Her stomach swooped at the casually delivered praise. They were standing so close together, she could feel his warmth and solid body and all of her was on fire with how much she responded to him.

She swallowed past a throat that was thick, and turned to look back down the corridor, towards the kitchen. 'I just made a pot of coffee, if you want one?'

He lifted his hand as though he couldn't help himself, his fingers curving around her cheek, so her eyes fluttered shut; the sensations were too overwhelming to add sight into the mix.

'Sure,' he said, but his thumb swiped across her lower lip and Rosie's insides tightened with a sparkling of desire that threatened to burn her from the inside out. 'But I might take a shower first.'

His thumb lingered in the centre of her lip. She resisted the urge—but only just—to lightly bite down on it.

'Care to join me?'

Water rained over them, plastering Rosie's fine gold hair to her face—making her look somehow even more beautiful, highlighting how fine her features were. She reminded him of a mythical creature, one of the fairies he remembered his mother telling him about, that as a girl she'd believed existed in the forests to the east of the country.

He found it impossible not to touch her. Being in the shower together, covered in droplets, her body was so tempting, and so close. His fingers traced lines over her arms, then found her breasts, circling her nipples, before running lower, to her hips.

She gasped as he gripped her on either side, her eyes startling to his, her head tilting, so it would have been a sin not to kiss her. Water doused them as he claimed her mouth, his body pressing to hers now so she was hard against the tiles, and he could wedge one knee between her legs. Rosie cried out, moving her hips, as if to satiate herself there, and he grinned against her mouth, the pleasure from her delirium almost unmatched.

He had no protection, and having not resolved the issue of pregnancy, he knew they couldn't be together here, but that didn't mean they couldn't have fun. What had started as a spur-of-the-moment offer for her to join him had morphed into the white-hot desperate need that always flamed between them the moment he'd touched her. Or had she touched him first? A tentative hand, lifting to his chest, her eyes trained on the gesture. Yes, she'd touched him, almost as if she didn't dare, and her uncertainty had broken something inside of him, some last vestige of control, so he'd sought to explore every piece of her, to feel her anew. And now this. Unmistakably, unsurprisingly, the culmination of any time they seemed to give in to this, there was an overwhelming need, building to a crescendo that simply had to be met.

He cursed inwardly, moving his hand between her legs, finding the part of her that offered satisfaction and teasing it at first, kissing her languidly, enjoying her rapturous little moans issued against him, her fingernails digging into his shoulders. Moans turned to pleas, and her head tilted back removing her lips, and he moved faster, glad they weren't kissing, because watching her climax was one of the most beautiful things he'd seen in his life. Her whole face seemed to glow when she cried out on a wave of euphoria. He smiled slowly, his hand still between her legs, even after her frenzy had slowed and she was looking at him again completely dazed and confused by why this kept happening.

'Better?' he asked, arching a brow.

Her gaze skimmed his face, something shifting in the depths of her eyes that he didn't understand, reminding him a little of the five months they'd spent married—and estranged—and how little he'd understood her. He hadn't known that beneath that buttoned-up exterior was a wild, passionate woman. He'd seen her as money-grubbing, social climbing, someone who had done all they could to ingratiate themselves with the king for their own personal gain.

He'd been wrong about her.

The thought was as surprising to him as this sexual chemistry; he pushed it aside. He'd been wrong in some ways, but that didn't change the fact that her loyalty lay with the king, and the king was not a man Sebastian could trust. Ever.

'For me, a little.' Her fingers lifted to his chest, tracing the droplets of water down the central line of his abdomen, stalling a little where his dark hair thickened at the top of his arousal. 'But not for you.'

His smile was tight. 'Unless you can see a condom somewhere…'

Her cheeks flushed pink, and she hesitated before speaking. 'I can't see one, but I suspect there's one available?'

Pleasure burst through him. At her wanting him. At her feeling confident to tell him she wanted him. At the prospect of being with her. 'Hold that thought,' he promised with a darkness to his voice that was at odds with the relief he was experiencing. He strode from the shower completely uncaring for the pools of water he left in his wake.

Mere moments later, like a moth to a flame, he returned to her, sheathing himself as he stepped past the glass wall, reaching for Rosie immediately afterwards. She came as he reached—it was just like that. An echo of one movement creating a wave of another. Her skin was so soft, reminding him of rose petals in the early morning dew. He lifted her even as she seemed to almost climb his body, her legs wrapping around his waist, her back against the tiles, so he could enter her and support her on the wall, his frame shuddering with relief as he felt her muscles tighten around his length, welcoming him back. All of him, buried so deep inside of her, and yet they both moved with a desperation that spoke of needing more. Somewhere in the back of his mind it occurred to him that he might never get enough of this. That if he had a billion days on this planet, and could spend them doing this with his wife, it might never be enough.

Ridiculous.

He dismissed any idea of a billion days, or even the next day, and focused instead on the delightful, intoxicating here and now...

CHAPTER TEN

ROSIE'S COFFEE WAS cold when she was reunited with it, but what did that matter? She could easily make more coffee. It had been so completely worth it for that. Her cheeks flushed as she replayed how they'd spent the last hour—in the shower, fast and desperate, and then in his bedroom, wet and uncaring, slow and languid, an exploration that had left her breathless for how thorough they'd been. When he'd caught her hands and pinned them above her head with one of his much larger hands, she'd felt imprisoned for his pleasure, and hers, in a way that had seemed to melt her spine.

'Hungry?' He entered the kitchen a moment after her, and when she glanced at him, her heart sped up a little. He had dressed in a pair of khaki shorts and a crisp white polo shirt with the collar slightly lifted. Her eyes devoured him as if she hadn't seen him in weeks, and the quirk of his lips showed exactly what she was doing. Mortified, she spun away, back to the coffee, trying to kick her brain into gear.

'I can make eggs,' he said. 'Or pancakes?'

She tried to catch her breath. 'I'm not really a big breakfast person. I'll just have an apple with my coffee.'

But he came to stand behind her, so close she could feel his warm breath at her nape. 'You might not normally eat breakfast, but do you usually expend that much energy this early in the day?'

Her cheeks felt as hot as the sun. She didn't turn around to face him, but she shook her head a little.

'I'm starving. Eat your apple, if you'd like, but I'll make plenty.'

In the end, he cooked bacon, eggs, grilled tomato and mushrooms, and it smelled so good that when he offered her a plate, she agreed with a small smile. 'Thank you. It looks too good to resist.'

'Hey, that's just what I was thinking,' he murmured, winking so she couldn't fail to understand his meaning. He sat opposite her at the kitchen counter and owing to the width of the bench—or lack thereof—their legs couldn't help getting tangled. Neither made an effort to move.

Sebastian ate with a kind of gusto that she now realized was inherent in him. No matter what he was doing, he pursued it with all of himself. Defending his mother, building his business, becoming the next in line to the throne of Cavalonia. Making love.

Her fingers trembled a little as she stabbed a mushroom—buttery and perfectly seasoned—and lifted it to her lips. She groaned a little at the delicious taste. 'You really are an amazing cook,' she said.

His laugh was a deep, husky sound that pulled at her insides. 'It's just a fry-up.'

'It's delicious.'

'I'm glad you like it.'

Their eyes locked and Rosie had the strangest sense that they were caught in a silent communication, as if their minds were speaking when their lips weren't. She blinked away, looking towards the horizon. Though they were inside, and the house was cool, she could already tell that the day would be warm.

'A storm is due this afternoon,' he said conversationally. 'We should make the most of the morning.'

She was familiar with Cavalonia's weather system, those summer storms that often seemed to break in the afternoon, or just as the evening wrapped around them. The smell of rain in the air, the electricity of lightning, the bursting of the day's heat.

'What do you have in mind?'

'How do you feel about hunting for our lunch?'

Her eyes flared. 'Hunting?'

'Well…' He grinned in a way that was boyishly charming. Her heart stammered. 'Fishing, at least.'

'Oh,' she said, relaxing. 'That sounds fun.'

And it did. But not because she had any particular penchant for catching fish, so much as the prospect of spending the morning with her husband was strangely alluring.

She told herself it was in the service of her stated aim, the purpose for this trip: to get to know him better. But there was a part of her that had begun to worry that the time they were spending together was coming to mean more to her than it should. That she was enjoying it more than she ought.

So what?

It wasn't reality.

It was a fantasy.

A bubble of escapism from her normal life, and their normal marriage.

She didn't care about him. Or maybe she did care about him, just a little bit, but so what? He was different than what she'd thought, but that just meant she'd been willing to revise her opinion of him. There was no danger in starting to respect the guy, in maybe even *liking* him a little. What mattered was that she didn't love him, and she never would. This was a perfectly sensible marriage of convenience with clearly delineated boundaries. They had a contract to that effect, for goodness' sake. There was no risk here. She had made sure of that!

And yet, was it any wonder that Rosie, who had such limited experience with relationships and affection, should be finding it difficult, at times, to remember that this was really, at its heart, pragmatic? Of course she was. She was only human, and this situation was *a lot*. Sebastian was a lot. But Rosie had spent her whole life avoiding entanglements that threatened her ordered, emotionally safe life—and of course she'd be able to do so now. No matter how attractive she found him, no matter how much she enjoyed their chemistry, she could handle this.

Before long, they'd be back in Cavalonia and when they returned to the capital city, everything would be different. Or rather, it would be the same as before.

Despite her desperate attempt to cling to rational thought, the idea of going back to the palace—and the way things had been before—brought a small frown to her face, forming a divot between her brows.

'What's wrong?'

She glanced at him, her frown deepening. What did she want? For more? More than the marriage they'd been living in for the last five months? For what they'd started to share on the island, but in the palace? He'd already said he'd never live there.

But she could move in with him.

She caught herself midway through the thought.

That's not what they were, and it was *definitely* not what she wanted. Was it? Confusion rattled through her.

She closed her eyes on a wave of nausea, as an image popped into her mind of Rowena—her father's fourth mistress, that Rosie could remember. She'd been a nurse, and very kind. She'd started coming to the house to spend time with Rosie, even when Grieg wasn't home. Rosie had liked her.

The ending of their relationship had destroyed Rowena. She'd still tried to see Rosie, but hadn't been able to get through even five minutes without bursting into tears.

Rosie heard, six months later, that Rowena had fallen asleep behind the wheel of her car on the way home from a late shift. It was plausible, of course, but all Rosie could remember was the older woman's plaintive cry that she didn't want to live without Grieg and Rosie in her life. She'd wondered, ever since Rowena's death, if she'd actually fallen asleep behind the wheel, or if it had been intentional. Guilt and grief had mingled together. Though she'd only been thirteen years old, she'd carried that burden a long time, wondering if she could have done something differently.

'Wife.' Sebastian's hand on hers shook her out of the memory. 'What's the matter? You look as though you've seen a ghost.'

Emotions swirled inside of her. Pain, sadness and yes, determination. Because those women had let their lives be destroyed by Grieg. He was like Sebastian in some ways: far too handsome for his own good, easily able to charm whomever he wished, and quite cold when needed. Rosie blinked across at Sebastian and had no doubts that Sebastian would cast her aside when it suited him, per their marriage agreement.

This was not real. This was not meaningful. And she refused to hope for more—not when it wasn't on offer, and not when even the desire for more could destroy a woman.

'I'm fine,' she said, resolute, removing her hand and forcing a brittle smile to her face. 'Fishing sounds great.'

In the end, despite the sobering of her mood, fishing *was* great. Unlike the handful of times she'd gone as a girl, and spent hours casting in a line, waiting and waiting, and catching nothing, Sebastian took them to a cove with an old timber jetty and they cast off from the very end of it. She caught her first fish within ten minutes, and almost as soon as she threw her line back in, another fish availed itself of the bait. Sebastian focused on the crab pots he'd dangled over the edge, and in a gesture of pure chivalry, handled the bait and fish removal for Rosie, so she didn't even have to get her hands dirty.

'Why do I feel like you do this a lot?'

Sebastian grinned. 'Because I do. Or rather, I did. Before.'

'Before you came home?'

He nodded once, his handsome features set in a firm mask of concentration.

'With Mark?' she prompted.

His eyes slid to hers. Her heart thumped, but she stole herself against such a silly response. 'He loved to fish. He loved all sports, actually, but fishing was one of those things, he always said, that combined his greatest loves— family time, because we would go together, the importance of feeling like you could keep yourself alive without all the modern crap, like supermarkets, and the peace, and time, to contemplate life. He was a deep thinker, and it wasn't unusual for us to spend a whole day fishing without saying a word.'

'Even as a kid?' she prompted.

'I liked it.'

'You were a deep thinker too?'

'I found I could keep my mind busy,' he said.

'Where would you fish?'

'There was a stream just a mile or so from our house. When I was older, I'd ride my bike down and throw the line in after school, always trying to impress Mark with my haul.' He grinned, but there was something behind the grin, something she wanted to understand.

'Was he impressed?'

'If there was reason to be. Mark was lavish with praise when deserved, but he didn't believe in gilding the lily.'

'It sounds like you were very close to him.'

'He raised me.'

'You loved him?'

Sebastian was silent. 'I am very grateful to him.'

'But?'

'But nothing. He made my mother very happy.'

She contemplated that for a while, trying to imagine what it had been like for a little boy to accept that reality. He would have been happy for his mother, even when he missed his father and grandfather and old life in Cavalonia.

'He was a great man. I wish he was still here.'

'I'm sure you do,' she said sympathetically.

'What about your father?' he asked, handing the rod back so Rosie could throw the line in. She did so, unaware of the deep frown lines that had formed on her brow.

'You said you're not close?' Sebastian prompted, when a minute passed without Rosie's response.

'We're not.' She'd been guarded about this conversation for a long time.

'Were you ever?'

She was glad he hadn't immediately launched into "why not?" because she wasn't sure how to answer that question.

'Perhaps when I was younger.'

They were quiet for several moments. Rosie moved her rod a little, but it seemed the fish had calmed down and were no longer biting the moment she cast in.

'Then something changed?'

Of course he wasn't going to let it go. He was taking a less direct approach, but Sebastian was not a man to have mysteries in his life. He wanted to know about this, and he was teasing the information from her in a way that was gentle and non-threatening. Never mind the fact he kept his own cards close to his chest.

She sighed a little. 'I suppose so.'

'Did you become a teenage rebel? Drugs? Alcohol? Wild parties?'

She sent him a droll look. 'If I had done any of that, don't you think the media would have dug it up by now?'

He arched a brow.

'I was almost depressingly straitlaced,' she said with a lift of one shoulder. 'I was more of a tea drinker than anything else.'

'So, what happened?'

She tugged on the fishing rod. 'It's hard to explain.'

'We've got time.'

She bit into her lower lip. 'I guess it wasn't just one thing. As I grew older, I became aware of things I couldn't have understood as a child. Lifestyle choices he made, for one.'

'Such as?'

'You know my mother is in a coma?'

'I remember that, from our wedding arrangements,' he confirmed with a nod, but his eyes had softened in a way that spoke of sympathy—something she hadn't expected from Sebastian—and her eyes stung with the threat of tears. 'She was in an accident?'

Rosie ignored the compunction at the small fib—one she'd used for so long that it was now an accepted part of her narrative. They didn't talk about what had really happened. For Rosie, it was too painful, a constant refreshing of guilt, of having been the instrument of her mother's demise.

'Yes. I never knew her—I was very young at the time. And my father never got over it. He's still not. He had a lot of affairs with a lot of women, and rather than explaining that he was still very much in love with his comatose wife, he led them on, fully aware that they were falling in love with him, and just not capable of caring.' She shook her head in an angry gesture of condemnation. 'I saw these women getting their hearts broken time and time again, and at first, I didn't understand, or perhaps I didn't want to put the blame where it belonged. But over time, I came to see that he was being ruthlessly cavalier with their hearts, that he was almost seeming to enjoy it. To punish them for living, with my mother in that state.'

Sebastian's eyes bore into hers. 'It is very difficult to accept the imperfections of someone we love.'

It was the perfect thing to say, because it struck at the heart of what she had struggled with. Loving her father, even when he'd disappointed her so badly.

It made her willing to continue, when she never discussed this with anyone, ever.

'At the same time, as I grew up, I started to look more and more like my mother. You might have thought that would make him care for me more, to see so much of her in me, but it was the opposite. He found it almost impossible to sit across the table from me and share a meal. He would drink too much and tell me not to speak, because even my voice sounded like hers.' The words were hollow, repeated from memory, and she tried not to let herself *feel* that pain again. 'He sent me away to boarding school when I was fifteen, and it was a saving grace. I no longer had to witness his litany of disastrous relationships, except when I came home on holidays, and then, he made himself quite scarce, because I continued to remind him of her.'

Silence, except for the gentle lapping of the ocean against the jetty supports, hung between them while Sebastian absorbed this.

'Do you see him often?'

'A couple of times a year. For his birthday, usually for Christmas.'

'And your mother?'

Rosie's lips twisted into a soft, melancholic smile. 'I see her more often. Usually every couple of weeks, whenever I can get away. I know it's silly, but I like to paint her fingernails.' She glanced across at him, wondering if he'd think it was a waste of time. 'It's something I figure we might have done, had things…if things had been different.'

'Is there any hope of recovery?'

'I gave up that hope a long time ago—it was too hard, otherwise. Doctors have always been honest with us. There is the possibility—you hear of cases, every now and again. But it's so rare. She is comfortable and cared for, which might be as good as it gets.'

It was depressing and upsetting to contemplate and yet she was glad they'd spoken about it. It was such a huge part of Rosie, had been for so long, that somehow it just felt right that Sebastian should understand this about her. Wasn't that the point of getting to know one another?

'Her name is Juliet?'

Rosie nodded.

'And you are Rosalind. Shakespearean?'

Rosie smiled. 'My mother told my father how much she wanted to name me after a Shakespearean heroine and thought long and hard about whom to choose. She had always felt that her own name disposed her to some form of tragedy or another—perhaps she was right. She wanted my name to be the opposite: a beacon of strength and confidence, and she definitely wanted me to have my own happy ending.'

'Like Rosalind?'

'Yes.'

He lifted a hand to her cheek, ran a finger over it. 'I'm sorry about your father.'

Her eyes shifted to his; emotions tightened in her chest. 'There's no point resenting him for any of it. He has made his choices in life. I've made mine.'

'And do you regret any of yours, Rosalind?'

Something yanked at her fishing line, but she was so captivated by Sebastian that she didn't register the movement. 'That's an almost impossible question to answer. Who doesn't have regrets?'

'I don't.'

'None?'

'Not really.'

She furrowed her brow. 'Oh, to be so self-assured.'

'I make decisions I'm willing to stand by.'

'Always?'

'To this point.'

She laughed a little unevenly; her line jerked again.

'But you don't?' he prompted.

'I don't know. What about our marriage?'

'What about it?'

'Surely you must regret it?'

'It was the only way to bring my mother home. I'm comfortable with that decision.'

Her eyes fluttered closed for the briefest of moments, while she processed a strange, tightening pain in her chest accompanied shortly after by a swooping of her stomach.

'Do you regret it?'

A week ago, she might have said yes, but even then, she'd been comfortable with the deal she'd made.

'No,' she answered, simply. 'I suppose there are times when I wish things were different, but we each got what we needed out of this deal. I can make my peace with it, by reconceptualising our marriage as a partnership—more of a business arrangement.'

'How sensible,' he drawled, and she wondered at the slight inflection of anger in his tone.

'Why does that bother you?' The time for obfuscation and pretence had passed. They had shared too much with one another, understood too much.

'How do you know it does?'

She rolled her eyes. 'Because I know you, way better now than I did even forty-eight hours ago. You're annoyed with me.'

'I'm annoyed with the sentiment.'

His eyes narrowed.

'I'm annoyed with your father, for demonstrating again and again all the reasons for avoiding relationships.'

'We're not in a relationship,' she said, her voice breathy and rushed.

'That's my point. Would you have willingly married a virtual stranger if it weren't for the fact your father has made you completely set against the idea of a real relationship?'

Her lips parted in surprise. 'I was engaged before you.'

'Yes, to someone else with whom you could have a loveless, transactional marriage.'

'How dare you?' she asked, but the words lacked fire, because he was right.

'You deserve more than this, Rosalind. You should never have agreed to marry me.'

'I told you—' she jutted her chin defiantly '—there is more than enough in our marriage to make it worthwhile. And before you start banging on about the money, you know that's not what I mean.'

'I know,' he said, surprising her by readily agreeing. 'I was wrong about you.'

Again, her lips parted, and her line trembled, hard enough now for it to finally get Rosie's attention. She was glad for the excuse to look away from Sebastian, to focus on pulling the fish from the water. She reeled the fish in but the more she reeled, the more the rod bent.

'It's big,' she said, over her shoulder, but it was unnecessary; Sebastian had seen and was moving to stand behind her, his bigger body and stronger arms working with hers, easily, seamlessly, like a well-oiled machine, combining their efforts to remove from the water an enormous black rucksack.

'Oh my God.' Despite the tension Rosie had been feeling only moments ago, she burst out laughing. 'Catch of the day?'

'You never know, it could have hidden treasure.'

'Or some poor kid's holiday kit.'

They drew it onto the jetty, a puddle at their feet, and Sebastian crouched down, unzipping it. 'Hat, sunscreen, water bottle, very waterlogged books. You were right.'

'Poor kid,' she said, smiling up at him. He smiled back, and everything was right again.

'We have enough,' he said, eyeing the icebox that had ten good-sized fish. 'Let me pull up the pots, and then we'll go back.'

'Oh.' Disappointment spread through her. She was enjoying herself.

'The storm is coming,' he reminded her, gesturing towards the horizon. 'By the time we walk home, it'll be here.'

'Right, of course.' She hadn't even noticed the darkening clouds. That was the Sebastian effect, she supposed. He was so much—too much—he just took up all of her oxygen and ability to focus on anything else. He drew in the two ropes to reveal several crabs in the pots and Rosie watched, fascinated, as he expertly hooked the pots together for easier transport. The crabs nipped their claws, but Sebastian wasn't worried.

The cove was not far from the house, and they didn't talk on the short return journey. Rosie was in her own mind, thinking about their morning, their conversation, about the ebbs and flows that made being here with Sebastian so interesting, even when it was tense. She supposed it had been a long time since she'd done this—gotten to know someone new. Besides the king, there wasn't really anyone in her life she talked to. It had been nice to open up to Sebastian, and even nicer when he responded in a way that showed he was genuinely interested in her life.

While Rosie showered, Sebastian set to work filleting the fish and preparing the crabs. While she'd enjoyed fishing, she could honestly say she wasn't sorry to miss either of those tasks, and she took her time blow drying her hair and rubbing moisturiser all over her body when she was done.

By the time she stepped out into the kitchen, the storm had arrived. Rather than the pristine blue sky, they were now engulfed by dark grey, and rain fell to the ground in big fat drops, slowly at first, and then much faster, like making popcorn but in reverse. Out at sea, lightning forked through the sky, so everything was momentarily overbright.

And she shivered, for no reason she could think of. She wasn't cold—this was still summer, and though the rain would cool things down, it would also bring humidity. No, it was more the darkness of the sky and the persistence of the rain. She couldn't help but feel an ominous weight beginning to bear down on her. If she were prone to superstition, she might think the storm was in some way a warning, but she had never been one to believe in mystical signs, and so she pushed the feeling away and stepped into the kitchen without any intention of letting a simple storm ruin her mood.

CHAPTER ELEVEN

IT RAINED AND it rained, so that as they sat down to a simple yet luxurious lunch of grilled just-caught fish and boiled, salted crabs, they had to halfway shout to hear one another. But despite how she fought it, there was something about the rain, its ancient reliability perhaps, the fact that like the oceans and the skies, the passage of time did nothing to change it, that got under her skin. As they sat and talked about things that were unimportant but not uninteresting, like their childhoods, the schools they'd attended and friends they'd cherished, and where they'd gone on holidays and what those experiences had been like, she had the strangest sense that the rain was almost washing clean their history and renewing it with moments like these. She wouldn't let it change what she wanted from this marriage, but it was impossible not to enjoy it.

She found herself smiling, and laughing, more than she'd ever thought she would when alone with her husband, and somehow, without the usual passage of the sun through the sky, time became strangely amorphous, so when Rosie happened to glance at the clock and saw it was nearly six, she gasped. 'It's so late,' she said, staring at the scraps of their lunch and aghast to realise they'd been sitting for hours while the storm raged.

'Got some place you need to be?' he responded, arching a brow.

Heat flushed her cheeks. 'Well, no, not for a few days, I suppose.' But she frowned then, because her clarity had only hardened during this week, and there was no longer any doubt left in her mind. 'But I should tell you, I don't think we need to take that long.'

He began to clear the plates. Such a routine gesture, and yet his back was ramrod straight and there was a tension to his shoulders that made her wonder if he was as casual about this as he was evidently trying to be. 'Oh yeah? Why is that?'

'Because I know you're going to be a great dad, and I know we can make this work.' She toyed with her fingers, ignoring the icy fear that stole through her, the idea of being fated to a life like her mother's. For as long as she could remember that idea had stalked her, the belief that if she were ever to get greedy and hope for children of her own, she'd be similarly cursed. It had been one of the points in favour of her previous engagement—her ex-fiancé had despised the idea of having children and swore he'd never change his mind. He would never have asked her for a baby. He had been focused on his career and his career alone. Nothing on earth would have induced Rosie to have children with *him* anyway. But Sebastian was different. The whole situation was different. What she also knew, but didn't say, was that if her worst fears came to pass, she trusted Sebastian to remember her to their child. She trusted him to do what was right. Conceiving a child was still terrifying, but it was no longer something she dreaded, as one might the prospect of stepping off an abyss into a shark-infested ocean.

'Are you saying you'll do this?'

She nodded slowly. 'Yes.'

'And this is your choice, Rosalind? I will not have our baby be something you regret.'

'I told you, I don't regret our marriage.'

'You should.'

Something sparked inside of her. 'Don't ruin this moment,' she said quietly.

He placed the dishes in the sink, then turned back to face her. 'I need to be sure.' He strode across the room, catching her wrists and lifting her hands between them. 'You were pressured into marrying me. You might not regret it, you might think the reasons you cling to for accepting the deal matter, but that doesn't change the fact you were pressured. I would not ever want you to say the same thing about this baby.'

She nodded and wished she wasn't feeling the sting of tears in her eyes.

'This has to be a decision you are making for the right reasons.'

Her heart twisted over. His concern for her was well beyond what she'd expected, given how important this child was to his claim to the throne.

'It is,' she promised him. And it was. This baby would be a gift to all of them, and she knew that no matter what, even if it meant her worst fears came true, that the safe delivery of their child would be worth any sacrifice she might make.

How was it possible that she already loved a baby which was very much just a concept? There was still so much to happen before then.

Lightning cracked, close to the house, and she jumped a little. A frisson of something ran the length of her spine. Adrenalin? Fear? Courage? Exuberance?

'I'm scared,' she admitted, and God knew that was the truth. 'But that's a normal way to feel with anything new, especially something like this. I want this, Sebastian. I really do.' She could just imagine their baby, whether a boy or girl, with his soulful dark eyes and swarthy skin. Perhaps the baby would be like her mother, too? The thought was instantly mollifying. Wasn't that how this was supposed to work? Descendants were a living testament to those who went before them, a way to always remember.

'Then when the time is right for you, we will start trying.' His eyes ran over her face, as if looking for something, or wanting to say something. She didn't know which, and she was concentrating on calendar maths anyway.

'Actually,' she murmured, her heart speeding up. 'The time now is perfect.'

He laughed softly. 'I meant for conception, but if you're suggesting we take this to the bedroom for other reasons, then I'm fine with that.'

Her cheeks flushed. 'I mean the same thing. This, right now, would be a good time for us to try.'

He sobered. 'Now?'

She nodded. 'If I remember my tenth-grade biology classes.'

He was serious. 'And, you're sure?'

She laughed. 'God, Sebastian, next minute you'll be making me beg.'

He gave her a rueful look. 'I could not live with myself, *cara*, if such a monumental decision was not your own.'

'You know me better now too, don't you? Do you seriously imagine I'd have a baby if I wasn't completely sure it was right?'

He tilted his head a little as he contemplated that, and then shook it once. 'No. You're too smart for that.'

His compliment pulled at her heart, but was he prevaricating on purpose? Was he now having doubts? 'We don't have to try this month,' she said quickly, to give him an easy way out. 'If you'd prefer to wait, we can.'

'No. Believe me when I tell you, I don't want to wait another moment.' His voice was so deep and raw that her whole body seemed to ache in response. When he scooped down and lifted her up, he carried her over one shoulder to his bedroom, and as they crossed the threshold, it was with a shared intention not to leave it again for many, many days.

Rosie loved her country, her king, and she loved her life, but when Sebastian's private jet touched down in Cavalonia, she didn't feel a rush of relief or gladness to be back. Not even a little.

She felt…regret.

The word sprang to mind easily, perhaps because of their conversations on the island. How could she fail to regret being back, though?

The island had been wonderful.

There, she felt as though so many things had happened, it was as if she was fundamentally changed in some way, and despite her every effort to keep him at arm's length, she felt as if Sebastian had become a physical part of her. They'd spent almost every moment together for a week and a day, and the last four of those had been spent almost completely in his bedroom, and absolutely naked.

Coming back had necessitated a shift.

They'd both dressed, for a start, but it wasn't just the requirement for clothes, so much as the type of clothes. Sebastian wore a suit, and Rosalind a tailored dress with high heels—the sort of thing she wore often in her role as princess. Her phone had pinged with many emails and texts, including one from the king telling her he was looking forward to seeing her.

They had sat separately on the plane, neither really looking at the other. Rosie didn't need to look at Sebastian; he was burned into her memory banks. Not touching him when they disembarked was a form of torture, but she was aware of the way he held back a little, so there was no need for either to brush hands, nor for him to put a solicitous hand in the small of her back.

And on the tarmac, two cars were waiting. It was a starkly visual reminder of their separate lives. One car was to take her back to the palace, and another to take him to his home.

She hesitated a little, midway between the steps of the plane and her car, and Sebastian was then beside her, looking at her quizzically.

'You're okay?'

She nodded, but frowned, and knew that she wasn't. But how could she explain it to him? She refused to ask when she'd see him again. She refused to do anything so desperate and needy, and thus confirm that she was every bit as vulnerable to handsome, suave men as her father's girlfriends had been.

'And you'll let me know about our project as soon as you know?'

It would be about a week before she could do even the most sensitive pregnancy tests. Was he planning not to see her for that whole time?

Her heart dropped to her toes. She wouldn't ask that either. She wouldn't say anything that might sound as if she was begging him to come to her. She'd hold it together, show him that she was strong and independent, even when she didn't feel it.

'Of course.' Her voice was brittle, her smile just a shadow. 'Well, goodbye then,' she murmured, turning to walk to her car. She took small, deliberate steps, as a nice woman from the protocol office had shown her for the wedding. Now it was because it physically hurt to walk away from him. When she was near the car, one of the security teams opened the rear door for her. She almost allowed herself to look back before sliding in, before reminding herself that she was stronger than that, and she simply took her seat, staring straight ahead, as if the week with Sebastian had just been a fun little getaway that was now behind her.

As if he wasn't integral to her body's functioning, and maybe even her ability to breathe.

Sebastian stared at her car for a long time, part of him wanting to go to her, even when he knew he wouldn't.

From the moment she'd put on that damned dress, he'd been forced to remember who she was.

Who she worked for.

Who she served.

Who she loved.

She would always put the king first.

She had married Sebastian at the king's behest, and despite Sebastian's numerous questions, he half feared she had agreed to this plan because a baby would put the king's mind at ease.

And he hated that.

He hated that the king was the last man on earth to deserve such loyalty, and he particularly hated that the king had it from Rosalind. Rosalind who should have known better, who should have valued herself more than to become embroiled in any of this. Rosalind who should have known her worth.

Rosalind who should have believed in fairy tales and happily-ever-afters, just as her poor mother wanted for her.

Instead, she was living in a drama that was almost guaranteed not to have a happy ending.

Nothing good could come from going after her.

It would simply be prolonging the inevitable.

Their week together had blown every single one of Sebastian's expectations out of the water, but so what? It didn't change anything.

When the king called, she would always go. Her loyalty would always be to him, and Sebastian couldn't live with that. He couldn't live with the thought of growing close to someone who didn't see things as he did, who didn't agree with him. He couldn't ever really allow someone into his life who defended the man who'd made his mother so miserable, who had exiled him as a young boy.

On the island, they'd formed a truce. An agreement not to discuss the king. It was too inflammatory, too dangerous for them. But here? Here the king was everywhere, and they couldn't continue to act as though he didn't exist.

If Sebastian went after Rosie, if he asked her to come to his bed that night, he knew she'd agree. But in exchange, he'd want more. He'd want her to switch allegiance, to agree with him that the king was awful, to admit that his hatred was warranted.

She'd never do that, and he wouldn't ask. He watched her drive away, knowing it was the right decision but wishing like hell he could stop time and take her back to the island, just for a little while longer.

Procuring a pregnancy test when you were a princess was not exactly as simple as popping down to the local pharmacy and simply buying one. In order to get the thing, she'd had to ask someone she trusted to buy one for her, which meant opening up to Laurena about the possibility of a baby, at least.

Laurena, who like the rest of the world, had no idea about the cause of Rosie's mother malaise, had shrieked with excitement before Rosie had shushed her. 'It's just in case,' she'd promised. 'It will probably be negative,' she said, keeping her fingers crossed that it was positive. Lord knew they'd given a baby every opportunity to exist with their days of dedicated trying.

And she so desperately wanted the baby to have been conceived on the island. There was just something so magical about the place, but more than that, there was something magical about who they'd been when they were there. Just two people, getting to know one another, without all of the impediments and constraints that existed here.

Laurena had taken almost two hours, because she'd explained when she returned, she'd driven to the other side of the city to shop in a place that was unlikely to have any paparazzi lurking. Rosie was grateful for her discretion.

Her fingers shook as she removed the test and read the instructions carefully, and when she took it, her breath burned in her lungs, and she found she almost couldn't bear to look. Her excitement and hope were at such a zenith level that she knew if it was negative, she'd be crushed.

Or maybe she wouldn't? Negative meant more trying, after all… Just the thought of that sent her heart into a frenzy. She glanced at the test. Nothing.

But it had only been a minute. She waited some more, and some more, and still there was no second line where one would be if she'd conceived.

Despite the consolation of more time with Sebastian, her heart felt as though it had been smashed into oblivion.

She wasn't pregnant.

'Oh,' she whispered, wrapping the test in toilet paper and shoving it back into the box. 'That's that, then.'

She told herself it was okay. That it was to be expected. But a single tear rolled down her cheek as she stepped out into her bedroom and looked around. Laurena had tactfully left, and Rosie was grateful. She didn't want to have to tell her aid, yet, that she was not pregnant after all.

But there was Sebastian. She'd promised to let him know. Should she do so immediately? It seemed wrong for her to have this information, and for him not to, and yet they were scheduled to see one another the following night at the ball to commemorate the closing of parliament for the holidays.

Should she wait until then?

And risk the moment being overheard or photographed?

No, she would tell him now, and she would keep it just as brusque and businesslike as befitted their relationship. Not the relationship they'd shared on the island. There, she'd have walked straight up to him and let him wrap his big, strong arms around her, holding her tight while she gave into a flood of disappointed tears. But here, they were not like that, and it was obviously how he wanted things to stay.

So much for new beginnings.

She picked up her phone and loaded a text message box. She began to type before she could reconsider the wisdom of this.

Hi.

She considered what to add. His phone was private, but there was always a risk, when putting things in writing, and so she wrote:

I said I'd let you know about our project. The answer is no.

She re-read it, hoping it was both cryptic but informative, and then sent it. And cried, because it made it all the more real.

She'd gone from desperately not wanting to ever conceive to suddenly feeling as though it were her purpose in life. She stamped her foot and stared up at the ceiling for a long time, waiting for the feeling to ease, but it didn't. A strange, heavy grief was pressing down on her. She knew it was irrational. They'd only tried for one month, and of course these things could take much, much longer. But she'd wanted, with all her heart, she'd wanted…

She lay down on her bed, glad she was alone, glad she could just stare up at the ceiling and alternate between utter silence and gentle sobs. She pressed a hand to her flat stomach, and tried to imagine it growing round, feeling all the things her mother had, once upon a time. An hour later, sometime near dusk, her door burst open in a manner that was totally surprising—no one ever simply burst into her apartment. On the contrary, one of her private secretaries always knocked first and announced visitors, in case Rosie wasn't available. But this was not an ordinary visitor. Sebastian stood just inside the door, an out of breath Laurena behind him, mouthing apologies.

Neither Sebastian nor Rosie noticed Laurena, and she backed away, closing the door behind her.

Rosie scrambled to sitting and then stood, straightening her outfit and mentally bemoaning her appearance. She must look dreadful.

But Sebastian was staring at her in a way that made everything all scrambled and confusing, just as he always did.

'I didn't see your message immediately,' he said with a voice that was a little different than normal. 'I came as soon as I read it.'

Her heart turned over. 'You didn't need to come here.' She was trying to be professional, to be reserved, just like she always had been with her husband, before the island.

He frowned. 'You're upset.'

A sound strangled inside her throat. 'Yes.' Why deny it?

His eyes lashed her face. She wanted to hide.

'I'm sorry,' he said, striding towards her, and stopping just short, not touching her.

'Why? What for?'

He frowned, as though he didn't know. 'We'll try again.'

She knew they would, but it would be different. She'd somehow fooled herself into thinking, on the island, that they'd been doing more than trying for a baby. That she'd meant more to him. This week had proved how wrong she'd been. How little he cared. How little she meant. The pain of that truth was instantly familiar. No one cared about her. Only the king, and even then...

She tilted her chin in an angle of defiance. 'I know that.'

'We can go back to the island, in a few weeks.'

She shook her head. Not the island. It was too magical. Too beautiful. On the island, she forgot. She forgot all the reasons she had for keeping him at arm's length, everything that could go wrong if she let herself want more from him than he'd ever give.

'We don't have to do that.'

His eyes flecked with something; she didn't bother trying to understand. Her heart was tattered.

'This might take months. Maybe even a year. We can't fly to the island every time we try.'

'Who says?'

Was it an attempt at a joke? If so, she wasn't laughing.

'I'll let you know when the timing is right, and our teams can sync our schedules.'

His eyes narrowed, as if with anger. As if she'd said the exact opposite of what he wanted. 'Excellent, and perhaps my private secretary can offer tips on our performance? Maybe there's a position we should be trying that we missed.'

'You're seriously snapping at me?' she asked, her tone rife with hauteur.

A muscle jerked at the base of his jaw. 'Yes, but I didn't mean it. I'm sorry. I wasn't expecting this.'

She realised then, with compunction, that she wasn't the only one who was grieving. This was the baby he'd been hoping for too. She glanced away, her heart breaking for a whole other reason now.

She didn't know how to do any of this, but she had to cling onto the boundaries they'd established. The island had made everything complicated, and though it had fundamentally changed her, it hadn't changed them. They were too different, and this marriage was only ever going to be this: a ruse.

Why fight that?

'We'll try again next month,' she said softly, swallowing past a lump in her throat.

'Yes.' He reached for her then, but she flinched away. Not because she didn't want him to touch her, but because she wanted it so, so badly, more than she could ever express, and she knew it would never be enough. One touch, one kiss, even if they were to fall backwards into her bed, it wouldn't be enough, because it didn't mean anything. Not to him, anyway. And to her?

She moved towards her bedroom door. 'And I'll see you tomorrow night.'

He nodded, but his expression showed distraction. 'You're disappointed. You really wanted this.'

'Yes,' she agreed. 'I'm sure it will happen. We'll just keep trying.'

'Right.' He hovered though, as if he wanted to say something else, but she needed him to go now. Her grief was all-consuming and if he lingered, she suspected he'd see it, and maybe see more than she wanted him to. Everything was such a mess.

He strode towards the door but stopped, just inside of it. 'Will you call me if you need anything, wife?'

Wife.

What a joke.

She used to think he was being ironic when he used the label—after all, they were hardly spouses in the traditional sense—but she'd never really *felt* the irony like she did now. It was like being taunted with something she wanted and could never have. The realisation of just how badly she wanted it all to be real was like an enormous rock boulder being dropped into a placid lake. Ripples emerged in every direction of Rosie's soul, leaving her bereft by how alone she was. Just like she'd always thought she wanted—just as she'd always been.

When had that happened?

She'd worked so hard on the island to remind herself that their marriage was just a means to an end, that the baby would be too. She'd told herself again and again that this was all just an arrangement for the good of the kingdom. When had she started to want the kinds of things she'd always told herself were off limits?

Her loneliness was a deep, soul-aching pain, because she'd glimpsed an alternative. For one brief week, she'd lived something else, and she'd never be the same again. Panic slicked her insides; she swallowed hard, paling imperceptibly. She recognised who she'd become: one of her father's girlfriends. Was this the desperation they had felt?

She straightened her spine. While she couldn't deny her feelings, she could certainly try to hide them from him. 'I won't need anything.' Her voice emerged pleasingly clear. 'Goodbye, Sebastian.'

She didn't look at him again; it had taken every ounce of effort she had left to dismiss him with such apparent coldness. If he stayed a moment longer, she was terrified she'd beg him to stay.

CHAPTER TWELVE

AFFAIRS OF STATE were neither here nor there for Sebastian. He'd been to enough formal events even before returning to Cavalonia to know the drill. He was generally nonplussed by them, regardless of how big and important they were.

It didn't bother him that this evening's party would feature the entire parliament and their partners, nor that dignitaries from all over Europe had been invited.

As he stepped from his limousine dressed in a midnight-black tuxedo, he could only think of Rosalind. He was anxious to see her, to reassure himself that she was fine.

She hadn't been fine the day before.

She'd been breaking, and he'd understood that, but hadn't known how to fix it. He had only been able to think of one way, and that wasn't a solution, so much as a stopgap measure. Making love to her might push the reality from her mind but it wouldn't actually change the fact that despite many, many, many attempts, they hadn't conceived.

But had he really expected to in the first month? Sure, it happened for some people, and he might have deluded himself into thinking it would happen for them also, but some solid researching he'd done overnight had convinced him that several months of trying was far more usual. Anything up to a year was considered standard. He refused to live and die by each month's attempt.

Besides…

The trying was fun.

If he was honest, he'd say he was itching to take her back to the island, rather than stay here in the city, but whatever. Wherever. Sex with Rosalind was its own kind of perfection; it didn't matter where they were. Suddenly, he was counting down the days to the right dates in her cycle to make this happen.

It wasn't just the sex he missed though, he admitted uneasily, his step faltering a little as he frowned deeply. Out of nowhere, unwelcome memories slashed through him. The way she would smile at him, the feeling of her hand brushing against his finger, her bravery in wanting to defend the cottage with a pepper grinder, her goodness and kindness. Realisations that burned inside his gut like acid, because he didn't want to feel any of that for his wife. For anyone. He had carefully charted a course for his life, and it didn't include the kind of sentiment that might predispose him to more rejection and disappointment. Those lessons had been etched into his soul as a boy, and he'd never forgotten them. Every day that his biological father shunned him had crystallised his determination to remain totally alone in life. Losing Mark had underscored the wisdom of that decision.

But he wasn't stupid enough to pretend Rosalind hadn't cracked through his carefully erected walls, just a little. He clung to the fact that it was temporary, that things would settle down again once they'd conceived. They had to—it was what they both wanted. A calm, easy marriage. No feelings, no risk.

But didn't Rosalind deserve more? Wasn't that part of the problem? He knew her now. He knew her in a way he hadn't when he'd first agreed to this, and he knew that while he was happy to wall off his emotions, she shouldn't have to. She was the kind of woman who should have so much more than this. She should have everything.

As he walked into the east wing of the palace, he glanced around, but he was so deep in his thoughts that at first he didn't see Rosalind step out from the shadows. And when he did see her, it was like being punched hard in the gut.

She was beautiful, and he knew that. It had been one of the first things he'd noticed about her, of course, even when he'd been seething with rage at her apparent devotion to the king. He'd noticed her flaxen hair and the way it was braided in a crown around her head, her delicate, graceful movements, her huge blue eyes and full, pale pink lips. She was beautiful no matter where she was and what she wore, but tonight, she looked like the kind of princess young children went to bed dreaming of. Her dress was a pale pink with a fitted bodice and a full skirt that had a fine sparkle to it. At her throat, she wore a diamond choker, and over her gloved hand, her wedding ring sparkled like an omen.

She must have been wearing heels because she was taller than when barefoot, and she walked towards him with so much poise and cool control that his admiration for her quickly morphed into something else. Something darker.

What would she do if he pulled her against him here and kissed her until the lipstick smudged and her nipples grew taut? What would she do if he pushed his hand into her hair and pulled it from that sleek golden bun, so it was loose over her shoulders? If he lifted up the many layers of her dress until he found the elastic of her underwear and slid his finger inside her sex?

'Your Highness,' she murmured when she was close enough.

He wouldn't do any of those things though. He wasn't an

animal, and they had a state event to attend. But that didn't change the fact that he wanted to unsettle her.

And so he leaned close, his voice gruff, and murmured in her ear, his lips brushing her lobe a little, 'You look good enough to eat, and believe me, I'd like to do just that.'

He heard and felt her gasp. A dark smile curved his lips.

'Sebastian.' Her voice trembled a little, a warning in her tone. But there was also a plea. Because she wanted him just as much as he wanted her?

'Would you like that, wife? Would you like me to pull you into one of these rooms and taste you, just like on the island? Would you like me to taste you and suck you until you are falling apart at the seams?'

'Sebastian,' she said again, but it was frenzied, need in every syllable.

'Say the word and I will do it,' he promised, running a finger over her hip. 'Even better if we could find something for these,' he moved his finger to her wrist, and pulled it behind her back a little. 'I like the thought of you tied up and totally at my command, mine to pleasure over and over again…'

She trembled and he pulled back, his eyes glittering dark when they met hers. Her cheeks were flushed, and her lips were parted. There she was! The woman he'd seen on the island, the woman who was flesh and blood and all for him.

'I can't—'

'Yes, you can,' he responded gruffly. 'Any time you want to, you can.'

Her eyes were wide, her features stricken. 'Stop it,' she said, but kept her body close to his, her lips parted. 'This isn't fair.'

'No?'

'No,' and then she did pull away from him, glaring at him

with barely concealed anger. And he was glad! Anger was so much better than grief, and so much better than coldness. Anger was an emotion he could work with. Anger, with them, always turned into something else, anyway.

But they were ushered into the ball, and both assumed a mask, the same mask they'd worn on multiple occasions, when they'd been forced to spend an evening together. To almost anyone looking at them, they seemed serene and content. A perfect young royal couple. But inside, Rosie was fuming.

Whenever she glanced at Sebastian, she felt her anger surge—as well as other feelings—but anger was a refuge and so she clung to it. How dare he blow hot and cold with her like that? How dare he act as though the week of silence hadn't happened?

Irritation stretched and built until she found herself wanting to slap him, then and there, in the middle of the ball. And what would he say if she did?

She thought of the way he'd carried her on the island over one shoulder, so easily, and she imagined him doing so now. Picking her up in front of all the ministers, the king, the entire delegation. Her lips quirked but not with humour, so much as resignation, because when she imagined such a scenario, it was with anticipation more than anything else.

She wanted to push him to that.

She wanted to push him, as he'd been goading her.

There was no chance though.

They were kept separate all evening by their various responsibilities, conversations with dignitaries the main purpose of their attendance. The king came to make a brief speech, towards the end of the night, and Rosie stood near him, so he naturally came to her afterwards and gave her a small hug, and a kiss on the cheek, remarked on how well she was looking. When he left, she glanced around the room, not looking for Sebastian, and yet her eyes found him as though she was a heat-seeking missile and he, her target. She shivered at the expression on his features and quickly glanced away again.

It was late before the event was finally over and Rosie was tired. She hadn't slept well the night before. Visions of their baby, lost in a room, crying, kept coming to her, and the baby was so vivid and real that she couldn't believe such a person didn't already exist.

As was their usual way, Sebastian accompanied Rosie from the function, but once in the private corridors of the east wing, he didn't relinquish his grip on her hand, as he ordinarily might. Instead, he turned to face her, and there was a look on his face that took her breath away.

'We need to talk.'

'Do we?' she replied, pleased when her voice emerged cool and crisp.

'We need to talk somewhere other than here,' he confirmed with a tight nod. 'Come home with me.'

Her heart began to race. It was everything she wanted, and yet it wasn't. On so many levels, she was terrified.

'I'm tired,' she responded.

His expression showed cynicism. 'Is that a "no"?'

She opened her mouth and closed it again. She *was* tired, but she knew that if she demurred and went to her room, she'd regret it. She'd get no sleep, anyway.

'No,' she said after a beat. 'It's not a no.'

His eyes flashed to hers and he began to walk, holding her hand. 'Wait, Sebastian—'

'Why, Rosalind?' His impatience was palpable. 'Haven't we been waiting?'

Her stomach twisted. Yes, they'd waited all week, and it had been awful. Silently, she followed him, out into the moonlit night, and as they approached the car, her body seemed to explode like a wave of ash.

It had been a spur of the moment invitation. He was acting on instinct and autopilot, with no forethought or planning, and once inside his limousine, he had no goddamned idea what he was going to say to her when they were alone. But not being able to talk to her properly had been stifling and beyond frustrating. At least at his place they could speak to one another, or even yell at each other, if they wanted to.

Except it wasn't enough. In the back of his car, all he was conscious of was her. Her nearness, her soft skin, her shallow breathing, the smell of her perfume and shampoo, the fact that he could reach out and touch her anytime. But photographers were everywhere, swarming the exit of the palace and continuing to follow them on motorbikes, which zipped in and out of traffic with scant regard for safety.

Each mile stretched like elastic in his gut, torturing him. At one point, his fingers glanced across her knee, and she gasped softly, so he knew he wasn't alone, that her desire was at the same fever pitch as his own.

He was angry, he was frustrated, he was worried about her, and he was furious with himself for his weakness, but God knew, none of that mattered anymore. He just needed to get her into his house and lock the damned door. For days, if that's what it took.

He didn't know exactly what he wanted to achieve, but he knew bringing her here was right and necessary.

The car turned into the street that led to his home, the gates swinging open, with a few paparazzi outside of them. He glanced at Rosalind, who now had a serene smile plastered on her face. Well, it might fool the press, but he was beside her, and the tension emanating from her frame was unmistakable. It was a tension he felt too.

She was so beautiful, but he hated that beauty. Not the beauty, he corrected, but the untouchability. This version of her was something he couldn't help but resent, having seen her wild and free on the island.

Once inside his house though, the façade cracked. She whirled around to face him, eyes latched on his. 'So?' she demanded, an awe-inspiring mix of hauteur and fury. 'What do you want to talk about?'

This he liked. Anger was real. Anger was passion, just expressing itself differently.

'The baby, for one thing.'

'There is no baby,' she ground out.

He clamped his teeth, then said, 'You're upset. Yesterday, you pushed me away. Tonight, you acted like it never happened.'

'And?' she snapped. 'It's fine. These things take time.'

'I'm aware of that, but it doesn't make it any easier—'

'It's not like I had a miscarriage,' she demurred. 'We just didn't fall pregnant. We'll try again.'

'When our staff sync our schedules?' He couldn't help reminding her, the words scathing.

She flinched a little. 'Sure, why not?'

'You don't think that's a little…cold?'

'I'd rather call a spade a spade.' She waved a hand through the air, and only the slight trembling of her fingers showed him how moved she was by their situation. 'Why pretend this is anything other than what it is?'

'Which is?'

'Two people in an arranged marriage arranging to have a baby.'

His eyes narrowed. 'You're so angry with me you're shaking, and I cannot work out why.'

She clamped her lips together, tried to gather her composure. 'I'm not.'

'Oh yeah?'

He took a step towards her, and her chest rose with the sharp intake of her breath. 'You weren't angry with me on the island.'

She glanced away, her throat shifting as she swallowed, visibly trying to rein in her temper.

'Do you blame me?' he asked, lifting a finger to the pulse point in her throat and feeling it rush against her delicate skin.

'For what?' she muttered, not looking at him, and not moving.

'For not falling pregnant.'

She shook her head, her expression—what he could see of it in profile—like thunder. 'I blame you for treating me like—' But she zipped her lips together, cutting herself off just in time. Or frustratingly, too fast.

'Like what?' he pushed, so close to hearing her say whatever was bothering her and needing that.

'It doesn't matter.'

'It matters to me,' he responded, his own voice rising a little.

She glanced up at him, her eyes darkened by resentment. 'It's my fault,' she said. 'I got carried away. I let myself believe we could be…friends. But that's not what we are. It's not what we'll ever be. I'm just a body to you. Someone to have sex with when it suits, and to forget about when it doesn't.'

He felt totally blindsided. 'What the hell?'

'Come on, Sebastian. There's no need to pretend it's not

true. What else explains the way you cut me out of your life the minute we left the island? You did your bit, and tried to get me pregnant at every opportunity, in the right window of the calendar, and then you disappeared out of my life. Excellent breeding stock work—you're a grade A bull, or stud, or whatever.'

He swore under his breath, wanting to deny it, but the truth held him quiet. He waited until he could trust his voice not to shake then said, 'That's what we agreed to.'

'Right, of course,' she snapped, pulling away from him then, stalking deeper into his house and making a sound of frustration. To his immense relief, it was Rosalind who reached up into her hair and began to remove pins, dropping each one onto the polished timber side table with obvious disdain. She continued to do so as she spoke. 'And nothing changed on the island for either of us.'

'Of course it changed,' he responded. 'We got to know each other, just like you wanted.'

'But I got to *like* you,' she said, and then obviously regretted it. Yet she angled her chin defiantly, as if daring him to mock the sentiment, her eyes locked to his. 'I got to like spending time with you. I thought that was real.'

He glanced away, his gut twisting. It had been real. So much of it. But her loyalty to the king made anything like a relationship impossible. He could explain that to her, but then they'd argue over the king, and there was no winning that fight. He simply had to accept she would always defend the man Sebastian hated.

'And then we got back to the city, and you made it as clear as crystal that you couldn't wait to go back to ignoring me. So, why are we here?' she asked, running her hands through her liberated hair, pulling it over one shoulder. 'Why bring me here under the guise of needing to talk when you have nothing to say?'

'Fine, I don't want to talk,' he said, stalking towards her. 'I miss you, okay?'

'No, you miss having sex with me, that's not the same thing. If you missed me, you would have called. You would have come to see me. You want to take me to bed. Right?'

Damn it, yes. But no. She was right, and she was wrong. He'd wanted to call her. He'd wanted to talk to her.

But to what end?

There was no point pretending they had some kind of future. The last thing he wanted to do was lead her on when there was this enormous barrier between them, maybe several. It was all so hopeless. So he hadn't called. He'd waited for her to reach out to him, and when she had, he'd gone to her immediately.

But he also ached for her on a physical level, and that was so much easier to understand and to explain, so he nodded. 'Yeah, I want to take you to bed. What do you want, Rosalind?'

She glared at him as if she truly hated him—and perhaps she did—but then she stamped her foot and nodded once. 'I want that too,' she said, but to show her annoyance, she pushed at his chest, once. 'And I hate myself for it. If you only knew how much I hated myself.'

'Why?' he challenged; but he knew. She'd told him all he needed to understand her. 'You're not like the women your father screwed, and I'm not like him. I'm not leading you on—you're not falling in love with me. You're the one who said it—we call a spade a spade and we always have.'

'Yes,' she said, but her eyes filled with angry tears. 'You make me so angry, but I want you.'

'Yeah, well, we're in the same boat. You make me angry, and I want you. What about it?'

And then she laughed, but it was rich with emotion and confusion, and he couldn't help but step forward and drag her against him, kissing her until she wasn't laughing, and she wasn't crying, kissing her until they were both simply existing in this moment, this need, this fierce, desperate flame arcing between them, as it always did.

'Damn you, Sebastian,' she said, as he lifted her against his chest and carried her to the nearest soft space he could find, which just so happened to be the lounge. 'Damn you to hell.'

He didn't tell her that he'd been living there this whole long, cold week.

CHAPTER THIRTEEN

FOR A MOMENT, in that golden hour of dawn's first breath, Rosie thought she was back on his island. The lighting, the feeling of waking up beside him, the satisfaction she felt deep in her soul, it was all so familiar. But then, she remembered. The last week. The negative pregnancy test. Their fight last night. And the smile that had breezed across her lips fell, as she woke up fully and looked across at Sebastian. Whether she'd moved in some way, or he'd just happened to wake up, his eyes were on her, and when they connected, they looked at one another and she felt a rush of something she couldn't explain.

'Good morning,' he murmured, scanning her face, as though he too was uncertain how to proceed, or perhaps how she'd react.

Rosie sighed softly, because she wasn't angry anymore. She was just…sad. There was something inside of her that made her want so much more than this, but she knew it was impossible. Was that the difference between herself and the women who'd had their hearts broken by her father? Was it just as Sebastian said? That they were honest with each other, and therefore nothing could go wrong?

'Okay?' he prompted, putting a hand on her shoulder tentatively, as if not sure that he should touch her.

She nodded slowly. 'Yeah.'

He frowned, like he was thinking something but not expressing it. 'Are you hungry?'

She was starving, but everything was so complicated and messy, and she didn't know what to do next. On the one hand, sex was sex. But on the other, something was shifting inside of Rosie, the feeling that they'd crossed a line that had been hugely important to her. Sex on the island was one thing. It was different; removed. But being here, together, it was blurring all the lines and making her forget what they were, and what she wanted. Nothing made sense.

'I'll make breakfast,' he said, and before she could argue, he was up and pulling on boxer shorts, walking out of the bedroom and damn it if Rosie didn't let him. Damn it if she didn't allow herself this one small indulgence of pretending that things between them were just this easy.

She flipped onto her back, eyes focused on the ceiling, her mind spinning and rolling.

Maybe she could put this down to the disappointment of her negative pregnancy test? Emotions were running high, so they'd slipped up and slept together. It didn't mean anything except that she was in a vulnerable place.

But if that were the case, why wasn't she scooting out of his place at the first opportunity and getting back to her real life? Why was she allowing herself the indulgence of playing make-believe with her husband?

She groaned softly as she got out of bed and dressed in her underwear and one of his shirts, scraping her hair into a loose ponytail as she left his room.

He was tipping scrambled eggs into the pan when she stepped into the kitchen, and two mugs of coffee were on the counter. Her heart skipped a beat.

It was just so normal.

So domestic.

In her heart of hearts, this, right here, was everything she'd ever wanted in life.

She'd wanted it so badly she'd never admitted that to herself, never let herself reach for it, nor hope for it, because the fear of not getting it had been almost paralysing.

And she still didn't have it.

This was the impossible dream.

She'd married for practicality, and the reality of that made her fantasies unattainable.

'I was surprised the other day,' he said, his tone soft. 'I was sure we'd have made a baby, and when I got your text, I felt so many things, *cara mia*. I was angry with myself, devastated for both of us, and all I could think was that I needed to see you, to make sure you were okay.' One side of his mouth lifted in a half smile. 'And then I came to you, and you were so dismissive, I handled it badly.'

'No.' She shook her head. 'Or if you did, I did too,' she conceded. 'I was angry with you.' She lifted her shoulders. 'I felt like you'd cut me out of your life so easily, and I just... I don't know. But the thing is, I think I needed to go through that, Sebastian, to really understand how much this matters to me. I've spent my whole life convinced that I didn't want children, but this week proved how wrong I was about that.'

He stirred the eggs, folding them neatly. 'And now?' he prompted, reaching for two plates.

She waited for him to continue.

'You're still committed to this?'

'Yes.'

He expelled a breath. 'We can make this work.'

Her smile was wistful. 'We don't have to. This was never about you and me. It's about the royal line of succession. It's about an heir.'

'That's not what you said before the island. Then it was all about getting to know one another.'

She shivered, remembering. It had seemed so sensible back then, but she'd had no idea of the can of worms she'd been about to pry open.

'Tell me something,' he said, placing the eggs on two plates and sliding one across the counter to her. It reminded her so much of the island that she had to dig her fingernails into her palm to anchor herself back to this reality.

'What would you like to know?'

'The not having kids thing. What's that about?'

She shook her head to demur. She'd spent a lifetime not talking about this to another soul. But with Sebastian, there was something that pulled to her. Even after everything they'd been through. Even after this past week, she still felt as though she wanted to open up to him. Why?

'Do you not like kids? Or the idea of childbirth?'

'I love kids,' she corrected automatically. 'But childbirth terrifies me.'

He reached for a fork and lifted some eggs to his mouth, chewing before speaking. 'But still,' he said, contemplatively. 'To decide never to have kids, that's a leap.'

She arched a brow. 'Not for me.'

He waited, forking some more eggs into his mouth.

'You know about my mother,' Rosie said, pushing her eggs around her plate, her appetite disappearing.

'That she's in a coma, yes.'

'But what you don't know, because no one really knows besides my father, is that she had a stroke hours after giving birth. It was a complication from the delivery,' Rosie said, not meeting his eyes. It was easier to talk that way, easier to think. 'I wanted to get to know you because I was worried that the same thing might happen to me. I mean, I've seen doctors, and they say it's not probable, but no one can tell me it won't happen. No one's been able to rule it out. So I just decided I'd never risk it.'

'I don't understand. Do you fear this might happen to you or do you think it's a genuine possibility?'

She frowned. 'I guess because of how alike we are, the latter. I look like her, I sound like her. I'm just like her. Why would that happen to her and not me?'

Sebastian drew in a sharp breath, drawing her gaze. 'Why didn't you tell me this?'

'I don't talk about it, generally. It's personal.'

'But relevant to us.' His voice was raw. 'Relevant to what I've asked of you.'

'Yes,' she conceded. 'But ultimately, this decision was mine to make.'

'I don't agree. If I had known this, I would never have asked you to fall pregnant.'

'That's not fair,' she responded. 'It's not your call.'

'I beg your pardon, but how do you think I would feel if that happened to you?'

Her heart stammered for no reason she could think of, and she leaned forward a little. 'I don't know. How would you feel?' And she held her breath whilst waiting for him to answer, hope a strange, strangling feeling.

'Guilty as hell,' he muttered. 'I would consider that I had essentially killed you.'

Guilt.

Not exactly a declaration of love.

And was that what she wanted from him? Rosie stood, eggs forgotten, pacing to the other side of the room, her whole body feeling as though it were in freefall. 'What are you saying? That you don't want to do this?'

'We *can't* do this. Good God, Rosalind. What were you

thinking, to keep this from me? If there's even the slightest chance our pregnancy would harm you, I will not do it.'

She flinched a little. 'You need an heir. The country needs an heir. And I am your wife.'

'Yes. But this is not a risk worth taking,' he responded, swiping his hand through the air. 'It's not a risk I will allow you to take. Not for me, and not for this—' he gestured from his chest to hers. 'Jesus Christ—'

She glared at him. 'What?'

'You're not really my wife, Rosalind. This is an arranged marriage. Two weeks ago, you said you hated me. You sure as hell don't care about me. Why would you be willing to put yourself through this?'

She stared at him, aghast. How could he think that, even after the island? How could he think her feelings hadn't changed? Was he really so obtuse? Surely, he knew that everything had shifted.

At least, it had for Rosie.

You're not really my wife.

Evidently, for Sebastian, this was still very much a contractual arrangement. She blinked rapidly, focusing on a point over his shoulder. Even after everything that had happened with them.

'Because the king needs this, right?' he asked, his tone hardening. 'First of all, you agree to marry a complete stranger, and now this? To risk your life because he demands an heir? What won't you do for that man?'

She dropped her head. It wasn't about the king. Not really. It hadn't been for a long time. This was about Sebastian, and it was about the baby that she now wanted more than anything.

'I wish I'd never told you.'

'Well, I'm glad you did.' They stared at each other, neither talking for several beats. She could see his mind working though, the wheels turning. 'Rosie...' It was the first time he'd ever called her that and her stomach swooped because far from sounding like a term of endearment, it terrified her. There was such finality in these two syllables. 'We're not doing this.'

She blinked. 'Doing what?'

'We're not having a child together.'

Nausea rose inside of her at the ease with which he was decreeing that. 'You don't understand. I want this.'

'Like you wanted our marriage? You sacrificed your whole goddamned life to help other people because you think that's what your mother would want you to do, and you're going to do it again and again unless someone stops you.'

'I want to have your baby,' she repeated, wishing he could understand. 'It's a leap of faith I'm willing to take.'

'And your mother?' he asked with intensity. 'Wouldn't she have said the same thing?'

Rosie opened her mouth but shook her head. 'I don't know.'

'You can't say for sure that this won't happen to you.'

'A thousand things can go wrong at any point in a pregnancy, or in life. If I can accept that, why can't you?'

Silence.

'This is ridiculous,' she said. 'I was explaining how I used to *feel*, not offering a genuine risk assessment—'

'It doesn't matter. Now that I know, it changes everything.' He paused in the doorframe, his back to her, his shoulders squared. 'Our marriage isn't worth this risk, Rosalind. Nothing is.'

Rosie glanced around for her dress and pulled it on quickly, her mind spinning. She hadn't expected this.

Because she'd had a long time to come to terms with her

mother's stroke, and to grapple with her own feelings and fear about it. She'd evolved from being terrified of having a baby to accepting that there was always going to be a small risk, but that she wanted to take it, because the gift of having Sebastian's baby suddenly felt like what she'd been placed on earth for.

He had to understand that.

No, it was more than that.

He had to understand what he'd come to mean to her.

Rosie's heart began to rush as she strode out to find Sebastian. He was standing in the kitchen, staring at the counter, as if the Magna Carta were inscribed into the stone.

'I want to have your baby,' she said softly, crossing the room. 'Not because of the king, not because you need an heir, not because you asked me. I want to have your baby because something happened on the island, and suddenly, everything I am became bound up in you, and the idea of us creating a new life together seems like the kind of gift I never thought I'd be given. I was devastated when I saw that negative pregnancy test because having your baby is genuinely the beginning and end of what I want.' She pressed a hand to her side, forcing herself to be bold. 'No, that's not true,' she whispered. 'I also want you in my life, Sebastian.' God, it was terrifying to put herself out there like this. She felt an echo of every single one of the women her father had hurt, felt a kinship with their vulnerabilities and susceptibility. But maybe it was also incredibly brave to face your feelings head on? Maybe what she was doing was simply stepping into a truth she'd been fighting for too long.

He stared at her, his eyes flinty. 'What are you saying?'

Really? He was going to make this that hard for her? 'I'm saying that somewhere on the island, I stopped thinking of this as an arranged marriage. I think you did too. I think that's why you don't want to take this risk.' She pressed a hand to his chest, her eyes beseeching. 'Could it be that you care about me too much to think of losing me?'

A muscle jerked in his jaw. 'I do care about you,' he admitted after a long, painful silence. His voice was raw, the words almost dragged from him. 'You're so different from what I thought, and if we'd met under different circumstances, if I was a different man, perhaps—' he shook his head a little. 'But there is no sense in playing that game. This *is* an arranged marriage, and it always will be, and at its heart there is a rotten, rotten core we will never be able to outgrow.'

Her eyes widened, her breath shallow.

'The king,' he supplied, taking a step away from her. 'You love him and will defend him with your dying breath. I feel the exact opposite. There is no way to get beyond that, Rosalind.'

Her eyes filled with tears. 'He is a part of my life, but he doesn't have to be a part of our marriage.'

'You are too loyal to draw that line, and too filled with goodness to accept my stance. You will try to reunite us, I know it. You will try to make me forgive him, and I can't. I won't.' His nostrils flared. 'Could you really be married to someone who despises, with every bone in his body, your precious king?'

Rosie flinched. 'Your relationship with him is complicated.'

He laughed harshly. 'No, it's not. It's simple. We have no relationship—that was his choosing.'

Her heart hurt for the king. The foolish king, who'd sent his daughter away rather than simply love her through the turmoil of her marriage breakdown. Rosalind had always seen his way, but even that had been shifting. Though she was not a parent, she'd spent the last few weeks imagining their child, and the love that had begun to form in her heart for that creation was a mother's love; she already knew there was nothing she wouldn't do for a baby, if she was lucky enough to have one.

'He was wrong to send you and your mother away,' she said, quietly. 'I think if you asked him, he'd admit that now.'

Sebastian made an angry noise, a sound of impatience and disbelief.

'But that's a separate matter.'

His eyes flashed to hers.

'I'm telling you that I've fallen in love with you, and I'm asking if you feel the same way.' She held a hand up to forestall an immediate response. 'I mean real love. The kind of love that doesn't give you a choice. The kind of love that demands you feel it and fight for it.' He stared at her, his face blank, but in his eyes, she saw a swirling of emotions that tied her tummy into knots. She didn't know what he was feeling, but she needed to. Urgency softened her voice, hastened her words. 'We aren't going to agree about everything—the king is a case in point. But I love you in a way that makes me want to fight through that, to reach out and grab this, you, this gift we've somehow stumbled upon, with both hands.'

He still said nothing. Her heart trembled. His nostrils flared as he inhaled, and his chest shifted. Finally, he opened his mouth to speak but the words that came out were like the cracking of a whip. 'I cannot decide if what you are feeling is wishful thinking, blind optimism or some kind of Stockholm syndrome.'

She gasped, his response, ever so slightly mocking, the very last thing she'd expected after all they'd shared. She stared at him, trying to reconcile his words with the man she'd come to know—and love—and failing. 'Sebastian—'

'Or is it that you are telling me you love me to try to get me to give in to you? To acquiesce to your desire to have a baby, no matter what? After all, it's what the king needs, so you must feel compelled to provide it.'

Her eyes hurt with the threat of tears. 'You think I'm manipulating you?'

A muscle jerked in his jaw. 'I don't know what to think.'

'Then stop thinking and tell me how you feel.'

'That's not a good idea.'

'Why not?'

'Because I suspect I'll regret whatever I say right now.' He crossed his arms over his chest. 'You should leave, Rosalind. Go back to the palace, go back to your king. Forget any of this ever happened.'

'You aren't listening, my love.'

Anger flooded his veins. It had been coursing through him all day, since Rosie had thrown a grenade into his life.

No, two grenades.

If I fall pregnant, I might have a stroke, or die.

Oh, and by the way, I'm in love with you.

What the hell?

How dare she lay that at his feet? The one thing he'd been clear that he *didn't* want. Would never want. Could never have. He sat up a little straighter, the final statement clawing at his insides. He'd drawn lines around his life, a barrier around his heart. He'd done it so long ago, and he'd been glad for it. It had kept him safe.

But what about Rosie? Hadn't she done the exact same thing? She'd chosen a loveless relationship once before, and then again with Sebastian. She'd entered into a practical marriage with a contract outlining what she was and wasn't prepared for that marriage to look like. She's protected herself fiercely too, and yet she'd let herself love him regardless. She'd let him in.

More fool her.

There was only darkness ahead for them if they forgot this was all make-believe.

'What's going on?'

He glanced across at his mother, but barely saw her. Until he did. Until he saw her serenity here, the way she seemed so completely at home, as much as the trees in the garden surrounding them, as much as the ancient vines that wrapped through their stems. This was her home—he'd brought her here. No matter what, it had been the right decision. Even if it led to Rosie's heart break?

'Nothing,' he muttered. 'Tell me more about your plans for the garden.'

But it was no use. The more his mother talked, the more Sebastian disappeared into his thoughts. His memories.

Rosie on the island, the sun making her hair glow like a halo, her smile, her laugh, the twinkle in her eyes whenever she told a story. Rosie in his bed, making love to him as though there was nothing else she wanted in life—as though he were her everything.

Rosie, as she'd been before the island, always so strait-laced, as though she didn't dare let her guard down around him. Had she known even then how out of control things would get, if they let it?

Had he?

Was that why he'd treated her with such disdain?

Never in his life had Sebastian kept a woman at such arm's length and gone out of his way to treat her with coldness. That had been about the king though, and Rosie's place in his life. Except, what if it hadn't? What if it had always been about the potentially explosive nature of their relationship? What if he'd intuited the potential for conflagration and had wisely chosen to stay away, until he couldn't?

He'd always charted a path of solitude. He was safer on his own. It hadn't even been consciously done, until Rosie. Until he'd had to actively remind himself why he wanted to keep all aspects of their marriage clearly delineated. It was better for both of them! Didn't she see that? Couldn't she understand?

Except, she loved him.

She wanted him in her life.

And he...

'Sebastian.' His mother pressed at his arm with her hand. 'You are worrying me now. What's going on?'

His eyes flashed to hers, probing, his heart twisting as though it were being mauled by a pair of angry, cold hands. He had spent so long hating the king that he hadn't even questioned the way that hatred had overflowed into his own life. Tainted it. Ruined it.

He looked at his mother, his features taut.

'Have you forgiven your father?'

Maria's face showed surprise at the question. 'No.' Her tone softened a little. 'But I understand him better.'

'What does that mean?'

'That I am not angry with him anymore. Not for sending me away.' She lifted a hand to Sebastian's cheek. 'Though it is impossible to forgive him for taking all of this from you.' She sighed. 'Why are you thinking about him now, Sebastian, when everything is finally as it ought to have been?'

Because Rosie had made him think. She'd made him look and see and understand. She'd pushed him when he didn't want to be pushed. She'd been brave time and time again.

Brave in a way he simply didn't know if he could be. He shook his head, confused, angry, lost.

'But it's not. You should not have been cut from the line of succession. You should be inheriting the throne.'

'I have no interest in the throne,' she said with a lift of one shoulder. 'I never did. All I wanted was to come home again, to be here.' She gestured to the garden.

Sebastian made a noise, a strangled sound. Rosie had every reason to run from commitment. She was just as scared of rejection as he was. She was utterly alone, and yet she was also brave. Was he really going to let her down? Was he really going to keep hiding, playing it safe, when she was willing to take such risks?

'But that's not what's bothering you.'

'It is, in part.'

'And the rest?'

The rest? The rest was everything. The rest was an awakening, a sense that he had made mistake after mistake, pushed away when he should have pulled closer, said no when he should have shouted yes, over and over again.

He dropped his head into his hands and let out a low, dark growl. 'I think I've done something really damned stupid.'

'What is it, darling?' Maria watched as he dragged his hands through his hair. When his gaze met hers, Maria saw a look of disbelief in the depths of her son's eyes, a look of shocked, confused disbelief and then, relief. Because finally, he understood, and he was ready to be brave, just like her.

'I believe I've fallen head over heels in love with my wife.'

CHAPTER FOURTEEN

AT FIRST, SHE'D CONTEMPLATED sending him away. Their conversation from the day before was still running verbatim through her mind, had been torturing her all night. She wasn't ready for round two.

But she needed to see him. She needed to prove to herself that she *could* see him. Yesterday, she felt as though the world had stopped spinning; today she needed to show herself that this was not the case.

He was just a man.

True, a man she loved.

But she was strong. She would conquer this: starting now.

She took her time checking her appearance. It was important to Rosie that she look poised and perfect—not broken, like she was inside. She coiled her hair tightly into a bun, inspected the suit she wore for lint, slipped her stockinged feet into a pair of heels then walked with a confidence she didn't feel towards her office, where Laurena had installed Sebastian.

At the door, she took a deep breath before pushing it inwards. He was standing, hands on hips, and every single pretension of poise fell to her feet.

Her breath escaped her in a single whoosh.

He looked so perfect.

Utterly, desperately perfect, but it wasn't about that.

She loved him.

And while she knew she would have to conquer that feeling, she could only look at him now and imagine a lifetime without him, without their intimacy, without him to talk to, and she wanted to curl up in a ball and cry.

She didn't though.

Outwardly, she kept her features in a neutral mask of curiosity. Inwardly, she trembled all over.

'Listen, Rosie,' he began as though they were halfway through a conversation, as though he'd been having this conversation with himself before she'd come into the room and was just bringing her in on it now. 'There's something you need to understand about me, something I should have explained yesterday, but honestly, I don't know if I even connected the dots then. Not consciously. It's not like I made a decision, at any point in my life, not to fall in love. These things happen in the background of your life, don't they? I do know that at some point, I decided that relying only on myself was the safest and best way to live my life.'

He moved towards her, his features taut. She held her breath. She wasn't strong enough to be close to him, but nor was she strong enough to back away. 'My own father excised me as though I were a gangrenous limb. My grandfather did the same. It didn't matter how much my mother or Mark loved me. Or maybe the more they loved me, the more I became paralysed by the fear that they'd one day stop. Nothing could ever make up for the sense of rejection I'd experienced, for believing on some fundamental level that I wasn't worthy of love. That I wasn't *enough* to be loved, no matter what.'

She sucked in a small breath, digging her nails into her palms to stop herself from reacting. She wanted to comfort him but was hurting too badly. Besides, he was unburdening himself in a way she suspected needed to continue unchecked.

'Maybe that's why I never felt a damned thing for any of the women I was with in the past, why it was always so easy to keep things light and simple. I think on some fundamental level, I just decided I would never again risk loving someone who might cut me out of their life.' He closed his eyes, his lashes dark against his tanned cheeks, drawing in a deep breath as though steeling himself for something important.

'Or maybe it was that I just hadn't met you,' he conceded quietly. 'Maybe there is just one person on earth after all who could make me love even when I know the flipside of that. Even when I know the pain of losing that love.' He pinned her with his gaze, and she trembled. Though they weren't touching, it felt as though every part of her was on fire.

'Yesterday, when you told me about your mother, all those old instincts wrapped around me, protecting me from the prospect of losing you, pushing you away before anything could happen and I was forced to live without you. Because if I *chose* that, it would hurt less, wouldn't it?' He shook his head at the rhetorical question. 'But you were so, so right. This isn't a choice. This is real love, the kind that takes hold of you without your consent and refuses to let go. My God, how did we spend five months married with no concept of what we'd lucked into? Rosie, you are my everything, and I know I stuffed it all up yesterday, but believe me when I tell you that I feel exactly the opposite of what I said.'

Her eyes filled with tears. She wanted to go to him, but she was too overwhelmed. 'Sebastian—'

He was quiet, respectful, waiting for her to speak.

'I didn't mean to blindside you yesterday, when I told you about my mother.'

He shook his head. 'I should have known then, how much trouble I was in. I felt as though I couldn't breathe. Just the thought of anything happening to you scared me senseless, but then the idea that it would be because I'd asked you to have my baby—' He dragged a hand through his hair. 'I should have known, and perhaps I did. Perhaps how much I love you is why I pushed you away so hard. I was terrified, Rosie, of a life without you in it.'

'Then let's not live that life,' she whispered, holding out her hand.

He took her hand in his and lifted it to his lips. 'Rosie, my darling, *cara mia*. My wife…' His voice rumbled with passionate possession over the last word. 'Will you move in with me?'

She pretended to think about it. 'On one condition.'

'Name it.'

'Can we go back to the island first?'

His eyes swept shut on a wave of relief. 'How soon can you be ready?'

'Oh, Sebastian. I've been ready for this my whole life.'

It was three days before they surfaced from his bedroom on the island for long enough to have a conversation more serious than to debate what they'd like to eat, but finally, as the sun set one evening, and the breeze grew cool, Rosie reached for his hand, forcing herself to be brave.

'I've been thinking,' Rosie said, her heart beating faster.

'Oh? Have you had time to think? Then clearly, I am not doing a very good job at seducing you senseless.'

She laughed. 'Oh, you've done an excellent job of that, don't worry.'

He kissed her hand. 'What are you thinking, my darling?'

Her heart rolled over. 'About our baby,' she said, teeth pressing into her lower lip.

'I've been thinking about that too.' His expression was wary. 'Rosie, I want you to have everything you want in life. If that means a baby, if you really want to do this, then of course we'll start trying again.'

She expelled a shaky breath.

'But first, I want you to see some specialists. I want assurances, as many assurances as we can get, even knowing absolute guarantees are impossible.'

She nodded. It was so like Sebastian, and so indicative of his love for her, that she couldn't help but agree.

'Except—' His eyes turned down a little, his features serious. 'What if we waited a little while?'

She tilted her head to the side.

'I know it's selfish, but I'm not ready to share you. I love you. I love everything about you, and yet still I feel like there's so much more I want to know. Every day I learn something new, and I want to keep learning about *you*, exploring you, loving you, worshipping you, building our life together as a couple before we become a family. What do you think, my love?' He came to crouch in front of her. 'As always, this decision is yours.'

Her heart soared. 'I thought you needed an heir,' she said with a lift of one brow.

'I need nothing but you.' He was now adamant. 'You tell me your heart's desire, and I'll make it happen.'

She sighed with contentment. Rosie knew that a child was in their future, but in that moment, she also knew that Sebastian was right. They had just found their way to one another, and she wasn't ready to share him yet either.

She pressed her forehead to his. 'I love you,' she said, simply, and in those three words, there was a lifetime of promise and hope.

It was an accident, in the end, and one with serendipitous timing. A few niggling symptoms in the weeks leading up to their first wedding anniversary had Rosie beginning to wonder. This time, when she dispatched Laurena to buy a pregnancy test, she expected it to be negative. They hadn't been trying. Sebastian had been emphatic about using protection, despite the fact every test under the sun had shown Rosie to have no increased risk factors. She took the test as a matter of course, glanced at it quickly before intending to toss the thing away, only to be stopped in her tracks by the appearance of a very dark second line.

'Oh my,' she whispered, lifting a hand to her mouth, her smile broad. Her other hand pressed to her stomach. Her heart soared.

A baby!

And a baby that had simply decided to swim into their lives no matter what they'd intended. It was as though the fates had pulled all the strings, shaped the stars, done whatever they could to gift this to the royal couple.

Although it was news Rosie felt bursting out of her, she didn't tell Sebastian right away. She felt a hint of guilt at confiding in only Laurena, but she needed her help to discreetly book appointments. Before she broke the news to Sebastian, she wanted to have every assurance she could give him: she knew he'd need that before he could celebrate, and when she told him, she wanted him to be happy.

And so appointments were organised with the royal obstetrician, scans completed, more tests undertaken, and though Rosie couldn't be exactly sure, when she worked back the dates in her head, she became convinced that they'd conceived on the island, whilst celebrating Sebastian's birthday, two months earlier.

Their first wedding anniversary was marked with a formal dinner. Many dignitaries were in attendance, but it was notable to Rosie because the dinner also included Maria and the king, and for the first time, she witnessed them have a private conversation. Concern frayed at the edges of her mind, because Maria had looked pale and walked out quickly afterwards, leaving the function for almost ten minutes. Rosie, as the guest of honour, had been unable to follow and make sure she was okay.

Sebastian only had eyes for his wife and hadn't noticed the conversation.

For her part, Rosie wanted the formal event to be over, so she could be alone with her husband, and finally tell him their news.

At the first opportunity however, she excused herself and went to her mother-in-law.

'Hello,' she said, taking a seat beside her and smiling.

Maria smiled back. 'You look radiant, my darling, utterly radiant.'

'Thank you,' Rosie frowned though. 'Maria, I wanted to make sure you were okay. I thought you might have been upset earlier.'

Maria waved a hand in the air, but her lips trembled, and her gaze travelled across to the king. He was locked in conversation with the prime minister.

'I hadn't realised until tonight how much I needed it,' Maria said, her voice soft.

'Needed what?'

'His apology.' She shook her head. 'I had given up all hope of hearing it, and then tonight, out of nowhere, he told me how much he'd missed me. How much he regretted his decision. He said he'd been wrong, and if he could undo any one thing in his life, it would be his failure to stand by me. He said it had been like the knocking over of a domino that had tracked through the rest of his entire life, and that he will always be grateful to Sebastian for finding a way to bring me home. To bring Sebastian home.' Maria squeezed Rosie's hand. 'Can you imagine how I felt to hear these things, darling one?'

Rosie's mouth dropped. 'I had no idea he was going to speak to you.' She had pulled back from her official duties in recent months, seeing less and less of the king, and working instead on her key charities.

'He has asked me to stay here for a while, to spend time with me.'

'Are you going to?'

Maria sighed softly, her eyes shifting then to Sebastian's. 'I will never forgive him for what he took from my son,' she admitted. 'But then, he has also given Sebastian the greatest gift in life. You.'

Rosie's cheeks flushed pink.

'On balance, I am inclined, I think, to let bygones be bygones.'

Rosie wanted to cry with happiness, but she didn't. She smiled instead, and in her heart, she felt a lightness that spoke of a bright future and a truly happy family.

The plane touched down on the island a little after midnight, and it was ten minutes after that before they were at the villa on the edge of the water, but Rosie wasn't tired. She was buzzing and humming, almost incapable of believing that after weeks of waiting, she could finally reveal everything to her beloved husband.

'We need to talk,' she murmured, draping an arm casually around his waist and drawing him onto a balcony that overlooked the ocean. The evening was cool, and the moon was high and silver like a shiny coin.

'About my mother?'

'You saw?' she asked, surprised.

'He spoke to me too.'

Her brows shot up. 'Did he really?'

Sebastian turned and wrapped his arms around his wife. 'He told me you'd made him see the error of his ways. Or rather, that the only way to fix things was to admit his mistakes.'

Rosie's cheeks flushed. 'I didn't intend to get involved, but when he asked me for my opinion, I had to give it.'

'Of course you did,' Sebastian agreed, with a kiss to the top of her head.

'What did he say to you?'

'That he recognised his behaviour was impossible to forgive, but that he hoped we could forge some kind of relationship. He said he would never be able to make up for what he'd taken from both of us, but that he wanted to at least know me.'

Rosie held her breath. 'To which you replied?'

'That my own instinct has long been to walk away from him. However, as we both cherish and adore you, it makes sense for us to try—for your sake—to forge an easier path.'

Rosie shook her head. 'You don't have to do this for me.'

'Yes, I do. And what's more, I want to. For my mother, as well. If there's any chance of establishing a peaceful relationship, I want that. I will never agree with his decisions, but that's not to say that I can't learn from him. As you've pointed out, time and time again, he loves this country and has spent a lifetime governing it with grace.'

Rosie's smile was beatific. 'I'm so glad. But that's not what I wanted to talk to you about.'

'No?'

She shook her head.

'Then what, my dear wife?'

'Well, you know how we talked about waiting to conceive?'

'Let me guess,' he said, squeezing her tighter. 'You're ready to start trying?'

'Well, yes and no.'

He arched a brow. 'You want to wait even longer?'

'Well, the thing is, the decision has sort of been taken out of our hands.'

His expression gave nothing away, so she blurted out, 'I'm pregnant, Sebastian. It wasn't planned, obviously.'

'You're pregnant?'

His smile was instantaneous, but he sobered a moment later. 'How did this happen? How do you feel? *When* did this happen? When did you find out? Are you okay?'

'So many questions,' she laughed. 'Let me start at the beginning.' And she began by describing the few niggling symptoms that had started to add up in her mind, to the pregnancy test she took just to know for sure that she wasn't pregnant, only to get the shock of her life in discovering that she was in fact expecting.

'I knew you'd worry, and I wanted to be able to offer you reassurances when I told you, so I've been seeing an obstetrician and I've done a heap of tests and scans. Sebastian, everything's fine. Everything is just as it ought to be, and he has a plan for managing the later stages of my pregnancy to keep the risks as minimal as possible.'

'Good God,' he said, shaking his head. 'I can't believe it. I feel as though it's a miracle, Rosie.'

'Oh, you haven't heard the rest of it,' she laughed, taking his hand and pressing it to her no longer super flat stomach. 'It turns out, it's twins.'

'Twins,' he practically spat the word. 'What are you talking about?'

'I know. Twins. Who would have thought?'

'Two babies—' he let out a low whistle. 'How do you feel?'

'Actually, I feel great. Excited. Nervous. But mostly, just…so blessed.'

He drew her closer and pressed his brow to hers. 'We're both blessed, my darling.'

And they were. Six months later, via an early, scheduled caesarean, Her Royal Highness Princess Rosalind al Morova was safely delivered of a son and a daughter. They both had dark, spiky hair and pale blue eyes and even as newborns, their hands seemed to reach for one another, linking their tiny little fingers as if in a pinkie promise that they would be best friends, always.

The pregnancy was mostly without complications, and the delivery went as planned. Not the least afraid, once the babies had been born, Rosalind was swept up in such an intense rush of love for her little ones, her husband, her country, and also her mother, to whom she now felt an irreplaceable bond. In that moment of cradling her twins, she knew for sure that she and her mother had shared a similar experience, had known a similar sense of overwhelming love, and it would join them for all time.

They named the children Antonio and Emilia, two lesser-known names from Shakespearean plays, a subtle tilt of the cap to Rosie's mother, who was always and forever more a part of their family.

Far from reliving her mother's terrible health fate, however, Princess Rosalind went on to have three more children, in three more healthy pregnancies, and the king lived to see all five royal descendants arrive.

He was a doting great-grandfather. It was as if he recognised that he'd been given the most valuable of all second chances in life and was determined not to waste it. Bit by bit, over time, and with effort, his relationship with both his daughter and grandson improved. The king was nothing if not stubborn, and once he'd set his mind to making amends, he spared no effort. At every opportunity, he did what he could to show how much he valued his kin, and gradually, love won out. There was no going back and fixing things, but time helped heal a wound that had at one point cut very, very deeply.

Sebastian never saw his father again, but in becoming a father himself, he overcame something else he'd been unknowingly terrified of all his life: that he wouldn't know how to love his children. That he wouldn't know how to put himself on the line for them. As it turned out, Mark had taught him all he needed to know on that front, and in addition, his heart had been ignited by his love for Rosie, and there was no switching it off again.

Seven years after Rosie and Sebastian's marriage, after a family dinner with much food and laughter and happiness, the king died peacefully in his sleep. Death is, of course, always sad, but in his passing, all who'd loved him could say with sincerity that they had no regrets. The king had erred, but in recognising that and finally making amends, he'd also showed humility and forged a family connection that would prove lasting and valuable.

King Sebastian and Queen Rosalind were by then beloved figures in Cavalonian society. Far from Sebastian being considered an outsider in any way, his people had claimed him with a ferocity that at times made him laugh. But he was proud—oh so proud—of this country, his people, his family, his life and most of all, his commitment to make things better for every single person who lived in this land. To this end, both he and Rosalind worked tirelessly, lobbying the government, and using his considerable personal wealth to build state-of-the-art schools and hospitals in areas that were financially disadvantaged. Their goal to create one of the most educated and literate societies in the world was something they worked towards all their lives, and which they instilled in their children.

At the start of their marriage, both Sebastian and Rosalind would have laughed at the very idea of fairy tales. They were just make-believe stories for children, after all! Except they weren't. As it turned out, they'd stepped into their very own fairy tale with a big, bright happily-ever-after, and they never stopped appreciating that. With every breath, every smile, every sigh, they lived and they loved and enjoyed the life they deserved—side by side, for all time.

* * * * *

Did you fall in love with
Unwanted Royal Wife?
Then don't miss out on these other
intensely emotional stories
from Clare Connelly!

Twelve Nights in the Prince's Bed
The Sicilian's Deal for "I Do"
Contracted and Claimed by the Boss
His Runaway Royal
Pregnant Before the Proposal

Available now!

MILLS & BOON®

Coming next month

ACCIDENTAL ONE-NIGHT BABY
Julia James

Siena took a breath, short, sharp, and summoning up her courage, stepped into the lift that would take her to the one man in the world she did not want to see again.

Vincenzo Giansante.

'He'll think you're chasing him – and he's made it clear he's done with you.'

Siena's mouth tightened. Vincenzo Giansante had, indeed, made it crystal clear he was done with her – had walked out in the briefest way possible in the bleak light of the morning after the night before.

Well, now she was walking back into his life – to tell him what she still could scarcely believe herself, ever since seeing that thin blue line form on the test stick.

He has a right to know – any man does – whether I want him to or not.

The lift jerked to a stop, the metal doors sliding open. For a moment she just wanted to be a coward, and jab the down button again. Then, steeling herself, she walked forward.

Continue reading

ACCIDENTAL ONE-NIGHT BABY
Julia James

Available next month
millsandboon.co.uk

COMING SOON!

We really hope you enjoyed reading this book.
If you're looking for more romance
be sure to head to the shops when
new books are available on

Thursday 27th February

To see which titles are coming soon, please visit
millsandboon.co.uk/nextmonth

LET'S TALK

Romance

For exclusive extracts, competitions and special offers, find us online:

- **MillsandBoon**
- **@MillsandBoon**
- **@MillsandBoonUK**
- **@MillsandBoonUK**

Get in touch on 01413 063 232

For all the latest titles coming soon, visit
millsandboon.co.uk/nextmonth

Afterglow Books is a trend-led, trope-filled list of books with diverse, authentic and relatable characters, a wide array of voices and representations, plus real world trials and tribulations. Featuring all the tropes you could possibly want (think small-town settings, fake relationships, grumpy vs sunshine, enemies to lovers) and all with a generous dose of spice in every story.

♪ @millsandboonuk

◎ @millsandboonuk

afterglowbooks.co.uk

#AfterglowBooks

For all the latest book news, exclusive content and giveaways scan the QR code below to sign up to the Afterglow newsletter:

SCAN ME

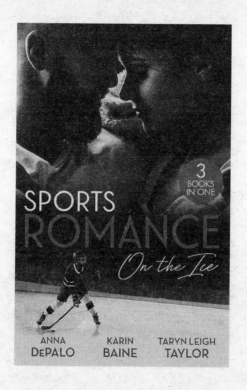